D0871261

A PLACE FOR VANISHING

Books by Ann Fraistat

What We Harvest

A Place for Vanishing

A PLACE FOR VANISHING

ANN FRAISTAT

DELACORTE PRESS

Content warnings for *A Place for Vanishing* include:

• Mental health themes: suicide (discussed attempt, ideation), bipolar disorder (cyclothymia/bipolar III), anxiety, depression, self-harm (cutting), hallucinations, and delusions

• Graphic violence

• Overdose (discussed)

• Bullying/cyberbullying (mentioned)

• Strong language/profanity

• Mild sexual content

Visit us on the Web! GetUnderlined.com

Educators and librarians, for a variety of teaching tools, visit us at RHTeachersLibrarians.com

Library of Congress Cataloging-in-Publication Data is available upon request.
ISBN 978-0-593-38221-9 (hardcover) — ISBN 978-0-593-38223-3 (lib. bdg.) —
ISBN 978-0-593-38222-6 (ebook)

The text of this book is set in 11-point Maxime Pro.
Interior design by Cathy Bobak

Printed in the United States of America
10 9 8 7 6 5 4 3 2 1
First Edition

For those of us with divergent minds, who see things differently.
Never forget: the world needs us.

AUTHOR'S NOTE

WHILE I WOULD DESCRIBE *A Place for Vanishing* as a mental health recovery story—one that carries hope and growth and a hell of a lot of fight—this book centers on a character recuperating from a suicide attempt. At times, she struggles with lingering suicidal ideation, and she reckons throughout with a recent bipolar III diagnosis. Another character has wounds that appear to be self-inflicted by cutting. Please use your best judgment about whether this story is right for you.

If you or someone you know is considering self-harm, please visit 988lifeline.org or call or text the National (US-based) Suicide & Life Crisis Lifeline at 988. Support is 24/7, free, and confidential. The International Association for Suicide Prevention also offers additional lifelines and international resources at findahelpline.com.

Above all, please take care of yourself.

CHAPTER ONE

DAYS LIKE THIS MADE ME WISH I'd never come back from the dead.

Since the doctors dragged me back six weeks ago, life sometimes felt foggy, like a strange dream. But *nothing* was stranger than this: sitting in Mom's road-weary sedan, gaping through my window at the house towering over the yard, the street, our car. Us.

The house stared back.

The crumbling Queen Anne Victorian was massive. Solid. It sank into the earth like it had roots coiled five hundred feet down.

"Do you like it, girls?" Mom turned to me in the passenger seat and my thirteen-year-old sister in the back. Since I'd returned from the psych ward, her every word came glazed in honey. The way you might talk to a five-year-old—if you were bad with kids.

I couldn't find the breath to answer her. I rolled down the window, that thin veneer between me and the house, inch by inch. The summer air climbed into the car with us, sticky and suffocating.

This was the house Mom had inherited from her parents? The one that Mom—a real estate agent—had ignored for decades? Had never even tried to sell?

I was stunned by the sheer size. The extravagance. The house had to be over a century old, with its spindly spires and lacy woodwork. In places, the white trim was still so shiny and marshmallowy that it hurt my teeth. But age and rot had left their marks, too. Faded cobalt paint encased the house's shingled body, peeling like sunburned skin. Weathered wood boarded every window. It was like the place was guarding against a hurricane decades in the making.

And it was like the neighbors knew. Football-field-sized gaps sat between our property and the single-family ranch homes on either side. They hunkered low, less than half the height of our monstrosity.

The longer I stared, the more my chest tightened under my seat belt. The house's steep rooflines towered with octagonal turrets and sharply gabled dormers, masking the layout inside. It felt like the kind of puzzle that if you stared long enough, revealed a whole new picture. One hiding smugly just under the surface. There had to be some reason it had sat empty so long. Maybe the neighbors and their flinching houses knew something I didn't.

Worse, maybe *Mom* knew something I didn't. All this time, she'd been holing us up in a two-bedroom apartment a couple counties over, and she'd made this place sound like some rinky-dink shack.

"Mom . . . ," I said finally, "I thought you said this house was worthless."

"No!" Mom hid her hands in her lap, tearing at her thumb's cuticle. A habit I'd inherited, but she'd tried to kick, to set an example. "It wasn't the best fit for us before, but I couldn't have said 'worthless.' "

She'd definitely said *worthless.* It was only since my stint in the hospital that Mom had started singing this house's praises. Suddenly decided this was the place for us after all. Anything to get me into a new school before the fall crept up on us.

I looked over my shoulder at Vivi, hoping she'd help me call Mom out. She'd been there for the same conversations I had.

But she ducked my glance. "It's great, Mom," she said, though her chirping voice came out uncertain. A little thin. "Maybe we could check out the inside. Right, Libby?"

Likely, she was prodding me to play along for Mom's sake.

And she was probably right—I should. For better or worse, this was our new home, and I *wanted* to love it. The old-timey embellishments weren't without their charm. The size was astounding. I just couldn't shake the strange sensation gnawing at my brain—that something was wrong.

Maybe it was me who was wrong.

I'd caused a lot of misery lately. I owed it to Mom and Vivi to make them feel good.

"Sorry, Mom. I was just surprised," I lied dutifully. Once I adjusted to my new medicine, Dr. Glaser said it would get easier to smile. For now, I had to settle for a stiff flash of teeth and hope I didn't look as much like a grinning skeleton as I felt. "Give us the grand tour."

"The grand tour, yes," Mom echoed with new life. A little color flushed back into her white cheeks, and she fluffed her shoulder-length brown curls like it was showtime. This time, I'd said the right thing.

I followed Mom and Vivi out of the car, past the white spiked fence.

On the cracked front walkway, I craned my neck until it twinged, peering at the house overhead. This place delighted in asymmetry. The whole thing felt unsteady, like any second it might topple down to crush us.

And yet I couldn't look away. You didn't take your eyes off a snake sizing up your ankle. Somehow, this place filled me with the same uneasy impulse.

"Don't you love all this ornamental trim? That's called 'gingerbread'—isn't that sweet?" Mom cooed, in full saleswoman mode. "And the yard needs some sprucing, but can you believe the potential?" She swept her arms around like the star of some musical, inviting Vivi and me to join her onstage.

We nodded, and managed the appropriate murmurs of admiration. But the yard was a patchy yellow, sun-dried to straw. Even the stray dandelions had been reduced to scraggly stems. Maybe it had been less bedraggled when Mom had lived here as a kid, but decades of neglect had amounted to decades of decay.

Strangely, the only plants thriving were the shaggy bushes that wrapped around the base of the house and the inner perimeter of the fence. Glossy leaves, blue buds. They pulsed with cicadas, buzzed with wasps. And they bloomed in the early July heat, oblivious to the steaming roads and sidewalks.

"Blue roses," Mom told us, "if you can believe it. I don't remember much from my time in this house when I was little, but those made an impression. Usually, florists have to dye roses blue. They aren't supposed to grow in the wild."

I glanced down the street, expecting to spot them in nearby yards if they were local to the area. But the rest of the block was all puffy popcorn balls of hydrangeas and cheery pink crape myrtles.

This tangle of impossibly blue roses was ours alone.

I examined the nearest bush, with its clusters of thorns and red-veined leaves. The petals, arranged in mesmerizing swirls, were velvety-soft against my finger but oddly thick for a rose. Almost meaty.

Floral perfume billowed into my nose, so heavy it was practically mind-altering.

I'd never seen or smelled anything like it.

Still, for Mom's sake, I was grateful. She'd always had an appetite for gardening, swamping our old apartment patio with herbs and the poor tomato plants that died no matter what. A real yard like this could be the escape she needed.

And if Mom had couched those roses as a scientific anomaly to capture Vivi's attention, then well played. My sister was practically buried headfirst in a nearby bush. Mom had to pry her away so we could continue our tour.

As she led us across the creaking wraparound porch to the front door, the moment of truth approached. The inside of the house might not feel as strange as the outside. I might even like it. *Please, please, please.*

The knocker was also a rose—a silver hunk the size of my fist. Its petals were rendered in breathtaking detail, thin and rumpled, the edges burnished with age. Custom-made. No doubt expensive.

It should make me feel better: Someone had once loved this place. It was possible to love this place.

Mom threw open the front door. "Welcome home, girls!"

We were greeted by a whiff of fresh lemon, one of Mom's inviting real-estate-agent tricks.

But the second I stepped inside, a musty ripeness closed around me like a fist. Rotting logs and honeysuckle. Like under the skin of this wallpaper, the house's guts were a pulpy mash of mothballs and mildew.

Light trickled in from the open door behind us, but beyond the cramped foyer, the house gaped as dim as a mouth. Not even the faintest rays slanted in through the windows.

It took me a second to realize why. The windows weren't only boarded from the outside. They were boarded from the inside, too. I'd thought the point was to protect the house from the outside world, not the other way around.

Metallic dread gummed up the back of my throat, even as I fought it.

Vivi also hung back, hovering in the doorway behind me.

Mom winced at our lack of enthusiasm. "Uh, hang on!" She fumbled toward a floor lamp in the foyer, complete with droopy shade and dripping fringe. It flickered to life with all the conviction of a candle in a cave. "The windows were supposed to be uncovered by now. I'll give the contractor another call."

A brassy gleam caught my eye. Across from the front door, a plaque clung to the wall, mottled with oxidized patches. Its deep-etched lettering read: MADAME CLERY'S HOUSE OF MASKS. EST. 1894.

I squinted at the words, as if an explanation might appear if I stared hard enough. "Mom, what is this?"

"Oh!" Mom turned back, with an absent-minded smack to her forehead. Not like someone who'd actually forgotten their keys, more like someone who wanted to *indicate* they had. "Right. This house is something of a local landmark. Apparently, your great-great-great-granduncle and his wife were entertainers. So you'll notice a bit of kitsch here and there."

"What does it mean, though?" I asked. "'House of Masks'?"

"Sweetie, that was . . . what? A century and a half ago? I can't claim to know all the history."

Mom had just called this house a local landmark. And she was a complete nerd about houses and their histories. Even if no one in the family had told her, did she really want me to believe she hadn't looked this up?

She was avoiding my eyes again.

Guess I'd have to look it up myself.

The plaque lay on top of cloudy blue wallpaper. Past the dust, a faint gold glinted. I swiped away a palmful of grime to reveal a filigree design: Winding vines and bugs creeping through leaves. Beetles and ants and butterflies, centipedes and praying mantises . . .

If this is what Mom meant by *kitsch,* it wasn't what I'd been expecting.

"Hey, this is kind of cool . . . ," Vivi said, stepping closer to trace over the nearest gold caterpillar. A shadow of her old smile played across her face.

Vivi *loved* bugs. For years, Mom and I had prayed it was a phase, but now she was an up-and-coming teen and an aspiring entomologist.

Maybe she'd bond with this house after all.

I did want that for her—for her to find a new happy place—but if the house won her over, I'd be the only one with actual reservations. Yet again, the problem child.

My bare arms itched. The dust of this place was settling over me like a second skin.

"How long has the house been empty, Mom?" My voice came out small, muffled by what had to be a million rugs and drapes, sure as a hand clapped over my mouth. "Has anyone been in here since you and your—"

I stopped myself. Because she didn't like to talk about her parents.

The unspoken words hung heavier than if I'd said them outright.

Mom tried to hide her discomfort. "Not lived here, no," she said. "But people have *been* here. To check on the place."

So this house really hadn't been a home in decades. Over forty years.

Not since Mom's parents had died here, and she moved in with Great-Aunt Carol.

"I know the house needs some—well, okay, a lot of love." Mom fidgeted, almost like a kid worried she'd done something wrong, committing to this house without showing us first. All three of us shared the same deep-brown doe eyes, and hers were now painfully plaintive. "But we're not afraid of a fixer-upper, are we, girls? A motivational family project?"

Through the foyer's open arch, the waiting rooms leered from the dark. The dim shapes of an overgrown Victorian dollhouse, with the velvet love seats and oriental rugs to match. *Family project* felt like a stretch to me—but I could see how much Mom wanted the label to fit. Anything to get us back on the same team.

Vivi and I must've hesitated too long, because Mom rushed to fill the silence. "Well. I'll get some more lights on. Why don't you two check out the upstairs before the movers arrive? You could choose your bedrooms."

Vivi froze, like the mere prospect of alone time with me had her debating fight or flight.

I stifled my sigh. Once upon a time, I couldn't have gotten rid of Vivi even if I wanted to. As I'd brushed my teeth, she'd knock my elbow, practicing ballet positions in our cramped bathroom, babbling about the soldering iron she'd used to melt copper during science lab or an especially fuzzy caterpillar she'd bottled up. When she'd had a nightmare, she'd crawl into my bed and shock me awake with her cold feet.

But that was before. For the past few weeks, she had honed the art of using Mom as a buffer, avoiding one-on-one time with me like the plague. Which truly took talent, since we'd shared a bedroom. When my presence was inescapable, she kept in earbuds. I wasn't sure she was even listening to anything.

Never mind that the last thing I'd wanted was to hurt her. Never mind that I was hurting a thousand times worse and she was supposed to be supportive.

Never mind, never mind, never mind.

Anger, sharp as bile, welled in my throat, but I swallowed it down. I slathered on the fake-bright cheer as I turned to her in the foyer. "Sure, let's look together."

"If you want." Vivi fiddled with one of the elastics that bound her hair in two big puffs at the top of her head, although she succeeded only in knocking it and the decorative purple scrunchie out of place.

My fingers twitched with the old impulse to fix it—she used to ask me to do her hair every morning before school.

Instead, I stuffed my hands into the pockets of my jeans. She wouldn't want me touching her anyway.

"You girls go ahead, then!" Mom was way too pleased with herself for engineering this excuse to shove us together. She was mid-exit, blending into the shadowed dining room, when she paused. "Oh, and the last two rooms on the hall are spoken for, okay?"

Two rooms?

Major upgrade from our previous apartment, where Mom had given us the bigger bedroom and taken the smaller one for herself.

"You're using both?" I asked.

Mom stiffened. "No. One's mine. The other is . . ." She flushed a strange shade of pink. "There are some structural issues. Just steer clear. Please. That leaves you girls with four bedrooms to choose from. I hardly think it's a serious inconvenience."

With that, she slipped away.

Before I could ask any more questions.

By our phones' flashlights and the few flickering bulbs we managed to turn on, Vivi and I stumbled toward the staircase. The saggy steps moaned under our feet.

Honestly, I felt like a trespasser. This house had spent decades stewing in its own silence, solemn as a closed crypt. And here we were, not just disturbing it but moving in. Claiming it as our own.

We shouldn't be here, my brain whispered. A nonsensical warning.

The beams from our phones cast jagged shadows over the upstairs hall. Tiny dark shapes squiggled away, ducking into corners and crevices. I full-body flinched.

Bugs.

They weren't only in the design of the foyer wallpaper.

"Didn't Mom say she'd called an exterminator?" I asked.

"Yeah, they fumigated. Twice." Vivi's distaste was obvious. She didn't like "murdering" insects. "Why?"

She was behind me. She must not have caught the squirming flickers in the hall, diving for cover.

"I think they missed a few . . . ," I muttered.

My phone's flashlight rippled over patchworked plywood, which covered the wall opposite from the staircase landing. An enormous boarded-up window, framed by floor-length lace curtains. I couldn't wait for that plywood to come down. It was way too dark in this house.

I ran my hand along the grimy wallpaper beside us and found a switch. I flipped it, and the glass sconces studding the long corridor flickered to life. At least, half of them did. The murky bulbs cast whispers of light over the dizzying blue wallpaper that coated the top of the halls. Dark wood paneling lined the bottom up to my waist.

Paralyzed at the staircase landing, I peered down the corridor and counted the doors. Too many. All closed, except the one to our immediate left. Mom had said there were *six* bedrooms. Plus there must be bathrooms and who knew what else.

I suddenly felt very small.

On a good day, Vivi was a scrawny four-foot-eleven shrimp, but she'd shrunk in on herself, too, hugging her knobby elbows tight across her purple tie-dyed T-shirt. Her brown skin was tinged gray in the dim light.

I could only imagine how pale *I* looked. As Vivi had once so lovingly informed me, the only foundation lighter than the one in my stage-makeup kit was the white face paint. Performing was something she and I used to have in common—acting for me, ballet for her—until this past spring, when both of us had quit.

Now, here we were, in a house sunken as low as we had. From what little Mom had told us, I'd known it wouldn't be perfect.

But the more she had promised this fresh start for the three of us, the more I'd envisioned it: a real house, after our dull-walled, spongy-carpeted apartment.

A home.

But no part of this place bore *any* resemblance to the soothing safe haven I'd imagined. I'd wanted sunny, picket-fenced, cozy. This was bloated, bug-infested, its spiky metal fence painted white like a lie.

The back of my tongue clenched. Heaviness dripped from my infuriating brain down into my shoulders, through my limp arms. A hopeless cloud was settling over me.

This was more than some seasick gut feeling.

Misfiring brain chemicals.

Tangling my thoughts and feelings until I couldn't tell what was real.

My official diagnosis had come only a few weeks ago: cyclothymia, aka bipolar III, a milder form of the disorder that was trickier to clinically detect than type I or II. Dr. Glaser said one of my biggest triggers was disappointed expectations. So no wonder my body was trying to crash into a low, one of those depressive episodes that, if it sank its claws in deep enough, would crush me into a catatonic lump.

Clearly, this house was in need of, as Mom put it, "a lot of love." But was anything truly *wrong* with it—or was I only seeing, yet again, my own mental distortions?

My brain might not be entirely to blame. Vivi had also stalled in the doorway. And she was balking now, too.

"What do you think of this place?" I asked quietly. Conspiratorially. "You don't actually like it, do you?"

Vivi hugged herself tighter. "Libby. Don't," she hissed under her breath. "Could you at least *try*? You know how much this means to Mom."

The accusation, like I was being difficult for the sake of it, hit me like a slap.

I am *trying,* is what I wanted to say. To scream.

But I was the big sister. Three years older, three years theoretically wiser. If one of us bore the onus of putting on a good face for Mom, it should be me. And we were both painfully aware of that.

"You're right," I managed. "It'll be better once the windows are unboarded. The house just needs more light."

"Exactly!" Vivi nodded, too desperately. "More light."

I pulled my brown curls aside to fan my sweaty neck, and couldn't help mumbling: "And another fumigation. A deep scrub. A total redecoration. Possibly an exorcism."

Vivi didn't laugh. She glared at me.

Pressing my lips together, I glanced away, and my eyes caught on a shape fluttering out of the open bedroom. Dingy ivory, like a used handkerchief.

I gasped and grabbed Vivi's arm.

"What?" she demanded. "What are you—?"

The shape darted toward us, its path wild and choppy.

A white bat?

I shrieked and tried to drag Vivi out of the way.

"Libby! Calm down!" Vivi pushed me off and let the creature land on her.

It settled over her heart, fluttering its ghostly wings. Not a bat. A butterfly, big as a luna moth. Big as someone's flexing hand.

The butterfly gleamed with a satiny sheen. Its gossamer veins wove lacelike patterns, hypnotic in their dips and dives and swirls. But its wings were tissue-paper-thin, torn and flecked with holes. I was surprised the thing could fly.

Vivi stood stock-still as an awed smile curved across her face.

Footsteps crashed downstairs. "Girls!" Mom raced into view at the bottom of the staircase, her face blanched paler than her white button-down shirt. "Are you all right?"

My shriek. Any sound of distress from one of us was enough to send Mom into overdrive these days.

"Yeah, sorry," I called down to her. "Just a bug. Startled me, that's all."

"Look, Mom!" Vivi grinned, pointing at the butterfly clinging to her shirt.

"Oh. That's nice, sweetie." Mom wiped a trickle of sweat from her forehead. "Well, I'm going to rescue the milk and ice cream from the car before they turn into puddles, like the rest of us. Make sure you look at those bedrooms, okay? The movers should be here any minute."

We called back our okays, but Vivi's full attention still belonged to the butterfly clinging to her chest. "What would a butterfly be doing in here?" she murmured, half to herself, half to the butterfly.

No way had something that delicate survived two fumigations. "Bugs must still be finding their way in," I said.

"Yeah. I hope this one didn't pick up any leftover poison." Vivi frowned at its tattered, sickly wings. "Maybe there are more butterflies where this one came from." She ducked into the room beside us, and I followed her in.

There was no overhead light. I flicked the switch by the door, but it turned on nothing. My phone's flashlight landed on an abandoned bed frame and armchair, dull blue walls, and the glint of spiderwebs in the corners. More plywood covered a large window, framed with frothy curtains.

No extra butterflies popped out to greet us.

Vivi glanced at the dust-caked armchair before parking herself cross-legged on the floor—which, honestly, looked cleaner. She examined the butterfly crawling from her chest to her shoulder. Strangely, it seemed to have no intention of leaving her.

The minor miracle was perking her up, the gray tinge in her cheeks fading. "It's not like I believe in signs, but this butterfly almost feels like one, doesn't it?" she asked. Against all odds, this house was winning her over. "I feel like I should pick this room. Unless . . ." She threw me a slightly panicked glance. "You didn't want it, did you?"

I shook my head. "Take it. It doesn't matter which room I get."

At my reply, her eyes narrowed.

So, somehow, that was still the wrong thing to say.

She wanted me to embrace our new home. She wanted my investment—the one thing hardest to give her.

I sighed. "I'll look at the others."

Vivi nodded, the hurt crease between her brows smoothing back into hiding.

I left her murmuring soothing nothings to the butterfly and stepped back into the hallway.

Alone, I liked it even less.

I glanced down the dim corridor. At the haphazard shadows, the cold winks from the dagger-like crystals hanging from wall sconces.

Something looked different this time.

When we'd come up here, every door except one had been closed. And now . . .

The room across from Vivi's stood wide open.

I faltered, pulse stuttering.

I could've *sworn* that door had been closed. And there were no open windows, no cross drafts to explain how it could've moved on its own.

"H-hello?" I said, bracing myself as I stepped into the room. I scanned the shadowy humps of scattered old furniture for the slightest hint of movement. "Mom?"

No answer but the rasp of my footsteps.

Nobody here.

Logically, I'd known there wouldn't be. Every part of me had known, aside from the clenched fist hanging at my side. I made myself open my hand, shake it out.

It was a loose door on decaying hinges. That's all.

And I was acting more and more ridiculous by the second, jumping at butterflies and a house in disrepair.

This space was smaller, L-shaped, with a sloped ceiling and nooks I might've called cozy if the angles weren't off. A little too sharp. A little too asymmetrical.

But a patch of tinted sunlight filtered down from the ceiling, pouring a pretty pool of blue onto the hardwood floor.

At last, an unboarded window!

A circular skylight. It'd only been fifteen minutes since I'd entered the house, but I'd been starting to feel like I'd never see natural light again.

I stood beneath and stared up, into a stained-glass rendering of an indigo sky, complete with a full white moon and smattering of stars.

Finally, a piece of the house that I liked. My chest unknotted the tiniest fraction. It felt like somewhere to start.

And it made me wonder what lurked under the plywood boarding up all the other windows.

Across the room, there was a covered window, situated over a wooden bench built into the wall. I walked over and tugged at the bottom corner of plywood until a piece splintered free.

My phone's flashlight glinted off a border of green and purple glass, and the barest patch of the scene it framed: a log and a blue beetle as big as half my thumb.

There was no escaping bugs in this house.

The glass beetle's back glimmered, iridescent. I ran my finger over the silver seams dividing it into three sections. Vivi had once told me that the word *insect* traced from the Latin word *insectum* to the Greek word *entomon,* which meant "cut into pieces." *Because that's how their bodies look. See?* she'd said, pointing at a drawing in one of her awful insect books. *Head, thorax, and abdomen.*

Pieces stitched into something whole. Like stained glass.

Well, I didn't love insects, but I *did* love how stained glass made fragments look so beautiful together. Made it feel like they were better off broken.

A very pretty lie.

Lies—pretty or otherwise—might have been this house's specialty. I hadn't forgotten those words from the decaying brass plaque in the foyer: *Madame Clery's House of Masks.*

I still wasn't sure what that meant, but if I wanted this "fresh start" to mean anything for me and Mom and Vivi, I'd have to wear an invisible mask of my own—swallow my fears, give this house a chance.

I could do that. I *had* to.

Last time I'd stopped believing in new beginnings, all I could see was the ending.

And I wasn't allowed to do that anymore.

I tapped my phone to life and stared at the lock screen. In

therapy, one early assignment from Dr. Glaser was to change the picture to something that reminded me why I was still here. What I wanted my life to look like.

Of all things, I'd settled on an image of an old family Polaroid. I wouldn't have had the guts to parade such a cringe-inducing photo with me around school. But school was out, and I intended to have zero contact with my peers this summer.

So here it was: My ninth birthday. My cheeks puffed like some ridiculous hamster as I took aim at the candles on a chocolate-frosted Funfetti cake. Vivi leaned over, puffing her cheeks, too, because she was six then and didn't give a crap whose actual birthday it was. I'm shoving her away, and she's shoving me back. We're both laughing, and the picture is blurry—Mom's arms were shaking with her own laughter as she snapped the shot.

I touched Vivi's grin in the picture. And then my own.

My tongue tightened.

I wanted to feel like that again. Happy in a way that was real and warm, secure like a hug.

I wanted to wake up one morning, any morning, and look forward to something. Anything.

I didn't need my old friends back—they hadn't been real friends anyway—but I did need Mom and Vivi. I needed to feel like part of my family again.

I hoped Mom was right, that this busted home could bring us all back together. Maybe there was something beautiful hiding beneath all the dirt—more treasures like the stained glass.

In any case, this bedroom would have to do. The skylight was the one thing I loved about this house so far. Any redeeming factor was more than welcome.

That low mood was still clawing at my ankles, groping for purchase. Sometimes I could stave it off before it got a hold on me. My new medicine was supposed to help, but it was clearly far from infallible.

Keep moving, I told myself. *Just keep moving*.

It was dangerous to stay still if a low was stalking me. Linger long enough, and it liked to pounce.

I pocketed my phone, turning away from the stained-glass beetle and the rest of the obscured window. "Hey, Vivi," I called. "I found my—"

But the words caught in my throat.

I'd left the bedroom door gaping wide behind me. And now . . .

It was closed.

I stiffened.

Had Vivi shut the door while my back was turned? No, the floorboards were too creaky. I would've heard her.

It had to be the hinges again. Or maybe the doorway was set crooked.

Claustrophobia squeezed my chest. The irrational fear that I was trapped—that suddenly the door would refuse to budge.

I raced over and grabbed the knob. With one hard jiggle, it opened.

Of course it did.

Outside, a cacophony of beeps broke out, making me jump more than it should have. The moving truck was here, backing up on the street.

Vivi and I had chosen our rooms just in time. Or, in a way, they'd each chosen us.

I stepped out into the hall. Ready or not, time to start building our new home together.

CHAPTER TWO

WE STARTED WITH THE MORE BREAKABLE boxes and lamps and screens we'd piled into Mom's car, dodging movers as they clunked through the house, carrying bookcases and dressers, entombing us deeper with every piece of our furniture that found its home here.

Eventually, I seized the chaos to sneak peeks at the rest of the upstairs. Most of the doorknobs were stuck. I jostled them free, but they only led to more dark rooms with boarded windows, cluttered with old furniture. Stuffy and cobweb-kissed as the original furnishings were, we were lucky to have them. Our accumulated possessions could've filled two or three of the rooms, max. At least our stuff would suggest the new occupants were *vaguely* aware it was the twenty-first century.

Mom's room was the largest, attached to a private bathroom with a claw-foot tub. Her wallpaper teemed with blue roses and thorny vines, so lifelike they looked ready to burst through the paper.

As I stood at the foot of her bed, my stomach turned to

concrete. That *Something is wrong* whisper scratched inside my skull like a desperate rat. I couldn't pinpoint what it was about her room: Some deeper latent stench? The disorienting design of the wallpaper?

I had to leave.

The room across from hers, the one she'd told us not to enter, was locked. The doorknob, modern and nickel-plated, didn't match the ornate silver and gold hardware throughout the rest of the house. That lock had to be new. Likely installed by Mom, before she chanced bringing us over here.

She'd claimed it was off-limits because it was structurally unsound. But with all her nail-picking and nonanswers, I was sure she was hiding *something*. Maybe that something was behind this locked door.

Or maybe it was just a locked door, and my imagination was running wild.

But even the movers seemed to tread more softly inside this house. While unloading our apartment, they'd been shouting to each other, laughing, joking around. Here, none of that. Hushed tones, hushed footsteps. One of them clipped the hall corner with Vivi's desk, and I swear he mumbled an apology to the wall.

So maybe I wasn't the only one who felt like eyes were hovering over my shoulder. Like the house itself was taking measure of us.

Mom and Vivi and I worked all afternoon, long after the movers were gone, reshuffling furniture and boxes, swiping away sweat, and taking turns running outside for the occasional lungful of fresh air.

Finally, our stomachs' grumbles turned into roars, and Mom asked me to order pizza for dinner. She probably figured that something comforting, something familiar, would be welcome.

For me, it would've been. Only the pizza place sounded shocked when I gave them our address, then they put me on hold for several minutes before agreeing to fill the order. When a car horn sounded an hour later, I peered outside to see the delivery person dropping the box on the grimy sidewalk outside our unlocked front gate.

To be fair, if I'd had the option of driving away when I first saw this house, I would've done the same. And it was even more tempting now, as the sky colored from hazy blue to bloody red. As the daytime hum of cicadas faded into the nighttime chirp of crickets.

In the mountainous shadow of our house, I walked down to the gate to rescue our dinner from the ants. I grabbed the steam-softened cardboard, and was about to retreat, when I felt it—the same spine-tingling sensation I'd learned to dread the past few months at school. That made me feel like every particle of my exposed skin was on fire.

Eyes on me.

The delivery driver was long gone. These eyes came from across the street. A guy my age had stopped in the middle of the sidewalk.

I froze, staring back.

Under the glowing haze of a streetlight, he stood. Tall and hard and lean, dressed too warmly for the weather, in a red-and-black-striped sweatshirt with the hood pulled up. A shock of burnt-copper hair raked across his forehead. Freckles dusted his cut cheeks and jaw.

At the sight of him, warmth dripped thick as honey between my ribs, down to my stomach. Down farther than my stomach.

I'd *thought* social contact was the last thing I wanted. That I needed every day of the eight remaining weeks of summer to transform myself into someone acceptable—or at least invisible—before facing potential classmates.

But I was transfixed, melting over the fact that he'd noticed me, too. Or at least, he was staring back like he didn't mind the view. And he was even wearing all-black Converse high-tops, which happened to match my favorite pair. The pair I hadn't been allowed to take with me to the psych ward (apparently, I was no longer to be trusted with dangerous objects like shoelaces).

I raised my hand in a weak wave, attempting a smile.

Somehow, that gesture shattered whatever spell had been holding him captive. His gaze darted between me, the house, and our car parked out front—likely performing the mental math that I was here to stay.

And something changed.

His shoulders stiffened like he was bracing for a fight. With a frown, he jammed his hands in his pockets and strode off down the street.

I had no idea what I'd done wrong, how he could take one look at my smile and already know he wanted no part of me. But I should've known there was nothing fresh, nothing clean, about starting over.

I allowed myself one last glance as he faded down the block, melting into the day's last shimmering heat waves—the ones that made every tidy little home past our front gate seem like a mirage. Like a world that no longer existed for me.

If I really wanted a second chance at life, I needed to become someone new.

Or at least find a more convincing mask.

So far, I wasn't fooling anyone, not even strangers.

* * *

The second I started unpacking my bedroom, I would truly be accepting it: We lived here now. We would make this tilting, creaking creature of a house our home.

I did my best to put on a good face, but every room was too dim, every shadow too long. The first time I'd tried to wash my hands, the bathroom faucet sputtered and spat. Clanging thundered through the walls, and when the water came, it came soupy as swamp water. Left a rusty ring around the drain. We'd had to run every faucet for fifteen minutes before the water ran clearer. Not clear. Still tinged pink and brown.

But we'd already eaten dinner here—gnawed on our pizza in the overly large dining room, with its twelve-seat mahogany table and oppressively blue wallpaper. And I needed a bedroom before bedtime.

My new room came equipped with a rusted, overwrought brass bed frame, a bedside table, and a couple old-lady lamps. I'd moved in my small wooden desk, scarred by marker from my five-year-old self's "artistic" phase, and its accompanying rickety chair. My four-drawer dresser had never managed to fit half my wardrobe, but my new closet was huge.

I began unpacking my clothes, a small exercise in torture. Everything I owned was too small, too old. Sweatshirt cuffs were frayed. Bare patches had worn into the thighs of my jeans. Then there were the fashion-disaster trophies from Mom's misguided thrift-store hunts. She didn't shop in thrift stores out of necessity. It just gave her a special thrill to reclaim trash into treasure. She couldn't stand the idea of anything going to waste.

"How lonely," she'd say, when she saw something chipped and forgotten, sitting on the shelf.

I was always struck by that: *How lonely.*

As if the rocking horse knew it was broken. Knew no one was coming back to ride it.

In the end, I guess it was inevitable that she had reclaimed this abandoned house, no matter how long she'd tried to avoid it.

I waded deeper into the closet to hang my most embarrassing sweaters, and a strange gleam caught me off guard.

At the back wall.

This closet didn't have a light, so it only revealed itself once I was practically on top of it: a mirror.

A cracked, skinny full-length mirror mounted on . . . a door?

I fumbled around in the murk, grasping for a knob. Yes. There was one, as ornately carved as my bedposts. I twisted it, but it wouldn't budge.

Another locked door, in addition to the room down the hall.

This mirrored door had to be part of the original house. Maybe another owner down the line had wanted more storage, and they'd slapped a bigger closet over top of the first. No wonder this house was so twisty and strange, if nobody bothered to pitch out the old before glossing over it with the new.

To embrace the new, you had to annihilate the old.

Actually. That was a good reminder for me, too.

I batted past my clothes to free myself from the closet. There'd only been so much space for clutter in my previous shared room with Vivi, so I didn't have *that* many bags and boxes to unpack. But I still felt like I was drowning in my old stuff, the stuff that made me the old me. The broken me I couldn't be anymore.

And there was an easy enough fix for that.

I pulled out the box that Mom had labeled LIBBY'S DECOR—a generous effort to make my useless crap sound fancy—and started pitching old posters and drama-department playbills into a trash bag. Since I'd started acting, Mom had saved every program, dating back to my role as Narrator #3 in *The Lion, the Witch, and the Wardrobe* in fifth grade.

My fingers found the program for this past spring's production of *Romeo and Juliet.* And the deepest part of me cringed.

The show should've been a happy memory. Against all odds, I'd landed Juliet, my first lead. It had felt like a dream. Even if the casting had scandalized the entire drama department.

Everyone had expected the lead to go to my friend Gemma. With her sparkling laugh and bouncy hair and honey-nectarine perfume, she was born to play the love interest. But I'd put in the work for that audition, and it showed. Gemma tried to be happy for me, but she couldn't be—not really. And that also showed.

So my friend group was already splintering before the *Romeo and Juliet* cast party in March. But that was the night when the cracks between us widened into gulfs. The first night I drank.

Already high from our closing performance, I'd blissfully chugged one plastic cup of sugary spiked punch after another. I didn't realize—didn't have the vocabulary to describe it then—I'd slipped into what Dr. Glaser called "hypomania." Not as intense or long-lasting as mania, she'd explained, but nonetheless, an intoxicating burst of energy more than capable of clouding judgment. I'd experienced that kind of thing before, but *never* so publicly.

That night, I was drunk on more than punch. My overeager brain chemicals flooded me with energy, whispering that I was invincible. Every idea was a good—no, a great—no, *the best*—idea. That secret crush on my castmate Mason, aka Romeo, was worth fighting for. Even if sober me had been pretty sure it was Gemma he liked. The whole party was cast in glittering gold, all fruity booze and grins.

At least, that's how it was playing out inside my head.

In everyone else's reality, I'd been a drunken, awkward mess. Raw and overbubbly, with too-wide smiles. At one point, Mason literally shoved me off the arm of his chair. Even then, I'd assumed he was teasing—I crawled right back on.

And everyone had the videos to prove it.

Around the time I started throwing up, Gemma and my other friends got so embarrassed that they stranded me without a ride.

They were gone before I crashed, hard, slumped on the bathroom floor.

Maybe it was different for people with bipolar I or II, but in my shitty adventures with bipolar III, I'd found my mood swings didn't always linger for days. Sometimes it was hours. With the right triggers, they could even switch straight from high to low.

Once I saw my friends' coats were gone, overheard Mason reaming me to his friends, my sunshiny energy flatlined.

I couldn't get up, not even when people started pounding on the door.

There were videos of all that, too.

And of Mom, who I eventually had to call to pick me up.

My mistakes hadn't been huge, but they'd been splashy. And the humiliating aftermath proved that my friends weren't the friends I'd thought they were.

The ensuing isolation at school over the past few months was the most obvious contributor to my downslide into depression. But really, the worst dangers were the ones nobody else could see: the lies my brain kept whispering to me, the chemicals that weighed on me, heavier and heavier, exacerbating my lows, robbing me of every tiny happiness, every tiny hope, until . . .

Well. My mood swings had been increasingly vicious since middle school—tearing me down, heaving me up, hurtling me back and forth. Mom had dismissed it first as puberty, and then as teenhood. We'd pretended that's all it was. She'd let me wade through life like I was wading through the same waters as everyone else. Like the tides weren't tugging me harder, dragging me under.

The awful truth is, it could've been anything that finally drowned me.

Still, right now, it felt a little too good to tear the *Romeo and Juliet* program. Down the middle. To the side. Then again. And again and again and again. Into choppy flecks.

If only I could tear the memory out of my mind, too.

Into the trash it went.

At the bottom of the DECOR box was my stuffed bear, Freddie, with his worn fur and chipped butterscotch-brown eyes. My constant bedtime companion, age zero to . . . Well, I'd still been keeping him under my pillow.

My hand holding him hovered over the trash bag.

But I knew I couldn't keep this little-kid crap. If, by some miracle, I found any friends at school this fall, I couldn't risk them spotting Freddie on my bed.

"Oh no, sweetie. Not Freddie." Mom's voice jolted me from the doorway.

"Mom! How long have you been there?"

"Just got here. Knock, knock." She rapped on the open door, like that wasn't beside the point, and came to kneel with me on the floor. "Luckily, I'm in time to rescue poor Freddie."

I was already regretting propping that creepy door open. But I wasn't allowed to close my bedroom door anymore. Privacy, as it turned out, was a privilege—one I'd lost. Still, I could've let that door swing shut on its own, like it had no doubt wanted to, and feigned innocence.

Mom pulled Freddie away from me. "Remember how you

used to insist on taking him in the bath with you? I told you it would break his music box, but you didn't care. Until after he got soaked and you kept trying to wind him up." She smiled at the bear, running her fingers along his torn fur.

Of course I didn't remember. I was what, two? "I didn't even know he had a music box," I said, and snatched the bear back. "And I'm not two anymore. So."

I stuffed him into the trash bag.

"Lib, no. I'll keep him for you, then. Out of sight, I promise." Mom dug him out and frowned into the bag. "I don't understand why you're throwing your stuff away."

I couldn't stay beside her anymore on my bedroom floor, watching the crow's-feet crumpling around her clouding eyes. I stood and crossed to my bed. "People change, Mom. They're supposed to, right?" I fiddled with the sheets on my mattress, stretching them to grasp at the corners. "Change is good."

She watched me from the floor. "It can be."

The unspoken part hung there, too.

She certainly hadn't been the same since that awful day.

For one thing, she'd stopped working. She had some flexibility as a real estate agent, so at least she wasn't at immediate risk of getting fired. But the longer she stayed home, the more it felt like something important was draining away.

Like my actual mom had gone into hiding.

She even looked different. Her wardrobe used to be an ode to sherbet, button downs in a million pastel shades. Lately, she wore whites and creams—a solid ivory if she was feeling daring. Her curls used to bounce around her shoulders, free and frizzy, but now they were crunchy with hair spray, brushing against her skeletal collarbone. It didn't look good, but she couldn't see that. It was like this knock-off version of her couldn't let anything bad be real. Maybe that's why whatever reservations she'd had about this house—whatever had stopped her from moving us in before—had mysteriously melted away.

All I knew was that I hated this careful wall of sunshine she'd started holding between her and the rest of the world, especially between her and me. I wanted to grab her by the shoulders and shake her until that artificial sweetener fell out of her mouth.

I missed how she used to talk to me—like I was a person.

I missed *her*.

"Aren't we supposed to start over in this house?" I asked. "We all need that. So let me try. Is that too much to ask, or do I not get to make any of my own decisions anymore?"

"Okay." Mom's voice was flatter now. "You're the expert, Libby."

She stood and moved toward the hall, taking Freddie with her. "Remember," she said, touching my door, "leave this open."

Salt in the wound, thanks.

Late that night, once we'd split into our separate rooms and gotten into bed, I realized how far away Mom and Vivi felt. Our apartment had nestled us together. But this house—this big, big house—stretched the air thin between us.

Instead of Vivi's whistling snore, the sounds of night settled in.

This house creaked. It moaned. Groaned.

Calls of the crawly things hiding in the rosebushes seeped in through the boarded windows. If only a fresh cross draft would seep in, too. Mom had gotten centralized air-conditioning installed, but it wasn't proving up to the challenge. At least she'd promised the plywood would come down from the windows tomorrow.

Just had to make it through tonight.

The feverish July heat ripened the house's pervasive floral stench, along with that strange sour undercurrent. The final whiff at the end of my every breath: rot.

Something had probably died in these walls.

My sweat was soaking my nightshirt and my sheets. With a groan, I kicked them off and flipped flat on my back.

I would've stripped off the nightshirt, too, except for my door rule. I'd propped it open with my trash can. The gap leered at me, yawning into the deeper dark of the hall.

In the psych ward, they'd insisted on open doors, too. There, the hallway lights were always on. Their incessant fluorescents had buzzed into my skull—a mocking hum that never let me forget: *This is not home. Home isn't a place for people like you. People who've done what you've done.*

Here, the drone of insects outside was too similar for comfort.

This is not home. Home isn't a place for people like you. . . .

I glanced at the clock on my nightstand. Midnight.

I'd positioned the bed under my skylight, the one view to the outside world. Overhead, the real moon lined up with the fake moon in the glass. A half-moon. Half-light, half-dark.

Bump.

The sound jerked me up in bed, spiked my heartbeat. It came from above me.

Another water pipe banging?

But then came shuffling, skittering. Creaking wood.

That was no water pipe.

Something was *moving* above my ceiling.

Part of my room jutted into the open air, where the moon

filtered through my skylight, but the rest was masked by the choppy rooflines overhead. Likely, there was an attic up there. And that's where the noises seemed to be coming from.

I held still, listening.

Scritch, scratch, scriiiiiitch . . .

My mouth was too dry, my heart rate ticking up. How many bugs did it take to make such big sounds?

They could be nesting in the attic—squirming, living mountains of them.

But after two fumigations, shouldn't whatever was up there be dead?

I grabbed my phone from the nightstand and searched: *Can pests survive fumigation?*

Wi-Fi wouldn't be installed until tomorrow, so my phone had to fall back on its own network. The connection crawled. The outside world seemed reluctant to reach inside this house's walls. Couldn't blame it.

The results finally loaded, and I clicked through them, my toes curling as I read about cockroaches and termites and wood-boring beetles and rats and every icky crawly creature that can dig its way into your home.

Fumigation should've killed them all. Although some bugs might linger a few weeks after treatment. And reinfestations were possible.

Maybe we needed one more fumigation, to be safe.

Unless . . . Mom was lying about having brought an exterminator here. I couldn't imagine why she'd do that. It was just hard not to be suspicious of her, after her baffling attitude reversal about this house. She'd spent her whole life past the age of four ignoring it, and suddenly, in the last six weeks, she had some burning desire to move here. And she kept ducking questions.

I blew out a sigh of musty air and tapped my restless fingers against my phone. I hadn't looked up my new house yet. The "local attraction" status that Mom refused to explain. The House of Masks name.

I might find something I didn't want to know. But nothing on the internet could be worse than what my shivering brain would imagine—lying awake as the night deepened around me, tormented by that persistent *scritch-scritch-scratch*ing above my head.

I typed *House of Masks* into my browser and hit GO.

Slowly, choppily, the screen filled with text.

The top hit was from some sketchy site: RealHaunted Houses.net.

You had to be freaking kidding me.

I clicked on it, unleashing a sea of yellow text on a black background. The cherry on top of the trying-too-hard sundae was a banner complete with shittily animated lightning.

In a font that mimicked dripping blood, it read **HOUSE OF MASKS**, followed by a block of text:

> House of Masks was founded by the renowned spiritualist Madame Ellen Clery, in 1894. Known for its masked séances, magnificent stained glass, and a twisty hedge maze of blue roses (yes, really!!!), the local attraction operated for just a few years before Ellen Clery and her husband, Joseph Cragg, went missing.
>
> And they're not the only ones.
>
> At least nine people moved into House of Masks and never moved out. Some even think the house is responsible for a tenth

disappearance—a neighbor who vanished in 2017.

No one has lived in House of Masks since the 1970s, and for good reason. Think twice about stopping to smell the blue roses!

A long shiver slid down my sweaty spine.

Masked séances?

Since the original owners, people had been vanishing from this house?

In other words, *my relatives* had been vanishing in this house?

Mom had never really explained what had happened to her parents here. She'd said they'd died in an accident when she was four. She'd definitely never mentioned any disappearances.

If rumors like these were circulating, that might explain why the delivery driver had abandoned our pizza on the sidewalk. Why the hot neighbor who'd caught my eye had bolted for the hills.

I couldn't believe this website was right. Otherwise, why the hell would Mom have brought us here?

Then someone screamed. And I jolted upright in bed. The terrified wail ripped through the walls—through the house's muffling velour padding and lacy curtains and thick, swallowing rugs.

It came from down the hall.

It came from Mom.

CHAPTER THREE

"MOM!" I SHOUTED, THOUGH I KNEW she would never hear me over her own wail.

I jabbed on my phone's flashlight and burst out of my bedroom. Vivi was in the hall, quivering and panicked. Together, we raced toward Mom's room. My legs were so shaky I had to fight not to trip with each step.

Sometimes Mom had vivid nightmares. Once, I'd caught her sobbing in her sleep. But I'd never heard her scream like this. Mom was shrieking like she was fighting for her life.

I shoved her bedroom door open and slammed into a thick wall of rosy fragrance. Under that, the deeper stench of decaying logs and dirt squirming with earthworms.

I gagged.

"Mom," I choked out.

My phone's flashlight found her: upright in her four-poster bed, clutching the quilt to her chest, backed against her headboard.

Swollen shadows collected in the pockets of her room. The

only window was boarded, like all the rest, blocking out even the weak light of the moon.

My phone's beam tracked her stare to her closet door.

It was open, its mirror reflecting her wide-eyed, white-lipped reflection.

The rest of the room . . . was empty. Practically echoing with the terror of Mom's shrieks.

"What's wrong?" I stepped toward her, slow and stiff, and Vivi followed.

Mom snapped her head toward us. "G-girls?" she stammered, as if just noticing us. "What are you doing out of bed?"

Um.

I glanced at Vivi, who looked as bewildered as I felt. "Mom, you were screaming your head off," she said.

"I was?" Mom smoothed down her sweaty nightgown with trembling hands, like she was trying to make herself presentable. "I—I hope I didn't scare you. I must've had one of those—what do they call them?—night terrors. I dreamed something was here. Standing at the foot of my bed."

As much as I didn't want to believe anything I'd read on RealHauntedHouses.net, the timing of Mom's night terror prickled every micro-hair up and down my spine.

The phone slipped in my clammy palm, and I gripped it even tighter, fighting to hold the beam steady. "You're sure it was nothing?" I asked.

"I'm sure," Mom said. "It was impossible, what I saw."

That didn't necessarily make me feel better.

We moved in slow motion to join her on the bed. I had the irrational fear something might grab me or Vivi. The bed felt like the only safe spot in the room. Some holdover from childhood, where that was the one place monsters couldn't touch you.

Vivi crawled up to the headboard and wrapped her arms around Mom's shoulders. I sat closer to the edge, but I couldn't help pulling my legs up, out of reach of the dark space under the bed. I clicked on Mom's bedside lamp, and the golden glow was a tiny refuge.

But the blue roses and vines covering the wallpaper loomed around us. The blooms were printed in velvet and, by lamplight, they looked like sour lumps of mold.

"I really am sorry I scared you." Mom pushed her unruly curls from her face. Her eyes darted to the closet again. "I just could've sworn I closed that door."

"My bedroom door moves on its own, too," I said. A weak attempt at comfort, but all I had to offer.

Mom nodded. "The hinges are on their last legs, I'm sure."

"I'll close it." Vivi stood.

"No," Mom gasped. She lunged, grabbing Vivi by the nightshirt.

Vivi turned to stare. I stared, too—at Mom's suddenly wild expression, Vivi's top knotted in her fist.

Mom caught herself then, with a weak laugh. Released Vivi and rubbed her own chest in soothing circles. "Sorry, I'm still a little worked up. This was my room when I was a little girl. Being here is bringing old memories to the surface."

"Memories?" I demanded. *Memories* were responsible for Mom screaming like she was being murdered?

"Nightmares," Mom clarified. "Old nightmares."

It was probably a losing game to press further. Whenever Vivi or I pried into Mom's past, she looked like we'd stabbed her in the stomach, but I couldn't ignore the opening, not after reading about the supposed disappearances in our house. "Nightmares about your parents?"

Mom winced. "Not quite. Tied into losing them, I'm sure."

I knew she wouldn't want me to ask. Knew it would be bad if I did. But.

"Mom . . . ," I said slowly, "you said it was some kind of accident, but how exactly did they die?"

Mom froze. Then she and Vivi both turned on me, shocked in a way that demanded loud and clear: *What is wrong with you, asking a question like that here and now?*

I withered in on myself. "I read online that people had disappeared in this house," I mumbled, "so I . . . I wondered . . ."

"Disappeared?" Vivi demanded. "What do you mean, 'disappeared'?"

I had her full attention for what felt like the first time in weeks. Never thought I'd so desperately crave validation from my little sister, but it felt better than I wanted to admit that she was listening to me how she used to, even for a second.

"It didn't really explain. See, look." I still had the page open on my phone. I held it out.

"Libby!" Mom snatched it from me before Vivi could. Her lips moved silently as she scanned the contents, brow furrowing like she was fighting to remember something. "Nine disappearances?" she mumbled. "Maybe ten?"

My phone trembled in her hand. And for the first time since I'd returned from the hospital, the honeyed tone she'd been smearing over her every word was gone.

I was sorry she was so unnerved, but relief softened the tightest knots in my shoulders. I hadn't realized how much I needed to hear Mom sound like her actual self again.

"Mom, what is it?" I asked. "Do you know something about the disappearances?"

"I . . . ," she started to answer.

But then she blinked, that slight glaze of the past six weeks returning to her eyes. Like someone had reached into her brain and pressed SKIP on the troubling song that was playing. "Libby, these are just wild rumors."

She shook her head at my phone. "What even is this site . . . ? RealHauntedHouses.net? Come on, sweetie. What happened to my parents was . . ." Her honeyed tone was back, even as her fingers tightened on her sheets. "Well, I promise I'll tell you girls once I've gotten my bearings. But, trust me, that kind of freak tragedy could happen anywhere. Maybe, in a strange way, we're actually safer here. Lightning never strikes the same place twice."

"That's a myth about lightning," Vivi replied automatically. At Mom's frown, she bit her lip. "I mean, maybe, though. You never know."

"Anyway, that's enough of this morbid talk." Mom turned to me. "Promise me, Libby, no more half-baked Internet 'research.' "

I hesitated, maybe longer than I should have, and Mom's eyes narrowed. Talking about the disappearances—even if the rumors were as off base as she claimed—was obviously rattling her. But she had at least promised to share the full story about her parents once she was ready. It was only fair to respect that.

Finally, I nodded. "Okay, okay."

"Thank you," Mom said. She closed the browser before handing my phone back.

As I set it down beside me, my hand brushed something on the bed.

A half-balled moth-eaten yellow blanket.

I pulled it out and spotted stitching in the corner. The initials *SF*, same as Mom's: Sharon Feldman.

"Mom, is this yours?" I lifted it up.

Mom startled. Like she was seeing a ghost. "That looks like

my old baby blankie. I had no idea that was still in this house," she said. "Did one of you girls find it?"

Vivi and I both shook our heads.

Mom frowned, reaching out a reluctant hand. "Let me see it."

I held it out, and the blanket in my hand squirmed.

I shrieked, dropping it on the bed, and a writhing fistful of cockroaches spilled onto the covers.

I leaped out of the bed in one direction. Mom leaped out in another.

And Vivi leaned in closer.

The cockroaches scurried madly, some digging under the stirred-up sheets, running for cover, others falling over the edge of the bed.

They met on the ground, and—as one horrifying gleaming swarm—they scuttled through Mom's bedroom doorway, across the hall, and vanished under the opposite door. The locked one. The one Mom had forbidden us to enter.

The sudden squirm of the blanket in my hand. The writhing cockroaches and their escape under that locked door across the hall. Even once the three of us were sequestered back in our rooms—Mom insisting she was fine, just fine—the scene kept replaying for me.

Those cockroaches had me thinking: If the locked room was structurally unsound, maybe that's because it was sheltering a burgeoning nest of bugs, gnawing at the wood. I'd asked Mom about it, but she'd insisted the exterminator had been thorough: *Fumigations reach the whole house. Sometimes bugs linger a little afterward, that's all.*

That's all, huh?

Vivi swore she hadn't put that blanket on Mom's bed. I knew *I* hadn't. All I could think was that a mover found it today and, trying to be helpful, laid it out for Mom.

Even if this house wasn't haunted in the way the internet claimed, Mom's history was lying in ambush at every turn. Whatever happened when she was a kid must have been horrific. One night here, and she'd already woken up screaming. And her hand had trembled when she read over that website. It seemed like she'd been on the cusp of remembering something.

Her past trauma had to be the reason she'd never wanted to move here before.

But I still didn't understand why she'd brought us here now.

Yes, we had to move *somewhere* to get me away from my old school, and, yes, since Mom already owned it, this was the most financially sound option. But the dreamy way she'd started talking about this house, only in the past six weeks, made me think it wasn't as simple as finances.

She'd *wanted* to come here.

And I couldn't think of one sane reason why.

All I wanted was to leave. Repack the few things we'd managed to unpack. Load up the car and drive away. Far away.

My head was pounding. I paced my worn rug and kneaded my chewed fingernails into my tense scalp.

From the corner of my room, the closet door gaped like a mouth. Mom had been so sure she'd closed hers. I couldn't help wondering if she had a second door at the very back, like I did. If our pest problem was bigger than bugs, something might have eaten through that inner door and nudged the outer one open.

Now all I could picture was hungry rodents chewing through

the back of Mom's closet. *My* closet. Me falling asleep, then waking up to wriggling shapes under my sheets. Something gnawing on my toes.

I shuddered and shook away the vision. I hadn't noticed any holes in that secret, inner door in my own closet. And it was stuck shut.

To be sure, I crossed to my closet, shoved my clothes aside, and checked again.

The mirrored door at the very back was still closed. Still intact. But I retreated quickly and shut the outer closet door, then wedged my desk chair under the knob.

Above my head, something skittered across the ceiling. And I winced.

Suddenly, the last thing I wanted was to be walking around barefoot. I was lucky I hadn't already stepped on any bugs. The thought made the soles of my feet crawl.

I climbed back into bed and started counting my breaths, like Dr. Glaser had instructed me to practice.

Inhale: one, two, three, four.

Exhale: one, two, three, four, five . . .

Thud.

Above my ceiling.

Sweat dripped down my forehead, but I pressed my pillow around my ears to muffle the house's scuffling and scratching.

The most ridiculous part was, the only thing that brought me any peace was imagining Vivi's snore. I pretended to hear it until I finally drifted off.

Dread followed me, like a fog, all the way to the morning light.

* * *

I woke up feeling deader. Deader than I had before I'd gotten into bed.

I'd been hungover once, and this was worse. I couldn't do another night like that.

I peeled off my sticky pajamas and pulled on fresh clothes to sweat through.

Downstairs, clangs and bangs announced that Mom was already awake, and maybe Vivi, too.

I dragged myself to the kitchen. Despite the efforts of the stained-glass pendant light above the island, the boarded windows kept everything dim and murky. The walls were a dingy blue. Because the wallpaper was blue everywhere in this godforsaken house.

The enormous room was cluttered with boxes, some half-empty, many still sealed. Cabinets hung open—a few plates here, a few glasses there. Mom didn't have a tidy system for unpacking. So far, it looked more like: Grab what you need. If you can find it.

The counter closest to the dining room was covered in a hopelessly chaotic stack of papers, and the corner of a pale-pink brochure caught my eye as I walked past.

I didn't need to see the title. I remembered it too well: "After the Emergency: Caring for Your Family."

A careful title. With careful subject headings throughout like "What to Know" and "How to Help" and, my personal favorite, "Moving Forward—Together."

I doubted Mom had meant for me to see it, but she'd left it in the mail-table stack before, and I'd bumbled into it not long after returning from the psych ward. Maybe it should've made me feel good, seeing all the parts she'd underlined. Instead, it had left a taste under my tongue, bitter as crushed aspirin. And every time she asked how I was feeling today on a scale of 1 to

5, or directly quoted one of the pamphlet's suggested sympathy lines, like "I'm sorry I didn't see how much pain you were in," I tasted it all over again.

For me, the worst part was the page titled "What Not to Do," because that's where I saw that Mom had underlined "Don't blame yourself" and "Don't blame the person who requires treatment." She must've felt she needed the reminders.

Ironically, she hadn't bothered to underline "Don't ignore what happened and expect things to get better." And yet when she wasn't quoting that pamphlet at me, nine times out of ten that's what she was doing instead.

I sighed, and Mom looked up from the stove.

"Good morning, sweetie!" she chirped with Disney princess levels of zeal. She had a big skillet out, and the counter was littered with bowls and dirty measuring cups, flour and sugar. "Blueberry and lemon okay?" She waved her spatula at the sizzling stove top.

Pancakes.

Mom didn't even like cooking. She'd mostly left meal prep to me or take-out restaurants when she was working. Now, here she was, flouncing around wearing a pinned-on grin and the frilliest apron we owned—a misguided Hanukkah present from Great-Aunt Carol that had made Mom grit her teeth when she'd received it several years ago.

On her, the apron almost looked like a costume. Like she was auditioning for Mary Homemaker in a 1950s sitcom. It was so transparent how much she needed this house to feel like home. How much she'd strain herself to make that happen for us.

The effort was kind.

But watching Mom bend herself into unfamiliar shapes made me feel a little nauseous.

And that big vase of blue roses she'd stuck in the center of the counter—with their wafting syrupy perfume—wasn't helping.

I did my best to play along anyway. "Blueberry and lemon. Great."

"Great!" Mom turned back to the stove and to flipping. "I'm sorry again for that . . . excitement last night. I hope you got back to sleep all right?"

Excitement was one hell of a euphemism for shrieking night terrors, but Mom clearly needed this to be a picture-perfect morning—our first sit-down breakfast together in our new home. Vivi was already perched at the kitchen island, her place mat set, phone in one hand, OJ in the other.

So I stammered, "Y-yeah. I slept okay after that. Did you all?"

"Mm-hmm, very well!" Mom said. Quickly. Tightly. Like that was something she didn't want to discuss either.

"Fine. Good," Vivi said. But her voice was off kilter, betraying an obvious lie.

Maybe I wasn't the only one who'd spent the rest of the night tossing and turning and barely breathing.

I cleared my throat. "By the way, did anyone else hear the sounds from the attic last night? I noticed them through my ceiling before Mom's nightmare. On and off afterward, too."

"I didn't hear anything," Vivi said, though she'd probably been wearing headphones.

She side-eyed me. A clear enough message: *Can you just not? For once, can you not?*

For Vivi's taste, I must've been veering too close to unpleasant topics—brushing up against Mom's nightmare, raising problems with the house. But it's not like I was pouring salt in the pancakes. I was raising a real concern, as gently as I could.

Unfortunately, Vivi was stumbling into another "What Not

to Do" from the recovery pamphlet: "Don't make your loved one feel guilty for having bad feelings." It was far from the first time. I wasn't sure if Mom had shared the pamphlet with her, but I knew Vivi had met with people at the hospital, who'd run through guidelines about how to support me. Surely, they'd covered this. Surely, she could manage the basics if she bothered to try.

Her side-eyeing made me feel sicker. But I had to ask anyway: "Mom, are you sure we don't need one more fumigation?"

Mom shook her head. "Fumigations are expensive, sweetie. And we'd have to move out and stay at a hotel. The exterminator said we might still notice bugs for a few weeks. If they're here after that, then we can talk."

A few weeks? That was an eternity. "For now, could we take a quick look in the attic to check for ourselves?" I asked. Although, now that I considered it, I hadn't noticed any obvious attic door. "How do you even access it?"

"The attic?" Mom's shoulders rose a solid inch. "I—I don't think going up there is necessary. Most of the house is perfectly safe, of course, but the attic hasn't been well maintained. We don't need anybody stepping on the wrong floorboard and falling through."

The *structurally unsound* excuse again—same as with the locked room upstairs. Plausible enough. Except that Mom kept avoiding my eyes.

I couldn't shake the sense that she wasn't telling me something.

"But, Mom, the sounds were loud. I mean, we're either talking about a hell of a lot of bugs, or something a hell of a lot bigger than bugs."

Mom laughed that off, one of her dismissive *Oh, everything's fine* laughs. "It was probably squirrels playing on the roof, Lib. Don't let your imagination get away from you."

My imagination.

Was it?

I wasn't positive where the attic started or the roof ended above my bedroom ceiling. I'd *thought* the sounds came from the attic. But I could have been wrong. I'd like to think it was squirrels.

I didn't. But I'd like to.

"Have some pancakes." Mom nodded at the chair beside Vivi's. She'd already set a place for me, folded napkin and everything.

My meds were tucked beside a glass of juice.

My new antidepressant. And my mood leveler, lithium. I did think the pills were working. I felt flatter overall, like there was a dam in my brain, holding back the flood of my most extreme emotions. I needed that dam—this house was one unsettling trigger after another.

I washed down the pills with a big gulp of OJ. And we ate our breakfast together at the island, our attempts at conversation every bit as fluffy, as artificially lemony-bright, as our pancakes.

It was a relief when the heavy chimes of the doorbell rolled through the first floor. Our new house's first visitor: the contractor arriving to unboard the windows.

Vivi and I hopped to dishwashing duty as Mom invited him in. Over the splashing sink and rattling pipes, I heard him tell Mom he'd spend the day peeling the plywood back from the outside. Mom told him we'd peel it back from the inside.

Which was news to us.

After the contractor retreated outdoors, Mom returned to us in the kitchen. "How about it, girls? Let's get the plywood off these windows today," she said. "I think it'd be best if you two teamed up." If her scheme to enforce Libby-and-Vivi bonding time wasn't transparent enough, her sly little smile was poking through again.

I flinched, and Vivi nearly dropped the skillet she was drying.

But I thought of the picture on my lock screen and the very real grin I'd shared with Vivi over birthday cake. I needed to claw back to that place.

I wanted so desperately to believe Dr. Glaser that healing—real, true healing—was possible for me. That Mom could be right, that fixing up this house, reconnecting with Vivi, was somewhere to start.

After we finished in the kitchen, I brushed my teeth, tied back my hair, and spent several minutes practicing deep breaths before I was ready to face a one-on-one day with my sister.

Finally, I met Vivi in her room and held out a hammer to her. Too busy poking glumly at her phone, she didn't notice me standing there.

"Who died?" I asked.

She stiffened, and I realized, of course, that was a terrible opener.

"Leia's having a pool party today," Vivi mumbled. "No one bothered asking me. They assumed I can't go because we live, like, an hour away now. They're gonna forget about me. It's already happening." She clicked her screen to black and chewed her chapped bottom lip.

I knew this was my fault. I was the reason we'd moved, forcing her to abandon her friends and her ballet studio. And she had to be thinking it, too.

When I'd shared that guilt with Dr. Glaser, she'd reminded

me that Vivi would meet more people once she got back to dancing. But as I glanced around her new room, I noticed an obvious omission from her decor. "You're not putting your ballet posters up?" I asked, changing the subject.

Vivi shook her head, indicating a dead end to this line of questioning.

That struck me as deeply wrong.

Vivi had been in love with ballet since she was six years old. And she'd kept a poster of her idol, Misty Copeland, over her headboard for nearly as long.

Her fantasy had always been to play Odette in *Swan Lake,* because Misty Copeland had played Odette in *Swan Lake.* This past spring, Vivi's studio had announced auditions for the show. The day she got the part, she came home with a glittering grin, the starriest eyes, bursting to share a second-by-second replay of discovering her name on the cast list.

I wanted to support her, like she'd supported me when I'd landed my own dream role of Juliet. Not only had she squealed when I told her and thrown her arms around my waist, she'd promised to run lines with me whenever I needed her. Ultimately, I needed her so often that she learned Romeo's lines better than my costar, Mason. I caught her mouthing along as she sat with Mom in the front row at every performance. She'd even tacked the program on her bulletin board in our old room, with my name circled in little stars, until I'd made her take it down.

But by the time Odette came along for Vivi, depression had its chokehold on me. I said the rightish things, managed smiles when I could.

Then came that point when I couldn't give *anything* anymore. Two weeks before opening night.

I hadn't meant to do that to Vivi. I just . . . ran out of time. But I'd been kidding myself that she'd still have *Swan Lake.* I should've realized Vivi would have to drop out.

It was only a show, but for Vivi, it had been a dream. More than once, I'd caught her ghosting through the steps she'd never gotten to dance onstage. Then she stopped dancing altogether, like I'd stopped acting.

I'd been assuming it was temporary, but now she was refusing to hang her posters. Some of the light that used to shine in her eyes had been snuffed out.

I asked uneasily, "Vivi, you *are* going to start dancing again, right?"

"Are you going to start acting again?" Vivi shot back, with barely concealed venom.

It landed like a knife between the ribs. Dr. Glaser and Mom wanted me to get back into theater at my new school. At least audition for the fall production. But the thought of all those eyes on me, all those people depending on me . . . I'd forgotten how to do anything but let people down.

I turned away from Vivi, even as her glower burned into my spine. This was why we couldn't talk about anything real anymore—we both got too tight, too touchy.

"Where's your butterfly?" I asked instead, forcefully pleasant. Her desk was primed for insect collecting, armed with jars and airhole-poked shoeboxes, but I didn't see the butterfly inside.

Vivi was appalled at the question. "You don't keep a healthy butterfly in a jar, Libby."

"I thought it wasn't healthy?"

"No, it's much better!" Vivi said. "I tried releasing it outside, but it wouldn't go. I gave it some blue roses, though, and that worked wonders. The caterpillars love them, too." She pointed to a jar on her desk, stuffed with blue rose branches. Caterpillars wound around the thorns like oversized maggots.

Mom's pancakes turned in my stomach. "Where did the caterpillars come from?" I asked.

"Oh, I found them hiding in the curtains! That's probably where the butterfly is now, too." She nodded to the curtains framing her boarded window.

The one we were about to unboard.

No wonder the caterpillars and butterflies liked those curtains. That lacy yellow-white was the perfect camouflage. There could be a million wriggling through the fabric, and you'd never know.

If Mom's plan for pest extermination was nothing more than to wait a few weeks, then we were stuck with them. Stuck pretending this was normal. Or remotely sanitary.

And now I had to stand beside them for the next hour, or however long it took to pry off this plywood.

I took a deep breath in and out and passed Vivi a hammer.

CHAPTER FOUR

LUCKILY, AFTER FIFTEEN MINUTES OR SO of prying out rusty nails with my rustier hammer, I could see that Vivi's window was stained glass, too.

But I wasn't noticing any way to open it—no cranks, no liftable panes. If all the windows in the house were sealed, this southern summer was going to roast us alive.

And when we broke down the last of the plywood and stepped back to admire the artwork, it was . . . strange.

Very, very strange.

The scene in Vivi's window featured a humanish figure: a long-limbed blue body draped in an old-fashioned cloak. It hovered, with elegant wings, above emerald grass crawling with caterpillars, and was surrounded by a swirling cloud of butterflies. One sat poised on the tip of its finger.

The figure wore a mask that extended out from the window. A half mask, shaped like the body of a butterfly: tufty white feathers rippled down its nose, and ivory lace wings extended over the forehead and cheeks.

I'd never seen anything like it—the rest of the window was flat, but that one piece, the mask on its face, was protruding. Sculptural. Made of feathers and lace. It looked like a separate piece that had been attached. Almost like it could fly straight out of the window.

So House of Masks did come equipped with some masklike decor.

At the bottom of the portrait, a stained-glass banner with Gothic lettering proclaimed: THE BUTTERFLY.

The image reminded me of a tarot card, something you'd spot alongside the Magician and the Fool.

Vivi sighed up at it like she was falling in love. Butterflies were her favorite insects, after all. Which said something—*every* insect was practically her favorite insect.

But the window gave *me* a different feeling. Underneath the butterfly mask, the figure's stained-glass chin was a flat panel of empty swirling blue. Except for one feature: A wide white smile. Sharp and curved as a crescent moon.

That smile didn't look sweet.

And this window had been waiting, hidden under plywood, in the same room where Vivi had found butterflies and caterpillars—ones that *very closely* resembled those featured in this artwork. That was too eerie to be a coincidence, and yet I couldn't fathom any meaning.

Vivi frowned at whatever face I was making. "You don't like it."

"No, I do! I . . ." But she was only getting stonier, so I stopped lying. "Well, don't you think it's *weird* that you're finding butterflies—butterflies that match this window—in what is apparently the Butterfly room?"

"Hmm." Vivi scrunched her nose in that way she'd done

since she was small. "Maybe the butterflies came first," she hypothesized. "Maybe they're drawn to this room for some reason, and that's why they installed this window here."

"Maybe." I realized that for Vivi this was an exciting mystery, a puzzle to explore. I couldn't explain the sinking weight in my stomach.

Vivi pointed at the figure's protruding feather-and-lace mask. "Hey, do you think that piece is wearable? Like, it can pop free from the window?"

I squinted up at the mask. Small silver hooks gleamed around the edges, suggesting that it might be removable. But, even sitting untouched, the mask's starched lace was saggy and torn, weathered as the wings of the butterfly we'd found on our first day. I doubted it would survive poking and prodding.

I opened my mouth to say as much, but Vivi was already dragging her desk chair over, preparing to use it as a step stool to reach the mask.

"Vivi, leave the window alone!" I grabbed the chair from her and thunked it back beside her desk. "You're going to break it. Or break yourself, trying to get to it. Come on, let's unboard the one in my room."

"Fine," Vivi grumbled. She glanced more than once over her shoulder at the window, and I could practically hear the gears in her head cranking. But she did follow me across the hall.

Previously, I'd only picked away enough plywood to spy a chunky rectangular border and a lone blue beetle on a log.

Little by little, we revealed the rest and then stepped back to see what we'd uncovered.

Like Vivi's, my window featured a mysterious humanish figure. This one was stocky and sturdy, shimmering in blue and gold glass. It sat cross-legged on the ground, hemmed in by mossy logs studded with beetles. Its hands were palm-up, each balancing an entire log vertically—two wooden columns jutting into the sky—with total ease.

The figure also wore a three-dimensional mask. But the mask was simpler than the one in Vivi's room. No feather or lace. Just smooth, transparent glass, poured to mimic the shape of a beetle's back.

Again, the rest of the window was flat. Only that one piece bulged out, mounted on silver hooks.

At the bottom, the portrait read THE BEETLE.

If butterflies truly were drawn to Vivi's room, I didn't like what this window portended for mine. I swallowed thickly, staring up at it.

The Beetle stared back. Glassy and unblinking.

And I was tempted to take all that plywood we'd removed and hammer it right back up.

I sighed and swiped a sweaty arm across my sweatier forehead. I didn't see any way to open this window either. At least the light spilling through, scattering slices of sapphire and emerald and amethyst across my room, was sweet relief in this dim cave.

So we left the Beetle glistening in the sunshine, and we went to work on the giant hall window across from the staircase landing. It had to be at least six feet tall and ten feet wide.

Several splinters and swear words and piles of broken plywood later, the hall window revealed itself as the eeriest yet.

It depicted a scene of lush grass and blue rosebushes teeming with insects. In the center, framed by Grecian columns, was a white table with thirteen chairs.

Each chair held a figure draped in a cloak, wearing a bright mask. The masks weren't life-sized or three-dimensional, like the ones in our own windows, though. They were flat depictions. Some of the masks were full-faced. Others reached halfway down, but there were no faces underneath. No chins past the masks' bottom edges, no eyes under the eyeholes—only panes of swirling blue glass. The figure at the head of the table was entwined with blue roses. Vines wound around its arms and legs, twisting up to meet its silver crown.

The whole image could've come straight out of a storybook—a gathering of some grand faerie court.

At the bottom, in the same Gothic stained-glass lettering, this one read THE RITE OF THE STARS.

Vivi and I gawked at it.

"'The Rite of the Stars,'" she read. "What do you think it means?"

I chewed at my thumbnail. The image reminded me of what I'd read on RealHauntedHouses.net about House of Masks and its séances. "It must have something to do with the first owners," I said. "The kinds of events they used to host here."

Vivi nodded slowly. "Actually, yeah, the table in the picture looks like the one in the backyard." She pointed out past the window.

I hadn't had the chance to explore outside yet, but I squinted through the paler-blue panels of glass. Our actual backyard appeared massive, ringed with blue rosebushes. And Vivi was right—tucked toward the back, a solid white table rose out of the ground, framed by high-backed stone chairs and columns.

This window was an overlay of the backyard itself. Standing in the middle and looking straight out, the lines all matched: the glass table with the real one, columns with columns, chairs with chairs . . .

Thankfully, there were no masked figures in the actual backyard.

My nervous teeth tore too deep, ripping a hot stripe of pain into the side of my nail. I sucked in a hiss at the tiny throb and yanked my fingers from my mouth before I did anything worse.

The Butterfly, the Beetle, the Rite of the Stars.

No doubt, relics of Madame Clery's original House of Masks.

How many old secrets was this house hiding? Or, rather, it occurred to me, looking down at the hammer in my hand: It wasn't the house that was hiding them. Someone else had boarded up these windows. Someone else had built bigger closets over the first. Someone else had done a lot of work to seal away this house's secrets.

We were the ones unburying them.

Over the course of the day, all the plywood came down. Every window was stained glass, *none* of them opened, and each was stranger than the next—portrait after portrait of humanoid figures surrounded by bugs.

There were five on the ground floor. Dining room: THE HOUSEFLY. Kitchen: THE ANT. Living room: THE CRICKET. Parlor: THE MOTH. Bathroom: THE CENTIPEDE.

And at least five on the top floor. My room: THE BEETLE. Vivi's room: THE BUTTERFLY. Our shared bathroom: THE MOSQUITO. The open bedroom near mine: THE WASP. The open bedroom near Mom's: THE CICADA.

But unlike in my and Vivi's windows, none of the other figures had three-dimensional faces—no sculptural masklike pieces. Instead, most only had flat panes of blue glass, framed by empty silver hooks.

It looked *wrong*.

Incomplete.

Like they must have once had masks and someone had picked them clean off.

Then there was Mom's room, which broke the pattern: it wasn't bug-themed, and aside from mine and Vivi's, it was the only other portrait that still had its face.

Mom's window hung over her bed, perfectly framed by the top of her headboard and bedposts. We walked in as she removed the final traces of plywood.

The portrait featured a silver-crowned figure, entwined with roses, like the one at the head of the table in the hallway mural. Winding vines curled around its body, latching on to its arms and legs.

The protruding mask was a porcelain oval, half overlaid with the velvety outline of a blue rose blossom. Faint silver dusted its hard cheeks, and a Mona Lisa smile shimmered on its rosebud lips. From its crown of twisted metal, a white veil dripped down, pulled off to one side like long gauzy locks.

The bottom banner read ROSE.

"Rose. That's right." Mom was lost in a haze, reaching reverently to touch the glass. "This face . . ."

As if remembering Vivi and I were there, she dropped her hand and stepped back. "I'd forgotten about these windows. Seeing them again is . . ." She shook her head. "Well, I *much* prefer this design to all the bugs." Then she clapped a hand to her mouth. "Oh! Sorry, girls. The other windows are nice, too, of course!"

No, they weren't.

But I found Mom's more disturbing—the utter iciness of the figure's expression, the vines digging into its body.

"Mom . . ." I cleared my throat, afraid this would be taken as inexcusable criticism of the house. "I know they're stained-glass and all, but don't you think some of these windows could use replacing?"

Vivi gasped like that was sacrilege. "Not mine."

To some extent, I understood. Each window almost felt holy. Like some kind of altar. They reminded me of the stained glass in the synagogue Mom had taken us to once or twice. Or maybe more like the kind you'd find in a cathedral—the ones that depicted martyrs. Beautiful on the whole, disturbing in the details.

"It's just . . . some of them are pretty freaky," I said, "and not a single one opens."

"True." Mom nodded. "They *are* historic, but . . ." She laid a palm against the rose window over her bed. "Well, let's live with them for a bit. See how we feel. Meanwhile, I'll run out today and get us some fans to cool the house down."

Fine, then. Mom was the one who had to sleep under the rose-bound figure's vacant eyes—ocean-blue voids from corner to corner, no whites, no pupils.

I wasn't keen on contending with the Beetle either, but with nowhere better to go, I curled up in the window seat underneath its glassy stare for my weekly session with Dr. Glaser, late that afternoon. Her office was a full hour and a half away now, reduced to a tiny square on my phone, what little of the soothing soft greens I could make out past her head.

Of course, she asked how I was adjusting to the new house. Her brow furrowed when I told her it wasn't what I'd expected.

"That's always tough," Dr. Glaser said. Through my phone's speaker, her level tone sounded tinny, more distant than ever. "Disappointed expectations is a common trigger, and we know that's come up in the past for you."

"Yeah, but it's more than that . . ." I glanced at my partly open bedroom door and dropped my voice, hoping Mom wouldn't hear me. "It feels *wrong* here. Everything is crooked, and the art in the stained-glass windows is creepy—"

"Creepy?" Dr. Glaser thought I was exaggerating, I could tell.

"You should see the one in my bathroom. Mosquitoes feasting on a dead sheep. Like, *Jesus.*" I shivered.

"True, old art can be macabre," Dr. Glaser said. "But remember, Libby, even if you can't control the way your new house looks, you can control the stories you tell yourself. You don't have to like every window, but they also don't have to signify that something is *wrong.*"

I glanced at the Beetle looming overhead, the surreal, serene figure balancing enormous wooden columns like they were nothing. The three-dimensional masklike face that felt like it was staring down at me.

"I guess," I said finally.

"Just keep taking stock of those feelings when they arise. See what happens if you challenge them. Do you remember what we discussed regarding depressed self-talk? Thinking in absolutes—'always' or 'never,' or even 'right' or 'wrong'—is rarely helpful."

"Right." Whoops. I corrected myself. "I mean, yeah."

"I know how much we all want this to work—you recovering at home with your family. Try to keep an open mind."

I *hated* when she brought that up. She couched it as a reminder, but it always felt more like a threat. "I am," I promised. "I will. I am."

I really was trying. To swallow my worst feelings. To be as helpful as possible. To prove that my place at home shouldn't be provisional.

When my telehealth session with Dr. Glaser ended, Mom was out buying us fans to cool down the house. So I set the table and warmed pizza leftovers in the oven, making sure dinner would be ready when she came back. I offered Vivi the first shower that night—even though she always took forever since she'd started shaving, terrified of nicking herself or, gasp, missing a spot. When my turn came, I tried to ignore the clattering pipes and the rusty tinge of the water, and to focus on the soothing warmth.

But the positive attitude was harder to maintain once the sun had faded from the sky and the time had come for bed.

At least the fans Mom had bought each of us were the industrial kind, two feet wide, loud as an airplane turbine. I wheeled mine as close to my bed as the cord would stretch. It stirred the stale air, wicking the sweat from my hairline. And I was relieved when the screech of crickets and katydids melted into the fan's blanket of white noise.

No sounds from above yet either. A major mercy.

Dr. Glaser had hammered home how important a consistent sleep schedule was to managing a mood disorder. As it was, my temples beat with an exhausted ache. My triceps and shoulders burned from a day spent unboarding windows, stretching and reaching and prying.

Tonight, I would keep my promise to Mom and stay off the internet, away from sketchy searches about our house. No matter how creepy those windows were. How curious I was about them.

Tonight, I *needed* sleep.

I tucked myself in, as tight as I could bear. And, pride be damned, left my bedside lamp on.

I couldn't help flicking paranoid glances at my bedroom

door. At the shadowed swatch of hallway. At my outer closet door, though it remained closed, like I'd left it, a chair wedged under the knob.

What did I expect to see—some childish nightmare? A too-tall silhouette filling the bedroom doorway? The closet door cracked, a glowing eye behind it?

The real moon rose, creeping into view through the fake moon in my skylight. Soon, the scrapes and scratches came from above. I tried not to hear them. To focus on the fan's steadfast roar.

I desperately wanted Mom to be right, that the noises were squirrels running across the roof. But I was even surer tonight—they weren't coming from the sloped part of my ceiling with the skylight.

I knew, I just *knew,* those sounds were coming from inside the house.

The attic.

Which was apparently unstable. What if pests gnawed away at the attic floor until it buckled? If my bedroom ceiling caved in with one big explosion of plaster and clattering hardwood, and whatever was hiding up there crashed down on top of me. A slithering pile of rats and cockroaches and caterpillars. Crawling and gnashing and squirming.

No. Enough, I told myself. I hugged my sheets to my chest, curling into a sweaty ball. *Nothing bad is going to happen tonight. It's time to relax now. It's time to go to slee—*

My lamp cut out before I could finish my thought. My alarm clock went dark. And my fan sputtered to a stop, taking its soothing wall of white noise with it. This old house must not be able to keep up with all these appliances.

A fuse must've blown.

The shadows around me swelled, the darkness broken only by the milky moonbeams trickling in through my skylight and the Beetle window across the room.

Thud. The noise boomed from overhead, flooding cold through my body.

I winced, as if ducking my head an inch would keep me safer.

Now I'd have to decide which was worse—reckoning with the dank, sticky air and sounds coming from my ceiling or ruining Mom's sleep by begging for her help with the fuse box.

Maybe I could ride it out. Maybe—

Scritch, scriiiiiitch.

The sounds traveled into my bones, like the squeaking of chalk.

No. Riding this out was not an option.

I forced myself from the safety of my sweaty bed and jammed my feet into slippers. Grabbed my phone and tapped on its flash light, which was too quickly becoming indispensable.

My heart pounded harder than it should as I tiptoed into the hall. The staircase that twisted down to the first level was as black as one big gaping throat. Leading to an open gloomy belly.

I was pretty sure Mom had mentioned that the fuse box was in the cellar. Even if she came with me, did I really want to hazard the trek all the way down there?

I glanced down the snaking hallway toward Mom's room. With the wooden paneling running halfway up the walls, the corridor reminded me of a forest that had been chopped off at the knees.

A sharp creak came from close by—not overhead. *Beside me.* I jumped, nearly dropping my phone.

But the shadowed hallway was empty.

The creak came again. Weight shifting over the floorboards. This time, I could tell it was coming from behind Vivi's closed door.

I exhaled shakily. It'd be a relief if she was up, too. The last thing I wanted was to be alone.

"Vivi?" I whispered, leaning in close to her door. "Are you awake?"

She didn't answer.

I tried again: "Vivi, did your power go out, too?" No light was coming from under her door, but I thought maybe I heard the whir of her fan.

Still no answer.

I was on my own, then. Either she was ignoring me or those creaks were just the old house settling—whatever that meant. The expression had always made me picture some gargantuan creature with a rattling skeleton made of glass and rotting planks and rusty pipes, shifting restlessly in its sleep.

The thought made my bones feel crushable. The hairs on my arms prickled, my skin mottled blue and green by the moony wash leaking in through the enormous Rite of the Stars window.

The real backyard was masked by this eerie facsimile. Stained-glass insects swirled through the panes. Looking more closely, I could see that bugs enshrined in the windows throughout the house were all here—together. And aside from the figure at the head of the stone table, the one sprouting into blue roses, those filling the other twelve seats wore insect masks.

It was almost like the windows in this house were trying to tell a story.

Maybe that's *exactly* what it was like.

Then, beyond the window, came a flash of motion. In the real backyard, something near the white stone table moved.

More than one thing. Several things.

My breath came in shallower and shallower gulps. *Stay calm,* I told myself. *Stay reasonable. That movement could be anything—deer, raccoons.*

I pressed up to the window, squinting out through rippled glass. The backyard was dark, contoured black with night, but the moon cast its ghostly gleam over the stone table. And over the thirteen chairs, in which . . .

There were thirteen masked and cloaked bodies.

CHAPTER FIVE

WRITHING PANIC EXPLODED UNDER MY SKIN. Thirteen person-sized shapes, wearing masks and cloaks. Like the image in the hall window. Only these were really out there, really in the yard.

Before anything could see me, I ducked into the ivory curtains by the window's edge.

Then, an inch from my flushing cheek, the lace fluttered.

Out burst flapping wings, nearly catching me in the eye, and I recoiled. Clapped a hand over my mouth to stop my shriek.

Another butterfly, lacy as the curtain it had been sleeping in.

At least I'd swallowed my cry, but I'd moved too quickly, too suddenly.

I hazarded a glance back to the table. To the figures I thought I'd seen . . .

They were still there.

Really, actually there.

And the one at the head of the table turned its blank white mask toward the house. The window.

Its shadowed eyeholes locked dead on me.

My heart seized—a sharp stab in my chest. I staggered back from the window.

Whatever it was, it had seen me.

It knew I'd seen it.

I didn't know what else to do. I ran.

Thudding all the way down the hall for the second time in as many nights.

"Mom!" I felt like a useless child, but I had no better idea than to wake her up. I threw open her door. "Mom, someone is in our yard!"

That woke her up, all right.

"Someone's in our yard?" Mom was scrambling from her bed, on her feet. She ran after me to the hall window.

Vivi's door flew open, and she charged out in her nightcap and pink PJ set, but there was no trace of sleep in her wide, round eyes. "What's going on?"

"Trespassers," I gasped, clutching at my thudding chest. "Outside!"

Mom threw the curls from her face and peered out the stained-glass window. "Where are they?"

"There!" I couldn't stand to look again, but I pointed toward the white stone table. "Right there!"

Mom and Vivi followed my finger.

And then Mom paused. "Lib, I don't . . ."

"No one's there," Vivi said.

"Huh?" I pressed up against the glass, staring out. "No one . . . ?"

Vivi was right.

The table was empty. The whole yard was empty.

"They must've run after they saw me!" I said, flustered. "They were right there, I swear!"

"Okay. It's okay, Lib," Mom said, in her overly soothing tone, the one better suited to toddlers. "What were they doing?"

"I have no idea *what* they were doing." Too much energy thrummed through me. I was pacing, hugging myself so tight I was practically choking the air out of my body. "Some creepy gathering at the stone table! They were wearing cloaks and white masks, and there were thirteen of them, and who the hell does that in the dead of night—*in someone else's backyard*?"

My words were coming too fast. I could barely hear myself over the relentless pounding of my blood.

Vivi's nose scrunched in puzzlement. "They were wearing cloaks and masks?"

Something in Mom's face was changing, too. Her big blaring panic shifted into a deeper, quieter sort of alarm as she turned away from the empty yard and fixed her attention firmly on me. "You mean . . . like the image in this window?"

"Yeah! Well, they weren't wearing bug or rose masks. I told you, just plain white masks, but . . ."

Mom and Vivi exchanged meaningful glances.

A silent conversation had begun, one I wasn't meant to be a part of.

"Sweetie . . ." In a gentle voice, Mom asked, "Are you sure this wasn't a bad dream? These windows can be so evocative. Do you think you might've been sleepwalking?"

"What?" I stopped, my pacing frozen to a halt. "No, Mom, I really saw them!"

I was sure.

Pretty sure. I . . .

I replayed the last ten minutes. "No, I couldn't have been dreaming. I hadn't even fallen asleep yet. At first, I was in bed, but a fuse blew—"

"A fuse blew?" Mom looked past me, at my room. "But your light is on."

"No, it's—" I turned.

Past my propped-open bedroom door, there was the yellow glow of my lamp. The whir of my fan was going strong, too.

Mom frowned. "If the fuse blew, the power shouldn't come back on its own. . . ."

That was true. And yet.

I blinked again at the glow from my lamp, so suddenly gone before and so suddenly back now.

"Maybe a brownout." Mom turned to Vivi. "Did your power cut out, too?"

Vivi shook her head. She chewed her lip and avoided eye contact like she felt sorry for me.

She didn't believe me. Worse, she downright *pitied* me.

And it wasn't just because the backyard was empty or my power was on. It's because I was raving, wasn't I? I was pacing too fast, breathing too fast, talking too fast. Too shrill.

No, she didn't believe me because my story was unbelievable—*I* was unbelievable.

Frustrated tears pricked the back of my eyes as I turned to Mom. "Mom, look, I don't know what happened with the power, but I *did* see something outside. Should we call the police?"

But now, Mom was biting her lip, too, mulling—a certain suspicion firming under the heavy crease of her forehead. "Well, let's . . . hold off and monitor the situation, okay? If someone was out there, they're gone now. For tonight, maybe it's best if we all try to get some sleep."

She wasn't going to do anything? Anything at all?

My shoulders sank. "Mom . . ." I hated how small my voice sounded. "Do you think I'm making this up?"

"Of course not, sweetie. I know you wouldn't make up something like this."

But she obviously didn't believe me either.

She must've been settling into her theory that I'd been sleepwalking.

Or . . .

Or . . . oh no.

Did she think I was *hallucinating*?

Dr. Glaser said the symptoms associated with my type of bipolar disorder tended to be more mild. I wasn't likely to experience hallucinations, and Mom knew that, too. But my diagnosis was so recent. What if it wasn't what they thought?

Was I hallucinating?

I wanted, so desperately, for that to be impossible. But it wasn't.

And what if Mom told Dr. Glaser that she thought I was?

Maybe my psychiatrist's calm, flat eyes weren't unshakable after all. Reporting hallucinations could be the tipping point to push my care from outpatient to inpatient.

I'd stayed in that psych ward for only three days the first time. But if I went back, I doubted it would be to a short-term facility. We could be talking months. Months and months of shoes without laces, shitty art therapy, scratchy tissues, and staring out windows at a view of the parking lot, killing time by counting the spaces—worst of all, with no control over when I got out.

Holy hell, I should *never* have told Mom what I saw tonight. I should never have let her see me like this.

If it wasn't too late to undo the damage, I had to try.

I made myself laugh, even if it was sputtering. Nervous. "You know, the more I think about it, you, uh, you might be right, Mom. I could've been dreaming."

Mom was overeager to laugh along with me. "That could've been it." Her shoulders sagged in relief. "This house lends itself to vivid dreams. It was my turn last night, after all."

Vivi managed a weak smile, too. "Yeah," she said, "probably just a dream."

The worst of our tension drained from the hallway, even if fear had turned my tongue to metal. Even if my heart still railed against my ribs.

Even if I'd sold myself out. Utterly.

Mom and Vivi retreated to their rooms, so I retreated to mine. But I couldn't stop replaying what I'd seen, pacing and pacing and pacing, gnawing at every fingernail. Stripping away cuticles. Biting into blood.

Stop, body. Stop.

Pacing. Chewing. Shredding. Mom and Vivi thought I was hallucinating.

Did my power really go out? Were those intruders really in our yard?

The crooked angles of this house. The creeping stench of sour-sweet mildew and syrupy blue roses—was any of that real either?

Was I imagining *ALL* of this?

No, this house couldn't be totally normal. Vivi had been nervous, too, when we first got here, even if she pretended like she wasn't. Even the movers felt it. It wasn't *ALL* me. But how much of it was?

Creak creak creak creak creak creak under my pacing feet.

Scuffle scratch drag scratch scraaatch over my throbbing head. The sounds from the attic whispered through the drone of the fan—scraping, raking at my skull.

Were *those* real?

Mom and Vivi hadn't noticed the noises. I was the only one. How could I be the only one?

The poised figure of the Beetle in my stained-glass window was mocking me, sitting so calm. So balanced, holding up those enormous logs like they were twigs. Like the weight was nothing.

"Fuck you," I whispered at it.

Why am I talking to a window?

Scritch scratch overhead.

"Fuck *you,*" I whispered at that, too.

Why am I talking to a disembodied goddamn noise?!

This house was hell, my brain was hell, and together, they were insurmountable.

Sit down, stop pacing, stop biting your nails. You're losing your mind. YOU'VE ALREADY LOST IT.

No. Shh. I made myself breathe out. Imagine Dr. Glaser. In moments like these, I was supposed to climb outside of myself, out of the moment. Get perspective, if I could.

Label what was happening.

Hypomania. The worst kind of hypomania.

I hadn't experienced the happy, on-top-of-the-world kind since the *Romeo and Juliet* cast party. For months now, my hypomania had manifested as high-octane dread. I did also have generalized anxiety disorder, but I knew *this* wasn't as simple as anxiety alone, because I felt drugged. Like my thoughts weren't my own. Like some separate being had hijacked the controls of my body and kept mashing random buttons. My heart thudded so fast and hard it hurt.

Okay, so it's hypomania, I told myself. *It's temporary. Ride it out. Slow down. Breathe. Breathe, breathe, breathe.*

Bed. Get into bed.

I got into bed. Packed the sheets around myself, in spite of my sweat. My hands, they wouldn't stop shaking. My heart, it wouldn't stop pounding.

Maybe I really *was* hallucinating.

My medicine was pretty new. This could be some sick side effect. I'd check the bottles, except that Mom insisted on managing my prescriptions, on doling out my pills herself.

I searched online, but didn't find many mentions of hallucinations as a side effect for lithium. As for my antidepressant, it was possible, slimly possible. Very rare, it said. Tell your doctor right away.

But I couldn't tell my doctor. Because I didn't know if my medication was to blame or if my brain was to blame. Or if neither was to blame, because what I saw was *real*. And I had no idea which possibility was worse.

Thoughts darted in and out like a slippery school of fish. I could barely touch one, get my fingers around it, before it'd wriggled free and three more brushed up against my hand, and I didn't know which one to grab and—

With a frustrated growl, I spiked down my phone, thumping it hard against my mattress, and sat up, pressing my head hard to my knees. Rocking faster than was actually soothing. But it was the best I could do.

Someone, please, let me off this ride.

Static roared through my veins—energy, too much energy, pushing and pushing from the inside, screaming to escape.

I wished I could tear off all my skin.

All night I listened, not only for the sounds from above, but for any sounds from below.

What did I expect to happen—that the intruders I thought I'd seen were going to break through our stained-glass kitchen doors and drag me from my bed?

Of course not.

But also, maybe.

By morning, I was exhausted.

If I'd slept, it was in the tiniest, fuzziest blips. The whole night was a wash of shadow-smeared terror.

I still had no idea what had happened, what I'd seen or hadn't. The most harmless option was, like Mom had suggested, that I'd been sleepwalking and dreamed I saw people in the yard.

That's what I *wanted* to believe. By daylight, that was the only part I knew.

After breakfast, I would check the backyard. If anyone had been there last night, they must've left behind proof. Footprints, or an empty chip bag, or . . . Hell, I'd take anything.

I found Mom and Vivi downstairs in the kitchen. Now that the windows were unboarded, it was almost too bright. Sun poured through the stained-glass doors and window, splashing color over the dingy faux-tile floor.

Mom had set my pills out for me, waiting beside a fresh glass of OJ.

I grabbed them automatically and then paused, staring down at the round white pill, the oblong pink capsules. I wasn't sure if I should take them—not if they might be to blame for last night.

But skipping the medicine didn't seem advisable either.

After burning through hours of frenzied energy, I felt down this morning. My limbs were heavier, the world drabber and drearier. It was the kind of mild low I could try to fight through.

Those lows sucked, in their own special way—I felt even more pressure to claw through the day, pretend I was fully functional.

But wouldn't I like to keep it that way? A light low. A functional low.

I grimaced as I swallowed the pills.

Breakfast felt, in every way, like leftovers. Mom had microwaved the remaining pancakes from yesterday. Each of us was worn down further than we'd been the day before: staler smiles, less to say.

I didn't think I was imagining that both Vivi and Mom looked worse. Vivi was oddly twitchy, her leg jiggling against the wooden support bar on her stool with choppy, relentless squeaks. She kept massaging her forehead like she had a headache. And Mom rubbed at her eyes, pinched the bridge of her nose, her every reaction a couple seconds too slow.

I apologized for being the one to wake them up with a nightmare, and was rewarded with more relieved nods. Both Mom and Vivi loved the idea that the masked trespassers were only a dream—that I *knew* they were only a dream. Mom asked if I'd gotten better sleep afterward, with the kind of misplaced hope that made me want to lie.

So I did.

As soon as escape was possible, I told them I "wanted to get some sun"—the kind of wholesome sentiment Dr. Glaser would've praised—and pushed past the kitchen doors onto the patio. I had to know if what I'd seen last night was real.

The sun's rays greeted me, the heat sticky as plastic wrap, even on this hazy morning. This was my first actual foray into our backyard. And the sight stopped me short.

I usually found the outdoors soothing. I used to walk in the park by our apartment. It wasn't big or fancy, but I'd put in my earbuds and listen to the kind of melancholy music that felt like poetry, and it was something. A place I felt safe. From others. From myself.

That park had even featured in the safety plan that Dr. Glaser made me fill out after my hospital stay—as one of the locations I could turn to for comfort. A place where I could shut out my worst thoughts. The only ones I could come up with were my side of the bedroom, our old kitchen, and that one park. When we moved, I'd lost all three.

Here, there were no slouchy elms or glossy magnolias, like I was used to. No trees at all in our yard. They peered in past our metal fence, rubbernecking at our property like they were eyeing a car crash. Squirrels and wrens and mockingbirds darted through their branches, lovely and lively.

The only life here was tangled blue roses and insects. Humming, buzzing, wriggling. A clashing cacophony of whirring wings and rubbing legs and rustling bushes.

The far side of the yard was consumed by the sprawling hedge maze mentioned on RealHauntedHouses.net. I followed the winding path over to the entrance and squinted up at it through the sun. The rosebushes, thick with vibrant blue blooms, had to be ten feet tall.

I was almost curious enough to poke my head in, but the maze had grown wild, half consumed by vines and thorns. Mom had mentioned over breakfast she'd be working on tidying our rosebushes. If that included the maze, she had her work cut out for her.

I backed away. Instead, I took the narrow path toward the white stone table—that small patch resembling Athenian ruins near our back fence.

If there was a concrete foundation underneath, scraggly grass had long overgrown it. The table and high-backed chairs appeared to grow straight up from the earth. The area was hemmed in by a rectangle of white columns and rosebushes, with a gap at each end for entrance. There was no roof. The columns poked up at the blotchy clouds and blistering sun. At night, though, I bet you could see the stars.

The roses here were especially potent. Their musty perfume swirled into my nose, half-dizzying.

My chest tightened. My footsteps fell softer. It felt like I was the one intruding. Like I'd blundered into some world I didn't understand.

But this was our yard now.

I walked closer to examine the table. At the very center, a crystal ball was mounted, held in place by three stone petals. A blue rose made of what looked like velvet was suspended inside.

And that wasn't even the most ornate decor. The chairs themselves were elaborately carved. The towering throne at the head of the table was engraved with sinuous roses and thorns. At the top, there was a face—an oval with hooded eyes. A stone veil spilled from its crown, dripping down the chair's back.

The design matched the figure from Mom's stained-glass window.

The other twelve chairs were carved with insect motifs. I circled them all before my hand fell, almost magnetically, on one beside the rose throne. This one was . . .

Beetles. The same kind enshrined in my bedroom's stained-glass window.

Of all the chairs, I'd just happened to be drawn to this one?

With an uneasy twist in my stomach, I yanked my hand away.

I shook my head and scanned the area for evidence of recent activity. In front of the ant-themed chair, drops of white wax marred the table. Some clumps of grass nearby were matted.

Possibly footprints.

I crouched to check.

But I was no detective, and it infuriated me to admit—I couldn't tell what I was looking at. They might have been footprints. Animal prints. Tangled grass.

The examination of the whole area was inconclusive.

A dead end.

I turned back toward the house, which sat so tall and smug as I rooted around in its shadow, digging futilely for evidence. Failing to exonerate myself.

It almost felt like this house wanted me to fail—to doubt myself and my sanity.

And it might have been working, because I'd just entertained the notion that a pile of wood *wanted* to sabotage me. *Wanted* anything.

The mounting mysteries of this place were eating away at me like a parasite.

If the backyard had no answers, then I'd have to look elsewhere.

I'd promised Mom to avoid sketchy internet research, and that was probably for the best. Crashing into random sites wouldn't do me any good.

I needed reliable sources. And as for the library?

Well, I'd made no promises about staying away from that.

CHAPTER SIX

THE NEAREST PUBLIC LIBRARY WAS ONLY a few blocks away. Lucky for me, since I couldn't drive.

I walked, while the sun cooked me from above and the asphalt cooked me from below. By the time I arrived, I was a mess of sweaty curls, my lower back damp against my tank top, but it didn't matter how I looked. It's not like I knew anyone in this town.

After two days immersed in our otherworldly house, I was desperate for anything plain and ordinary. The library seemed like the perfect escape. Outside, white brick. Inside, clean green carpet and orderly metal bookshelves. Unlike our house, all the angles here made sense—crisp lines meeting corners just where they should.

And yet, somehow, the longer I looked, the more all the library's right angles felt wrong. So tidy they almost made me nauseous.

My family was changing the house, peeling back its dusty

exoskeleton one plank of plywood at a time—but what if the house was changing *us*, too? Recasting our sense of normal in its own warped mold. If I ever managed to feel more at home there, would I only feel more out of place everywhere else?

Stop it, I warned myself. Dr. Glaser would remind me not to tell myself unhelpful stories. This reverse seasickness was just the temporary shock of a different environment. I needed to embrace the reprieve as much as I could.

I shook my head and rubbed my arms. They kept this library cold as a fridge, and the air against my sweaty skin was making me shiver.

Mercifully, it was Tuesday morning, and the library was pretty dead, aside from story time in the kids' corner. A woman in a polka-dotted blazer read aloud to a circle of restless kids and parents about the misadventures of Bunny and Fox.

I hoped she wasn't the only librarian, or I'd die waiting at the front desk. I tried my luck and dinged the bell.

Someone answered from an open office door behind the counter, "One minute!"

The mystery worker's voice was far from what I was expecting—male, and intriguingly raspy. I waited until, finally, he stepped through the door, and I stiffened.

"Can I help—" He stopped talking as he made eye contact.

Of all people, it was *him*.

The elusive boy next door, tall and lean, with wildfire hair. This time, he was sporting a cherry-colored hoodie. An industrial barbell glinted through the top of his ear. And the last place I'd expected to find him was under a bubble-lettered banner featuring a cartoon owl in round glasses, who proclaimed READING: IT'S ONE HECKUVA HOOT!

He really worked here?

His gaze swept over me, and I remembered how I must look—sweaty, with frizzy curls, in the world's rattiest tank top and short-shorts. Not a pretty picture.

A tiny, agonizing eternity stretched between us.

Eventually, he cleared his throat. "Can I help you?" he tried again, in a guarded customer-service voice.

"I, um . . ." Clearly, he didn't recognize me—or was pretending not to, which was even more painful. I picked at the fraying hem of my shorts to avoid picking at my fingernails. "I was wondering if you had archives of the city paper, or anything like that. I just moved here, and I was hoping to do some research on local history."

The vague pretense felt less uncomfortable than admitting I was researching my own house because I was scared of it. I hoped he didn't notice how my voice shot up an octave.

"Local history, huh?" he asked, his eyebrows raising in what felt like a challenge. "The city paper's archives are on microfiche. You'd need someone who works here to help you with that."

He didn't offer. He shrugged, like my problem was unsolvable, and started sorting books on a nearby cart.

What the hell?

When we first met, I could've sworn we'd shared a moment. For at least a second, he'd wanted to know me. Then everything changed, and I still didn't know why.

Could there be some misunderstanding? If it wasn't too late to repair this awkwardness, I'd better try. He was my neighbor, probably headed to the same school this fall. And with the story-time librarian busy reading away, he was my one ticket to the microfiche section.

I swallowed my nerves and held out my hand. "I'm Libby, by the way."

Isabel, really. It had always felt too elegant for me, so I was only Libby. Always Libby. Which I hated.

And this could have been an opportunity to introduce a new nickname.

Dammit. My chance to reinvent myself, and my imagination was already failing me.

He regarded my outstretched hand, and a slight hardness in his shoulders caved. Grudgingly, he reached out to me. "Flynn."

We shook. I tried to keep it quick, so he wouldn't notice my anxious tremble, but he must have. Surprise flashed over his face, and I winced. In my experience, if someone was being asshole-ish, showing fear was the *last* thing you wanted to do. It was like admitting you were easy prey. I almost expected him to squeeze harder or get meaner.

Flynn's grip did change—but only to give my hand the smallest reassuring press before releasing me. "Listen, uh, you look a little familiar," he said, his eyes averted almost guiltily. "Did I see you on my block the other day?"

It felt like a peace offering.

If that's how he reacted to a stranger's anxiety, maybe he was a smidge nicer than he'd let on at first.

I nodded, relieved. "Yeah, I think I saw you, too. You live nearby?"

"Not far. And you live in . . . uh, *that* house?" He said it with weight. Like the house loomed larger than I did.

"What do you mean?" I asked. I suspected I knew what he meant—that my house's creepy reputation was known beyond RealHauntedHouses.net. But I wanted the confirmation. "Do you know something about my house?"

"About House of Masks? *Everyone* knows something about

House of Masks," he said with a slight smirk. "I assume that's what you're actually here to read up on."

So he *had* seen right through my "local history" excuse.

"It might be a slight area of interest," I admitted.

"Uh-huh. I was surprised to see your family moving in," he said. "You're renting the place?"

"No, my mom owns it," I told him.

Flynn blinked. "You're the *owners*? The actual owners? But that house has been empty for decades. Why come back now? You're not really planning to stay, are you?"

He seemed bizarrely invested in our business, but I guess that's what happened when your house was a local celebrity. "Well, my mom wants to stay, for a while anyway. But I—I'm not sure it's such a good idea."

"Hmm." Flynn mulled that over. For the first time, he leaned toward me and dropped his voice, like we were sharing a secret: "For what it's worth, I think you're right about that."

A shiver rattled my spine, and I wished I could blame it on the overactive AC.

Validation of my fears. Exactly what I wanted. Also, incidentally, exactly *not* what I wanted.

At least Flynn was finally warming up. He stepped out from behind the desk. "Okay, then. I'll get you the info you need."

Suddenly, he was only an arm span away, and I was noticing that his eyes were green. That stubble glinted along his jaw.

"Nice shoes, by the way," Flynn said.

I was wearing my all-black Chucks, the same ones he'd been sporting when I first saw him. That he was still wearing now.

A foxlike smile had curled over Flynn's lips, and my stomach gave a wobbly little drop, as if it was about to hit the first hill of a roller coaster.

Oh, please, no. I knew this feeling way too well from my disastrous crush on Mason.

I tried to take the compliment in stride. "Oh. Thanks. You too," I said. But extra heat was flushing into my chest. I made myself look away, fixating on a half-peeled sticker someone had failed to remove from the front of the counter—a melting strawberry ice cream cone.

I wasn't sure why it felt like I was melting, too. Because he was the first guy who'd paid attention to me in months? Or maybe it was because he'd noticed I was anxious and he got kinder, not meaner. Because he was the only one treating me like my feelings about my house made sense.

"Follow me." With another flicker of that addictive smile, Flynn led me to the side room. "I'll have to pull each microfiche for you. Library policy."

So we were about to get some quality time. Equal parts thrilling and nerve-racking.

He set me up in front of a machine that looked part microscope, part prehistoric computer. "Let me guess," he said. "You're here because of the disappearances?"

Just like that, the weight of my house crashed back down on me. "The disappearances?" I squirmed in my plastic-backed chair. "So there *have* been disappearances?"

"Oh, yes." Flynn wasn't smiling anymore either. "Many."

"Do you happen to know about my grandparents? They died in an accident—it would've been in the seventies. I forget the exact year." I grabbed my phone from my pocket. "Hang on. I can look it up."

But Flynn looked confused. "You don't even know what happened to your own grandparents?"

I hesitated. As much as I didn't appreciate Mom's secrecy, I couldn't help feeling protective of her. Probably because she'd promised to tell us about her parents when she was ready and yet here I was researching them behind her back. "Like I said, I know they were in some kind of accident," I said defensively.

"An accident?" Flynn asked. "That's what your mom told you?"

I stiffened. "It . . . wasn't an accident?"

Flynn shook his head. Now he looked downright disturbed. "The article you want is from October 1979." With that, he disappeared among the wooden file cabinets.

I wasn't sure which was more unnerving—how much I *didn't* know or how much Flynn *did*.

"How did you know that?" I asked as he returned with the slide. "The exact month and year?"

"Oh." Flynn tensed, the wall that had started melting around him icing back up. "I did a paper on House of Masks a couple years ago," he said. "Freshman history. We did projects on local landmarks." He ran a restless hand along the back of his neck, maybe because he'd outed himself as my house's fanboy.

But that did explain a lot.

"Anyway, this article is useful," he said. "It outlines the other disappearances, too, and it . . . Well, you'll see." He leaned over me, and I caught an intoxicating waft of warm cedar and sharp orange. I held stock-still as he laid a flat piece of film on the glass tray, wheeling the knobs on the machine to focus it. "There you go."

As he stepped back, his hand accidentally grazed the sticky skin of my bare shoulder. The touch seared into me, electric and alive, jolting me so much I jerked.

"Sorry." Flynn jumped, too, and stuffed the offending hand in his pocket. "Didn't mean to . . ."

"No, no, I'm just jumpy," I said. "This house stuff . . ." I bit my lip, my cheeks burning, and glued my eyes to the monitor.

The article was dated October 27, 1979:

Disturbing Mystery Deepens as Eighth and Ninth Victims Vanish from "House of Masks"

> Over the past century, the local landmark known as "House of Masks" has garnered an unsettling reputation. Once home to spiritualist Madame Ellen Clery and her profitable séances, it is also the site where nine people have now gone missing—most recently, Peter and Margaret Feldman.
>
> The disappearances began in 1897, when the original owners, Ellen Clery and Joseph Cragg, vanished, leaving behind all of their personal effects.
>
> Ownership of the house passed to Joseph Cragg's older brother, Calvin. By the following year, in 1898, Calvin, his wife, Harriet, and their eldest daughter, Mary, would all vanish in the same fashion.

The article recapped the chain of ownership as the house passed down the family line, first to one Cragg after another, and then, after Protestant Laura Cragg married a Jewish man named Louis Feldman in 1917, one Feldman after another. Not everyone who owned the house moved in. For many stretches, the house had stood alone and abandoned. Some owners attempted to sell or rent the house, but with no luck.

And whenever the owners *did* move in, it happened again. More "disappearances."

1897: Ellen and Joseph.

1898: Calvin, Harriet, and Mary.

1913: Cedric (the son of Joseph's youngest brother) and his wife, Cora.

And then a long empty stretch until the 1970s, when my grandparents, Peter and Margaret Feldman, took their chances and moved in.

And the article was very clear about how that went . . .

> The Feldmans' four-year old daughter was the only witness. She escaped from the house and appeared at a neighbor's door, sobbing in distress. When police questioned her about her parents' whereabouts, the girl replied, "The monsters took them."
>
> While monsters make for poor suspects, even as Halloween approaches, police are investigating whether such a reference is the work of a frightened child's imagination, or if it might indicate actual intruders at the house, possibly wearing masks or costumes.
>
> So far, there is no evidence of a break-in, and the personal effects of Peter and Margaret Feldman, including wallets and driver's licenses, were untouched. Their only car was found in the driveway.
>
> By all appearances, Mr. and Mrs. Feldman have vanished.

The article ended, and I had to close my eyes. There it was, in black-and-white: my grandparents *had* disappeared.

A headache squeezed my forehead, and everything felt a little blurry. I rubbed my eyes—I couldn't tell if I needed glasses or if the information was a sickness of its own, worming its way into my brain. My body was rejecting it.

It was one thing to read about missing people on a dubious website. Another to see it here, in the local paper.

And whatever had happened to my grandparents, Flynn was right—it didn't sound like an accident. The one theory police had was intruders. Intruders wearing masks or costumes.

Masks or costumes like . . . *those masked and cloaked figures I'd seen in our yard?*

There was still the chance I hadn't been dreaming or imagining things. That what I'd seen was true.

Suddenly, I was keenly aware of the library's fluorescents humming overhead, like I was back in the psych ward. I flinched. The real world kept feeling less and less real.

"Are you . . . okay?" Flynn was leaning against the nearest filing cabinet a few feet back, allowing me some space.

Of course I wasn't okay. But I needed to know how deep this rabbit hole ran. I made myself turn to face him. "Isn't there a better explanation?" I asked. "Another article that says where any of these people went, or why?"

"No. There are other articles, but with even less detail. Afraid that's as clear as it gets."

"Well, what about the most recent disappearance?" I said. "I saw online that one *more* person might've gone missing seven years ago." I figured we had to have better investigative tech now than they'd had in the '70s. Surely, modern detectives could've found something more helpful. "That must've come up in your paper, right?"

Flynn went strangely still, like I'd said something wrong.

"That disappearance isn't confirmed. And that person didn't even live in the house," he answered with a fake sort of ease—overly loose, overly languid. Except for his jaw, coiled tight. "In my opinion, that's a dead end."

I had to wonder if that end was quite as dead as Flynn wanted me to think. Either way, he wasn't interested in discussing it.

"Why are you looking into this anyway?" he asked, almost like he was afraid of the answer. "Because of the rumors, or did . . . something happen?"

"I'm not sure," I admitted. My own brain didn't count as a reliable witness. Clearly, Mom and Vivi didn't think so. "I thought I saw someone in my yard last night. Several someones."

My words hit Flynn as hard as a shove. "Really? Like, prowling around?"

"No. Gathering at our backyard table. Wearing masks. And cloaks."

"Hmm." Flynn quieted, staring off into the distance.

"What?" I asked. "What are you thinking?"

"Nothing." But something had changed. He'd iced over again. "Just, as I understand it, that table is where Madame Clery used to host séances." He turned to me, but his green eyes were stone. "Some people think it's haunted. You're not saying you saw *spirits*?"

I couldn't read that sudden chill in his voice—if he believed seeing spirits was possible or impossible. What he even wanted my answer to be.

I shook my head regardless. "Of course not. But what if it's, I don't know, a cult or something?"

"A cult, huh?" Flynn whistled, low and slow, like that possibility was even more far-fetched. "Someone's been watching too many true-crime documentaries."

Excuse me. He was talking about spirits, and wanted to paint *me* as the unreasonable one?

"What am I supposed to think?" I pointed to the screen. "The disappearances are too far apart to be the work of one person, but they *could* be the work of one group."

"Well, either way, maybe you shouldn't be wandering around your house at night. Doesn't sound very safe. Not if something is haunting your yard."

Why did he have to say it like that? Not "someone"—"some*thing*"? Goose bumps swarmed over me. "I never said 'haunting'! I don't believe in hauntings."

Flynn shrugged. "I guess that's lucky, given where you live."

I couldn't tell if he was screwing with me, and I hated that it might be working. I frowned at him.

"Whatever the cause," he continued, "all those people disappearing? Look, I agree with you—that's no coincidence. And I think it's really weird your mom moved you into that house without telling you about it."

So did I. Was it possible that Mom was so traumatized that she'd forgotten what had happened to her parents? That she honestly didn't know that so many members of our family had gone missing?

To be fair, Mom had never connected with the rest of her family, not beyond Great-Aunt Carol, who'd passed away years ago. If Mom hadn't heard about the disappearances from her, she might never have learned the full history. Especially not if she dismissed local gossip as outrageous.

That didn't explain, though, why Mom's hand started shaking when she read about the disappearances on my phone after her night terror.

But what was the alternative: Mom *did* remember what

happened to her parents, she *had* known about the other missing people, and she moved us in anyway?

I shook my head. "Mom thinks what happened to her parents was some standalone freak tragedy," I told Flynn.

"This article proves it wasn't, though. Here." Flynn stepped in close and clicked some options on the screen. "I'll print it for you."

This time, he was all business—careful not to brush me. And I was careful not to brush him.

The printer spat out a couple pages, and he slapped them into my hand, still warm. "Show this to your mom."

That had been my plan, actually. But Flynn's sudden pushiness was setting my back teeth on edge.

Without a word, I placed the article face-side down on the desk to dry.

"Look, you're the one who said your family shouldn't stay there," Flynn pointed out. "Your mom has to understand it's not safe. If not for her sake, then what about you? What about your little sister?"

My little sister?

On the one hand, it was a point in his favor, recognizing Vivi and me as sisters. Some people stopped at the skin tone—saw I was light and Vivi was dark, because our white mom used a white donor for me and a Black donor for Vivi. They didn't always bother looking further, to notice that both of us, and Mom, too, shared identical deep-set brown eyes. Hard, arched eyebrows. In many ways, Vivi looked more like Mom than I did.

But any point he might've gained, he forfeited if he'd been spying on my house. Especially if he'd been spying on Vivi.

"What do you know about my little sister?" I demanded.

"I was walking past your place and saw her out in the yard.

Your mom wouldn't want anything to happen to her, right?" He hit me with a meaningful look. "To any of you."

I hesitated. That almost sounded like a threat.

Had I imagined that kind little squeeze of my hand earlier, when he felt me tremble? The guilty peace offering that came after?

Maybe there was nothing nice about him, after all. Maybe Flynn *was* trying to scare me. Haze the new girl. He'd mentioned working on his House of Masks paper a couple years ago in freshman history, so he must also be heading into junior year this fall. Before I set foot in that new school, I'd be a walking joke. Just like before.

Or he really had gotten sucked into local urban legends. Had drunk the haunted Kool-Aid.

Either way, a sobering reminder: I knew nothing about this guy. And maybe I'd be better off keeping it that way.

I thanked him for his time and grabbed the printout, then I left the library—as fast as I could.

CHAPTER SEVEN

I CAUGHT MOM IN THE KITCHEN, fresh from gardening, arranging a vase of blue roses. She looked, for the first time in a long while, sun-soaked and satisfied, and I felt terrible that I was going to ruin her day. All the same, I shoved the article into her hand.

"What is this?" she asked. Her face blanched as she skimmed the headline. "'Disturbing Mystery Deepens'?"

"I know you wanted me to leave this house's history alone, Mom, but the disappearances aren't some overblown internet rumor. We have to talk about this."

"Libby . . ." Mom set the article down and returned to the roses, trimming stems with sharp, hard snips.

Was she not even going to read it? "Mom, I swear I'm not trying to ruin this house for us. But you said your parents died in an accident—and this article says they didn't."

Mom slapped the scissors onto the counter. "I told you I'd share what happened when I was ready. But I guess I wasn't ready fast enough for you," she said tightly. "I don't think you understand how painful . . ."

She blinked watery eyes and pressed a steadying hand to her chest before she squeezed out, "If it weren't for what happened this past May, I'd say that was the worst thing that ever happened to me."

That punched the breath out of me. What happened in May was my doing.

She'd survived unspeakable trauma in losing her parents to "monsters," and, even still, *I* was the worst thing that had ever happened to my mother.

But deep down, I'd already known that, hadn't I?

She was the one who'd found me on the bathroom floor. I'd pictured it so many times I'd given myself an imaginary memory: Her coming home from work and spotting the bathroom door cracked open. I could see her trying to open it all the way—and the door bumping into my heap of a body.

Her hand clapping to her shrieking mouth. Her purse dropping to the ground. Mom falling to her knees beside me on the puke-soaked tile . . .

That's when I'd pictured her finding the note I'd left on the sink.

But when I'd asked her about my note in the hospital, she'd looked confused. *Note? What note?* Maybe, in her frenzy to reach me, she'd knocked it aside. Or maybe it had stuck to one of the EMTs' boots when they hauled me away.

So I edited the note out of my mental re-creation, but I couldn't stop imagining the rest.

The whole thing was sick, really.

And now here I was, traumatizing her again. Dredging up the second-most-painful piece of her past and thrusting it in her face.

The issue was bigger than that, though. "I'm sorry, Mom. I really am. But this article suggests intruders might be behind the disappearances. Maybe even intruders wearing masks and costumes, and after what I saw in the yard last night . . ."

Mom stiffened. "I thought we agreed that was a nightmare." I doubt she meant to, but she sounded so disappointed in me.

I had to bite the inside of my cheek, to focus on a different kind of pain. "I hope it was a nightmare," I admitted. "But *nine* people from our family have gone missing here, not just your parents. Would you read the article? Please?"

"Nine people? From our family." Mom blinked. She reexamined the headline, as if staring through a fog—the article in one hand, a rose in the other. "That's right. I . . ."

I recognized this expression. It was the way she'd looked at the information on RealHauntedHouses.net, like she was on the cusp of remembering something. And I was afraid she'd do the same thing—blink away whatever she was about to remember.

"You . . . what?" I prompted. "Mom?"

Her eyes weren't all the way focused. Concentration creased her forehead.

Then I saw Mom's hand, the one holding the rose. She was squeezing the spiky stem so tightly that blood ran down her wrist. Droplets slipped to the counter, one by one.

"Mom!" I snatched the rose from her, and she jolted back to life.

"Oh! Oh, these thorns are so sharp. I didn't even realize." Mom laughed her weak laugh and ran her hand under the kitchen sink, washing the blood down the drain. "I'll have to be more careful."

I nodded, queasily eyeing the tiny red puddle on the counter. The stained tips of those thorns.

"What were you going to say?" I made myself ask. "You do know something about the disappearances, don't you?"

"Of course not." She busied herself with paper towels, wiping off the counter, and then her hand. I couldn't help noticing—and hating—that she'd prioritized the counter. "No. I . . . No," she stammered, but her brow was so scrunched.

Then she shook her head, and it was gone.

"Anyway, I will read this article. After dinner." Her lips formed a tight line as she folded the printout and tucked it into her back pocket. "And I'll think about what you're saying, Libby. We can talk about it tomorrow."

I understood that I'd been dismissed, but I stayed, staring at her. Searching for that one tiny thread of her that still made sense to me. The thread that had to be in there somewhere. I knew trauma shattered people into awful shapes, but the way Mom kept fogging out about these disappearances was mystifying. I'd have to ask Dr. Glaser about it in our next session. Maybe a professional could make sense of it.

In the meantime, I made myself walk away. Mom had agreed to read the article. If nothing else, that was a small victory.

But at what cost?

Before I left the kitchen, I glanced back and caught Mom wiping her eyes, leaning on the counter like she couldn't hold up her own weight.

And I felt smaller than the tiniest squirming bug.

Unease simmered in my stomach for the rest of the day and night. It was even worse after dark, once Mom and Vivi had closed their doors, and I was alone in bed.

My fan whirred away beside me. I kept it on low, terrified

it would knock out the power again. Terrified it would kick off another chain of events like those from the night before. But low wasn't quite a match for this house's humidity. I plucked a sweaty curl from my forehead and tucked it, for the thousandth time, behind my ear.

The moon clicked into place in my skylight. It was after midnight, later than the time last night that the real moon lined up with the fake moon in the glass.

Tonight, the house's moans and groans, the scuffling above my head, struck an even more ominous chord. I couldn't shake the sense that the shadows were reaching out for me. Clawing in from the walls.

Then, across my room, my metal trash can—the one holding open my bedroom door—tipped. On its own.

It fell onto its side with a crash, spewing its contents. Tottering back and forth until it ebbed to a stop.

And my bedroom door swung, silent as a ghost, until it closed. Sealing me inside.

I bit my tongue, clenching my sheets.

The weight of the door must have mounted against the knee-high trash can, pound by pound, hour by hour, until it finally tipped. The floorboards in this house were so uneven, practically mushy in places. Everything here wanted to tilt. Wanted to fall.

That's all it was.

I ground my teeth. This house was trying to steal the last shreds of my sanity, but I couldn't let it win. I forced myself out of bed. Anxious shivers ran up from the soles of my bare feet as I tiptoed to the fallen trash can.

The can had littered the floor with sticky wads of tape from unpacking and stray remnants from unboarding the windows—a few rusty nails and splintery shards of plywood.

I stooped to collect them. My trembling finger was one inch away when the plywood *moved.*

I gasped and yanked my hand back.

The tape moved, too. Even the nails. One rolled away like it had been knocked, when my hand was nowhere near it.

An iridescent shimmer winked at me. A blue back, half the size of my thumb, unburied itself from under the plywood. Another squirmed out from under some tape. Another. Another. And another.

My skin squirmed with disgust. I swore and stood, took two big strides back.

The trash was swarming with beetles. Beetles that were the same brilliant blue as the ones enshrined in my stained-glass window, gilded with identical golden legs and antennae.

A perfect match. Like Vivi's butterflies in her room and in her window.

They writhed, on all those clicking little legs, over the trash and over each other, sluggish and almost drunk. Weak as the first butterfly that had clung to Vivi's chest. Like something was wrong.

Had they snuck in after the fumigations, too? Ingested enough lingering poison to be sick and stumbling but not quite dead?

My stomach lurched. The sight of them all was almost enough to make me sick, too.

I backed away from the beetles, from the trash, from my room. Fled through my door and into the hallway, hugging my shivering arms. My room was too much. This *house* was too much.

A creak sounded behind me, and I whirled around, my heart slamming inside my chest.

The noise was coming from Vivi's room again. It was dark

under her door—lights out. But as I stared, a blacker shadow flickered under the doorframe. Movement from inside.

And the worst part of my brain whispered: *What if something is in there, with my sister?*

"Vivi?" I called softly. My voice came out strangled, desperate.

Nothing answered.

No more shadows. No more creaks.

This was all my imagination. All it needed was to hear the word *haunted* a couple times, and that was enough to send it careening through my brain with these nonsensical nightmares.

Pathetic.

If anyone was in there ignoring me, it was Vivi herself.

My breath was coming too shallow again, but I was *not* going to let myself be terrified into another hypomania. I knew I should march right back into my room and clean up the trash, and the beetles with it. Or, if nothing else, leap over them, dive back into bed, and beg Vivi to collect the bugs in the morning.

But now that I'd retreated into the dark hallway, I couldn't help eyeing the enormous window beside me. I was almost afraid to look out at the backyard beyond—like the second I did, I'd spy masked figures in the flesh, and yesterday's nightmare would start all over again.

More delusional thinking.

To spite my brain—to prove it wrong—I made myself look.

The night sat hot and heavy. No wind. No breeze. There was only the shrill chirp of hidden crickets, filtering in through the glass.

And then, in the backyard, something moved.

Shadows.

Shadows in white masks.

No.

I pinched myself—first hard, then harder.

But I wasn't waking up. And the shadows weren't disappearing.

In fact, they crept closer. From a crack in our fence over to the stone table. To the chairs.

The masked figures were back.

The masked figures were *real.*

My trembling body moved for me, tucking to the side of the enormous window—careful, careful, quiet—gently enough not to disturb any butterflies lurking in the curtains. I peeked out with eyes so wide they watered.

At the head of the table, one figure stood, mask bobbing like it was speaking. It gestured, grand and sweeping, and its cloak flicked aside. Revealing, underneath, a flash of red.

A popping cherry red.

I knew that color.

I had a sudden hunch. Furious and awful. One that changed everything.

Flynn's words from the library stabbed at me all over again: *Maybe you shouldn't be wandering around your house at night. Doesn't sound very safe. Not if something is haunting your yard.*

What a sick little game.

My hands balled into fists. My fear was melting into boiling fury.

Before I knew what I was doing, I was charging through my house, dark dots scurrying out of my way.

I slammed open the doors to the backyard, rattling their stained-glass windows. "Hey!" I thundered into the night. "What do you think you're doing?"

All the figures turned to look at me.

The one at the head of the table spoke: "Oh shit."

Then, all at once, they scattered like cockroaches—the way cockroaches are supposed to—in different directions, sprinting for the back fence, the side fence. But I knew which one I was after. I chased the masked ringleader, who was beelining for the back.

Adrenaline was powering me, full speed, and I was gaining ground, thudding after him through the long, slick grass.

I closed in on his fleeing cloak and reached out to snatch it.

He lurched to the right—a feint—then dashed to the left. Straight for the hedge maze.

"Stay out of our maze!" I shouted.

The entrance was clogged with overgrown rosebushes. Snatching thorns. No way he'd make it through that. As soon as he saw, he'd realize.

He reached that treacherous tangle of bushes.

Then he wrapped his cloak around himself, ducked down, and charged straight in.

I cursed to myself. I didn't have a cloak, and my pajama top was tragically short-sleeved, but I ducked down and charged after him.

My arms knocked against velvety petals, bobbing rose heads. Thorns tore into my skin with needless vengeance. Barefoot in the dewy grass, I barreled into the maze, deeper and deeper, even as the ten-foot-tall bushes pressed in on me. That thick scent billowed up my nose, down my throat, until I was practically drinking it—rancid and floral, sour-sweet. "Get back here," I yelled. "You'll never find your way out!"

The bushes ahead crashed as the intruder plunged deeper into the maze, flinging branches forward so they'd swing back and whip into me.

One popped me right in the chest, petals exploding like a tiny blue firework. My pajama top snagged on an especially sharp thorn—

And the flash of his cloak disappeared around the bend. He was getting away.

I ripped my top free, tearing open a small window to my midriff and a stinging scratch from belly button to hip, and darted around the corner after him.

But there was nothing waiting for me except knee-high grass and massive bushes.

I strained, listening for movement. A night breeze whispered through the winding roses. Concealed bugs hummed through the maze with deep drones and high whines. . . .

He must've found a hiding place. If I got close enough, though, he'd have to move and I'd hear him.

The path ahead forked. I'd have to choose.

The nubs of my nails pressed into my palms. I *had* to catch him. For the last several months, I'd proved nothing but how weak I was, and I wasn't going to do that anymore. This time, in my second life, I was going to be strong.

I raced down the path and chose at random: the right.

The corridor was long, straight, and narrow. Maybe close to the middle of the maze? I couldn't tell. I couldn't orient myself at all. Halfway to the upcoming bend, I heard a rustle from the parallel path.

He'd taken the left fork, and the pounding of his steps was steady, like someone who knew exactly where he was headed.

I turned the corner and skidded to a halt.

A dead end.

"Dammit!" I yelled. He was just on the other side of these bushes—so close. And yet totally out of reach.

From the path beside me came an answering, taunting laugh. A delighted bark of "Ha!"

My fists clenched tighter than I'd known they could clench.

Then I spotted a slight gap in the bushes. A few paces ahead, the maze wall was thinner, a spot I *might* be able to squeeze through.

Before I could talk myself out of it, I buried my face in the crook of my arm and plowed into the gap.

I winced, bracing for scraping thorns—but none came. I pulled my arm away from my eyes, and somehow, I was already on the other side of the wall.

It was like the roses had *moved.*

Out of my way.

I couldn't believe my luck—Was it luck? How was that possible?—but I was still running and now it was too late to stop, and I barreled straight into the intruder I was trying to catch.

CHAPTER EIGHT

MY SHOULDER CRASHED INTO THE INTRUDER'S chest with a hot punch of pain, sending us both tripping and tangling.

Intertwined, we crashed down to the grass. The thud rattled in my teeth and rippled through the hedge maze, stirring flapping bugs from the bushes around us. My knees and shoulder and right elbow throbbed, but at least we had landed on grass. We were in a small clearing, and the back of his head had hit only two feet away from stone.

I was amazed I'd actually caught him.

I scanned over the wall of roses behind us, but couldn't find any evidence of the opening I'd passed through. None at all. Like the impossible seam that had opened for me had sewn itself right back up.

Like I'd imagined the whole thing. And yet . . .

"What the hell! Where did you even come from?" My captive twisted under me.

I stopped gaping at the roses and refocused on the more immediate problem. I straddled him, my thighs hugging his waist, squeezing against every shift in his lean torso as he thrashed. For once, I was too mad at him to be mortified, to focus on anything except: *You're not getting away with this.*

His mask was thick white plastic, a plain half mask, with holes for his eyes and nose. I grabbed it.

"Hey, don't!" he yelled, reaching for my arm, but I ripped the mask off.

There he was, in panting pink-cheeked glory.

Flynn.

"I *knew* it! The second I saw your red sweatshirt," I cried. "After all your 'help' at the library, too!" Hot spitting poison seeped through my chest—he'd played me.

At least he had the decency to look embarrassed. "Libby, I . . ."

Dew formed long before sunrise in this humidity, soaking both of us. Clammy stains pressed into my pajama pants, making me shiver even in the summer night. And I didn't think I was imagining that slight tremble in Flynn, too. The scent of smoky herbal incense clung to his cloak. His green eyes were dilated dark as he lay under me, pinned in the grass.

He was slim, but tall enough, toned enough, that I knew he was letting me hold him down. Maybe he didn't mind me straddling him.

In different circumstances, I wouldn't have minded either.

I released him with a flustered growl and climbed to my feet, swiping at the wet patches on my knees. "You've got about three seconds to explain what you're doing here before I call the cops."

"Oh, really?" Flynn said, scowling. My threat had killed his brief flash of repentance. He brushed himself off and rose to his feet, too. "That's how you wanna play this?"

Excuse me? Oh, no. He did not get to be the indignant one here. I narrowed my eyes as he sized me up, his challenging glare sizzling over my bare feet, my baggy plaid pants—which were, as he no doubt noticed, pocketless, and couldn't be concealing a phone.

And then I remembered that rip in my shirt, the naked gap through to my stomach. I locked my arms tight over my torso. "What are you doing here?" I said—too quickly, too loudly. "Did I interrupt your little cult meeting?"

"Cult meeting?" Flynn barked out his stab of a laugh. "I told you there's no cult."

He seemed to mean it. If so, there went my one vaguely coherent theory about the disappearances. And about why the hell Flynn would be skulking around my property, shrouded in a mask and cloak.

"Look, the truth is . . ." He sighed, raking a hand through his hair. "This is the second time you've crashed my séance."

"Séance . . . ?" I said, confused. "Like the kind Ellen Clery used to do here?"

"My operation isn't half as elaborate, but someone's got to keep the tradition alive, don't they?" He tossed that off like he didn't want me probing deeper. "After you interrupted us last night, I had to reschedule. I was *hoping* you'd take my hint not to go wandering—"

"Uh, I'm allowed to 'wander' in my own house. You, on the other hand, should not be here under any circumstances. Why would you want to keep a creepy tradition like séances alive?" Especially if it meant sneaking onto someone else's property. Either Flynn was some screwy occult adrenaline junkie or . . . "Wait, are you doing this for money?" I asked. "Are people paying you, like they paid Ellen?"

Flynn hesitated. Then, with a sigh, his shoulders slumped

in resignation. "Well, it beats minimum wage at the library," he said. "Besides, we wouldn't want the spirits getting lonely." Another deflection, blown at me like a puff of smoke.

I crossed my arms tighter, glaring at him. One thing I knew was that there are only two reasons to wear a mask—you have something to protect or something to hide.

I wondered which it was for Flynn.

He watched me judge him. When no out-loud verdict came, he shrugged, a bitter little *Think what you want,* and strode across the clearing to retrieve his mask.

It had landed at the foot of a stone statue, a woman bedecked in roses, standing alone at the center of the concrete circle. Ellen Clery, if I had one guess. Judging by the plaque in the foyer, she'd been eager to memorialize herself. But her legacy had fallen into decay. Her ruffled Victorian gown was cracking. Her face had weathered flat. Several of her fingers had broken off, lying in pieces on the ground.

The statue was hardly a monument—more of a crumbling ghost.

Flynn's mask had fallen among the broken clumps of Ellen. He leaned down to grab it and coughed. "God, that stench." He straightened up and covered his mouth with his midnight-blue cloak.

I sniffed the air. "Stench?" I couldn't smell anything beyond the grapey haze of blue roses.

"Like a sewer," he said. "I always notice it around Ellen. Coming from down there, I think." He gestured to a square stone panel in the ground near the statue. It looked like a door, equipped with a rusty metal hoop like a bull's nose ring. "You don't smell it?"

I stepped closer, but still only smelled roses. I shook my head.

Flynn frowned at the door. "Why can't anyone else ever smell that?"

"Anyone else . . . ?" I blinked. "You take people into this maze, too?"

"All part of the pre-séance tour. Or it was, anyway, when this place was abandoned." He scratched and then slapped his wrist. "These damn ants again!" He shook off his mask, and the bugs that must have been clinging to its edges. "Your yard has a major ant infestation, by the way. And they bite. So much to enjoy here."

These were the first ants I'd seen since we moved in, but I was glad they were biting him. Clearly, they were on my side.

"Okay, you know what?" I said. "It was one thing for you to barge in here and play occult tour guide when the place was unoccupied, but this is my family's home now. So whatever weird séance racket you've had going, it's officially over."

"Is that right?" Flynn sneered in an amused way that made me want to punch him. He turned on his heel and cut back to the nearest corridor.

Presumably, the way out.

I tromped after him. "Oh, I'd better be right," I said, "because if I catch you out here again—"

A protruding branch he'd pushed aside thwacked me in my chest. He kept walking.

I gritted my teeth. "Very mature."

"So sorry. That was an accident," he said. Not at all sorry for the not-at-all accident.

I followed him back to the maze entrance without a single wrong turn, which proved he really did know his way around my backyard. Way better than I did, at least, which was infuriating.

I tailed him to the stone table and chairs. The tabletop was littered with tea lights, still flickering, curling up small plumes of smoke. A couple had overturned, splashing white wax across the table. Flynn didn't bother picking them up. He righted a black duffel bag near the butterfly chair at one end of the table.

The contents had spilled out—taller candles, gauzy veils, incense, a wooden Ouija board.

"What is all this stuff?" In spite of myself, I was curious. But I made sure to throw in plenty of scorn when I asked, "Do you think you're, like, psychic, or a medium or something?"

"A lot of people in town think I am." Flynn smiled, elusively, as he wrapped the Ouija board in fabric and tucked it into his bag.

Not quite an answer to my question. Which, from his smile, he clearly knew.

It was like he was laughing at his own private joke. Like he knew so much I didn't.

The more I spun through Flynn's possible motives, the ones he refused to disclose, the more questions I had. "Tell me something," I said. "You believe in spirits, right? Does that mean you think people are disappearing because this house is haunted? And you're holding these séances anyway?"

I didn't believe that's why people were disappearing. But if *he did*—and he was encouraging these hypothetical spirits—what kind of person did that make him?

"Whoa, now." Flynn held up a hand, like I was way off base. "Just because there are spirits here, that doesn't mean the disappearances are their fault."

The frank way he said it was the most unnerving part of all.

So he did believe in spirits. He believed spirits were *here.* And he also seemed to believe that spirits weren't my house's scariest secret.

A tea light sat in his palm, and he was one puff of air away from blowing it out when his eyes wandered to my dark house jagging into the skyline. His smirk snagged on the sight and unraveled, into a much grimmer line. "Libby, you might not believe me, but I honestly thought it was win-win if you could convince your family to leave. I didn't make up those disappearances, or that article. And I meant what I said: this place isn't safe."

I stared at him, the warm light twisting gently across his face—fighting not to notice his dimpled chin and sharp jaw. And, even now, failing miserably.

"If you really are staying here, then maybe you could use my help," he said.

"Help with what?" I demanded.

"A medium could be what you and your family need. You want answers, don't you?" he prodded. "I promise you, my séances are harmless. Let me keep doing them—once or twice a month, that's all. In return, I'll get you the answers you need."

I rolled my eyes. "Oh, come on."

"I can prove I am what I say I am. A quick séance sample. And then you can decide."

He was actually standing here, trying to convince me he was a true medium. And I wanted to laugh in his face, to prove I wasn't the gullible dipshit he took me for. But . . .

After midnight, hemmed in by shrill insects and the drug-heavy perfume from the blue rosebushes, I found myself hesitating.

The scene from earlier in my bedroom replayed in my head—my trash can tipping on its own, teeming with blue beetles that matched my window. Then those bushes in the maze that I could've sworn had parted for me . . .

There was too much here that was unexplained, that felt *unexplainable.*

One way or another, Flynn did know way more about this house than I did. If there was even the slightest chance he could help me find answers, it wouldn't hurt to hear him out.

He was the only one who even agreed that we should be looking for answers. That something was as wrong with this house as my gut knew it was.

"A quick sample," I said finally. "And then *maybe* I'll agree to consider it."

I caught the flash of Flynn's upturned lips before he returned the lit candle to the table. He sat in the end seat closest to him, the butterfly chair, and gestured to the other open chairs. "Take a seat."

Circling the twelve-foot-something-long table, I settled into the beetle chair. The stone under my arms crawled with etched ovals, elaborate bug-shaped detailing that made me wince, remembering the beetles squirming from my toppled trash can.

And yet . . . somehow, the chair was surprisingly comfortable. It was almost a smidge soft, a smidge warm, like a welcoming hug.

Plus, it was practically as far from Flynn as I could get—which seemed wise, given that in spite of everything he'd done, part of me was still tempted to close the distance.

"Really?" Flynn's tone was deathly dry. "Since there are only two of us, I admit I had something a little more intimate in mind," he said, from the opposite end of the table. "Unless, of course, you're too scared."

He was so transparently goading me, and it was so transparently working. "Too scared of what?" I snapped back.

Flynn reached into the black bag beside him and withdrew

the Ouija board. He unwrapped it and set it on the table. I hated how my fingers clenched into the arms of the beetle chair. I'd seen horror movies where one wrong Ouija session led to blood-stained havoc.

But, then, those were only movies. If Flynn wanted me to scare me, he'd have to try a little harder. "I'm not scared of Ouija boards," I said.

"Okay, then." Flynn gestured to the open chair beside him.

I peeled myself up from the beetle chair and took the chair to his right, adorned with carved praying mantises. Unlike the beetle chair, this one wasn't comfortable at all—it was hard and stiff, unyielding like stone should be.

I had to be imagining the difference.

"By the way," Flynn said, "it's a spirit board, not a Ouija board."

"What's the difference?"

"Ouija boards are a patented kind of spirit board, sold commercially. This spirit board belonged to Madame Clery herself. See?" He traced a finger over the blue stars lining the border. There were thirteen, each with too many points. "It's custom."

"Uh-huh. And how would *you* have something that belonged to Madame Clery?" I asked. "Did you steal it from our house?"

"What? Of course not!" Flynn scowled. "I . . . Never mind."

I did believe he hadn't stolen it. But, in that case, no way did I believe it had belonged to Madame Clery.

"Anyway," Flynn said, "don't get your hopes up too high. Technically, you'd want a minimum of three people for a proper séance—a medium and two sitters to strengthen the spiritual energy. With just the two of us, it'll be harder to achieve a strong manifestation."

"You don't say." I used that same wry tone he liked to point at me. Here came the caveats, setting up preemptive excuses for why nothing was going to happen. "Well, I'll try and make my spiritual energy extra-strong to compensate for—"

"Libby?" A voice behind me spoke. "What's going on?"

"Vivi!" I said, my stomach sinking. I turned to face her. "What are you doing out here?"

"I saw you through the window." She hovered by the columns a few feet behind my chair. She was bedecked in her favorite pajamas, with a galaxy print, and her wary eyes were locked on Flynn. "Who is this?"

"Flynn. Nice to meet you." He smiled, sharp and toothy, uplit by candlelight.

Vivi's brow furrowed, but she stood her ground. "I'm Vivi."

"Well, care to join us, Vivi?" Flynn gestured to the table. "I was about to show your sister what a séance feels like when performed on the grounds of a real haunted house."

"Haunted . . . ?" Vivi looked at me, eyes big, and I could've killed Flynn on the spot. But she regrouped. "First of all, there's no such thing as haunted houses," she informed Flynn. "Second of all"—she stood her full shrimpy height, pushing out her chest—"you're in my chair."

"Your . . . ?" Flynn leaned back, examining the chair underneath him. He shrugged, then stood with a *Be my guest* gesture.

Vivi took her seat, the stone-rendered butterfly mask peering out from over her shoulder. Flynn took the ant-adorned chair beside her, across from me.

"Well, here's your third person," I said to Flynn. "No excuses now."

"Oh, yes," Flynn agreed. "With séances, it's always the more the merrier." He rustled in his bag, digging out a couple cloaks and masks he'd managed to collect, and held up a pair to her. "Want the full experience? Put these on."

Vivi did, and Flynn slid a matching costume toward me. "You too," he said. "This is a séance, not a pajama party."

I sighed, but realized the grass-stained cloak would give my ripped top some extra coverage. I knotted it around my throat and slid on the mask—a flimsy half mask covering my forehead and cheeks—with a plastic crinkle. Apparently, the masks he lent to guests were cheaper than the one he wore.

"One last thing . . . ," Flynn said. He stood and rearranged the tea lights, rekindling the few that had fallen, to form a circle around the crystal ball embedded in the center of the table.

The light danced off the ball's gleaming surface and the blue rose it encased. Like a mirror, it reflected everything—the candles, the stone chairs, our own reflections—but twisted the images upside down, bloated, and strange.

Vivi leaned in, eyeing her distorted crystal-ball counterpart. "What is this thing anyway?"

Flynn resumed his seat. "This crystal ball has been here since Madame Clery's House of Masks opened in the 1890s. Supposedly, it was her original conduit for channeling the dead." He dropped his voice, like speaking of such things required reverence. "An open invitation for spirits to join us."

"But why would we *want* spirits to join us?" Vivi asked.

"Oh, spiritualists believed speaking to the dead provided countless benefits to the living," Flynn assured her. "For instance, you and your sister might be hoping for answers about the past. Most commonly, people want closure—to contact a dead loved one."

Vivi flinched at those words: *dead loved one.* Her eyes darted my way.

Suddenly, I was grateful for the cover of the flimsy mask. I pressed it tighter against my flushing cheeks.

"I can see why someone would want to talk to their dead family," Vivi mumbled. "Even if just to yell at them."

Yell at them? Even six weeks later, Vivi had barely spoken to me about anything real. If she wanted to talk to me—*yell* at me—I was right here.

"Uh, sure." Flynn tilted his head. "Or see them one last time. Clarify last wishes. Apologize. Whatever it is."

Wordless, Vivi nodded. She stared down at the table.

Something was odd about her tonight. Something had been odd about her all day. She'd spent hours in her room, door shut tight, even before bedtime. And that twitchiness I'd noticed at breakfast seemed magnified. Maybe she was just nervous, but she couldn't sit still, fiddling with her mask and cloak, shifting constantly. Now she was firing cheap shots—in front of a stranger, no less.

"What are the other reasons?" I prompted Flynn, too high-pitched. "You said there were other reasons people might want to talk to the dead."

Flynn measured the painful silence between me and Vivi, performing some mental calculation. Finally, he played along. "Well," he said, "many spiritualists, Ellen included, believed spirits were not only superior to humans but that they could make us wiser, stronger—even gift us with supernatural abilities."

"Abilities?" Vivi snapped to attention. "What kind of abilities? Could they make someone fly?"

What a strange first impulse. I frowned at her. "Vivi, come on. That's not—"

"Actually, yes," Flynn said. "Levitation was a mainstay of Ellen's séances."

“Levitation,” Vivi echoed quietly, as if making a mental note to research this further. A new light shone in her eyes, one that burned deeper than the gleam of candle fire.

I knew that look. Her brain had latched on to something—and it was churning, hard. But hadn’t she been insisting, just a moment ago, that haunted houses weren’t real? I couldn’t tell what had changed for her—why she was starting to take Flynn seriously. Whatever it was, I didn’t like it.

“Now, if there are no further questions . . .” Flynn paused, but Vivi shook her head. “Then who should we call? With a house as haunted as yours, you have so many options.” He slipped his white mask over his face and lifted the hood of his cloak, melting into the same figure that had twice terrified me from the hall window.

“I could reach out to one of your relatives,” Flynn offered. “A grandparent? Someone who disappeared?” He smiled at me, moonlight glinting off his white teeth. A challenge: *Nothing to lose, right? Unless you’re chickening out.*

“Sure. Why not?” I returned the daring smile. “Let’s try Grandma. Margaret Feldman.”

“Margaret Feldman.” Flynn nodded. He positioned the spirit board in front of Vivi, with the triangular planchette in the center.

I started to reach for it, but Flynn stopped me with a gesture. “First, we do the invocation. We want to call Margaret Feldman specifically—not anything that comes knocking.”

Anything that comes knocking. The little hairs at the back of my neck prickled.

“Lay your hands on the table, palms up,” Flynn said. “Repeat after me.”

Vivi and I laid out our hands.

"Margaret Feldman," he intoned, in a practiced flat chant, "wandering and restless spirit, we welcome you."

"Margaret Feldman," Vivi and I echoed, "wandering and restless spirit, we welcome you."

"If you are here, please join us at this table."

We said that, too.

And we waited.

A restless itch begged me to take my hands off the table, to pick at my nails in my lap. But the dark hung around us, hot and heavy and empty. The insects in the surrounding bushes maintained their steady, insistent *scree, scree, scree.*

After a moment, I breathed easier again.

"Seems like Grandma isn't out tonight," I said.

Flynn held up a hand to silence me. His eyes were squeezed shut in concentration. "Just because you can't see her, that doesn't mean she isn't here. In fact"—he paused and turned his head, closed eyes and all, like he was following an invisible presence, one drifting closer and closer to Vivi—"she's hovering around us now."

Vivi followed the direction of Flynn's unseeing stare, scouring the darkness behind her. "I don't feel anything. . . ." She reached out.

Then, with a high squeal, she jumped in her chair. "What was that?" She grabbed her cloak and bundled it to her chest. "Something tugged my cloak!"

Hmph. To me, it didn't seem like a coincidence that she was sitting next to Flynn.

Although, admittedly, I hadn't seen him move. Or lean closer to her. And Vivi was looking at the opposite side of her chair, not the side near Flynn. . . .

"How did you do that?" I demanded.

"I didn't do anything." Flynn grinned but held up innocent hands. "Seems like it's time to try the spirit board. Place your fingers lightly on the planchette but don't apply pressure. We won't be the ones moving it. We're offering up our spiritual energy."

I was having trouble taking the phrase *spiritual energy* seriously and was grateful that it was giving me a little distance from the séance. The roses breathed over us with their drunken smog. Light and shadow from the candles crawled over the spirit board like living creatures.

We set our fingers on the planchette. At first, it was just me and Flynn, and my pinky brushed his. I hated that it made my finger jump and my chest flutter. I also hated that he saw it all and smiled at me—slyly again—like he knew exactly why he made me so twitchy. And like he was enjoying it.

Then Vivi squished her fingers onto the planchette, too, and there went those vibes.

Flynn cleared his throat. "Now, Mrs. Margaret Feldman, could you confirm that you're the spirit who is currently with us?"

We waited, the planchette still under our fingers.

Then it started to slide. Slowly across the board, toward the top left corner, toward Flynn.

"You're moving it, aren't you?" I asked him.

"It's not me," he insisted.

The planchette stopped, its glass lens framing the word YES.

"You're definitely moving it," I said. "Vivi, do you feel him pulling?"

Vivi glanced back and forth between us uncertainly. "I—I can't tell what's moving it."

"I can," I said. Even though I couldn't. But it *had* to be Flynn. It wasn't me. And I doubted it was Vivi.

Flynn sighed. "Are we going to argue all night about who's moving it, or do you have any actual questions for your grandmother? It's best to start light and conversational. Ask something I wouldn't know, if you want proof I'm not controlling the planchette."

I mulled that over but was coming up blank. Mom's refusal to discuss our grandparents meant they'd barely existed for us.

"Ooh, got it!" Vivi said. "We could ask about her birthday."

"Perfect." Flynn nodded at her. He closed his eyes and asked, "Mrs. Feldman, would you tell us your birth month?"

The planchette sat still. Then it lurched to life, dragging across the board to J. Back across to A. It crawled its way through every letter, spelling out J-A-N-U-A-R-Y.

Vivi sucked in a sharp breath. "That's the right answer! Mom said once that my birthday was a couple days from our grandma's."

Maybe so. But what Vivi didn't know was that Flynn had a freakish amount of knowledge about our house, potentially even about our relatives. Birthdays were a matter of public record.

I tried a different tactic. "Small talk with ghosts doesn't do us any good. If she's real, if she's here, that means she died on this property, right?" I said. "I want you to ask her what made her disappear. What killed her."

Granted, I didn't know the answer, so I couldn't instantly verify a true or false response. But I was 99.9 percent sure that Flynn was the one controlling the planchette. The pressure to prove he wasn't a fraud might get him to cough up something useful—if he actually knew anything.

Flynn hesitated. "Remember how I said to keep things light and conversational? That question is about as traumatic as it gets.

An awful truth like that can take time—even multiple sessions—to bring to the surface."

Oh, really? That sort of timeline seemed pretty convenient for Flynn.

"For our own safety, we need to know who did this to her. If someone hurt her," I said. "You did say you could get me answers," I reminded him. "Actual answers."

"Fine. I'll ask. Don't blame me when she refuses to talk." Flynn rolled his eyes at me before fluttering them shut. "Mrs. Feldman, I know this question is a little abrupt—*extremely* abrupt—but would you share with your granddaughters what happened to you? Did someone hurt you? Did someone make you disappear?"

We all held our fingers on the unmoving planchette, waiting for something, anything.

But nothing came. No motion. No answer.

Dammit. Flynn didn't know anything, did he? He wasn't going to bother faking an answer. He was going to pretend the ghost was giving us the silent treatment.

I waited for Flynn to wrap this up. To make excuses. To gloat. But he just sat there, strangely still, eyes closed.

Waiting.

Waiting, waiting, waiting.

"Maybe we could ask something else," Vivi finally suggested.

Even then, Flynn didn't move. He didn't open his eyes.

He'd made his point. I didn't know why he was still doing this. It was starting to freak me out.

And then the night's heartbeat, that rhythmic pulse of insect wings, stuttered to a stop.

In the crystal ball at the center of the table, something flickered. Behind Flynn's reflection, a white shadow.

I gaped and leaned closer, but it was already gone—as quick

as it had come. It must've been some trick of the candlelight, but my heart sped up all the same.

"Flynn?" I said, my voice breaking. "Never mind, you can stop now."

His mouth dropped open. A low, scratchy moan leaked free, one so small and sad and scared.

Vivi and I jerked our hands away from the planchette, flinching backward in our chairs.

A slow bleed of steam wisped from his mouth, from his nose, like the temperature around him was plunging. Like he'd entered his own separate climate.

The moan kept coming—an endless groan clawing its way out.

Vivi grabbed her arms and rubbed them for warmth. "Wh-what's going on? Libby!"

"What happened before . . ." A new sound tore from Flynn's throat—a new voice. Weak and crusty. Words flaking as fast as mummified skin, crumbling to nothing as soon as they were spoken. *"Will happen again. Is happening now."*

The voice was *wrong*. It sounded nothing like Flynn's. I fought the urge to clamp my hands over my ears.

"Flynn, stop," I said, as firmly as I could manage. "It's not funny."

"Libby," Vivi whispered, "I don't think that's Flynn."

"Of course it's Flynn!"

Vivi shook her head. To my horror, she leaned in closer, even reached out and laid her hand over his, where it still rested on the planchette. "Grandma Margaret?"

Flynn turned his neck toward Vivi one vertebra at a time, as if only now remembering how to operate it. In impossibly slow motion, he faced her.

And then, at last, his eyes opened.

Only they weren't his eyes. They were pure white orbs—glowing softly, terribly.

I shrieked and leaped from my chair, clutching my hands over my thudding chest. Vivi, brave as she was trying to be, pulled her hand away with a horrified squeal.

But Flynn caught her by the wrist, tugging her back toward him. Fixing her in that glowing stare. His mouth hung like he was going to speak.

Instead, he wheezed.

A ragged, desperate sound.

Flynn clutched his throat. He hunched over the table, hacking—clawing at his windpipe.

The choking had to be fake, but it sounded so real it made my own throat clench.

"Enough!" I charged over to them and ripped Flynn's hand from Vivi, grabbed his shoulder, and shook him.

But his coughs kept coming. Choppy and clogged. Maybe there really was something stuck in his throat. Maybe he was actually suffocating.

I thumped him on the back, as hard as I could.

With a dreadful wretch, Flynn lurched forward.

A shiny brown ball flew from his mouth onto the spirit board. And unfurled itself, into a gooey tangle of legs and antennae.

A cockroach.

Alive. Squirming, even with three of its legs crushed, half dangling.

It was dripping with saliva, tinged pink with what looked like blood.

Blood that must've come from Flynn's throat. When he coughed again, red flecks spattered his lips. His chin. "What . . . What is . . . ?" He spoke in his own voice.

The ghoulish light had drained from his eyes, and he looked nothing but horrified. He wiped his mouth and stared, first at the bloody spit on the back of his hand. Then at the cockroach writhing on the board. As if putting the two together. "H-holy shit! Did that come *out of my mouth*?"

He ran his tongue along his teeth and gagged on the taste. Frantically scrubbed his mouth with the sleeve of his shirt.

This cockroach was one bug even Vivi wouldn't closely examine. She squirmed to the opposite end of her chair, perching on the stony arm farthest from Flynn. Observing with horror-struck fascination.

I was frozen beside him, shaking.

The world was knitting and unknitting itself around me. I had no idea what had happened. What was real. What was fake. And the more I replayed it for myself, the more I was mystified.

"Libby . . ." Flynn turned to me, one hand hugging his throat, his voice scraped raw. "Nothing like that has *ever* happened before. I . . . I don't know what that was." He was pale. Shivering. "You have to believe me."

God help me, I did. He looked so horrified. There had to be ways to fake what he'd done, but it was hard to believe he could be this good of an actor.

I opened my mouth to admit it.

Then the cockroach righted itself and scrambled in a gooey trail back toward Flynn. With a cry, he leaped out of his chair. Something clattered from his sleeve.

He cursed. And tossed a panicked glance at me—one that told me everything I needed to know.

He didn't want me to see that, whatever it was.

So I swept in and grabbed it first.

"Wait," Flynn said desperately. "That isn't what you think—"

I held it up to the candlelight: a miniaturized grabber tool.

Oh.

Oh, it was *exactly* what I thought: This must be the trick he used to tug on Vivi's cloak. He would've had to slip this into place just before starting the séance, right under our noses. Otherwise, it would've fallen out when I tackled him in the maze. Clearly, he was skilled at sleight of hand.

Say, the kind you might need to fake coughing up a cockroach.

For a second there, he'd almost had me, too. That voice, those eyes . . .

Flynn snatched the grabber from me, slipping it out of sight. But it was way too late.

Furious heat flushed up from my chest. It wasn't only me he'd had the nerve to trick, but Vivi, too. No one screwed with my little sister—except for me.

"What is wrong with you?" I cried. "Listen, none of that was okay. I don't know how you did that glowing-eye thing, and I don't care. You can't—"

"Glowing-eye thing?" He touched his face, with the nerve to pretend he didn't know what I was talking about. This asshole wanted to stand there, acting innocent and feeding us nightmares about our new home.

"Just get out of here," I said.

For once, Flynn was stunned. "Are you serious?"

"Yes, I'm serious!" I stripped off my cloak and mask and slapped them on the table. "Next time I see you on our property, I'm calling the cops."

"Wait, Lib . . . ," Vivi said. She removed her mask and cloak, too, but stayed rooted by her chair. "We should hear what else he has to say." She was still rubbing her wrist in the spot he'd grabbed her. This séance had touched her deep.

Way deeper than it should have, for being a reeking pile of bullshit.

But of course she'd fallen for it. *I* nearly had, and I'd known going into this that Flynn was a scheming liar. I never should have let her sit down at this table.

"No, Vivi." I shook my head. "We've heard more than enough."

"But what if he's telling the truth? He might be our only chance to figure out—"

"The truth? He literally had tricks up his sleeve, Vivi!" I pointed at Flynn as he sank miserably into his chair. "He's probably trying to scare us out of this house so he can keep holding his freaky little shows!"

"He *did* scare you, didn't he?" Vivi called me out. "That's what this is really about. You say you want answers, but now you're too scared to hear them. To confront something you don't understand."

She was probably a little right. But only a little. And I definitely wasn't going to admit it, not in front of Flynn. I shook my head. "No, that's not it—"

"It is! And it doesn't even make sense." Vivi shook her head at me, bitter with disappointment. "If dead people scare you so much, why did you try so hard to become one?"

"Vivi!" My mouth went dry as ash. I flashed back to that stabbing, bitter taste inching up my throat—my stomach thrashing helplessly inside me.

She'd blurted it out. Just like that.

And now she realized what she'd done. Clapped a hand over her mouth.

But it was too late to take it back. Too late for Flynn to unhear it. His jaw had dropped. His eyebrows crumpled in worry.

So now he felt sorry for me. Like everybody else.

Of all the times for Vivi to confront me, it had to be here? In front of *him*?

"She's kidding," I blurted out. "Obviously."

Flynn blanched. "That isn't something to joke about." His voice came quiet. Grave as a funeral.

"No," I said, "it really isn't."

"But I . . ." Vivi wanted to say something, but she clearly had no idea how to recover. None of us did.

I seized her by the elbow, halting her midsentence, and dragged her into the house, where Flynn couldn't follow.

I glanced back once. And he was still watching. Standing alone in our nighttime backyard, duffel bag slung over his shoulder. Mask pushed up on his forehead, cloak hanging around him like a shadow. Staring at me like, of all the things in this supposedly haunted house, I was the most unnerving.

The entire reason we'd moved was to escape all the people who knew what I'd done to myself—so I wouldn't have to face them again this fall.

With one breath, Vivi had as good as told my whole new school.

CHAPTER NINE

IT TOOK EVERYTHING IN ME NOT to slam the back door as I ushered Vivi into the dark kitchen.

"What the hell is wrong with you?" My breath was choppy, my voice way too hot. "Don't you get it? You might as well have told *everyone* in my new class that I tried to kill myself!"

Vivi backed away, stumbling against the island. "I'm sorry! It just came out, and—"

"That was the whole reason we moved to this awful house in the first place—a fresh start for me—and you obliterated it!"

"A fresh start for you? Just you?" Vivi demanded. "You think you're the only one who needs that?" Moonlight filtering through the stained-glass doors caught in her eyes, and I realized they were bloodshot. The veins ate in from the outside corners, an angry red haze reaching for the brown. "Of course you do. It's only about you. Right?"

There it was again. That heavy shame, crushing my shoulders. "That's not what I mean. You know it's not, but—"

"No. I don't know!" It burst from Vivi, fierce, as a wet shine pooled in her reddened eyes. "Mom keeps telling me not to say anything—we're supposed to 'support' you. You. You, you, *you*! How do you think it was for me, after what you did? You think I'm okay? That *anything* feels okay anymore? You didn't even care what this would do to me and Mom. You didn't think about us for a second!"

Shock stole the words from my lips. Now I was the one stumbling backward. I found a counter behind me, something to grab on to. "That's not . . . That's not at all . . ."

I'd been thinking of Vivi more than anyone. How much better off she'd be without me.

I'd spent all spring plummeting into the deepest pit. A catatonic crush that had stapled me into bed.

I couldn't get myself up. I couldn't do homework.

Mom had started bringing me frozen dinners on trays. She made me sit up in bed, supervised as I ate miserable bite after bite of hardening, lumpy mashed potatoes. Reheated cod fillet that no amount of ketchup could make taste like food.

I had to watch as the circles under Mom's eyes got darker. As Vivi's anxiety spiked.

My mind started whispering, *They'd be better off without you. Maybe they'd even be grateful.*

I'd thought it was a mature decision I was making, for the greater good, to take myself out of the equation.

My mind had twisted up a lot of things. Clutched them close, crumpled them tight. Cognitive distortions, Dr. Glaser called them. Even now, sometimes the lies felt realer than reality. I didn't always see them—obvious as they should be—until I slammed into one face-first.

Like here in the kitchen with Vivi, watching the desperate heave of her chest. The tears in my little sister's eyes.

"Mom told you she's the one that found you, right?" She clutched her elbows into a lonely hug and turned away. "There, on the bathroom floor? Covered in your own puke?"

My heart did stop then.

I'd been so careful to time it when I thought Mom would come home first.

But it wasn't Mom who'd found me.

"It was you," I said.

And I didn't have to imagine what Vivi's face must've looked like: A sickening mess of fear and disgust and abject horror. Crushed with disillusionment, abandonment. Hopelessness.

It was the face she was making now.

That's why she couldn't look at me. Why she'd been avoiding me all this time.

No. No, no, oh my God. I hadn't wanted her to see that. I'd never ever meant—

"There were pills in your throw-up." Her voice, stilted and strained, pushed past the sobs shaking her shoulders. "All these half-digested pills."

It was like there was static in my ears. I was going underwater. Tasting all over again, the metallic tang of those pills, the slimy coating they'd left behind on my tongue. I'd been trying to move faster than my brain. Even as the panic started rising from my gut. Even as my fingers shook harder and harder, I kept telling myself, *It's too late. Finish what you started. You chose this for a reason.*

Only it was the wrong reason.

Now, more than anything, I wanted to hug Vivi. I reached for her, touching her arm.

But she pulled away like I was toxic. "And your note: 'I love you. It's for the best. You'll see. . . .'" She was full-on trembling. "What kind of note is that?"

Mom had been confused when I asked if she'd found the note. Now it made sense.

"I flushed it down the toilet," Vivi said. "Did you think that would make us feel better?"

I had, actually. I'd thought . . .

"You were my best friend," Vivi choked out. "You were *everything*. And you . . ." Her breaths came in gulps and gasps like mine. "You did it anyway."

Because I'd been sick. Because of a million reasons Vivi didn't want to hear.

Wouldn't hear.

Couldn't hear.

"I—I'm sorry. . . ." I didn't know what else to offer her. It felt like all my insides had been scooped out, into one quivering, useless pile on the floor. "I really am. I am so, so—"

Vivi shook her head. "It doesn't matter," she mumbled. "In a couple years, you'll go away. To college. And then it'll be over anyway." She smiled weakly. Numbly. "Some sisters hate each other from the start, so we're lucky, really. We didn't always feel that way."

What was she saying—that she hated me now? Could she mean that?

When I looked at Vivi, I didn't just see her in the present. I saw snapshots of her over thirteen years, all the people she'd been as she grew up. I'd loved—and only kind of wanted to strangle—every single one.

To me, Vivi was grass-stained knees and a palm wriggling with caterpillars, her eyes so full of wonder they took up half her face. She was caramel-satin ballet slippers and glittering tutus. She was pacing and muttering and scribbling "serious scientific notes" on a unicorn pad with a lime-green gel pen. And, yes, she was stealing my lip gloss and fighting me for the remote and smearing boogers on me.

But she was also the perpetual tug on my sleeve, pointing at something I never would've noticed without her. Because everywhere she looked, she found something worth seeing.

Except, apparently, when she now looked at the two of us.

I was so stunned it was a moment before my tongue unnumbed. "You're counting down until I leave now? You're just giving up? On me? On us?"

Vivi's brow pressed down. Hard. "You gave up first."

There came that choking whisper again, from the back of my brain: *They'd be better off without you.*

It hadn't been true before. But now that I'd done what I'd done . . .

Vivi couldn't wait until I left. She wanted me gone.

For her, I already was, wasn't I?

As far as Vivi was concerned, her sister was dead.

Above our heads, the lights flipped on. A lemon-yellow glow ate up all the shadows at once, washed us in bright bleach.

In the arched doorway behind us, Mom stood, rubbing her eyes, clutching her robe closed at the neck. "Girls? What are you doing down here?"

The fight drained from Vivi. With a shuddering breath, she wiped her cheeks clean and turned to Mom wearing a limp, dull smile.

So quickly, she smothered that gigantic ache inside of her.

And it horrified me, how fast she flipped that switch. That's how much practice she had at doing this—for Mom. For me.

The last thing she needed now was an interrogation from

Mom. So I tried, too, to slap on that lying family smile of ours. "It's my fault, Mom," I said. "I couldn't sleep. I—"

"What did you do to your arms?" Mom ran to me and grabbed my wrists, examining my stinging scratches.

The accusation in her eyes. Did she think I was cutting myself?

I yanked my arms away. "It's from the maze, Mom!"

"The maze? What were you doing in the maze in the middle of the night?"

"I was trying to tell you, but . . ." I turned to Vivi, to give her the go-ahead for a clean getaway. "Vivi, uh, you should probably head back to bed, right?"

I doubted Mom would appreciate hearing that I was with a guy in our yard in the dead of night, but I deserved whatever lecture or punishment she came up with. I deserved a lot worse than that. And I doubted Vivi would ever forgive me, but I still had to try to make it up to her. One micromoment at a time.

She just looked at me, head sagging in exhaustion, then trudged away upstairs.

Mom and I stood in the kitchen, silent. She blinked at me in the light that was too bright for us both.

Finally, she said, "Sit down, Libby," and gestured to the island.

Misery roiled in my stomach as I sank onto a rickety stool. The adrenaline was evaporating from my pores, and all I could feel were the soggy grass stains soaking my pajama pants. The dirt that clung in cold clumps to my bare toes.

Mom kept eyeing the scratches raking my arms, the rip in my pajama top, but she said nothing more. She shuffled to the stove. The sole of one of her slippers was beginning to tear away, flopping against the vinyl-tiled floor.

"How about some tea?" She was already filling the kettle.

"Oh. Um, sure," I mumbled, squishing lower on my stool. "Thanks."

She grabbed a cutting board, a large knife, and two roses from the vase she'd set near the sink.

"You haven't had rose tea before, have you?" She stripped off the thick petals and chopped them into little blue bits. Then, instead of fetching our familiar mugs, she trekked to the china cabinet in the living room and returned with a tray full of tarnished silver.

"Isn't silver a little fancy for two a.m. tea?"

Mom shrugged. "A set like this was meant to be used." I could see her all over again, the pitying looks she used to give abandoned toys in the thrift shop: *How lonely.* She placed the set in front of me. "Besides, it's so unique, don't you think?"

The whole collection was silver: the tray, the teapot, the sugar bowl, the cream pitcher, even the saucers and cups. Filigree garnished every piece, vines and roses and . . . silverfish. The slithery pests were etched throughout the design. They lined the lips of the teacups, unbroken circles of dead metal worms. With their squirmy legs, two jutting antennae in the front and three sharp prongs in the back. An oversized silverfish even crowned the lid of the teapot, curled up in the sickest satire of a cozy house cat.

Mom was right about one thing—the tea set was entirely "unique."

So unique I wanted to hurl it into the living-room fireplace. Tragically, I knew I wouldn't have much luck burning silver.

Mom carried the teapot to the stove. She scooped in the bleeding rose petals and filled it with boiling water. Apparently, more for the sake of ceremony than steeping. She wasted no time passing me a steaming cupful on a silver saucer.

The water's surface swirled with teeny bits of meaty petals, already dyeing the brew thick and inky.

Mom leaned against the opposite counter and cradled her own tea to her chest. "Tell me what happened."

So I did. Sort of. I told her the people I thought I'd seen last night had, in fact, returned—and I ran out to confront them.

"Libby!" If Mom had felt any relief that I hadn't been hallucinating after all, it was swallowed by new concerns. "Why didn't you wake me up? What if they'd been dangerous?"

I snorted, shaking my head. "They weren't. I recognized one of them—this guy I keep running into."

"Guy? What guy?" Mom tensed, like it was time to fetch the shotgun she didn't own.

"Oh, not like a creepy older guy! I'm pretty sure he'll be a junior this fall, too. He lives nearby and works at the library. He keeps saying our house is haunted, trying to freak me out, and he—"

I caught that honeyed warmth seeping through my chest again, and I stopped explaining, before it got even more humiliating. After the next-level shenanigans he'd pulled, I shouldn't want to *think* about him, let alone talk about him. "The point is, he's infuriating, but harmless."

Hopefully, Mom hadn't noticed my overinvestment.

"I see. In that case, this 'infuriating' guy"—she sipped her rose tea, a coy smile peeking over the rim—"you think he's cute?"

Dammit. She'd noticed.

"Mom!"

Now I was thinking about him all over again: the candlelight flickering over his green eyes and white teeth, his agonizingly addictive grin, the hard crush of his body against mine when I'd tackled him in the maze.

I took a tiny sip of my tea, to focus on anything else. And burned the tip of my tongue. The taste was electric—battery acid meets potpourri—and I gagged.

But Mom was savoring each drop. "I'm only thinking aloud here, but we just moved in and you keep running into him? He's even showing up in our yard . . . ?" God help me, her eyebrows started wiggling. Her grinning teeth were taking on a blue tinge from her tea.

"No! It's not like . . ." I clinked the cup down. "He's more into the house than into me, okay? Forget it."

I had *not* expected this enthusiasm from Mom. She'd never been one for romance herself. Hence, the sperm-donor route for me and then Vivi. Or . . . Well, I wasn't quite sure if she was ace or aro. She didn't use those terms herself, though she seemed interested when I showed her the definitions. Then she got bashful and played the *We'll talk about this when you're older* card.

Regardless, she was so invested in me reconnecting with my peers that she didn't seem to care what form that socialization came in—romantic or otherwise. This earnest hopefulness of hers . . . turns out it was more annoying than if she'd been pissed.

I sighed at my far-from-empty cup. "Anyway, Mom, I'm tired." More like exhausted. Wrung-out. My brain overstuffed with creepy-crawly questions and a dreary ache. The last thing I wanted to do was talk about boys—raising even more quandaries that would keep me awake tonight. "I'm going to bed."

I unhooked one leg from the stool.

"Hold on," Mom said, strangely sharp.

I froze.

But then she smiled, and that habitual honey was back in her tone: "You've barely touched your tea."

I sank back onto my stool and raised the cup to my lips,

braving the etched silverfish around the rim, to keep her appeased. I slurped the tiniest sour sip and flinched.

She nodded at me. "What's going on with you and Vivi?" she asked. "You didn't look cozy when I got down here."

That was Mom nice-speak for: She'd heard us yelling. She knew the simmering bad feelings between us had finally boiled over.

I dug too hard into my thumb's cuticle—and winced at the answering sting.

I could lie, or downplay it, but that's what we'd done before my suicide attempt. And where had that gotten us? "Why didn't you tell me?" I asked. "That Vivi was the one who found me?"

Mom choked on a gasp. "She told you?" She flopped in her broken slipper to the stool beside me and sat, clutching her mug like a lifeline. "It was probably wrong. To ask her to lie."

I cut my eyes to her. Mom always did admit fault after the fact, like that made it better that she'd done it in the first place.

"I didn't want to lose you again," she muttered, red-faced. "If we'd told you what really happened, you only would've tortured yourself more." She reached out and wrapped a gentle hand around mine—the one that had been picking at my bleeding thumb.

I hadn't realized I was still doing it.

She squeezed slowly but deliberately to make me stop. "I don't know why you keep hurting yourself. Yes, bad things happen, Lib, but why do you always have to point them in at yourself?"

I'd never thought of it that way before. I didn't have an answer for her, but heat welled in my eyes. She was right—I was always hurting myself. In big ways and little ways. Even the nail-picking was an example. And the scariest part was that I couldn't make myself stop.

Mom sighed. "I thought if I could keep your pain and Vivi's pain separate—stop you from directing it at each other—then it'd be less hard on both of you. But maybe that's not true."

"Yeah, Mom, it's not. Like, *really* not." I snatched my hand back from hers. "You made Vivi play pretend for weeks. Do you have any idea how much she hates me now?"

Mom blinked, eyes moistening. "She doesn't hate you, Libby. She might be angry, but . . . If I made things worse, that's not what I intended. Not at all." She gripped her cup so tight that her knucklebones strained against her skin. "Let me worry about taking care of Vivi. You focus on getting healthy again, okay? That's the best thing you can do for her, too."

I didn't know anymore what healthy looked like.

And I wasn't sure Mom did either.

She was a paler and paler imitation of herself, the color sucked from her cheeks. She'd chided me for picking at my nails, but the skin on her own thumb was ripped and raw.

I didn't think this place was good for her. I didn't think it was good for any of us.

"Mom," I said slowly, "did you read the article about the disappearances yet?"

Mom drained the last of her tea, eyes closed, like she wanted to be anywhere but here, having this conversation. "I thought we solved the mystery of what you saw in the backyard. That doesn't make you feel better?"

"It helps," I said. And it did. "But it doesn't explain why so many of our family members have gone missing."

"Missing." Her forehead crinkled. "Right." She drew the article from her bathrobe pocket and smoothed it on the counter between us. She'd been carrying it with her. She'd moved it from her jeans to her bathrobe—she must've been reading it. But she stared at it through hazy eyes, like she was having trouble recognizing it. "I did read it. It reminded me—a long time ago, your Great-Aunt Carol mentioned something. . . ."

Mom was *finally* remembering whatever she'd been shoving down.

I seized up tight. "Great-Aunt Carol did tell you about the disappearances?"

Mom winced. "It was a long time ago, I guess. I can't explain why I've had such a hard time remembering."

She knew. All this time, she'd been sitting on this. The only reason I wasn't shouting that was because Mom seemed so confused herself. So disturbed. I didn't think she'd been lying on purpose.

In some ways, that was even scarier.

"Mom." I made myself speak slowly. Evenly. "If you knew about this, why did we come here?"

She looked as puzzled as I felt, fighting to recall a decision she'd made only six weeks ago. "I . . . Well, I always used to stop by the house from time to time, to check on things. I never stayed long. But last time, it was while you were in the . . . you know, facility."

Psych ward. *Psych ward* was the term she was dancing around. I just nodded, because we had bigger problems right now.

"It was a difficult time. I needed something—anything—beautiful in my life. And those roses. When I saw them and smelled them, they touched me in a way I hadn't felt before. Even afterward, I kept dreaming about them, and I *knew* it was time to come here. We had to move anyway, and . . ." She cast a dreamy look at the vase of roses on the counter, and a strange peacefulness settled over her. "All those reservations that had been holding me back, I understood then: They weren't good enough. Weren't even real."

"But they *are* real," I reminded her, tapping the article between us.

A chasmic scowl—one I'd never seen before—carved Mom's face. This time, she didn't even look at the article. She stood and strode over to the teapot on the counter. She carried it back to the island and poured another serving into her empty cup. By now, the petals had steeped the liquid ocean-dark, the scent gaggingly floral. Without asking, she topped off my nearly full cup, too, then took her stool beside me and resumed sipping her tea.

The message was clear: this was as much of an answer as I was getting.

A clammy shiver ran down my spine. Was she really telling me that she'd known about the disappearances before we moved in, then smelled some roses and suddenly stopped caring?

That couldn't be the full truth. The Mom I knew would never put me and Vivi in that kind of danger.

Then again, I looked at her, hunched at the kitchen island, hugging her teacup. The stained-glass pendant overhead cast thin scales of color over Mom's skin, bruising her purple and green. Sallow as a corpse.

Maybe this person beside me wasn't the Mom I used to know.

It came out in a whisper: "I'm sorry, Mom, but . . . I think we should leave."

And it took me a second to realize why I was whispering: I didn't want the house to hear me. Total nonsense. But I felt it in my gut, all the same. What I was saying felt blasphemous. The one thing that, within these walls, should be unspeakable.

"Leave?" Mom was so startled the teacup slipped in her hand.

A splash of blue sloshed over the rim, staining her robe, and she didn't even notice. "Leave the house?"

I wished she'd keep her voice down. I fought the wild urge to shush her.

"Yeah." My throat was so dry. I glanced down at my own teacup. The velvety skin was slipping away from the strangely thick petals, coating the surface like algae.

I couldn't take another sip of that tea.

"Come on," I begged. "This house isn't our only chance for a new beginning. We could get another apartment. I know it would be small, but Vivi and I don't care about that—"

"No," Mom said. "We can't leave. We can't do that."

Of all things, she smiled at me—blue tea clinging to her teeth in a film, running between the cracks. "Libby, every flower needs the right environment. The right soil, the right amount of sun . . ." Her eyelids hung heavy. It was almost like she was high. Like she'd latched on to some Profound Truth that maybe, if you were sober, wasn't so profound after all. Maybe wasn't even true.

But she squeezed my hand, and with utter conviction, she told me, "This house is the garden where we were meant to be planted. Can't you see that?"

My hand lay lifeless in hers, my mouth open.

She patted my hand and drew her own away. "I'm sorry I didn't realize sooner. But it'll all be better now that we're here. Promise me you're giving this place a real chance, Lib."

"I . . ."

She fixed me with those heartbreaking doe eyes, long-lashed and pleading.

I was so tired of making Mom cry.

She couldn't hear me anyway. I knew now—something

fundamental in her had broken. No matter what I did, she would never let us leave.

"I promise." It slipped from my mouth quietly.

But it was enough. Mom smiled at me, realer than any smile she'd given me so far tonight. "That means a lot, sweetie."

She lifted the article and tore it into soft, snowy bits. Slowly but surely, to absolute shreds.

Like I'd torn that *Romeo and Juliet* program. As if she were ripping this article, once and for all, out of her mind. As if she could rip it out of mine, too.

Then she tapped one of her long nails against my full forgotten teacup.

"Now, drink up," she said. "You're not going to let that tea go to waste, are you?"

I drank the tea.

The first sip had nearly choked me. But with each subsequent swallow, more and more, I found myself craving that shocking, sour kiss. Even as I felt it dyeing me blue all the way down. My throat, my stomach, everything. Pulsing and electric.

I hadn't known what else to do.

When I'd been the one spiraling, I hadn't realized it at the time, not totally, but I had expected Mom to know how to fix me. How to save me. Every tiny thing she'd said wrong, every misguided gesture, had made me feel more alone. Impossible to help.

I had hated her for that. For having a brain that worked differently from mine. For not having been through this herself so she could shepherd me through safely.

What an ugly truth.

It stemmed from a basic childhood fantasy: Mom always had the answers.

But now that this eerie, disembodied dreaminess had seized her, I had no idea how to bring her back. She was slipping away from me, just like Vivi.

After leaving her in the kitchen, I rushed upstairs to my and Vivi's bathroom. The tea thrashed in my stomach almost as hard as all those pills had, and the echo of that sensation was drowning me in a cold, blinding panic.

I needed it out.

I jammed my finger down my throat and splashed that shocking blue all over our porcelain toilet bowl. I knelt there, shaking, as the stained-glass mosquito window watched over me. A faceless figure offering its arm for mosquitoes to suck.

At its feet lay a mangled sheep, riddled with holes, swarmed by more mosquitoes.

The figure held its other hand up toward a waning moon, its long, blue fingers dripping with glass rivers of red. Like it was the one who'd punched those holes in the sheep in the first place.

If Mom ever let us replace any of these windows, I wanted this one gone first. But now she was so in love with this place I doubted she'd let us change a thing.

We were stuck here. Trapped.

I shuddered and hugged my arms like Vivi had in the kitchen tonight. My poor sister. I had made my trauma her trauma, and it was eating her alive. I thought of her bloodshot eyes, this newfound hungering fury that felt so foreign.

My body was getting heavier and heavier. A warning—I was falling toward a catatonic low.

I should get up.

Body, please.

But the low had seeped into my limbs, locking them stiff. In front of the blue-splashed toilet.

Here I was again on the bathroom floor, ground zero for all my worst moments.

They'd be better off without you. My mind had renewed that insidious whisper.

No.

I could *not* go back to that place.

You have to move, I told myself. *Move any part of yourself.*

My shins ached under me, bruising against the hard tile. Even still, my legs wouldn't let me stand. Time was losing meaning, the world an unfocused smudge to my vacant stare.

This was pathetic. Utterly pathetic.

Your finger. You can move one finger, can't you?

My pinky twitched.

Yes. Another finger.

I lifted my thumb.

That's it. Move. Keep moving.

In slow motion, I fought through my fog.

One finger at a time.

Then my hands.

My arms.

Standing required too many muscles. Too much weight and too much movement.

So I did what I had to do—I crawled. From the bathroom floor, down the hallway, back to my bedroom. Praying the whole way that Mom or Vivi wouldn't see me. Every groan of the uneven floorboards was torture.

At my bedroom doorway, I stopped.

Trash from the tipped can was still strewn across the floor—broken plywood, twisted nails, who-knew-how-many beetles.

But now that I'd crawled this far, my muscles were a little less frozen. I used the doorframe to haul myself up and trudged like the undead to my bed. I collapsed on top of the covers, still in my torn, dew-soaked pajamas. I left my muddy feet hanging off the edge.

All I could hope was that this brutal stupor would fade into sleep. That while I slept, my brain chemicals would have mercy on me. And by morning, the hardest crush of this low would be lifted.

At last, the heaviness of my eyelids won out. Static drowned everything else until the world disappeared around me.

I woke up, and I couldn't breathe.

My chest, my lungs—they were squeezed flat.

I was stomach-down on the bed, arms and legs spread wide. My neck wrenched left, facing the stained-glass beetle window. My room was a thick indigo-stained murk.

Something was crushing my back. More than my back. All of me.

The ceiling. Had the ceiling collapsed?

There was no mess. There'd been no noise. All the same, some relentless weight was sandwiching me into the mattress. Compressing the air from my lungs, from between the cracks in my ribs.

I gasped for oxygen, sucking in sips when what I needed were gulps.

I had to move. I tried to push myself up.

But my arms didn't budge.

Was this a new symptom? What was happening to me?

Get up, I told my body. *Now.*

My legs wouldn't move either.

No, this couldn't be a low. My brain wasn't down anymore; it was racing. Pounding. Pulsing with white-hot fear.

I knew, just knew, this wasn't something my body was doing to me. This was something being done to my body.

The air barely wheezed through my windpipe, and every gasp was a stab. As if my throat were packed full of broken glass.

I was going to suffocate.

I was going to die, all over again—for keeps this time—and I was alone. Unbearably alone.

No.

Not alone.

A deeper shadow fell over me, darkening the pillow and sheets in front of my face.

Something was in this room.

Behind me.

A chill whispered over me, pricking every tiny hair on my body. It sank into my skin. Deeper than skin. Deeper than blood.

A screaming, bone-deep warning.

Look behind you.

Something was standing over my bed. Beside my stiff, helpless body. And my shivering gut told me that it—whatever it was—was the last thing I wanted to see. But if I didn't . . .

I made myself look.

Tried to make myself look.

My neck wouldn't turn. Not an inch. Not a centimeter. Not a muscle.

"Who's there?" I tried to ask.

But my tongue was lead against my limp jaw.

Who's there? Who's there?

What's *there?*

The floor shrieked under the impossible weight of the impossible shadow, its heavy steps tracking around my bed. Until, at last, it loomed into view.

A blue silhouette.

So very tall and so very hunched.

Its body wasn't quite a body. Like this house, the angles were all wrong. Its face wasn't quite a face. There were no features, just a flat, empty expanse.

I was still dreaming: that was the only explanation.

But it felt so real.

A rancid reek filled my nose: Putrid, like rotting roses. Bloody with iron.

The blue shadow leaned closer. Its eyeless face bent toward me, intent. The edges of its silhouette shifted and bled, blurring with the rest of the room. It wasn't clear, not exactly, where the house ended and the figure began.

What did it want? I had nothing to give it.

It reached for me.

I couldn't pull away.

I lay frozen as it grabbed my hand with its own. If you could call that appendage a hand. There were only two fingers, long and groping—smooth as glass, sharp as claws.

It tugged, urging me to follow.

It wanted to show me something.

As long as the shadow led the way, miraculously, I could move again. It dragged me up, and I stumbled after it, across the room to the Beetle window.

It touched my fingers to the glass.

The shadow had no mouth—no way to speak—but somehow, I understood what it wanted me to know: It was too late to escape this house. And there was only one way to survive.

I needed armor.

Lucky me, the shadow was willing to share.

CHAPTER TEN

STAINED SUNLIGHT SPILLED INTO MY BEDROOM, over my sweaty skin and grimy pajamas.

Morning was here, and I'd slept so deeply, so soundly. For the first time since stepping foot in this house, I felt rested.

But I wasn't in bed. I was lying on my stomach, wedged onto the wooden bench under the Beetle window. I yawned and stretched, too drunk on sleep to comprehend how I'd made it from bed to window seat.

Then the deepest part of the night—and that looming, misshapen shadow—flashed through me like an electric shock. I jolted upright, scanning my room for intruders.

But there was nothing. No one.

Dust motes dancing through rays of blue and green.

I pressed my back against the bench, clutching my knees to my chest. Gulping in air. The air I'd so sorely needed and couldn't get last night during . . . whatever that was.

A dream?

An episode . . . ?

The world was slightly blurry, as if I were wearing someone else's glasses. My forehead felt warm, feverish.

I tried to touch it, but my fingers didn't reach skin. They bumped against another surface altogether—slick as glass.

What the hell?

I patted my face, frantically tracing the glassy surface to the edge of my hairline. It stretched over my eyes and down my nose, except for nostril holes. Even covered my mouth and chin.

I wasn't still dreaming, was I?

I raced to my mirror.

A mask. I was wearing a full-faced mask made of glass.

My knees felt weak, and I pressed my palm against the mirror to hold myself up. The touch was cooling, grounding. I sipped in breaths, slow and steady.

The mask was clear glass, poured into the shape of an insect's back. A raised curve arced across the eyebrows, sectioning off the forehead like a thorax. Between the eyes and nose, there was a small upside-down triangle. A line descended from its bottom tip, cutting down the nose and chin so that the lower two-thirds of the face mimicked armored wings.

I knew this design.

I glanced across the room at the Beetle window. The three-dimensional mask was missing from the figure's face, only a placeholder panel of flat blue glass left behind.

I must've put the mask on in my sleep.

It actually felt good against my skin, slick and soft as a mud mask. From its edges, tingles radiated across my scalp, soothing as fingers running through my hair.

I turned my head, observing from all angles, but couldn't tell how the mask was secured to me. Nothing held it in place—no elastic, no ties.

With no help at all, the mask was *sticking* to my skin. My face.

A spike of panic drove through my chest. Like a vision from a nightmare, I could already see myself grappling for the edges, pulling and pulling. The mask refusing to budge. Clinging as I writhed, like the poor mouse Mom once caught in a glue trap.

I worked my fingers into the edges by my temples. With a small pop of suction, the outer rim peeled back, the tingling sensation fading.

I sighed with relief and ripped off the mask.

But the air swept in, harsh and strangely unwelcome against my face. An accompanying queasiness wormed through my stomach. My brain fogged over, the exhaustion of the past three days crashing down on me. Suddenly, it felt like I hadn't slept so well after all.

Worse, the low, the one I thought I'd shaken off, started seeping back in. Its heaviness was collecting in my shoulders, dripping down my limbs.

I swayed and blinked at my bleary-eyed reflection. Ghostly pale and tired.

The change was so drastic. So sudden.

A second ago, I'd felt fine.

Good, even.

And then I'd taken off the mask.

I turned it over in my hands, and my fingers sank into its surface. The glass was like firm taffy. Solid but tacky. Clinging to the threads of my fingerprints, as if it didn't want to leave me. Was it coated with some kind of adhesive—something helping it stick to my skin?

I tentatively lifted the mask back toward my face. It smelled stale and musty, but also syrupy-sweet like grapes. No, like blue roses. Exactly like the blue roses.

Intoxicating and dizzying, at the same time.

I frowned but pressed the mask back on. It sank into my skin, soft as a sigh. And my nausea and exhaustion faded. Even the miserable heaviness clawing at my mind.

The sudden lightness was a miracle.

How I imagined I might feel if I ground up and snorted my antidepressant. Or sucked in a huge hit of pot or dropped ecstasy or . . . well, what the hell did I know. I'd only ever gotten drunk before.

The mask was just a few millimeters between me and the rest of the world, but it made me feel like I was wearing mile-thick armor.

And to survive in this house, I needed armor.

Someone had told me that. It took me a second to remember who: that faceless blue shadow. I thought again of its hunched form leaning over me, its glassy claws wrapping around my hand.

My fingers flinched at the memory. Had that been the moment when I'd unconsciously reached for the mask, and my slumbering mind had contorted the action into a fever dream? That made a certain sort of sense, except for the fact that I'd never sleepwalked before.

I shivered. More evidence of my deteriorating mental health?

The truth was, wearing this mask did feel good—whether for psychological reasons, the barrier it created between me and the world, or something more toxic. Who knew what kind of strange, pre-FDA chemicals its makers might've used in its adhesive backing. God, the *last* thing I needed was to start actually hallucinating, to warp reality more out of shape than it already felt.

I ripped the mask off, even as my body and mind screamed in protest, and marched over to the Beetle window. Small silver hooks gleamed around the edges of the figure's blank face, where the mask had been attached.

Firmly, I slotted it back into place.

There it would stay.

Part of the window. Part of the house.

Not part of me.

I left the mask behind and stepped into the hall. Heading for the kitchen. Breakfast and medicine. Every step required double the effort as the low mood from last night lingered. It beckoned me back toward my bed. Whispered that I should give up and pull the covers over my head before this day even began.

But I figured I should at least try asking Mom about the masks in this house. She might not be willing to engage with much of this place's history, but surely she could tell me if she'd noticed them as a kid—ever tried one on the way I just had.

If nothing else, it would be such a relief if I could see Mom and Vivi looking closer to their old selves again: no more blue-stained teeth or red-veined eyes. I halfway hoped they'd be waiting for me downstairs, ready to play pretend that this was the perfect home and we were the perfect family. It wouldn't solve anything, but it would be closer to normal than how things had felt last night.

Vivi's bedroom was sealed, and as I passed it on the way to the stairs, I heard something. Behind her closed door, she was talking to someone.

I paused.

Was Vivi on the phone at eight in the morning? Her friends

weren't exactly early risers. And they tended to group-text, not call.

Suddenly suspicious, I forced myself to knock.

From inside: immediate silence.

Followed by a flurry of bumps and steps. A drawer slammed.

Then Vivi called out, "What?"

"It's me. Are you on the phone?"

"No." Quick and sharp.

I hesitated. She was hiding something, and I couldn't tell what. "Can I come in, then?" I tried the knob.

Locked.

I jiggled it to be sure. Yes, definitely locked.

Vivi didn't even lock the bathroom door when she took showers.

It stabbed me with a pang of panic. The kind of distrust that always made me so mad when Mom or Vivi directed it at me: *What* was she doing in there?

The door unlocked, with an indignant little click, and opened just a crack. Vivi poked out her head, blocking what she could of her room, with her short, slight body.

Her eyes were overwide, the whites streaked with red. Shadows hung like bruises underneath. She was exhausted, and yet very, very awake.

I was way too familiar with that look in her eyes. I'd seen it on myself, but I'd never seen it on her before. Vivi wasn't bipolar. Her usual excitement was bubbly, like a newly poured soda—fresh and fizzy, evaporating after a reasonable stay. Like healthy excitement should.

I gave myself a mental shake. Vivi was just stressed and overtired—likely due to our disastrous middle-of-the-night séance, and the aftermath of our fight.

"Can I help you?" Her bony shoulders were hunched high.

"I feel like we should talk," I said.

"About you? What you did?"

I nodded. "If you think it'll help."

"I don't." She moved to shut the door.

"Hey!" I blocked it with my shoe. "I get that you're not accepting my apology, but if you keep shutting me out, how do you ever expect things to get better?"

She still carried that deadened slump in her spine—the one that said she'd given up on things getting better. But the tiniest spark of hope flitted into her eyes. Finally, she said, "Promise me you'll never do it again."

"I . . ."

Claustrophobia crushed my throat. The idea of being trapped in this life. I knew I had to try—I *was* trying—for Vivi and Mom, but . . .

"You can't even . . . ?" Vivi shook her head. I'd killed her flare of hope. "Get away from me." She tried to close the door again, slamming it even harder against my foot.

"Ow, Vivi!" But I didn't move. "Okay. I promise! I do. I mean it."

And maybe I did. I wanted to mean it.

Vivi eyed me warily, a warning that we were nowhere near forgiveness. But her hand softened on the door, like she was considering letting me in.

Behind her shoulder, something fluttered—the dingy white wings of a butterfly—drawing my eyes into the bedroom she'd been trying to hide.

I glimpsed her desk, overflowing with shoeboxes and jars, the flexing shapes of bug bodies curling and crawling behind glass. There were too many containers to count. A hell of a lot more than Mom's maximum of three habitats at a time. The curtains writhed with butterflies and their pulsing wings.

I barely swallowed my gasp. "Jesus, Vivi, how many bugs do you have in there?"

Vivi tensed. "N-not that many," she lied. "You're not gonna say anything to Mom, are you?"

"I guess not, but . . ."

"Good. Just stay out of it, then." She slammed the door.

I stood helpless in the hall, hands clenched by my thighs as I stared at her locked door.

Yikes. This must be Vivi's version of therapy—throwing herself headfirst into bug collecting and ignoring everything else. And me asking one judgmental question was enough to undo my efforts with her this morning.

I sighed.

Well, I'd tried. I'd keep trying.

I went down to the kitchen and found Mom, like I'd hoped—but she wasn't making breakfast. She was on her hands and knees, working the edge of our largest kitchen knife under one of the floor tiles. Half the vinyl was already missing.

She looked up at me and flashed a smile so blue I nearly stumbled backward.

"Good morning, sweetie!" Her hair was pulled back in a wild bun, wisps flying around her face. Her bathrobe had been tossed over one of the island stools, and she was down to a long-sleeved nightgown. Forget her flouncy Mary Homemaker act; now it looked like she was auditioning for the part of a Victorian madwoman.

My plan to ask her about the masks melted into silence. "Mom, what are you doing?" I managed finally.

She paused at my tone, suddenly sheepish as she glanced

around the torn-up kitchen, at the pit stains on her rumpled nightgown. "Oh, I . . . couldn't sleep. I figured I should do something productive."

"Productive . . . ?"

"Well, I knew this stuff had to be covering up the original floor." She tapped the butt of her knife against it, eliciting a dull, plasticky *thwack*. "And I was right! My parents left this place to me, but when I was a kid, Great-Aunt Carol made a few updates, hoping to rent it out. When that didn't work, she boarded the whole house up. This cheap vinyl must've been her doing. She never had the best eye for interior design." Mom slipped me a conspiratorial wink. Like, good thing we both had much better taste than poor Great-Aunt Carol. "I thought I might find hardwood underneath, but *this* is spectacular." She yanked the square free and patted the floor underneath.

It was a dirty but colorful mess of tiny stone tiles. A mosaic. So far, the grand picture spanned from the patio doors to halfway past the island. No doubt it was lurking under the rest of the kitchen floor, too.

The artwork captured a menagerie of wild animals, gorging on meat, littering scraps across a lavish garden. The swirling greens and blues and browns were mesmerizing.

But there were reds, too. Under Mom's feet, a boar and a stag tore into an unidentifiable carcass, snatching sinew from bone. Their eyes were matte blue from corner to corner. No iris, no pupil. Actually, like all the eyes in this mosaic. In the stained-glass windows, too.

But deer aren't predators—they aren't supposed to eat meat.

I fought a shudder. No wonder Great-Aunt Carol covered this piece.

"It's really striking, isn't it?" Mom prompted.

"It . . . um . . . it's something," I stammered.

Mom nodded, knife in hand, surveying her work so far. "Unfortunately, the original mosaic has taken a bit of a beating over time." She gestured to patches of crumbling and cracked tiles. A five-foot section near the back doors had been smashed, rendering the artwork unrecognizable.

The damage looked like the result of violence. Like someone had attacked it with a mallet.

My stomach dropped. My mind spiraled, imagining some bloody battle with masked intruders. My grandparents cornered in the kitchen, only a few feet from the patio doors, and unable to escape.

Probably not what really happened. Police hadn't found evidence of a crime scene. But now I couldn't stop imagining it: my grandparents cowering, a hammer swinging down.

"Oh, don't worry, sweetie," Mom said. "We can fix that right up." I must've been making one hell of a face, but she wildly misunderstood why. "We'll get the mosaic back to its old self in no time," she assured me.

Its old self?

"You want to keep it?" I demanded. "The way it is?"

"Of course. The best way to honor a historic house is to restore it." Mom tilted her head, eyeing me like I was less well than she'd thought.

Only a couple days ago, we'd discussed an overhaul of the more disturbing stained-glass windows, and she'd seemed somewhat open to the idea.

But now, her eyelids hung heavy with the same drunken look she'd worn last night. "This house is living artwork," she said. "How lucky are we, to be immersed in that?"

I didn't agree quickly enough, and Mom sighed, like she

wasn't sure what to do with me. She turned to the teapot on the counter, the silverfish set lying out from last night. "How about some tea?" she asked.

Without waiting for an answer, she poured me a fresh cup and set it on my place mat. The inky brew curled with noxious steam, and I gagged. My body remembered this tea too well—the sour taste as I retched it up, splashing the toilet blue.

"Thanks," I mumbled.

She nodded, somewhat appeased, and dropped back to her knees to pry at the clinging vinyl.

I'd hoped Mom would be back to herself this morning, or at least, something closer to normal. But, if anything, her downward spiral seemed to be worsening by the hour.

In this state, she wasn't going to be much help to anyone.

My eyes flicked to the smashed tile by the doors. I still didn't know how or why, but I did know that bad things tended to happen to my family in this house. I thought of Flynn's chilling shock-white eyes at the séance last night. What he'd said in that strange voice: *What happened before is happening now.*

Dread pooled deep in my stomach. At the time, I'd decided he was making it up—putting on a show. But the longer we stayed here, the more my brain seemed to unravel, and the stranger Mom and Vivi got. Suddenly, it felt more difficult to dismiss Flynn's warning.

There *was* a lead I hadn't yet followed. Out of respect for Mom, I'd left the locked room upstairs alone.

But if she wouldn't let us escape this house, then I couldn't leave any stone unturned.

Here was my opportunity. Vivi was in her room, and Mom was fully occupied.

She didn't even notice when I dumped the cup of tea down

the drain. Instead, I swallowed my medicine with water and found a half-melted chocolate granola bar in the cabinet.

I left Mom on all fours, digging at the kitchen floor with her knife.

Alone, I slunk down the hall, toward the off-limits door, waiting at the very end.

I jiggled the knob, but it was still locked. I stretched up to check the top of the doorframe for a key. Couldn't reach.

So I slipped into Mom's open room across the hall, searching for something to stand on. The second I stepped over her threshold, my skin prickled.

There was an electric shiver everywhere in this house, an almost living buzz that felt like eyes watching me. But in Mom's room, it was so strong that I caught myself tiptoeing. Skipping every other breath.

Behind me, something rustled.

I whipped around to look, but nothing moved.

I could've almost sworn the wallpaper was whispering, like rosebushes in a breeze.

I swallowed thickly, rubbing the goose bumps along my arms. It was probably only bugs. Maybe cockroaches rooting around. But I didn't want to stay a second longer than necessary.

I snatched an armchair and rushed into the hall with it. Used it as my stepladder to reach the top of the doorframe.

There it was—the key.

For Mom to leave the key somewhere so obvious, she must not have expected Vivi or I would sink low enough to break in.

Sorry, Mom.

I clicked the door open.

I didn't know what to hope for. I was so desperate to unravel the house's mounting mysteries that I wanted to find something glaringly strange—a clear answer.

What actually waited behind the locked door . . . was an ordinary bedroom.

Stacks of cardboard boxes lined the walls. They looked old, not like the ones we'd just used to move. Otherwise, the room was well furnished. The king-sized bed was much fancier than mine or Vivi's, high-posted, with shiny caramel-colored wood. There were also two bedside tables, two wardrobes, a secretary desk, and a shaggy rug underfoot.

Mom hadn't repurposed any of this stuff? That, in and of itself, was a little strange, given how much she hated waste.

And the room didn't *look* structurally unsound, like she'd claimed. I stepped in, tentatively. The floorboards whimpered under my feet, but no more than anywhere else in this groaning house.

There were two stained-glass windows, which Mom must've snuck in to unboard. I frowned and stepped closer to examine the nearest one.

It was a shrine to stained-glass cockroaches. They feasted on a rotting rib cage in an apocalyptic landscape, under a dull orange sky. A skulking figure crept from the corner, wielding broken bones between its fingers like daggers. Shiny brown plating covered its shoulders. Extra legs, spiny appendages, hung from its human-like abdomen.

Its face was nothing but flat blue glass. Surrounded by silver hooks, as if there had once been a three-dimensional mask, like the one in my bedroom window.

The banner at the bottom read THE COCKROACH.

I shuddered but made myself examine the second window, too.

Lush magnolia leaves shrouded a figure at the center with the saw-toothed arms of a praying mantis, clutching a writhing lamb.

THE PRAYING MANTIS.

Again, the face was only a flat blue panel, surrounded by silver hooks.

If all these stained-glass portraits throughout the house were built to hold detachable masks, why were the majority now missing?

Maybe they'd been stolen as mementos by freakish House of Masks groupies like Flynn. This place had been abandoned for a long time. Breaking in wouldn't have been difficult.

I tore at my pinky nail and turned away from the windows.

I couldn't figure out why Mom had locked this room. Why she'd lied about it being unsafe.

Something else had to be hiding in here.

I squealed open the top drawer of the nearest bedside table. Inside was a jewelry box. I lifted it out and unlatched it, carefully, afraid the rusting hinges would snap. A few gaudy bracelets and rings sparkled up at me.

But what caught my eye was a tarnished gold locket. An oval etched with flowers, about two inches long. Which was big enough for a photo.

I cracked it open and found a faded picture of a youngish couple, with a toddler, standing in front of our house. The woman wore a ruffly brown-and-orange paisley dress. Vintage, but not 1890s; more like 1970s. She wore a chunky pendant around her neck—a five-petaled flower, gold with orange beads. Her long curls were gorgeously chaotic, like Mom's. The man beside her had a thick mustache, a denim jacket, and bell-bottom jeans. He held the toddler, raising her arm to wave at the camera. The sun was bouncing off his clunky silver watch and reflecting into her face. She was squinting, but her eyes were big and dark, her cheeks plump and pink, her brown curls tied back with a ribbon.

She reminded me of my own baby pictures.

"Mom." I touched the toddler like I could reach back in time and grab her out. Before anything worse could happen.

This had to be her parents' bedroom.

So Mom had locked away her trauma, neat and tidy and wholly unaddressed.

The room was frozen in time. It had been left like an empty hotel room, waiting for guests who were never coming back.

I wasn't sure why they had picked it over the larger rose suite across the hall. But, then, this house did make it feel like the rooms chose *you*, not the other way around.

Grandma's room. Grandpa's.

This was the closest I'd ever felt to them, standing among their forgotten relics, and I'd had to sneak into a locked room to accomplish even this much.

Vivi and I had so little family. Mom had never wanted to connect with relatives beyond our now dearly departed Great-Aunt Carol, even picking donors who had checked the confidentiality boxes to ensure that our biological dads would remain faceless.

Mom wanted it to be just the three of us. Turning only to each other.

But now that Mom and Vivi and I had slipped so far apart, none of us had *anyone* to turn to.

I tucked my grandmother's locket into the pocket of my shorts. If nothing else, I could keep this little piece of my family close.

I sighed and surveyed the rest of the room. The rickety rolltop desk was another spot to store potential secrets. Or, hell, I'd settle for basic information.

I riffled through, uncovering stacks of bills and papers, a clunky calculator so big it looked like a walkie-talkie. Another relic of the '70s. An old checkbook bore the name Peter Feldman.

Confirmation: my grandfather's desk.

The top drawer held a photocopy of a newspaper article, dated September 8, 1896. It featured a looming black-and-white picture of our house, and a headline that read:

Madame Clery and Her "House of Masks": A True Glimpse Beyond the Veil?

There is no shortage of séances which overpromise and underdeliver, and no shortage of phony mediums who traffic in cheap parlor tricks rather than true communication across the veil, if such a thing is possible.

I confess, I am a medium's worst nightmare: a Skeptic. I expected little from our supposed local treasure, Madame Clery's House of Masks. Rather, I attended last Saturday's séance hoping to sweep back the grand curtain and to reveal Madame Clery's tricks. But, Reader, I'm afraid this Skeptic must disappoint you. House of Masks has gotten the better of me.

According to Madame Clery, the origins of this mysterious House of Masks trace back to a small Massachusetts town in 1873, when Miss Ellen Clery, an

eighteen-year-old girl of simple means, met the traveling illusionist Mr. Joseph Cragg. Enchanted by his act, Miss Clery left with Mr. Cragg to become his assistant. Along the way, she met performing spiritualists and acquired the art of mediumship.

Soon, Madame Clery's following was stronger than Mr. Cragg's. When the pair married, she kept her own name, a decision as unorthodox as the woman herself. In 1886, after the fearsome earthquake rocked our city and grieving loved ones created a staggering demand for mediums, Madame Clery and Mr. Cragg moved here to join us. Madame Clery denies mercenary motives—however, Reader, it must be noted that for mediums, grief means profit.

The couple purchased an unremarkable Queen Anne Victorian in 1887, one that has since become an attraction in its own right. Saturday's séance was preceded by a tour of the property, complete with stained-glass windows and a sprawling mosaic mural, as well as a wander through the garden's vast maze of blue roses. Mr. Cragg mentioned a crypt attraction that they are developing as a finale for the tour, but it is not yet ready.

Then Mr. Cragg led us to the séance table, where the night graduated from strange to unfathomable. To my surprise, Madame Clery made no effort to contact the departed loved ones of anyone at the table. Instead, perhaps inspired by Mr. Cragg's original trade as an illusionist, this performance was purely about spectacle.

Many tricks were standard for a séance: mind

reading, table lifting, levitation. However, the execution was shockingly credible.

We've all heard of debunked mediums, known to lift a table with their own leg and pretend it was floating. And yet how did Madame Clery's full table of solid stone hover in the open air? How did she herself levitate seven feet from the ground, or seemingly bewitch rosebushes to move and grow before our very eyes?

These miraculous feats are performed outdoors, so the usual props employed in sham séances cannot be in service.

In fact, the only props Madame Clery uses are masks.

That line especially caught my attention, and apparently, it had caught my grandfather's, too. He'd underlined it in bold black pen. And he continued underlining sections below:

There are twelve masks shaped as insects and one featuring the house's emblem: the blue rose, a classic symbol of the impossible made manifest.

I cannot claim to fully understand their role in the séance. Madame Clery extolled their many glories but refused to explain how wearing them allowed her to perform such miracles, except to say that she had assistance from beyond the veil. When I inquired about the curious insect designs, she merely replied, "Spirits are our greatest teachers, encouraging us to evolve. What creatures better embody the miraculous process of metamorphosis than insects?"

Madame Clery's eyes took on a bit of a mad spark as she expounded, "The invisible underbelly of the world—the deeper truth about who we are and who we are meant to become—is at our fingertips. All one needs is the courage to look."

With that, she offered me a dreadful mask shaped like a cicada, and remarked, "Perhaps this one would suit you best? You journalists are of the loud and chattering sort."

Reader, I confess, not even for this story could I agree to put it on. Whatever courage is required to see what Madame Clery sees—the "invisible underbelly of the world"—I could not summon it.

In the end, this humbled Skeptic left House of Masks with the last thing a reporter wants: more questions than answers. I must ultimately urge you to attend Madame Clery's séance for yourself, Reader. Then, if you can, I beg you to sweep back the curtain for me.

In the margins, my grandfather had scrawled: *The masks are the key to this house.*

And underlined it three times.

I read the whole thing twice, frowning deeper and deeper. The masks were séance props? This article confirmed that there had once been thirteen, so most really had gone missing.

At least this somewhat explained the freaky theme of bugs, to Madame Clery's mind anyway—they represented metamorphosis. The blue roses were, as the article said, the house's emblem. *A classic symbol of the impossible made manifest.*

And they'd seemed to move on their own during the séance that reporter attended? Maybe the same trick I'd stumbled into while chasing Flynn in the hedge maze, when the wall seemed to open and close for me.

Assuming it *was* a trick.

I wasn't sure what to think about the roses or the masks or this description of Madame Clery's unearthly séance. Given this account, maybe I could trust my perception that the beetle mask had some real effect on me when I'd worn it this morning. The question was what caused it—how did it work? And this article didn't answer that, although it must have driven my grandfather to some conclusion. Some understanding that made him emphatically write and underline: *The masks are the key to this house.*

I couldn't afford to stand here forever, mulling it over. Eventually, Mom or Vivi was going to realize I was in the off-limits room.

Frustrated, I folded the article and stuffed it in my pocket, along with my grandmother's necklace. I wanted it with me, in case something clicked later. For now, I needed to finish exploring this room and get out of here.

And I needed to prioritize. There were too many boxes to look through all of them. Someone must've packed up everything my grandparents had left behind.

Most were sealed, taped shut.

One, on the far side of the bed, had been dragged out from the rest. Opened. But not with scissors. Not in a neat and tidy line.

Shredded cardboard hung from the corner. Something had chewed it, leaving a gaping hole bigger than my head.

I winced, the back of my neck crawling.

I *knew* it. *Knew* something else was living inside our house. Useless exterminator be damned.

I made myself pull back the chewed flap with two fingers, touching it as little as possible.

A box full of kid toys: a faded Raggedy Ann doll, with red-yarn hair and blushing pink cheeks, a silver piggy bank, a baby rattle with chunky plastic beads . . .

Mom's old toys. Had to be.

This was probably the same box that had housed her baby blanket. But the movers hadn't touched this room. It had been locked the whole time they'd been here.

In that case, they hadn't touched Mom's blanket.

So who the hell had?

I was frozen, one hand limp on the frilly skirt of the rag doll, which was stiff with dust and age.

From under it, something tickled me. Something that darted from inside the skirt to my fingertip to the back of my hand to my wrist to my forearm.

A cockroach.

I shrieked and smashed my palm down without thinking. Braced for a big smear of bug guts.

Instead, my hand hit the cockroach with a brittle crunch. Like the snap of a twig.

The smashed body fell into the box of toys, vanishing under a tiny rocking horse. But one of its legs stayed behind—its tip wedged under the skin of my palm. It stung like a splinter.

I plucked the leg free with a pained little hiss and held it up close for a better look.

It looked exactly like a shard of wood. If I didn't know better—hadn't felt it scramble over my skin like the very live cockroach it had been a few seconds ago—I'd say it *was* wood.

No guts, no goo.

But that was . . .

There was that word again: *impossible.* As impossible as blue roses.

The apparent symbol of this house.

CHAPTER ELEVEN

I LEFT MY GRANDPARENTS' ROOM, FEELING too much like the reporter who'd retreated from House of Masks with more questions than answers.

My pocket felt heavy with my grandmother's locket, my grandfather's article. I kept rubbing the sore spot poked into my palm by that splintery cockroach leg. It could've been some deranged séance prop. A windup toy I'd jostled into motion. Flynn might've used something similar when he'd seemingly spat up a cockroach.

As for the baby blanket and how that had appeared on Mom's bed . . .

Mom, Vivi, and I had each insisted we didn't know where it had come from, but if the movers hadn't touched it, then the most obvious culprit was Vivi. She might've assumed it would be a welcome surprise but balked once she saw Mom's horrified reaction. Or, hell, maybe Mom had been sleepwalking and had put the blanket on her own bed, the way I'd taken the mask from my window.

Whatever had happened, one of them—knowingly or unknowingly—was lying. And the three of us were becoming strangers to each other, with every fake smile, every lie we told.

I'd have to add breaking into my grandparents' room to the pile. Another secret to keep.

Guilt seethed in my gut as I snuck the key back on top of the doorframe and the armchair back into Mom's room. The hollow blue eyes of the figure in the Rose window seemed to follow me all the way out to the hall.

Even after investigating my grandparents' room, I wasn't sure why Mom insisted on keeping it locked. Was the only reason as pure and awful as trauma? She *had* lied about it being structurally unsound. And she'd used the same excuse to keep us out of the attic.

So what exactly was hiding up there?

Vivi's door was still shut, and I could hear Mom clattering around downstairs in the kitchen, so I searched the hallway ceiling for an access panel I might not have noticed. There had to be an attic door somewhere.

But, damn this twisty house, I couldn't find it anywhere.

When I finally went downstairs for lunch, Mom was still working on the floor. In fact, enabled by YouTube tutorials, she'd finished uncovering the mosaic and had begun repairing the damaged area with a tube of bonding paste and some extra colored tiles that she excitedly told me she'd found in the cellar.

"How do you know what the missing section is supposed to look like?" I asked, eyeing the area smashed beyond recognition. "Do you remember it from when you were a kid?" That seemed unlikely, but she was placing tiles with surprising certainty.

"Oh, no. I'm just feeling it out," Mom said. "Better to have a wrong *something* than a smashed-up nothing, don't you think?"

Actually, I didn't know whether I agreed with that or not.

But Mom worked all afternoon, and even as dinnertime approached, she was laboring in the corner. As far as I knew, Vivi didn't come out of her room all day—she might not have even eaten. My own stomach was rumbling. After scouring the fridge and cabinets, I'd given up and eaten a second granola bar for lunch. The few staples we'd brought with us were dwindling.

I asked Mom about groceries, and she promised she'd get to it. I asked when, and she didn't answer. But I did get her grunt of approval to order more takeout. Which, like the pizza, was again dropped outside our front gate.

I wiped the early-evening rain off the delivery bag, but enough had already leaked inside past the Styrofoam.

The three of us gnawed on our soggy chicken in the dining room as rain pattered against the Housefly window over Mom's head. The empty blue panel of the figure's face mocked me—like a puzzle missing its final piece. The image was practically buzzing with a swarm of houseflies and their jeweled red eyes. Near the bottom was a squirmy pool of white glass. At first, I'd thought it was meant to be snow. Then I saw the subtle ridges, the dark spots, the thin intestinal lines. Not snow. Maggots.

Some trailed up the figure's leg, nibbling at a crimson wound in its thigh.

Vivi had told me once how maggots could be used to disinfect wounds. To eat away rot and leave only clean skin behind.

Arguably, a cure worse than the disease.

A real fly, a living fly, crawled across the glass. And I thought of the flies that had sometimes appeared in our old apartment, desperately banging their bodies against the windows, fighting to get free. Fly away.

This fly didn't bother. It was crawling slowly, perfectly content. *None* of the bugs I'd spotted in this house ever seemed to be looking for an exit.

Mom smiled at me and Vivi with blue teeth and asked if we wanted rose tea with our dinner.

And I stopped chewing, the chicken on my tongue turning to mealy mush.

After dinner, I curled up in my bedroom's window seat and combed through the article I'd found in my grandfather's desk. Again and again.

The masks are the key to this house.

His underlined note in the margin kept plucking at my brain, an increasingly restless thrum. It was clearly some kind of breakthrough for him.

My grandmother's locket had been sitting in the pocket of my shorts all day. I pulled it out and cracked it open, staring down at the picture of her, Mom, and my grandfather—willing some kind of impossible mind-meld with him. If only he were here, to explain what he'd understood that I didn't.

Over my head, the beetle mask hovered, slotted into its place in my window. Its glassy stare burned against my neck.

The invisible underbelly of the world—the deeper truth about who we are and who we are meant to become—is at our fingertips, Madame Clery had said in the article. *All one needs is the courage to look.*

Then she'd tried to give the reporter one of her masks to wear. Only he'd been too scared.

Like I'd been this morning. That's why I'd stuffed the mask back into its slot in the window. And yet ever since, part of me had ached to take it back down. To smooth it over my skin and feel my clenching, miserable body relax.

What if my grandfather's note meant that *wearing* the masks was somehow the key to understanding the house? In that case, trying the mask back on was the responsible choice, really.

Or maybe I was just desperate for an excuse.

But I couldn't risk Mom walking past my open door and catching sight of me. No telling how she'd react, and the last thing I wanted was for her to confiscate the mask before I managed to investigate further.

I made myself wait. I slid my grandma's locket around my neck, hidden under my shirt, and brushed my teeth with rust-tinged water. Poked at my phone until Mom stopped by to say good night. Her breath and sweat carried a rosy reek as she kissed my forehead. And then I heard her say good night to Vivi, noting how quickly Vivi clicked her door shut afterward, snicking the lock, hard and final—before Mom could see her overflowing bug collection, no doubt. Or whatever it was that had such a rabid grip on her attention.

I guess I wasn't one to talk. If I'd had the option of locking my door, I would've done it hours ago.

Once I heard Mom's door close, I leaped into motion, lifting the beetle mask carefully from its silver hooks.

Strange. I was positive this mask had been clear glass. Now, a blue tinge blossomed under its surface.

I carried the mask to the mirror on my outer closet door, the one wedged shut with a chair, and held it near my face. The perfume of blue roses beckoned to me. Intoxicating and nauseating.

I pressed the mask on. Just like before, it clung to my face.

A cool rush of relaxation rolled across my forehead and cheeks, down my nose, out over my scalp. I closed my eyes, basking in the sensation. The little muscles behind my eyes were loosening, the tension wringing free from my forehead.

The soothing wave kept spreading. It was like the mask had started a leak—a pocket of water under my skin that flowed to places the glass wasn't even touching. Down my neck, through my spine.

Along with it came this sudden, deep reassurance: *All is well.*

It took *so much* these days to make me feel good. I wanted to lean into it. Let that calm wash all over my body.

Above me, the nightly noises began: *Scritch, scritch, scraaaatch.*

When I gasped, the glass lips moved with mine, hugging tight as lipstick. My shoulders hunched, but the soothing lull of the mask made it easier for me to drop them back down. To breathe out slow and steady.

A buzz darted past my ear, and I barely jumped. Something landed on the mirror in front of me—a beetle.

Like the ones I'd found in my trash can, which so eerily matched the design of the stained-glass beetles depicted in my window.

But this beetle was *glowing*.

The palest, ghostliest blue. Like a crawling splash of glow-in-the-dark paint.

Was this effect caused by the mask, too? I hadn't noticed anything glowing when I'd worn it this morning. Did things only glow at night? Was it only the beetles?

I stared, mesmerized, as the glowing beetle crawled across my reflection on the mirror—up my chin and nose, treading over my eye.

And then I noticed: *I* was glowing, too. The tiniest part of me. Buried in the black of my pupils, there was a bright pinprick.

Like someone had buried a blue-hot flare in my skull, and the smallest flicker was poking through.

The mask's transparent glass did cover my eyes—this could be some visual trick, an almost radioactive refraction. Or the sticky coating on the back truly was a hallucinogen, like I'd theorized earlier, and I was experiencing a contact high. Some people turned to drugs for spiritual awakenings. For all I knew, spiritualists had, too. Could hallucinogens have been Madame Clery's true secret?

I knew I should probably rip off this mask if there was a chance it was pumping me full of an unknown drug.

But that wasn't what I wanted.

I wanted to feel anything but bad. Just for a little while.

I wanted to watch the glowing beetle on my mirror, as it turned and trailed all the way to the floor and ducked under my closet door.

From underneath came the faintest blue light. Something inside my closet was glowing, too.

I pulled the chair out from under the knob and creaked open the door.

Glowing beetles dotted my clothes—scurrying out of sight and into my hanging sweaters—and I winced. So that's where they'd been hiding. Or some of them anyway. Who knew how many had been lurking around my room?

But there was another glow, too. At the very back of my closet, a faint rectangular outline bled from the edges of that secret, second door.

Something was back there.

A shiver squirmed through me. Part of my brain warned I was too fragile, too vulnerable, to pursue a mysterious glow behind a mysterious door by myself after dark. But through the filter of my mask, the calm rush pumping throughout my body, fear almost felt like excitement. A pure, clean thrill.

And I *needed* to know what was hiding behind that mirrored door.

I pushed through my clothes and turned the knob. It wouldn't budge.

I twisted a little harder, and—with an awful metallic pop—the knob broke off in my hand.

"Dammit!" I'd thought I was being gentle.

A few days ago, when I'd first spotted this mirrored door and tried to turn the knob, it had felt so solid to me. Immovable. And now . . . ?

I squeezed the useless knob in frustration. It crumpled slightly under my fingers, bendable as aluminum foil.

I jerked in surprise. How could metal corrode this much in three days, to become so soft?

I prodded the jagged remains of the doorknob mechanism—but now there was no way to work it. All I could hope was that jiggling the door would be enough to knock it open. I wedged my fingertips into the tiniest crack between door and frame, and started to pull.

The wood felt soft, softer even than the weirdly pliable doorknob. Weakened by mold or humidity or who knew what, it splintered, and I yanked back my hand. Somehow, I'd left an indent in the door's edge—a four-finger-sized gap.

Past the damaged wood, the eerie blue glow shone brighter.

I put my eye to the crack but couldn't make out the source.

Something warm and wet dribbled down my hand. To examine it, I held it up to the blue light eking past the edge of the door.

Blood.

A mammoth splinter had wedged itself under the nail of my

middle finger. And I hadn't even felt it happen. Wood shards poked out from my other fingers, too.

As soon as I saw it, I felt it—a sore pinch that was oddly distant. I'd bitten my nails enough to know how much these cuts should sting. It was almost like someone had numbed my fingers the same way dentists numb mouths.

Could the mask be dulling my pain? How hard had I squeezed the knob and door, without even realizing it?

Still, they shouldn't have broken. And no way was I strong enough to crush metal.

My heart thudded hard. I backed away, out of the closet, into my room. I slammed the outer closet door shut and leaned against its cool mirror, huffing for breath.

By the golden glow of my lamp, I could see too clearly: the crumpled doorknob in my left hand, the bloody splinters in my right. I picked the biggest shards free and instinctively sucked at the wounds, the taste of salty copper coating my tongue.

Above my head, something scraped at the ceiling. From outside, through the stained-glass windows that wouldn't open, came the stuttering whir of katydids, the tiny sharp shrieks of crickets.

Then, inside the house, a laugh split the air.

Shrill. Sudden.

A laugh I didn't recognize.

An intruder?

I dropped the doorknob with a terrible clang and froze, every muscle squeezing deathly still.

Whatever happened to my grandparents, was it happening to us now? This was the worst-case scenario. Even as a grounding steadiness trickled out from my mask, my terrified heart fought back, pounding against all my pulse points.

I stared at the darkened slice of hallway beyond my cracked

bedroom door, as the knob teetered at my feet. Its every metallic rasp against the floorboard was another chance that whoever had laughed would hear evidence of me, too. Peer in past my door.

I waited, petrified.

But nothing changed. No shift in light or shadows.

Had I imagined the laugh?

No. There it was again—a girlish giggle. But not Vivi's. Too high, too sharp.

Too piercing.

Too long.

It rose and fell and rose and fell. Champagne spilling over. Bubbles that wouldn't stop popping.

It sounded close. A room or two away.

I could wait here. I could hide and try not to breathe and hope this passed. I could tell myself the laugh wasn't real. As long as I didn't see anything, maybe I'd convince myself.

But if someone really was in our house, this close to me in my room, then they were close to Vivi, too.

Panic clutched at my chest. It had been so much easier to confront Flynn when he was trespassing in the yard, because I'd recognized his hoodie; I'd known it was him. This . . . I didn't know *what* kind of threat this was.

You are broken. Too broken to save yourself, let alone anyone else, that awful part of my brain whispered. *Face it: You are not strong. You are not brave. You are not enough.*

But for the first time, a new voice inside my head answered:
You are not broken.

You are strong. brave. enough.

The sudden conviction rumbled through me, a loud, impervious thunder. My voice, echoing back to me in fragments—rearranging my nastiest thoughts into beautiful new shapes.

Was I actually becoming my own advocate, like Dr. Glaser kept advising? She'd told me I needed to cultivate self-kindness. To learn how to talk to myself like a friend.

I'd honestly doubted I could.

But here I was. I was doing it.

I ground my teeth and balled my hands, even as my fingers, shredded by splinters, twinged in protest.

The laugh had gone quiet again.

I charged out of my bedroom and peered down the corridor for anything human-sized. But the hall was a tangled mess of shadows, dully lit by stained moonlight cast through the enormous window. And crawling with glowing dots. Bugs.

Through the eyes of the beetle mask, all the bugs were the same phosphorescent blue as the beetles in my room. They dipped through the air. Crawled down walls and disappeared into cracks. Huddled in the lacy curtains.

So many bugs—even more than I'd realized—living in these halls beside us. And I didn't have time to care. Not now.

I strained my ears, listening past the buzzing insects. And waited.

The laugh returned, bouncing off the walls, ripping its pixie-like fingers into my ears. Close. So close.

Vivi's room! It was coming from *inside* Vivi's room. But I knew my sister's laugh. This wasn't it. This wasn't right.

I ran to her door, but it was locked. I shoved it, as hard as I could—knowing it probably wouldn't work, shouldn't work. And yet the door flew open with a fresh spray of splinters.

I burst into her room, and wings flapped in my face. I gasped, swatting them away.

Butterflies. A whole darting cloud of them. Glowing as blue as the beetles, as the bugs in the hall.

The laughing was louder, but I couldn't spot the source. And I couldn't spot Vivi either. Her bed was empty, and her room was a fluttering sea of lacy wings. An impossible number of butterflies—where had they all come from? They flocked in the curtains, danced on Vivi's vacant bed, swirled upward.

In the back corner of the ceiling, the greatest mass of them writhed. They swarmed, like a living cocoon, over some curled-up shape.

I couldn't make out what it was.

But then, between their swirling forms, I caught a glimpse of human hair. Of pink and purple fabric.

Underneath all those butterflies, there was a body on the ceiling, curled into a ball.

Vivi.

She was lying on the ceiling as if it were the floor. As if gravity had nothing to do with her. Her body was loose and dreamy, her eyes sealed like she was sleeping.

And she was laughing and laughing that laugh that wasn't hers.

CHAPTER TWELVE

"VIVI!" I SHRIEKED.

Vivi's eyes flew open. A startled jolt ripped through her, shaking away the butterflies. She hung suspended from the ceiling, ten feet high, exactly as she'd been sleeping. "Lib . . . ?" she croaked out. She blinked at me, groggy and confused, like I was the one upside down.

Then she fell.

Plummeting toward the spiky brass bedpost beneath her.

I cried out and rushed toward her, but tripped over her pink Vans, scattered near the foot of her bed. I smashed to the floor with a *crack*. The impact clapped through my elbow and my chest, though it didn't hurt as much as it should have.

I was terrified about what must have happened to Vivi. I started to pull myself up to look.

Only to discover her kneeling by my side, helping me sit up. "Lib! Are you hurt?"

I exhaled in relief, though I had no idea how she'd gotten to me so quickly. I hadn't even heard her land. Disoriented, I rubbed my elbow. Scraped but intact. "Never mind me. Are *you* hurt? What . . . ?"

I met her eyes and lost my words. The face I was looking at—it was only half hers.

Her cheeks and forehead were covered by a mask: ivory white, shaped like a butterfly.

The mask from her window.

I shouldn't have been surprised. When we'd uncovered it together, she'd asked if I thought it was wearable.

I hadn't been able to see her clearly when she was on the ceiling, covered by butterflies, but she must've been wearing the mask then, too. The lace of its wings unfurled gracefully from the sides of her face, hiding the lingering baby fat of her cheeks. Feathers traced a perfect line down her nose. It was a half mask, unlike mine, leaving her mouth free.

So I could see how she was gaping at me. At my own face.

My own mask.

I'd forgotten I was wearing it.

Of all things, Vivi smiled, reaching out to touch my glass-covered cheek. "You realized, too—about the masks," she said. "That they're meant to be worn."

Something about her tone—an unquestioning deep devotion—worried me. But what worried me even more was her bizarrely calm reaction to waking up *on the ceiling*. "Vivi, forget the masks! You were on the ceiling! Y-you were surrounded by butterflies, and laughing in a voice that wasn't yours, and . . ."

I kept expecting what I was saying to land, for Vivi to freak out. Instead, she nodded, like none of this was new. "I was having the best dream," she murmured. "You don't think Mom heard, did you?"

That was her concern right now?

"I don't know, but, Vivi . . . how . . . ?" I didn't know which of my million questions I should be asking. Finally, my mouth settled on: "Has this happened to you before?"

"Yeah," Vivi said, easy-breezy. "When I wear my mask."

"Your . . . mask?"

"You really don't get it?" Vivi tilted her head, confused by my confusion—like this was basic arithmetic, and how could I not understand it by now? "But *you're* wearing your own mask. I thought you knew what they could do."

I couldn't quite get my brain to comprehend, but I tried to keep up. "I know that Madame Clery said the masks could help people see deeper truths about the world," I said. "Apparently, she used them as props in her séances. She claimed they helped her perform tricks, but . . ."

"Oh!" Vivi's eyes widened. "Duh! That makes so much sense!"

"Does it?" I demanded.

"Well, *yeah,* because . . ." She frowned at me with impatience. "Just watch this."

She stood back, centering herself against the backdrop of her stained-glass window. She gulped a big breath and held out her hands like she was steadying herself. Then she raised up, slowly, millimeter by millimeter, onto her socked toes. Not quite en pointe, but pretty damn close, especially without the proper ballet shoes or padding.

And then her spindly arms spasmed out to either side in a sudden stuttering flap. Her head snapped up, her gaze fixated on the ceiling.

"Vivi!" I started to get up.

"No! Wait, wait!" she choked out.

She started to get taller.

The line of her head, the top of her lacy mask, inched upward as she rose in front of the Butterfly window, panel by panel. First, her head only reached a bit above the panes of grass crawling with caterpillars. Then above the hovering figure's knees. Above the figure's waist.

In impossible slow motion, she inched up. And up and up and up.

Finally, I realized how: her feet had left the ground.

She'd gone from tiptoe to dangling in midair.

Like stage magic. As if she were attached to wires.

Levitating.

Vivi rose until her butterfly mask aligned with its usual spot in the window. There, she stopped. Striking the same graceful pose as the cosmic-blue, cloaked figure—one arm extended overhead, the other curled soft as a swan's wing around her body.

"Ta-da!" Her grin stretched wide, curved almost as sharply as the figure's crescent-moon smile in the window behind her.

A squeal ripped from my throat. Good thing I was still on the floor—my knees were trembling. If I'd been standing, they might have given out. "Y-you can do that on command?"

Vivi wasn't stiff anymore. She was floating, feather-light. "As long as I'm wearing the mask. It took some practice, but it's getting easier," she said. "Oh, and I guess you noticed, if I wear the mask while I'm sleeping, I wind up on the ceiling. But without the mask, I can't sleep through the night."

I thought of her all over again—that curled-up body on the ceiling, blanketed with writhing butterflies—and shuddered.

"What can *your* mask do?" Vivi asked.

"I don't know. I've barely worn it. I . . ." I considered. I hadn't noticed anything that suggested the possibility of levitation. And, honestly, levitation was the last thing I wanted if it meant waking up on the ceiling, crawling with bugs.

Even looking at Vivi now, floating above my head, was giving me the creeps. I didn't want to be down here on the floor, staring up at her anymore. As I pushed myself up, the bloody tips of my fingers gave a distant pang. And I remembered all over again—the crushed metal doorknob, the splintering wood. I'd even managed to burst through Vivi's door, probably breaking her lock. And I froze where I stood, suddenly afraid to touch anything else. "I think my mask makes me stronger," I said.

"Oh, of course!" Vivi seemed disappointed in herself for not realizing it first. "Mine's shaped like a butterfly, and it lets me levitate. Yours is shaped like a beetle. Some beetles can lift five hundred times their own weight."

So Madame Clery matched the shape of the mask to the stunt it helped her perform?

It was a theory anyway.

But I wasn't sure this kind of power was safe. Where did it come from? What *was* it? Some strange spiritualist trick . . . ?

Of course, that wasn't the only thing I'd noticed my mask could do. I told Vivi, "It has some impact on my mind, too—makes me calmer. Levels me out."

"Mine makes me happy," Vivi confided.

She did look happy. A wide grin curled above her chin. A glowing blue spark danced in the back of her deep-brown eyes, the same spark I'd noticed in my own eyes once I put on my mask tonight. Hers looked even brighter than mine.

"Can you see parts of the world glowing, too?" I asked, almost in a whisper. Embarrassed. Because it sounded so unhinged.

But Vivi nodded, her grin widening. "Don't you love it? All the bugs look like fireflies."

She gestured to the room around us and the bugs glowing like tiny blue stars. The largest mass of butterflies had settled in the curtains, clustering like roosting bats. On her desk, blue light filtered through the airholes of the shoebox habitats. Insects of all crawly shapes and sizes gleamed from glass jars, and so did the blue roses Vivi had stuffed inside to feed them.

If both Vivi and I could see the glow, then it couldn't be a hallucination. But it did seem to be mask-induced. "Do you have any theories about why only certain things glow?" I asked Vivi. Clearly, this was where she'd been pouring all her energy, and her investigative prowess was not to be underestimated.

But Vivi shook her head. "There's a lot I don't know yet," she admitted.

She was still floating, a few stray butterflies circling her. One landed on the edge of her mask. Its flexing white wings were delicate. Lacy. Its body was as tufty as feathers.

It looked so much like the mask it was sitting on I half expected Vivi's mask to start flapping its wings, too. To take off in sudden flight. Her mask almost did feel alive—the lace fluttered with Vivi's movements in the air. Tiny clear beads glinted in the feathers that ran down her nose, sparkling in the purple moonlight from her stained-glass window.

Come to think of it, when we'd first spotted the butterfly mask in Vivi's window, it had looked so withered and frail. I could've sworn the lace had been torn in places.

Now, I didn't see any tears or cracks. The lace had thickened, knitting together like skin. Flesh. Like someone had clapped an oversized ghoulish hand over the top half of Vivi's face.

Her mask had changed. Somehow flourished.

Earlier tonight, I'd wondered if my beetle mask was changing, too. If it was getting bluer.

I made myself peel the mask from my own face, even though it meant stripping back that soothing curtain of calm, and stared down at it.

Yes, the mask was definitely bluer.

And upon closer inspection, that slow-spreading blue wasn't uniform. Those were *veins.* The finest blue veins were blooming under the mask's hard glass surface.

My fingers flinched, and I had to stop myself from dropping the mask altogether.

I swallowed, through an increasingly dry throat. "Vivi, these masks are changing as we wear them. They're affecting our minds and bodies. I don't . . . Maybe you should take yours off, too."

Around the edges of her lively butterfly mask, Vivi's face crumpled. "How are we supposed to figure out how they work if we don't wear them?"

I frowned at the mask in my hands. There was no doubt that it allowed me to see a different side of this house, one my grandfather felt was so important. But . . . the shrill laugh that had terrified me echoed in my mind—the laugh that had sounded so little like Vivi.

Vivi dropped her floating hands to her floating hips. "Libby, wake up! This is *amazing*! Something to be studied, investigated, embraced! A discovery! When I'm wearing this mask, for the first time in weeks I can breathe again. How can that be bad?"

She did look lighter and freer than I'd seen her in an awfully long time. The last thing I wanted was to crush her happiness again.

Already, it was happening. The longer she stared at me, the lower she descended.

But I still had to point out: "Just because something feels good doesn't mean it isn't dangerous."

With a heavy sigh, Vivi dropped to the floor. "When I saw you in your mask, I thought maybe this was something we could do together," she mumbled.

I could see now how much she'd wanted that. She wouldn't say it, but I heard the undercurrent all the same: *I miss you.* She wanted these masks to be our shared secret—the thing that brought us back together.

The more I told her not to wear hers, the more I'd push her away. And I couldn't promise I'd never put my own on again. I might still have to, in order to investigate the house.

Shit. I didn't know what to do.

And then, behind me, came a noise.

The sound of an unlatching door.

I turned to look. Across the hall, my outer closet door—which I was positive I'd closed—was open.

And another creak cut through the house.

A strange, slow creak.

From deep inside my closet.

Vivi and I held hyperstill. Listening.

Silence now, in this too-large house.

Then Vivi darted past me, beelining toward my room.

"Wait," I whispered, charging after her. "What are you—?"

"We'd better check it out, right?" she said.

I had to wonder if her mask was making her bold. She didn't look scared; just intrigued.

I chased her to the entrance of my closet, where she stopped. So suddenly I slammed into her back.

Then I understood why.

The newly familiar scent of blue roses rolled out to greet me. That flowery fog, like sweet summer grapes left out in the sun. But this air carried a sour twist, a rotten undercurrent of mildew—like the fumes buried in the house's wallpaper, except stronger. Riper.

It was the stench of something freshly unburied.

And it came from the very back of the closet. The mirrored door, the one that had been stuck shut, hung open.

Vivi and I stared, stunned, past my clothes, past the open mirrored door, at gaping shadows. Earlier, I'd seen a glow hiding behind that door. Now, there was nothing. Only waiting darkness and the crawling stench of rot.

The partially open door reflected us in its cracked mirror: Vivi standing tall and curious in her lacy butterfly mask, and me shrunken and white-faced with fear. I clutched my beetle mask in my clammy hand.

Nothing was moving back there, not that I could see. By all appearances, the door had opened on its own.

I might've done just enough damage to loosen the door in its frame, spurring it to finally drift open. At least, that was the only logical explanation I could dredge up for why it had happened *now.*

Then again, logic and this house did not always go hand in hand. I had the eerie gut feeling that if I closed that door, it was going to open itself back up.

Vivi pushed past me, shoving my sweaters aside. "Only one way to find out what's back there!"

"Hold on!" I knew I was the one who'd been trying to pry

this door open earlier, pursuing that hidden glow, but now there was no glow and my heart was pounding. "At least let me get a light," I pleaded.

Too late.

She danced out of reach—beyond the mirrored door—and gasped. "Whoa, Libby, you've got to see this."

See *what*? It was unbroken darkness. The space could be teeming with rats or bugs. It could be rotten with holes. One careless step and then—*wham,* we'd plummet through floors and ceilings and splatter into mushy pieces on the cellar's concrete.

"Seriously, don't move, Vivi! Wait there!" I darted into the safety of my lamplit room and grabbed my phone from my nightstand. With every throb of my pulse, another second was passing with Vivi unattended—out of sight, in the dark, in a house where people were known to disappear. "Vivi, you're not moving, are you?" I called. I tapped on the flashlight function and raced back into the closet.

The glow caught on Vivi's white mask, and I exhaled in relief.

She squinted in the bright beam, shielding her eyes. "Would you chill?" she said. "We don't need extra light—look at all these stars!"

Stars? I didn't see any—not from where I stood in the main part of my closet, surrounded by clothes and hangers.

I gulped in one last fresh breath, and then leaned past the newly opened door. I still didn't see stars, but I did gasp. I'd been expecting the low, tight crush of a crawl space.

Not this.

My flashlight illuminated an area that wasn't especially deep and wasn't especially wide, but one that stretched up. Up and up and up.

We had to be inside one of the house's decorative turrets.

There were no windows. The only thing in here was a spiral staircase. Gleaming with honey-gold wood, it coiled like a snake with no head, up and out of sight. Leading in the same direction as the mysterious noises I heard every night.

And Vivi already had a foot on the first step, glancing at me impatiently. "Let's follow the stars!" she said. "Don't you want to know what's up there?"

The uncertainty in my gut swelled, shivery and flinching. I could practically taste the cobwebs on my tongue. "I don't see any stars. Maybe we should wait until morning. . . ."

Vivi slumped with an exaggerated sigh. "Put your mask on, dork."

Dammit. If I wanted to understand this house, there was no getting around these masks, was there? I frowned at Vivi but pressed the mask over my face. Calm dripped through me, the chill clutching at my spine released, and all around me the walls blazed to life.

I stumbled backward in surprise. The stairwell was speckled with stars. Stars with thirteen points—palm-sized sunbursts—and they were glowing. Blue. Strong and hot, like a flame.

They stretched up the walls as far as I could see.

Was this what my grandfather meant about the masks being the key to this house? They were peeling back a layer of reality to show us one deeper underneath—one painted like invisible ink all over this property.

I tapped off my flashlight app and turned to tell Vivi I could see the stars.

But she was no longer at the foot of the stairs beside me.

I jolted. "Vivi!"

From above, her butterfly mask poked around a bend in

the staircase, its lace backlit by starshine. "You see them, right? Let's go!"

I had to follow her. I couldn't let her go alone.

My breaths came too shallow, but cool and steady calm trickled out from my mask, bathing me with reassurance.

You are strong.

The new voice in my mind promised me. An inner conviction that whispered that everything was okay. I was exactly where I was supposed to be, doing exactly what I was supposed to do.

I couldn't remember the last time I'd felt that way. But I could get used to this.

"Come on already!" Vivi called. "Something's up here!" Her voice was starting to sound distant. How high did this staircase wind?

She'd vanished from sight, and the last thing I wanted was for her to get lost in our house's twisty walls.

"Would you wait for me? Vivi!" I followed her. I followed the stars.

Each step sank under me with the slightest sigh, reshaping around my feet, the same way the mask melded itself against my face.

"Ooh, I see brighter light!" Vivi's voice echoed from above. She may have been masked like a butterfly, but the expression "like a moth to a flame" came to mind.

I tried not to trip, taking the stairs a couple at a time. They kept winding and winding.

At last, the stairs opened up. The star-kissed dark melted into an embrace of creamy indigo. The stars were thicker here—casting the room in an eerie glow.

Something *was* up here. A room.

I stopped at the top of the staircase, gaping.

At the steeply sloped blue walls, gleaming top to bottom with stars. At the masses of junk cocooned in white cloth.

Vivi flitted around, creaking over ancient floorboards, ogling every detail. A Cheshire cat grin lit up the bottom half of her face.

"Well," she said, "I guess we found the attic."

CHAPTER THIRTEEN

THE ATTIC. THE ATTIC MOM HAD forbidden us from entering.

Other than Vivi's light footsteps, our moaning, groaning home stood silent around us. The torturous nightly noises I could've sworn were coming from up here, they *weren't* coming now. I didn't see any darting bugs or rats or bigger pests.

It was like the whole house was holding its breath.

The eerie weight of watching eyes that followed me everywhere, especially in Mom's room, was crushingly heavy here. And the house's undercurrent of mildew and rot had never been so strong. The attic had to be the origin. This reek like dead bugs, squashed caterpillar guts, was trickling down through the house, leaching out through the walls.

The putrid stench encased me. My bare arms felt sticky, coated in a thousand invisible cobwebs. As if I'd run through layer after layer of them on my way up the stairs.

The room was a giant rectangle, with a nonsensical number of staircase landings. To my right, three lined the long wall, in addition to the one we'd climbed. I craned my neck to look past the central mass of sheet-cloaked clutter—old furniture, most likely—and spotted three more landings along the opposite wall. The house's confusing rooflines and turrets must've hidden these secret passages, like the one built into the back of my closet.

There were only two windows—tiny circles embedded in the short walls at the front and back of the room. Under each, white sheets masked heaps of what had to be abandoned furniture, huddled like bent and broken ghosts. The stiff sheets were streaked with dust so thick it was downright fuzzy. In places, greenish-black splotches bled through.

The tallest hump of decaying belongings was the mountain in the middle of the attic. The stars glowing along the walls and ceiling cast the pile into pools of pale blue and deep pockets of shadow.

Were these the accumulated possessions of the previous owners—all the people who had disappeared?

If so, this attic wasn't just a holding spot for discarded antiques; it was a graveyard. A sad, dirty monument to every family who'd tried to make this house their home.

The relaxing effect of my mask warred with the painful clench in my chest. If Mom and Vivi and I vanished, was this where our stuff would go?

A sudden squeal from Vivi startled me. She'd been combing through the junk stacked against the nearest wall and was tugging at the leather handle of an enormous trunk. "Hey, Lib, check this thing out!"

I creaked over the old floorboards toward her, watching my step for the curiously quiet pests that *had* to be here somewhere. And I arrived in time for Vivi to blow across the top of the wooden chest, unleashing a cloud of dust.

"Vivi!" I coughed, waving the air away.

"Sorry, sorry," Vivi mumbled, honestly seeming way too caught up in this new adventure to be sorry. Behind her mask, her big brown eyes had picked up that fascinated sparkle at discovery upon discovery—and remarkably strange ones at that. Her small body was vibrating with energy. She swiped her arm across the wood to wipe it cleaner.

My own arm itched, watching her. I squinted at the top of the chest, awash in the blue glow of the stars from the wall behind it. The wood was intricately carved and painted, the colors chipped and faded. An enormous blue rose was at the center. Twelve circles surrounded it, each containing the outlined form of a bug.

"This matches the chairs at the stone table," Vivi said. "Look." She pointed to each circle in turn. "Beetle, moth, cicada, centipede, praying mantis, butterfly, ant, wasp, cricket, mosquito, housefly, cockroach."

She tugged at the lid, trying to see inside, but it fell with a heavy thud. "Ow! That's way too heavy."

Sounded like an excuse to test our theory about the beetle mask affording me extra strength.

"Let me try." I scanned for anything to cushion my hand from the dust, but the fuzzy white shrouds around us were no help. I grabbed the lid, bare-handed, intending to inch it up. But it felt so light that I flung it up way too fast, spewing more dust everywhere. "Dammit!" I sneezed into my elbow.

Vivi gaped at me. "That's incredible. Your mask really does make you stronger." She looked at me with glittering awe, the same way she sometimes had when we were younger. I'd forgotten how good it felt to be someone my little sister could actually admire. Even if the real credit belonged to the beetle mask, not me.

Vivi dropped to her knees before the trunk. If I'd tried that, I would've busted my kneecaps, but she still had that ballerina's grace. Tonight, it came through more than ever, her every gesture floating lighter on the air. She needed to get back to dancing. Even kneeling in a filthy attic, she was as elegant as a swan settling on a lake.

The underside of the lid was as ornate as the outside, the paint brighter, less faded by wear and tear: A caterpillar munched on a blue rose leaf. Above, in gold cursive, an inscription read METAMORPHOSE! ASCEND TO GLORY!

My body hummed with an electric sort of confusion. "Metamorphose . . . ?" I glanced over my shoulder at the starry attic behind us. At the glowing stars we could see only with our masks on.

Vivi ran her finger along the cryptic words with reverence. "You know how a caterpillar evolves from larva to pupa to butterfly? That must be what it means."

The chest held a small sea of black-and-white images, yellowing pamphlets and pages.

I grabbed a torn piece of paper, thin and curled, spotted with mold, and squinted to read the looping hand-inked cursive by blue light.

Luckily, I still had my phone. I tapped on the flashlight and held it up so we could read:

A Novel Approach to the Modern Spirit Circle:
Madame Ellen Clery's
"The Caterpillar and the Rose Leaf," December 1895.

As amended, in reference to "Science and a Future Life: With Other Essays" by Frederic W. H. Myers, 1893.

Knowledge of the future may be gained by scrutinizing the past.

This, naturally, is why we study history, but what if I told you the same principle applies to our own life spans?

In fact, Frederic W. H. Myers compared a living human to a caterpillar, a mere larva. Just as a caterpillar undergoes dramatic transformation to evolve into a butterfly, Myers believed that only in death could humans achieve their superior form.

To elucidate, let us suppose that a group of caterpillars sit together on a rose leaf—Myers suggested we envision a cabbage leaf, but in this House, do forgive me if I aspire to more poetic notions.

(Hold for laughter.)

Whoa, this was a script. Ellen Clery's séance script?

I'd thought it was an essay, but that was an undeniable stage direction. I kept reading:

Imagine that these caterpillars are discussing their purpose. They are well suited to their current existence on this rose leaf but cannot explain the vestigial structures built into their bodies, traits that are of no current use. A sole caterpillar suspects that these traits indicate that her species is meant for more. It is meant, someday, to fly.

And, lo, at that precise moment, a butterfly alights upon the rosebush.

The caterpillar sees the butterfly and confirms its traits as evolved versions of her own. She calls out to her fellow caterpillars, but before they can look, the butterfly flits away.

Now, although the caterpillar can no longer see the butterfly, and although her fellow larvae never glimpsed it, that does not diminish the Truth she discovered: Should the caterpillar be lucky enough to complete her evolution, this butterfly is indeed the future that awaits her.

So, truly, it is with humankind.

There is an undeniable similarity of structure between our own intelligence and an invisible intelligence.

Or, rather, should I say, invisible to you, my dear guests?

(Pause for effect.)

I need but don this mask and—

That's where the paper was ripped off.

Vivi grabbed it from me, frowning as she flipped the page and scoured the empty back. "Hmm, '*The Caterpillar and the Rose Leaf.*' I guess this explains the house's bug theme?"

I nodded. At least it reinforced what Madame Clery had said in the article from our grandfather's desk—she'd chosen insect designs for the masks to honor the process of metamorphosis. A process she was apparently obsessed with.

But the script left an awful lot of room for questions. Madame Clery seemed to be arguing that humans were better off dead, or at least that death was the only way they could achieve their "superior form," whatever that meant.

I was surprised by the answering pang in my chest—a conflicted twinge of validation. In my own way, I'd thought death was better than life, too.

But my eyes landed on the trunk's gold inscription again: METAMORPHOSE! ASCEND TO GLORY.

Just what kind of glory were we talking about here?

That phantom sensation rippled through me again—bitter pills sliming my tongue and sticking in my throat, my stomach thrashing with a pain so sharp.

Dying hadn't felt like glory to me. No matter how much I'd thought I craved it.

Maybe I misunderstood what Madame Clery meant.

I hoped I misunderstood.

Inside the trunk, a black-and-white picture caught my eye: a woman sitting at a desk in a dark room. The room had to be our downstairs parlor, because the hideous wallpaper still matched. The woman was surrounded by candles and flowers and a crystal ball. She held a metal-tipped fountain pen poised over a sheet of paper.

She wore a lacy gown and a full faced mask. The mask was attached to a pointed crown and a long veil, which was pulled over her face. Through the snowy mesh, the mask was visible enough for me to make out a doll-like face, with the outline of an oversized rose blossom on one half.

No mistaking it: The rose mask. From Mom's room.

A fine foggy mist, like cigar smoke, drifted from around the mask's edges. And behind the mask holes, the woman's eyes were nothing but light. As if they'd rolled all the way back in her head. And taken on a pale glow.

My stomach clenched at the sight. I'd seen eyes like that all too recently.

On the back, in scratchy ink, it said *Ellen communes with "Rose." 1894*.

I showed Vivi. "This must be the medium," I said. "Madame Ellen Clery."

"Her eyes . . ." Vivi squinted at the image. "They look like Flynn's did during the séance."

There it was. She'd said what I hadn't wanted to say.

Maybe because Ellen and Flynn were using the same cheap trick.

Maybe?

Less than a week ago, I'd come into this house pretty sure I knew what was possible and what was impossible. But tonight, I'd crushed metal in my hand. Vivi had levitated. We were hunkered in an attic full of glowing stars.

What did that mean about the other supposedly impossible things I'd seen? Like what happened to Flynn during the séance. He'd looked so terrified when he told me nothing like that had never happened before. And, yes, the miniaturized grabber had fallen out of his sleeve, so part of his séance had to be a trick. But what if it wasn't *all* a trick?

The terrifying truth was, I had no idea what to believe anymore. Maybe I wasn't losing my grip on reality. Maybe reality was losing its grip on this house and everyone in it.

"What does it mean, she's communing with Rose?" Vivi asked.

I wasn't sure. Mom's window, where the mask Ellen wore was kept, was labeled ROSE. But did the note on this photo mean that Rose was an actual person? Or rather, a dead person—a supposed spirit?

Ellen didn't appear to be talking to anyone. Her flat, glowing eyes were staring straight out, fixed on nothing. But she did have that pen in her hand. And on the sheet of paper before her, something was half drawn.

I couldn't see what.

Vivi grabbed a second photo, with the same setup, but this one with the mask and its attached veil removed. Ellen was far less unsettling with her own eyes, a Mona Lisa smile on her lips. She had hard, arched eyebrows and sharp features, covered with freckles. She held up her paper to reveal what she had drawn—the white stone table from the yard, a crystal ball in the center, the chairs filled with thirteen shadows.

At the top, it said *Rite of the Stars.* But the handwriting was like a child's. Hard, simple lines scratched too deep, slashing through the paper.

The caption on the back read: *"Rose" makes a humble request.*

"A request?" Vivi said. "What request?"

We scoured the front again.

No clues.

I squinted harder at Ellen. In a way, she really did remind me of Flynn—not only because of the glowing eyes and their shared freckles. More because her resting face seemed to land somewhere between permanently pissed and way too proud of herself.

Maybe it was a trait all self-professed mediums shared.

I dug deeper into the chest and pulled out another piece of paper. There were more underneath, a whole scrappy pile, scratched deep with fading ink.

Drawings. In the same style as the one Ellen held in the picture. They were designs—for the stained-glass windows, for the mosaic floors.

Vivi lifted one out. The back was labeled *Rose's design #14: "The Feast."*

"I'm pretty sure this is the original plan for the kitchen floor," she said. "You think Mom would want to see this?"

The drawing was intact, and remarkably detailed, including the part of the floor that had been smashed. Which apparently was meant to feature baby rabbits digging their teeth into a crying quail.

I shook my head. "Mom's already halfway finished, and I'm sure whatever she's coming up with is less disturbing than that. Better she doesn't see the original."

I dropped the drawings back into the chest and lifted out

another photograph instead. Dated 1895, it featured the stone table in the backyard, all thirteen chairs filled. "This looks like one of the séances." Every person wore a cloak and an ornate mask. In fact . . .

"All the masks from the windows!" Vivi realized. "Look, my butterfly mask!"

My beetle mask, too.

"But so many of these masks are missing now," Vivi mused. "I keep seeing empty spots where they must've been."

I wasn't surprised she'd noticed, too. Every room with a stained-glass portrait either contained a protruding mask or a space where one was slotted in previously. Except the kitchen, with the Ant window. I hadn't seen any spot for a mask there. But there was an ant mask in this picture. So the ant mask had to be in the house somewhere—or at least, it used to be.

Vivi scanned the hulking objects cluttering up the attic, hidden by white sheets. "You think these things were also séance props?"

Before I could answer, Vivi embraced her trademark *Only one way to find out* methodology. She stood and yanked the closest white sheet—in another puff of dust that sent me reeling—revealing a towering armoire. When she squeaked open the reluctant doors, there were thirteen cloaks on thirteen hangers.

I stepped forward to look and stumbled. My socked foot had kicked something—a soft, dark shape, bigger than the palm of my hand. I pulled back.

A dead rat? Please not a dead rat.

I sucked in a sour breath and made myself bend down to check.

No, it wasn't a rat. It was square-shaped.

"What the hell?" I muttered, retrieving the dusty thing from the floor.

A tattered wallet. Probably another discarded belonging.

I opened it, expecting it to be empty. But it was stuffed full of cards. Even a couple crinkled twenties. No one would've thrown this out on purpose.

I glanced at Vivi, to see if she'd noticed, but she was busy rummaging around in the armoire.

I pulled out the driver's license and shone my phone's flashlight on it.

It read:

DRISCOLL, JOHN CLERY

DOB: 08/21/1972

ISSUED: 07/27/2010, EXPIRES: 08/21/2018.

So this wallet had likely landed here sometime between 2010 and 2018. It could've been a contractor Mom had hired back then. Only it seemed awfully strange that this guy's middle name was Clery, matching Ellen's last name. And the listed address was on our street, a couple numbers lower than ours.

I wondered what Vivi would make of this. She'd moved on from investigating the armoire to the massive white-sheeted object propped against the wall beside it, still oblivious to my discovery. "Hey, Vivi—"

She ripped back the white sheet, and under it was . . .

An enormous balled-up body.

Shiny and brown. A tangle of six spiky-haired legs as long as my own. Skinny, ribbed antennae as long as my body.

A cockroach.

A seven-foot cockroach.

* * *

Vivi and I screamed.

I grabbed her and yanked both of us back from the prehistorically huge insect. My horrified brain clawed for purchase on reality. *Run. Should we run?*

But the unexpected will to fight grounded my legs as sure as concrete.

The beetle mask—did it make me strong enough to win?

I shoved my phone and the ratty wallet into my pocket and scanned for anything to use as a weapon.

"Wait! Libby!" Vivi tugged at my shirt, pointing. "It—it's not alive."

Not alive?

I stared at it, my pulse pounding in my ears. The cockroach husk glistened, backlit in neon splotches by the attic's glowing blue stars. The thorny spines on its twisted legs were each as long as my hand.

But Vivi was right. The cockroach wasn't moving. Its back was torn open, split down the middle.

Inside, there was nothing.

A hollow shell.

"It's . . ." Vivi's voice dropped into an awed whisper. "Is it an exoskeleton?"

Incredibly, it did look like one. I'd spent too much time cringing over Vivi's collection of cicada shells to miss the similarities.

Vivi stepped out from behind me, growing bolder. "Hold on, though. Ridiculous size aside, even the shape is wrong for a cockroach," she said. "The abdomen should be rounder, but the way this one curves in and out is more like . . . um, a human?"

I saw what she meant. This shell didn't totally mimic the barrel-wide segmented body of a cockroach. The abdomen looked more like a torso, with the rough structure of a chest and waist, even hips. Swollen, deformed, oversized, but still recognizable.

My stomach turned and acid burned my throat.

I didn't know *what* could produce an exoskeleton quite like that. But it could only be some kind of monster.

Vivi approached the cockroach shell cautiously, as if ready to leap back in case the hulking husk wriggled to life. She ran her hand along the nearest leg, poking at one of the spines. And it snapped off, brittle as a twig. "Ow!" She pulled back, examining her finger. "That thing gave me a splinter!"

"A splinter?"

She held up her finger to me.

A sharp and skinny shard was wedged under her skin. As for the cockroach leg, where it had broken off, the shiny caramel finish gave way to raw wood, same as the inside of ruptured tree branch.

Déjà freaking vu.

I yanked the shard from her skin. "This shell is made of wood," I said.

Like the smaller cockroach I'd smashed earlier today. And if my theory about that small cockroach being a séance prop held true, then . . . "Oh! Vivi, it's gotta be a costume."

Vivi stared at me, blinking.

"Remember?" I said. "Ellen Clery's husband was an illusionist, and they were holding *bug-themed* séances for profit, right? They probably wanted them to be as dramatic as possible. Hard to get more dramatic than that." I pointed to the enormous deformed shell.

Vivi burst into a laugh—relieved, and slightly unhinged—strong enough to set the pale lace of her mask fluttering. "A costume. Of course!" she said. "The split in the back must be so someone could climb inside."

Right. Yes. Not any indication that a cockroach existed in such a preposterous size—or actually, a little larger, because that's how exoskeletons work, right? Bugs split out of their old skins because they get too big to fit anymore.

I shuddered all over again.

Then, behind us, on the other side of the attic, something rustled.

Vivi and I froze.

The noises I'd heard through my ceiling—were they starting up again?

Rustle, rustle, scraaatch—

I whipped around.

The attic was dim, still lit by only stars. I pulled out my phone and shone its flashlight on the other side of the room.

Mounds buried beneath sheets. Suffocating clutter. And . . . Had one white sheet moved?

The flashlight glinted on something protruding from behind a sheet—something I hadn't seen before.

Something green and spiny.

Vivi whispered, "Is that . . . another costume?"

Oh God.

I'd dismissed the clutter up here as old furniture, but the outlines underneath—hunched backs, spindly points poking up against the sheets . . .

They had to be costumes. Had to be. A rat had moved under the sheet and exposed something new, that's all.

Rustle. The shiny green spiny bit—it shifted again.

"What *is* that?" Vivi took a step toward it.

"Girls! *What* are you doing up here?" Mom cried.

With twin gasps, we turned.

From the top of the steps, Mom stared at us.

A flashlight hung limp in her hand, pointing down at the floor.

She was in her nightgown and bathrobe, curls half fallen from a bun. Her breath came in pants. She hadn't heard us down the hall in Vivi's room earlier, but our screams when we saw the giant cockroach must've carried through her bedroom ceiling. Her pale face was practically as white as the sheets around us.

"And *what,*" she demanded, "are you wearing?"

Before either of us could figure out how to answer, Mom's flashlight landed on the mammoth cockroach behind us.

Her mouth fell open. She didn't scream. She didn't make a sound. She stood there, eyes popping out of her head, gaping as if she were choking on the air.

"Girls," she said in a hoarse whisper, "take off those masks. And get downstairs now."

Without our masks, all the stars went black. Ironically, this made us way less safe, which I'm sure was the last thing Mom intended. But Vivi and I were too scared to argue. Once we made it down the starless stairs and emerged in my room, Mom tutted at the damage to the inner closet door. She slammed it shut behind us, so that it stuck fast in the frame. For good measure, she slammed the outer closet door, too.

"Put those masks back in your windows," she ordered. "And never take them out again. They aren't toys."

The worry in her face was raw and real. But how few questions she was asking gave me pause. She'd looked around the attic like she hadn't seen it before, or at least hadn't seen it in a very long time, but how much did she know about the masks? If she was aware of their eerie powers, little wonder she was so freaked-out to see us wearing them.

I started with the less risky question: "Mom, did you know that the masks in our windows were wearable?"

"Put. Them. *Back.*" Her voice came out closer to a hiss. "Or do I need to confiscate them?"

Her eyes were so wild, her stress honed into biting fury. I couldn't tell which version of Mom I was getting—my old Mom springing back to life, desperate to protect us, or this strange new version, desperate to protect this house's secrets.

"I'm sorry, Mom. We didn't mean to freak you out," I said. "Something strange is going on in this house, so we were just—"

"I told you," Mom said, "there's nothing wrong with this house."

She swiped a trickle of sweat from her hairline with her sleeve, inadvertently streaking something across her forehead.

Dirt?

I blinked. No. Not dirt.

Blood.

"Mom, you're bleeding!"

With a flustered groan, she wiped at the smudge, only smearing it into a wider splotch. Her nightgown's sleeve rode up, revealing the skin of her forearm.

It was torn. Jagged and bloody.

"What is . . . ?" I reached for her arm.

She yanked down her sleeve, hiding her pale skin and the bloody marks. "Oh, it's from the roses, girls. You know how spiky they are."

My own scratched arms could attest to that, but Mom's wound was deeper than any of mine. Deeper than what looked like an accident.

Could Mom be cutting herself? I thought that was something teens did. I'd never imagined my mom might be doing it.

"That looks a little deep for a rose scratch," I said softly. In a mild voice I'd learned from her. One I'd thought I hated.

"I told you, it was the roses," Mom insisted. "It was an accident."

Vivi spoke, nearly as quiet as the creak of the floorboards underneath her feet. "Then why are you getting so defensive?"

Mom sucked in a sharp breath like she'd been stabbed in the back. Not even by me, the Failure Child. By Vivi, the Good One. "Girls, I'm glad to see you two are getting along—for tonight, anyway—but it's not fair to gang up on me. I need you to stop whatever little game you're playing with me."

"What game?" I asked.

She squeezed her eyes shut, like she was praying for strength. Like it was taking everything in her not to fly into a screaming rage. As much as I'd longed for her to snap out of her distant, dreamy behavior, this piercing anger didn't feel like the Mom I knew either. That little glimpse of her looking panicked had been closer to recognizable, but this . . .

When her eyes opened, they were cold. And hard. "How about the baby blanket, for starters?" she said. "I know one of you put that on my bed."

She said "one of you," but it was me she was staring down.

I knew *I* hadn't. I glanced at Vivi, but she looked confused, not guilty. As weird as Mom had been acting, I was more inclined to believe my sleepwalking theory—that she'd put that blanket on her own bed.

"Mom," I said, "w-we didn't—"

"Libby." Mom's eyes narrowed at something around my chest. "What is that you're wearing?"

I looked down to find Grandma's necklace swinging free from my pajama top, in plain sight, and winced. "Just a necklace I found," I said, reaching to tuck it back into my shirt.

But Mom yanked it, so forcefully it dug into my neck. She ripped it off over my head and turned it in her hands. Something was working behind her eyes—an old memory, an emotion, a suspicion.

She clicked it open and gasped at the picture inside. "My parents. This was my mother's." Her head jerked up, with a sudden glare. "Where did you get this?"

"F-from . . ." I couldn't even say it.

But Mom already knew. "You went into their room," she said. "After I expressly asked you not to."

I couldn't help it. I took the slightest step backward. Away from her wild eyes. Her pupils were stabbing pinpricks.

"You *did* put that blanket on my bed," Mom snarled, baring her blue-tinged teeth. "And you broke into the attic. Are you looking to cause problems? Do you hate this house that much? Do you hate *me* that much?"

Whoa, whoa, she was completely spiraling. This didn't sound like her. It didn't feel like her. "Hate you? I—I don't hate you," I sputtered in shock. "And it's not that I hate the house either!" Although I did. "I only checked the locked room and the attic because I know you're hiding things from us—"

"Okay, keep it up, Libby," Mom snapped. "Go ahead. Maybe I need to talk with Dr. Glaser about all this."

That sucked the breath from my chest. "Dr. Glaser? What do you mean?"

But I knew what she meant. That was a threat. A threat about reporting my behavior, about getting me back into a facility.

Vivi looked back and forth between me and Mom with increasing uncertainty. Even fear. "Mom, you wouldn't . . . ?"

All three of us fell silent.

I gripped the beetle mask in my hands. It was made of glass, but it was strong. And I could be, too. I could stand here and not cry.

Mom blinked, as if finally registering what she'd said. "Oh. Oh, Libby, I'm sorry. I shouldn't have said that." With a ragged sigh, she reached out and touched my shoulder. But her hand on me was as limp as a dead thing.

It was all I could do not to jerk away.

To stay still and not throw off this supposed peace offering.

"I didn't mean it." Mom sounded so tired. And she looked it, too. Her eyes were shadowed. Her hair hung lank and greasy from her scalp.

"It's okay," I muttered. Because, more than anything, I wanted her to stop touching me.

That did the trick. She removed her hand from my rigid shoulder and rubbed hard at the bridge of her nose, like she was fighting off a headache. A hangover. "Just . . . leave all of this—the attic, the masks—alone," she said. "Okay?"

We stammered out our respective okays. And Mom nodded, like all the strength had been drained out of her. "Let's leave it at that." She smiled a watery smile.

"Oh," she said, "and do try to get some sleep, girls." The faintest flicker of her old self.

But then it was gone. She walked out of the room, her soft footsteps fading down the hall until her bedroom door closed behind her.

The floor, the entire house, felt unsteady under me.

I had no idea what to make of Mom's aggressive outburst. Although she *had* shown me a flash of this ugliness once before: the deep scowl that had carved her face that night in the kitchen when I'd pressed her about the disappearances being real. The more she caught me delving into the house's secrets, the more this abnormal rage vented through her.

But the more I played along that things were fine, the more she spun off into her dreamlike daze.

Either way, Vivi and I were losing her.

Mom, as I knew her, *was* disappearing. In plain sight.

CHAPTER FOURTEEN

MOM LEFT ME AND VIVI IN suffocating silence, until my sister's half-choked sob leaked out. Tears spilled down her cheeks as she clutched the butterfly mask to her chest, stroking it like a beloved pet.

I held out my arms for Vivi—an old reflex. And then I realized there was no way she'd accept that kind of comfort from me anymore. I started to pull back, but Vivi darted over, tucking into me. In a hug I hadn't known how much I needed.

My eyes teared up. Out of habit, I fought to hold them back.

But, then, Vivi wouldn't judge me. I didn't have to hide myself. So I stopped fighting the tide. I leaned my cheek against the top of her head, breathing in the artificial green apple of her shampoo. And we both let ourselves be sad and small and scared. At least for a moment.

"We didn't do anything that bad, did we?" Vivi asked as she clutched my waist. "I know she didn't want us in the attic, but . . ."

"Yeah." I pulled myself together. "I'm not sure how much that was actually about *us*."

I couldn't pretend to explain Mom's behavior. But we needed more than ever to figure out what had happened to our family members in this house. And whether that was happening now to Mom.

Unfortunately, she'd ordered me and Vivi to stay away from both the attic and the masks—the two biggest leads we'd discovered so far.

"Well." Vivi wiped her eyes and stepped back, also regrouping. "She doesn't know what she's talking about. And I'm *not* going to stop wearing my mask." She jutted her chin in the air, like she was daring me to pile on, too.

I bit my cheek. My own mask was still clutched in my hand, and I didn't know what to make of Mom's opposition. Whether she wanted us to avoid the masks because they were dangerous, or because wearing them could lead to some deeply guarded truth.

Maybe both.

I'd feel better if Vivi would stop wearing hers, at least until we understood how they worked. But she'd never agree to that—not after the masks had illuminated an attic full of glowing stars—and I wouldn't gain anything by opposing and alienating her. As much as I hated to admit it, I needed her help figuring all this out.

The weight in my pocket reminded me—the attic had given us one more clue. For now, I steered away from the topic of masks, and showed her the ratty wallet. "Hey, I didn't have time to tell you, I found something else upstairs. . . ."

Success. Vivi's attention was redirected.

We sat down on the edge of my bed, examining the contents.

"Hmm, 'John *Clery* Driscoll,'" Vivi read from the driver's license. "Wait." She held the plastic card two inches from her nose and squinted, like she couldn't believe what she was seeing. "Lib, did you look at the picture . . . ?"

"Not closely. Why?"

Vivi thrust the license at me, and I saw for myself.

John Clery Driscoll's face struck an uncomfortably familiar chord: freckles, sharp angles, distinctive coppery-red hair . . .

Shit.

Those rumors of a tenth disappearance—a neighbor. Wasn't it interesting how Flynn had dodged discussing them?

I grimaced, a new suspicion settling into my gut as Vivi and I searched his name on our phones.

Within seconds, we landed on the same headline from seven years ago: LOCAL MAN MISSING: 10TH DISAPPEARANCE ON THE SAME BLOCK. The subhead read: IS THE INFAMOUS "HOUSE OF MASKS" TO BLAME?

Here it was—the neighbor's disappearance. John Clery Driscoll, who'd lived three doors down.

The Clery middle name *did* link him to Ellen. As the article explained, House of Masks had passed to Joseph Cragg's relatives—i.e., *my* family. But after Ellen disappeared, her sister had moved nearby, searching for her without success. That branch of the Clery family had stayed close to House of Masks over the years. Maybe too close.

The article offered no proof that the house was to blame for John Clery Driscoll's disappearance. He'd never lived in it. All the same, he'd vanished as mysteriously as the other victims.

And he'd left behind a family—a wife and kid. A nine-year-old boy.

The photo in the article jumped off the screen at me: a

freckled, copper-haired boy gripping his mom's hand. And as small as he was, the scowl on his face was one I recognized.

Yes, I might have been cut off from the attic. Might not know what to make of the masks. But *this* was a lead I could follow.

So the next morning when Mom came down for breakfast, smiling with her blue teeth like nothing was wrong, like nothing had happened last night, I played along. I didn't tell her about the wallet. After I'd watched her shred that article about the disappearances to snow, she was the last person I trusted to help me uncover the truth.

Instead, I asked her about the neighbors. And endured her sly little wink, as she misinterpreted my interest.

Luckily, there weren't many families on this street that counted a redheaded teenage dirtbag among their number.

Only the Driscolls, across the street and three houses down. Living at the same address as the one listed on John Clery Driscoll's abandoned driver's license.

Time for a field trip.

The Driscolls' house was squat and ramshackle. One story. No cover over the concrete front porch.

I squinted up at the July sun as I pushed the doorbell. My fingertip came back grimy. Didn't seem like they got many visitors.

I wasn't positive I was doing the right thing coming here. The wallet felt like it was burning a guilty hole through my jeans and into my thigh. No way sharing it wouldn't be traumatic.

Don't wimp out, I told myself firmly. *You deserve answers. We all deserve answers, no matter how much Flynn might have lied.*

For an excruciating mini-eternity, I stood on the porch,

sweating as the sun seared my scalp. Until the inner door opened with a rusty squeal.

A frizzy-haired blond woman peered out at me, baffled. I recognized her from the online article as an older, wearier version of John Clery Driscoll's widow. She kept the screen door locked and asked, "Aren't you a little old to be selling Girl Scout cookies?"

"I . . . What?" That one caught me off guard. "No, I just moved in down the street. I—I'm here to see Flynn."

Her pink forehead wrinkled. "You mean, you're one of the girls that moved into . . . ?"

I nodded, and she scowled ten times harder. She hesitated, swiping her arm across her sweaty face. It had to be at least as hot in the house as it was outside. No air-conditioning greeted me through the door.

"Well, come in," she said finally. She unlocked the outer door and bellowed over her shoulder: "*Flynn!*"

I shuffled into the foyer, a simple tiled square that opened into the living room. The walls were a faded honey yellow, not blue, blue, *blue*—and I sucked in a breath refreshingly free of our house's rotting potpourri stench. The smell here was more like vinegar and oranges. And a faint edge of . . . dog dander?

Yep. Barking pierced the air, followed by the clicking nails of a heavy basset hound. The dog bounded toward me, past an obstacle course of scattered kids' toys—building blocks and stuffed animals, picture books scribbled over by crayons.

The hound stopped by my feet, snuffling thoroughly. I reached down to offer it my hand, and the dog peered at me from under its baggy brow. At last, it gave me a slobbery lick of approval and huffed off to settle on the faded leather of the living room couch.

I held my drool-covered hand a few inches from my body, hoping it would air-dry before I had to touch anything.

"Can I get you lemonade or something, hon?" Flynn's mom asked, but then a burned smell wafted from the kitchen. She cursed before re-noticing me and clapping a hand over her mouth. "One minute. Excuse me!"

She dashed off. Something clattered on the stovetop, followed by muffled swearing.

"Flynn!" she bellowed again, even louder.

"Mom, you calling me?" Flynn shouted from the hall to the left. "You want me to watch the kids or not?"

"I'll get them. Just get your friend!"

"What friend?"

The bafflement in Flynn's voice was pretty telling. Confirmation I wasn't the only outcast living on this street.

I wavered by the front door, glancing wistfully at the sweltering outdoors I'd been so eager to escape. Flynn's family didn't seem to have time for any interruptions, let alone one this upsetting. It would be so much easier to run before Flynn saw me. Before I had to see *him* and his annoyingly attractive smirk and then shatter it to pieces by traumatizing him with his dad's wallet.

This was a huge mistake, wasn't it?

Too late. Flynn stepped into the living room, his coppery hair mussed, his arms filled with a squirming toddler, who was bawling and clutching fistfuls of Flynn's long-sleeved T-shirt.

When Flynn saw me, he froze. He stared at me as though I were a ghost. Like some supernatural occurrence must have summoned me, because there was no plausible reason why I should be here, standing inside his house.

Given how we'd left things, I couldn't blame him.

"Sorry," I squeaked out, backing toward the door. "Seems like a bad time. I can come back later, or—"

The toddler spit up all over his shirt.

Flynn sighed. "You've got to be kidding me." He leaned the crying toddler against his shoulder and rubbed her back, murmuring in the practiced tone of someone with baby-minding skills I'd probably never possess. And he threw me a cutting glare. "Don't you go anywhere."

I stood frozen in the foyer as Flynn strode into the kitchen after his mom. I couldn't make out their words, just aggravated tones. The hound on the sofa gnawed on a bone-shaped toy and stared at me.

Finally, Flynn returned, toddlerless. Before I could say anything, he charged forward and caught my arm, escorting me out of the house and onto the sun-drenched porch. "How? How do you even know where I live?" he sputtered. "What do you think you're doing, showing up at my house like this?"

I ripped my arm away. "Kind of disconcerting, right? When someone shows up at your home uninvited."

Flynn growled in something like disgust, but he couldn't argue. He sealed his arms across his juice-stained chest. "What do you want? To rat me out to my mom? To threaten to have me arrested again?"

I shook my head. "No, I . . ." When I'd mentally rehearsed this conversation, I'd told him about the wallet right away. But now my tongue felt way too thick for my mouth. "Is there someplace you and I can talk privately?" I asked.

"I . . ." Flynn's arms unclenched. "You . . ." He squinted at me, like I was some mirage under the heat of the sun. "Privately?"

Whoops, I might've broken his brain. It was somewhat

reassuring I could short-circuit him, after all the times he'd knocked me off guard.

After a moment, he nodded toward the side of his house. And I followed him to a picnic table with peeling paint, slouched under a fat elm tree. The bench was scratchy under my thighs—I hadn't let myself put on anything fancier than my embarrassingly short shorts. If I'd dressed up even a little, like I cared what Flynn thought of me, I was afraid he'd notice.

He didn't seem bothered by my slapdash appearance. Or his own—not that he needed to be. He raked one hand through his hair and, stained chest aside, would've looked right at home on a concert stage. It wasn't fair—he was wearing another cherry-red shirt, this one long-sleeved with hideous lime-green cuffs, and somehow he'd made dressing like cherry limeade look iconic.

I doubted he was forging his own personal brand on purpose. He came across like he didn't care what was in fashion, or what people thought of it.

I actually really liked that about him.

Not that I liked *him*. Just, literally, that one thing.

The wallet was heavier than ever against my thigh. Flustered, I peeled my ever-expanding curls out of the way and fanned the back of my neck. "Aren't you hot?" I asked. I was stalling, but it was true—the humidity had me clenched in its swampy fist, and I was the one in shorts and a T-shirt.

He was wearing long sleeves.

"I'm always cold," Flynn said with a rueful little shrug. "But you, uh, want something to drink? Lemonade?"

Guess lemonade was the hot-ticket item in this house.

"Sure, thanks."

He nodded and then hesitated. Almost tripping on his steps. "It's just the powdered kind."

And that, I recognized: the self-conscious shift in his stance, how quickly he glanced away. I couldn't count how many times I'd downplayed something I'd said or done or felt because I'd been sure my friends were about to judge me.

Flynn had no idea how much we had in common.

"The powdered kind is better anyway," I assured him.

"Way better." He smiled, his shoulders dropping back into place. "Be right back."

After a few nail-gnawing minutes, Flynn returned with two sweating glasses of lemonade, ice cubes clinking.

"Thanks." I took a big swig, letting the tangy crystals dissolve on my tongue.

Across from me, Flynn sat. He'd changed out his shirt for something spit-up-free. This one was black, printed with a dazed yellow happy face that had X's for eyes and a squiggly mouth with a tongue poking out. In all caps at the top, it said NIRVANA

"Nirvana?" I knew they were a band, but that's about it.

"It was my dad's," he said, with an automatic frown. A painful topic, and I already knew more than I'd bet Flynn intended to tell me.

I winced. But there it was—as much of an opening as I could've hoped for. "About that . . ." I said, inching my hand into my pocket, the worn leather sticky under my fingers. "Look, I know about the tenth disappearance."

Flynn stilled, his green eyes narrowing. "What about it?"

I'd been hoping he wouldn't make me say it.

But one of us had to, and it clearly wasn't going to be him. "John Clery Driscoll," I said. "He was your dad."

Flynn scowled, though he didn't look terribly surprised. "So? Congrats on the sleuthing, Nancy Drew, but like I told you, there's no confirmation it happened at your house."

I ground my teeth, but the hostility was obviously a knee-jerk defense mechanism. With effort, I made my voice softer, not harder: "That's actually why I'm here." I slid the wallet from my pocket and laid it on the picnic table between us. "I found this in our attic."

Flynn stared at it, then at me, then at it. He reached for the wallet.

When he opened it, he gasped. He grabbed his dad's license and leaned in, as if magnetically drawn to the picture. "You found this in . . . in . . . ?" His raspy voice was hoarser than usual, and shakier, too. He looked embarrassed by the sound of it.

"In my attic." I jumped in with as much information as I could offer, so he didn't have to ask: "On the floor. It'd been there a long time, I think. The money's still in it. It doesn't look like anyone took anything."

Flynn flicked me a glance, and I added, "I didn't take anything either, of course!"

Flynn blinked. "Right. Thanks for not robbing my dead dad, I guess."

Not much to say to that. I sipped my lemonade and looked anywhere but at Flynn covertly wiping his eyes, giving what little privacy I could.

Apparently, he didn't consider his dad missing—he considered him dead. I probably would, too. Seven years was a long time to be gone.

"I don't know if you want to turn the wallet over to the police as evidence," I said finally. "I figured your family should decide."

"Evidence," Flynn muttered. "I guess it is. Not that the police have done much to solve *any* of these disappearances." He cradled the worn leather in his hands and swallowed thickly. "I always knew that house was likely behind what happened to

Dad. It was just easier to hope that . . ." He snapped the wallet shut and shoved it into his back pocket, out of sight. "Forget it."

"What made you think he disappeared because of House of Masks?" I asked. "Does it have something to do with him being related to Ellen? I know now that he was a Clery. Like you, apparently. Which you could've told me."

Flynn didn't apologize for hiding it, but he did smile bitterly, like he'd rip his heritage out of his body if he could. "We're descendants of Ellen's little sister. We inherited a few of Ellen's old séance props. And nothing else. Since Ellen and Joseph never had kids, the house—*everything*—went to the Craggs. First to Joseph's brother, and then down the line, all the way to your mom. You and Vivi."

The article had mentioned as much, but it was still awful to hear. "In other words, my relatives muscled yours out of the entire inheritance, because Ellen Clery was a woman?"

"History's fun, huh?" he said dryly. "That's what happened when a couple had no shared descendants."

"No shared descendants," I muttered to myself with a nod. Flynn and I were in no way related. I'd been pretty sure about that, but I couldn't help a satisfied sigh.

Flynn looked at me sideways. "Awfully relieved, aren't you?"

I froze. What was I supposed to say? *Oh, no big deal. I only would've* freaked *if we were even the tiniest bit related, because of the inappropriate thoughts I have about you.*

"Hmm." The ghost of Flynn's smirk returned, like he'd untangled that little mystery for himself. "Interesting."

And I nearly choked on a nervous swig of lemonade.

"Anyway," Flynn continued, "yeah, the Clery connection has everything to do with it. When I was a kid, Dad was the one who used to hold séances at House of Masks. Even took me with him at times, once I got old enough. We had some of Ellen's gear, after all, and she was right about one thing: dark tourism pays. But over the years, it became about more than money for Dad. He started spending more time over there alone, and . . ." He shook his head. "I don't know what happened. One night, he didn't come back."

I frowned, mulling that over. "After all that, you're still doing séances?" If Flynn had thought his dad had likely disappeared because of his involvement with House of Masks, then sneaking over regularly was a huge risk. "I know you said you want the money, but—"

"*Need* the money," Flynn corrected sharply. "A séance here or there makes a decent dent in the utility bills."

Huh. If Flynn's desperately earned cash went toward utility bills, he might have been hiding a good heart behind all these charades. From what I'd seen earlier, seemed like his mom depended on his help looking after the other kids, too.

I nodded, glancing toward the house. "You have a lot of siblings?"

"Just a little sister," Flynn said. "Mom runs a day care, but it can be a lot for her sometimes, and it's not like we have . . . Abby's dad isn't around either. I mean, good riddance. Best thing he ever did for Mom was leave. Unfortunately, he took a big chunk of her money with him."

"That's awful," I said. Then I admitted, "Vivi and I never had dads."

"You mean you didn't know them, or . . . ?"

I didn't blame Flynn for not following, but I was so tired of explaining this to people. "Nope, never had them. Mom did the donor thing. She isn't into relationships, but she was determined to have kids."

"Oh." Flynn's voice got quieter. "That part's kind of nice, right? How much she wanted you?"

"Yeah. That part is."

Except for how it must've hurt her all the more deeply that she'd spent everything to give me this life—and I'd tried my damnedest to throw it away.

Shame spiraled up from the soles of my feet, dragging me down. I felt heavier already.

And Flynn must've noticed, because his mouth tugged into that same worried line he wore after Vivi as good as blurted out that I'd tried to kill myself. No matter how sad or angry she was—how sad or angry she deserved to be—that was a dick move.

Embarrassment flared hot under my skin.

I cleared my throat. "Hey, uh, about what Vivi said about me the other night . . ."

"I thought she was joking," Flynn said. But he didn't meet my eyes.

"No, you didn't. And, look, I know you don't owe me anything, but if there's any way I could convince you not to tell anyone—"

"Why the fuck would I tell anyone?" Flynn demanded. He looked pissed-off, offended that I'd thought he might. "It's not my story to share."

That hit my chest with a strangely tender swell.

"A lot of people would," I said quietly.

"Then a lot of people are assholes."

"A lot of people *are* assholes." My smile was lopsided, too much experience weighing it down.

And Flynn returned it—the same tight, unbalanced smile. "I know."

What had people done to him? And when? Was it recent

pain? Old pain? I guess all that mattered was that it was the same kind.

My hand twitched with the impulse to reach across the rickety picnic table and touch Flynn's arm. And that scared me so much I clenched my treasonous fingers into a fist and hid them in my lap.

"Not that it's any of my business," Flynn said, "but you're not still . . . ?"

Suicidal?

People rarely wanted to say that word. I wasn't sure I wanted to say it now either. Flynn and I were coming cleaner with each other, but I still didn't know how much I could trust him.

So I shook my head, fast and tight. It was the easiest answer—the answer I'd already promised Vivi—and I didn't want to stop to evaluate it.

But Flynn was watching me too carefully, like he wasn't sure he believed me. "I always wondered," he said, "what really caused the disappearances. I never believed the intruder theory. I wondered if it was something about that house, that property, that got inside people's heads. If disappearing was something they did to themselves."

He still wasn't saying it, not outright, but I understood. He meant suicide.

A cold wave washed through me. "You mean your dad? You think he . . . ?"

Flynn smiled weakly. Humorlessly. More like the world's emptiest defense mechanism than an actual emotional reaction. "It's a theory. By the end, he wasn't acting like himself."

Wasn't acting like himself. My stomach twisted, thinking of Mom. And Vivi was getting strange, too. . . .

"Flynn, did you mean what you said during the séance—that you think what happened before in our house is happening now?"

Flynn frowned. "I don't remember saying that." His fingers grazed his lips, and his face screwed up in disgust like it had at the séance table, after he'd coughed up the cockroach. "Look, I'll admit to *embellishing* elements of that séance. People want spectacle, right? I did tug on Vivi's cloak using that grabber tool I dropped. And, yeah, I was moving the planchette. At first. Then something changed. I blacked out and when I came to, I was hacking up a cockroach."

I hesitated, unsure what to believe. "So that cockroach was real? I found a wooden cockroach toy upstairs and wondered if it could've been a séance prop."

Flynn shook his head. "However that thing wound up in my mouth, it didn't taste or feel like a toy. Not when I swallowed half its legs. They kept moving, all the way down my throat." He squirmed with a shudder.

The reaction looked visceral, not like something a person could fake. And I nodded slowly. "I don't know what's going on," I admitted, "but there *are* things in that house that feel unexplainable. Do you know anything about the masks Ellen used in her séances?"

"Not much. Just that she claimed they were the source of her powers."

"Well, I don't know how they work, but I think the masks did help her perform those tricks." Luckily, I'd come prepared. I pulled mine from my waistband. "For instance, this mask came from a window labeled 'The Beetle.' It lets me move things."

Flynn's eyebrows drifted up his forehead.

"Really heavy things," I clarified. "It . . . Oh, just watch."

I held it to my face, waiting for it to meld against me. Instead, it remained stiff. Hard. Cold, smooth glass. When I released my fingertips, it started to slip.

I squealed in panic, catching it before it could fall.

"What the . . . ?" I frowned down at it.

"Wow," Flynn said dryly, drumming his fingers against the shade-dappled tabletop. "Impressive."

I sighed. "Maybe the masks don't work here, but they do at my place. I can show you if . . ." It was halfway out of my mouth before I realized what I was asking. Suddenly, my cheeks were burning in a way I couldn't blame on the summer sun. "Would you, uh, want to come over?"

He hesitated.

So I kept babbling: "I mean, then I could show you the masks. And maybe you could help me and Vivi figure out what's happening in the house. Finally get some actual answers about the disappearances."

Dammit. The longer I babbled, the less Flynn managed to hide his smirk.

Before my nerves got even more obvious, I made myself ask, "You in or not?"

Flynn was quiet. He looked up at the elm leaves over our heads, the sun shining through them. Then he looked at me. "I'm in."

And the soft way he said it, the way his gaze flushed warmth through my whole body . . . it felt like he was talking about more than séances.

CHAPTER FIFTEEN

FLYNN HAD APPARENTLY SPENT YEARS TELLING people stories about our house, dressing himself as the local expert. Funny how he'd never been inside. Before, he'd only ever ventured as far as our yard. And his first steps into the foyer were hesitant, weighty. He marveled at the interior like he was on the world's most exclusive backstage tour.

As we walked in, I called out, "Mom, Flynn's gonna be over for a little while, okay?" And I braced myself for her to flit out from the kitchen, hopefully not still wearing a nightgown with pit stains.

But no one answered. My chest unclenched. Mom was probably outside in the garden, and Vivi was probably upstairs in her room.

Good thing, too. Flynn seemed overwhelmed as it was. It almost felt like I should leave—give him and the house a private moment together. I settled for keeping my mouth shut and standing aside.

He stared at the cricket-themed living room window and

the housefly-themed dining room window like he was trying to memorize them.

When he saw the kitchen through the Gothic arched doorway, he gasped. "Whoa!" He dashed in to gape at the enormous mosaic of animals feasting in a lush green garden. "This is . . ."

"Creepy as hell?" I autofilled.

"Couldn't put it better myself." Flynn crouched to touch the boar and the stag tearing into a mangled carcass. "I wonder what it means."

"You think it means something?" I asked. "Like, spiritualism-wise?"

"I'd be shocked if it didn't." He surveyed the rest of the kitchen floor, his mouth pressed flat. "The symbolism is . . . It's everywhere." He toed the tiles by the sink with his scuffed sneaker. "Songbirds eating meat? I'd say it has something to do with the corruption of the innocent. Unexpected betrayal? If you ask me, this is somebody's idea of a tongue-in-cheek joke."

I scanned the mosaic uneasily. "If it's a joke," I said, "it's not very funny."

Flynn shrugged. "Maybe we don't know the punch line yet."

Something about that snagged a shivering spot at the base of my spine.

Then my eyes caught on the previously smashed patch. To my surprise, Mom had already refinished it, and my jaw dropped when I saw what she had done with the tiles she'd been so inspired to place.

The newly completed section held baby rabbits, their soft fur smeared with blood. Their strangely sharp teeth tore into a quail, which was flapping in a futile attempt to escape.

It was the same design Vivi and I had found last night in the attic. *Rose's design #14: "The Feast."*

But Mom, as far as I knew, hadn't seen the design. The trunk upstairs had been covered with dust when we found it. No fingerprints. When I'd asked if she remembered the section from when she was a kid, she'd claimed she hadn't. That she was feeling out her new design.

So how had she managed to match the original art so closely?

Dread clutched my body, my tongue too frozen to explain any of this to Flynn.

Luckily, he was busy exploring the kitchen. But then he cried out, and I turned.

He'd tripped and was rubbing the toe of his shoe. "Why is that sticking out of the floor?" he asked, pointing at a raised bump.

The hazard must've been revealed when Mom tore up the vinyl. It couldn't have been so pronounced before. With all the boxes Mom and Vivi and I had been hauling around, one of us would've face-planted by now.

I came closer for a better look, and my breath caught in my throat.

It was a mask.

A red ant mask. With small holes for eyes and formidable mandibles stretching down the cheeks, framing the open chin. It was plated with the stone tiles that made up the rest of the floor—large extra-sculpted versions of them.

I'd noticed before that the window in the kitchen featured ants, but found it strange there were no silver hooks, no indication it had ever contained a three-dimensional piece. Apparently, because the ant mask had been lurking in the floor.

The piece jutted out from an oversized humanoid figure, facing us from the ground. On all fours, the masked creature crouched over the carcass of a bear cub. The cub was dead, tongue lolling onto the grass, blood pooling under its body.

Flynn was backing away, and I didn't blame him. "Another ant?" he asked. "Even your damn murals are infested."

He'd mentioned the ant infestation the other night, too, in the hedge maze. Personally, I still hadn't seen that many.

With a slight bit of grappling, I popped the mask free from the floor, leaving behind flat blue stone, smooth and empty.

"Well," I said slowly, "if you want to check out a mask first-hand, here's your chance." I passed it to Flynn. "I think this one likes you."

Flynn stared at the mask in his hands. He looked more tempted to smash it under his foot. "It *likes* me? What is that supposed to mean?"

Honestly, he was right—that was a weird thing to say. A weirder thing to believe. But it did almost seem like, one way or another, these masks found the people they wanted to wear them.

I shrugged uncomfortably. "Ants have been following you around the property, and you're the one who literally stumbled on that mask," I said. "Aren't you the kind of person who believes in signs?"

I wasn't. Not typically. But this house was making me think twice.

Flynn hesitated. He lifted the mask an inch toward his face. Then he stopped, and shoved it at me instead. "You're the one who lives here. Why don't you try it?"

I took my beetle mask from my waistband and waved it at him. "I already have a mask."

"You can only have one?" he asked. "That's, like, a rule?"

Fair point.

But . . . I looked from the blank eyes of the ant to the blank eyes of the beetle. After I'd worn it into the attic last night, my mask was bluer, its fine network of veins deeper. The edge above the forehead, which had been oval when I found it, had started to soften and dip, mimicking the curve of my widow's peak. The mask had begun to learn the shape of my face.

Unnerving. But there was also something increasingly familiar about it, like a pair of well-worn jeans.

The ant was a blank canvas of hard red tiles. Somehow, wearing it would've felt like trying on someone else's underwear.

I shook my head at Flynn. "If you don't want the ant mask, put it back."

I was about to pass it back to him when Mom, fresh from the garden, walked in through the back doors. "Hey, sweetie! I—" She saw Flynn. "Oh! Who's this?"

"Mom! Hi!" I staggered toward the island, hiding both masks behind my back.

Flynn raised his eyebrows at my flailing espionage. But he didn't say anything.

Flustered, I managed the barest of introductions: "Mom, Flynn. Flynn, Mom."

"Well, hi, Flynn. You can call me Sharon." Mom darted a curious eye my way, registering what had to be my extremely red face, my awkward huddle against the island. And then a knowing smile flitted across her lips.

She'd decided my jitters were because of Flynn.

That . . . was better, actually.

"I was gonna show Flynn around the house," I said. "You know, hang out for a bit. If you maybe had somewhere *else* to be . . ."

"Oh, sure, sweetie." Mom grinned, *way* too excited about me making social contact with someone my age. "I was about to pick up some groceries."

After watching her ignore my previous pleas for fresh groceries,

I doubted that was her original plan, but I was also relieved it was the excuse she came up with. Our fridge was down to a half-empty pack of shredded cheddar, some shriveling apricots, and soggy chicken leftovers.

"I'll just head on out now," she said.

"You're not gonna change first?" I asked.

At least she wasn't wearing a nightgown, but her gardening clothes weren't much of an improvement. Her faded jeans were streaked with dirt, a tear in one of the knees. On top, she wore a dull ivory shirt—long-sleeved, even in the heat. Her curls were so greasy they hung limp, practically straight, from the ponytail gathered at the bottom of her skull.

Regardless, she looked at me like I was the one out of line. "I'm sure this will be fine." She tightened her ponytail self-consciously. And there it was on her forearm, visible on her sleeve: a dark slashy stain.

Blood.

I flinched.

Had the wound I'd seen last night reopened? Was this a *new* wound? I should've paid more attention to which arm I'd seen that gash on.

When Mom caught me looking, she beelined out of the room. "Great to meet you, Flynn. Have a nice time, you two."

I didn't breathe again until the front door had opened and shut, and the keys had turned in the lock.

Flynn's stare burned into me. "Is . . . everything okay?"

He'd probably seen it, too—the blood on her sleeve. And there was no missing the blue tinge of her lips, stained by rose tea.

When I'd been unwell, I'd wondered if Mom was ashamed of me. To be seen with all my pain.

I did feel shame now, but not directed at her. At myself. Her suffering was obvious enough that anyone could see it, and I still didn't know how to help her.

"You know what you said about your dad?" I asked quietly. "That he stopped acting like himself?"

Flynn nodded, troubled. "But that took months. You all haven't even been here a week."

"That's part of what scares me," I admitted. "Can I show you something?"

He followed me to the corner Mom had finished. And frowned as I explained about the designs we'd found in the attic—how Mom had completed the floor without seeing them.

"You said the drawing was labeled 'Rose's design,'" Flynn said. "You know who Rose is?" He asked it like he already knew the answer.

And I hoped he did. "All I know is that the window in Mom's room is labeled 'Rose,' and there's a photo in the attic of Ellen wearing that mask and 'communing' with her," I told him. "I wasn't sure if that meant Rose was supposedly a spirit?"

"Right. Rose is a spirit," Flynn confirmed. "The first spirit Ellen summoned to House of Masks—a little girl who died in the earthquake of 1886."

A spirit. A little girl . . .

I blinked, trying to process that. "So according to Ellen, Rose—a ghost—designed the mosaic? And the windows, too?" Among the drawings from the chest, I'd seen the Rite of the Stars window attributed to Rose.

Flynn nodded. "That sounds like something Ellen would say. She also said Rose was the one who made all the blue roses grow."

The blue roses that swamped our entire property.

I could see why Ellen would want her guests to believe there was evidence of a spirit surrounding them. But as far-fetched as it was, the idea squeezed my chest with claustrophobia.

"So with no explanation, your mom happens to know Rose's original design. . . ." Flynn let out a weak scoff. "If I didn't know better, I'd say your mom has been communing with a dead girl."

He probably meant it as a joke. Even though Flynn believed in spirits, he had to know my mom was no medium. I wanted to laugh—but the sound shriveled in my throat.

Those baby rabbits smeared in blood stared at me from the floor with empty blue eyes. Across the room, the kitchen sink brimmed with dirty silver teacups and a cutting board, stained blue by chopped rose petals.

I doubted dead girls were involved, but Mom had been obsessed with those blue roses since we'd arrived.

No. Since *before* we'd arrived.

In fact, she'd told me they were somehow what convinced her to move us here.

And she'd chosen the room with the Rose window. When she'd unboarded it, Vivi and I had caught her lost in a haze, fondly reaching for the vine-tangled figure. Almost like she was reaching for an old friend.

The thought prickled the hairs on my neck.

"What I'm hearing is, we should try another séance," Vivi said from behind us.

I clutched my chest, startled, as Flynn and I whipped around to see her in the kitchen doorway.

This was the second time she'd snuck up on us, eavesdropping. And I was *not* loving the new habit.

"Vivi! What the hell? How long have you been there?" I demanded.

She ignored me, a sly smile creeping across her face as she eyed the two of us standing together. "By the way, fancy seeing *you* here, Flynn." She said it in an unbearable-little-sister voice. With obvious K-I-S-S-I-N-G vibes.

I glared at her, dying inside. And did *not* look at Flynn to see his reaction.

"Fancy seeing *you* here, you little gremlin," I said dryly. "What did you say about a séance?"

She rolled her eyes. "I heard what you two said about the mosaic and Mom and Rose," she said, then turned to Flynn. "You already proved you can talk to spirits. So if we want answers, shouldn't we try talking to Rose? Isn't that the next logical step?"

Logical might have been overstating things, but I didn't know *what* to do anymore. "Well, you *are* related to Ellen," I said to Flynn, thinking aloud. "And in the photo of her wearing the rose mask, her eyes glowed like yours did during the last séance." I couldn't believe I was entertaining this madness, but . . . "If you put on the rose mask and we tried a séance, what do you think would happen?"

Flynn stiffened. "I—I don't know. But last time, I wound up coughing up a cockroach."

Valid. Extremely valid concern.

Still.

"Mom's out of the house. I don't know if we'll get a better chance to look at the rose mask," I said. "It might be now or never."

Flynn raked a restless hand through his hair and glanced toward the front of the house—toward the exit—longingly.

"Please," Vivi begged. "Come on, what's the worst that can happen?"

"I wish you hadn't said that," Flynn grumbled. But he sighed, and I wondered if he was thinking about his own dad. I knew he wanted answers as much as I did.

"Fine," he said. "We can try. Just don't expect much."

Then again, that's what he'd said before the first séance, too.

The three of us crept into Mom's room. Yesterday, I'd snuck in and out as quickly as I could. This time, we'd come to linger. And it was even more of a betrayal now that I'd brought company with me. Reinforcements.

I made myself scan the room fully, wincing at Mom's nightstand, which was a tangle of roses in vases and of empty blue-stained teacups. The roses in the wallpaper might as well have been real—the house's potpourri-ish perfume hung thick as smog. It lodged in my nostrils. Throbbed behind my forehead like a migraine.

I felt like an ant targeted by a magnifying glass—crisping and curling under some invisible, merciless scrutiny.

Above Mom's bed, the Rose window sat waiting, the white mask watching.

The mask looked as cold as ever, with the hard lines of its arched brows and sharp nose, crowned with twisted metal and a frosty lace veil.

Flynn eyed it warily. "You want me . . . to put that on?"

"Seems like it worked for Ellen," Vivi said.

"Right." Flynn chewed his lip and lifted the mask off the hooks that held it onto the window. Like the beetle and the ant masks, it popped out at the slightest touch, like it was waiting to break free. "It's just . . ." He paused, glancing at the image. The vine-wrapped figure poised high and mighty on her throne.

"What's wrong?" I asked.

"Well, Ellen always said Rose was a little girl," Flynn said. "But then the way Rose is represented in this mask and the window doesn't make sense."

Oh.

He was right—nothing about the face or body looked like a little girl's. The porcelain mask was a little dollish, sure, but it was too long, too oval to represent a child.

"Well, Rose is the one who designed the window, right?" Vivi pointed out. "Maybe it's what she hoped she would've looked like someday. If she'd had the chance to grow up."

A sad thought. Vivi had spent too much time thinking about death, and I frowned, knowing it was my fault.

"Could be," Flynn murmured. He glanced around the strange room, adrift. "You all should know, by the way, I've never tried a séance without my gear. I guess we'll see what happens."

At our last séance, he'd taken care to set the scene, with all his flickering candles and props. I knew well enough from theater that settings mattered. "Is there anything we can do?" I asked. "To make it more . . . séance-worthy?"

We were the ones who'd insisted on this séance here and now. The least we could do was make Flynn as comfortable as possible.

He flicked me a small smile, like he appreciated the effort. "Well, if nothing else, let's turn off the lights," he said. "Spirits like the dark. We should be doing this at night, not on a sunny afternoon, but that'd be a start."

Vivi flipped Mom's lamps off. Without them, the room was surprisingly dark. The only window was the stained-glass rose mural above Mom's bed, and it was a choked patchwork of rich blues and greens. A few sunbeams slipped through, dust motes dancing in their streaky blue haze.

In the dim light, the illusion that we were at the heart of the hedge maze was too convincing for comfort. The roses seemed to pop out from the wallpaper, to hug us in all the more tightly.

A wasp whizzed past my nose, past Flynn, and landed on a fake blue rose behind him, its thorax pulsing.

I cringed and hugged my arms. "Wasps? We have wasps inside the house now?"

"Oh, yeah." Vivi waved that off like it wasn't new information. "There are wasps and centipedes and praying mantises and—"

She saw my horror and stopped.

The three of us sat, forming a small circle on the creaky hardwood by the foot of Mom's bed. Vivi had brought a stack of scrap paper and a pen from her room. She set it down in front of Flynn. "In the picture, Ellen had paper with her," she told him. "She was wearing the mask and drawing."

"Ah." He nodded knowingly. "Automatic writing, a method even older than spirit boards. You call the spirit into your body and let it write through you."

"You've done it a lot?" Vivi asked.

"Well, no. I haven't done it at all," Flynn admitted. "But I know how to play Pictionary, so how hard can it be?" He laid the pen and paper in front of his crossed legs and picked up the rose mask. "Here goes."

He lifted it to his face fast, the way Vivi used to cannonball into a cold pool.

And then he pressed it on.

But it was . . .

Something was wrong.

The mask didn't conform to his face. It was slipping away from his forehead, his cheeks, his chin. "Didn't you say these things are supposed to stay on?" Flynn asked.

"Maybe press it harder," Vivi suggested.

Flynn tried. But the best he could do was balance its attached crown on his head. The mask itself hung loose—his eyes blinking through its gaping sockets.

But, then, this wasn't the mask that this property had led Flynn to. It had led him to the ant mask in the kitchen. The one he'd rejected.

I think this one likes you, I'd told him. For some inexplicable reason, I believed that.

Now, for an equally inexplicable reason, I sensed that the rose mask *didn't* like Flynn. Not at all.

This wasn't going to work, was it? Even if it had been the longest shot, I was desperate enough to feel a shred of disappointment.

But Flynn seemed relieved, almost traitorously relieved, his shoulders loosening, his chest rising and falling more freely. I could only blame him so much for not wanting to, say, cough up another cockroach—but I had hoped he was going to give this his all.

"All right, then," he said. "Let's call Rose."

The three of us held hands. And Flynn began the chant: "Rose, wandering and restless spirit, we welcome you."

We echoed him, repeating the same incantation he'd led us through the last time. Then all of us stilled, our touching hands tense, breaths barely audible.

The faintest sound touched my ears: a whispering scratch.

A rustle.

Like I'd heard when I snuck into this room yesterday.

It didn't come from the ceiling above us. It came from behind me. Then on one side, then another.

It came from the walls.

My heart started thudding a little too fast.

Bugs. Just bugs, I told myself.

Even though it sounded like bigger pests. Something under the wallpaper, behind the plaster.

Vivi glanced uneasily at the shadowy room around us. "Is . . . Is she here?" she whispered.

"Let's find out." Flynn poised his pen over a blank sheet of paper. "What do you want to ask her?"

I cleared my throat, even more self-conscious than I had been the other night at the séance table. This time, I'd dared to hope—even if it was the smallest do-or-die part of me—that this would work. But I'd made Flynn go this far. I had to see it through. Entertain the chance that spirits were real, that *she* was real.

"Right," I said. "Uh, hi, Rose. If you're here . . ." I was aiming for light and friendly, a tone that might coax out a shy little girl. Flynn hadn't mentioned how old Rose had been when she died. "We were wondering if . . . We wanted to ask . . ."

Vivi was fed up with my floundering. "Hi, Rose. First of all, we're really sorry you're dead. Second, do you know what the deal is with this house? Why do people keep disappearing?"

"I told you they don't like to talk about that," Flynn grumbled. He sighed before closing his eyes and touching his pen to the paper. "Rose, will you please answer us?" he asked. "Why are people disappearing?"

Again, the three of us paused.

Again, the rustle scratched at my ears.

A little louder.

And not from one wall at once. From every wall.

It was the worst sound—almost like someone was running their fingers along the wallpaper, only from the opposite side.

I scanned the room, but nothing was moving. The shadows hung still. The tangled roses watched our every move.

My skin prickled, like bug legs were crawling over the back of my neck.

"We should try an easier question. You wanna maybe ask her favorite color or something?" Flynn asked. "Because I don't think—"

"Uh. Flynn," Vivi said with sudden urgency. She was peering at his face, and then I realized why.

Tendrils of smoke leaked from under the rose mask, near the top of Flynn's forehead. Winding up through the twisted metal crown and fogging into the air.

"Flynn, the rose mask, it's . . ." I choked on the strangeness of the words and pointed to my forehead.

"Hmm?" Flynn touched near his hairline. "What about it? It feels a little warmer, but—"

The mask, with a lurch, latched on to his face. It didn't smooth over his features, meld and soften with them—it touched him as little as possible. The top edge gripped the center of his forehead, off-kilter, the bottom half dangling.

The eyeholes of the rose mask screened over: blue.

A hard sharp glow.

And all around us, the rustling exploded into ripping and tearing.

In one blooming burst, blue roses and vines erupted from the wallpaper. Full and fat and impossibly alive, stinking of rosy rot.

Vivi and I shrieked, but I was too afraid to move. To run. Thorny vines slithered over the dark walls, over each other, like snakes. And the rose mask, with those bright-blue pools of light for eyes, was fixed on me and Vivi.

There was nothing fake about this séance.

It felt like I'd tumbled headfirst into a nightmare. Some

impossible alternate reality. But there was no waking up. No turning back.

"R-Rose?" Vivi gasped.

The mask turned to her. With those empty blue eyes. Whatever Vivi saw in them, her jaw dropped slack.

And then, slowly, the mask turned to me.

My heart stuttered. Whoever was looking at me, my gut knew with deepest, most dreadful certainty—it wasn't Flynn. It was nothing like looking into the eyes of a little girl either.

When I'd tried to kill myself, when I'd started to die, long fingers of cold reached up from inside my gut, toward my heart, and started squeezing the breath from me.

If that feeling had a face, this was it.

It was like looking up into the vast night sky—and finding *all* of it staring back at you.

Just you.

And you were nothing. Dust.

I was dizzy with dread. And Flynn's body was so still I wasn't sure he was breathing. The rose mask, just the tiny piece grafted to his forehead, had clutched the rest of him to a halt.

Beside me, Vivi grabbed my arm, pressing close—her heart fluttering in time with my own racing pulse.

"Rose?" I asked. Her name made her feel more knowable. Smaller than her swallowing blue-sky eyes. "Is that you?"

Flynn's head lurched up. Lurched down.

A nod, you could call it. If you were being generous.

A spirit. I was talking to a spirit.

I nodded back to show her, in the smallest way, that we were the same—we could communicate. I could understand her, she could understand me.

"You heard us?" I asked. "You're going to tell us why—?"

In a flash, Flynn's arm stabbed down, dragging the pen through paper like a knife through flesh. It tore all the way through, but he didn't seem to notice, not past the blue screen over his eyes.

"Wait!" I started to reach out, to grab his arm.

But I couldn't bring myself to touch him, not if Rose was the one moving him.

I drew back, tucking Vivi behind my shoulder.

With fierce urgency, Flynn's body kept carving:

13

That was all. The number thirteen.

He threw the torn paper aside and grabbed a fresh sheet. Again, his pen ripped through with determined violence, chewing up everything in its path.

13

He chucked that paper aside, too, shredded as broken butterfly wings. Grabbed another. And another. And carved and carved and carved. Each time larger and deeper and faster:

13

13

13

He'd splintered past the finish of the floor, and tore into the raw wood underneath. The pen cracked into fragments, its blue ink spilling and seeping between his fingers.

He ran out of paper. He jammed the shards of his pen straight into the floorboards. That open wound of wood.

13

1—

"Stop!" I didn't grab for Flynn's arm. I grabbed the mask. "Flynn!" With a ferocious tug, I ripped it away.

The glow vanished from his eyes, as if I'd ripped that away with the mask.

And the roses blooming from the walls withered—curling and twisting, and melting into nothing at all.

I blinked at the impossible sight, but the roses and vines were gone as suddenly as they'd appeared. The wallpaper was whole and still. No rips, no tears.

Flynn was gasping, like someone had shoved and held him underwater. He clutched his heaving chest, smearing blue ink all over his dad's old Nirvana shirt.

The rose mask was warm in my hand, the back where it had touched his forehead sticky. It had snapped from this animated creature, with eyes of its own, back to a piece of porcelain decorated with blue velvet.

I rushed the mask back to the window and secured it in place. I didn't want to touch it anymore. I didn't want to look at it. I didn't want *it* to look at *us*. But I still felt the weight of eyes coming from its direction.

Meanwhile, the beetle mask remained tucked in the back of my waistband, softly hugging my spine.

My mask.

What the hell was I supposed to make of that after the rose mask had jolted to life and latched on to Flynn's face? Was there a connection between that mask and Rose's spirit? If so, what did that mean for my beetle mask? Was it connected to a spirit, too . . . ?

I shivered against the touch of my mask. But that eerie puzzle would have to wait.

"What just happened?" Flynn's raspy voice came out hoarser than ever, ragged, like he'd forgotten how to use it.

The floor was a ruined mess of ink and carved lines. Overlapping 13s.

And he startled like he was seeing it for the first time. He jumped to his feet, backing up. Away from the slashy mess he'd made of the floor. Away from us. "Did I do that?"

"Well, Rose did," Vivi said. "Right?"

Flynn's lips were parted, like he was trying to summon up some answer—any answer. Their usual pale pink was off, tinged blue. I hated that I knew what color Flynn's lips were supposed to be. But I did. And this color was wrong. His teeth were chattering.

"I don't know," he finally said. "I was here, and then I wasn't. I wasn't *anywhere*. I . . ."

He looked down at his shirt, realizing what he'd done. "Oh shit." The blue ink was smeared through the yellow-printed smiley face, its Xed-out eyes.

I stepped in closer, hoping to reassure him. Hoping he might reassure us. This was his world, after all. I'd been wrong, and he'd been right. Against all odds—all reason—spirits weren't the stuff of fantasy. I'd seen and felt and lived proof that at least one was inside my house. And Flynn was the only one of us who might have any idea what to do about that.

"Did you black out, the way you did at the last séance?" I asked. "I don't get why these two were so intense. You've been talking to spirits on the property for years, right? This isn't what normally happens?"

"No! This isn't what 'normally' happens." Flynn laughed, sharp and choppy and broken. "*Nothing* is what normally happens, because spirits aren't . . . ! They're not even . . ."

Vivi and I exchanged an uneasy glance.

"They're not even what?" I demanded.

Flynn shook his head. "I hope you got the answers you needed. Because I . . ." He glanced at the doorway. Ran a hand through his hair, mussing it ten different ways. "Look, I can't help you again."

Halfway to the door, he paused. With one last glance at me, he said, "I'm sorry. I can't do this. I really can't."

CHAPTER SIXTEEN

I STARED AT THE EMPTY DOORWAY Flynn left behind. The stench of roses and rot hung in the air, and my legs were trembling with residual shock.

But I couldn't let Flynn leave. Not like that.

"Wait!" I charged after him, rushing down through the house and out the front door to catch him on the rickety white porch.

"Flynn!" It burst out of me. "I . . ."

He turned back toward me, dazed and corpse-pale. In spite of the heat and the sweat that had dotted his hairline almost instantly, he rubbed his arms like frost had bitten through to the deepest layer of his skin.

"I don't understand," I admitted. "I'm scared, too, okay? But aren't you supposed to know what to do in these situations? You talk to spirits all the time."

"No. No! You don't get it. I . . ." Flynn leaned back against our spindly banister, rubbing the center of his forehead, the pink spot where the rose mask had bonded to his skin. "Libby, I *pretend* to talk to spirits. I've made an entire show out of *pretending* to talk to spirits."

My stomach dropped.

What he'd started to say inside.

Spirits aren't even real. That was the full sentence, wasn't it?

He'd already admitted to "embellishing" aspects of his séances, sure, but upstairs, half an hour ago, he'd been spouting shit like "Spirits like the dark." And now he was telling me he didn't even believe in them?

"You've *never* believed in spirits?" I asked, crossing my arms over my tightening chest. "But during the first séance you did for us . . ."

"I told you, I've been doing this for *years,* and nothing like that *ever* happened before," Flynn replied. "I wanted to believe I had, I don't know, some kind of fit, and a cockroach flew in my mouth, but now I don't know, I don't know . . ." He kept repeating "I don't know" like a mantra. In a trembling voice, one on the edge of breaking.

But I was replaying our past interactions, seething hotter and hotter. "So this whole time, you've been lying to me? What was the plan when you insisted that you could get me info with your séances? To string me along with useless tricks while you kept earning money on the side?"

Flynn frowned, but he had the guts to keep facing me, not to turn his back. "At first, I planned to do more research. To answer questions I knew the answers to. And if I could scare you and tip your family toward leaving, I genuinely thought that might be best for everyone."

I tried to stand tall, even as the towering doorway dwarfed me. "And that was your plan today, even after I thought we were finally being real with each other?"

"I didn't . . . It's not like I had some detailed master plan. But you and Vivi asked me to do the Rose séance, and you were worried for your mom, and . . . For what it's worth, I wasn't going to try to scare you. I was going to say Rose wasn't answering." His shoulders caved. He knew this was wrong. "I didn't know how to tell you the truth. So I played along. That's what I do. I'm a fraud."

I didn't want to look at him anymore, so I stared past our twisted metal fence, at the empty street instead. At the July heat waves so spiteful they melted the road into liquid shimmers.

At last, Flynn gave up on me responding. "I really am sorry," he said. "And I'm never going to do this again—to anyone. No more séances."

I didn't have it in me to forgive him. Not here and now. He'd lied and lied. He'd never expected the séances to work. But he *had* helped us, even if accidentally. And in the process, he'd endured the misery of real spirits hijacking his body.

I sighed. The worst of my fury had steamed through me, leaving me hollow.

What did fights like these really matter, compared to what I now knew was waiting inside my house?

"Well," I muttered, "it's a little late for 'no more séances,' isn't it?"

Flynn hesitated, newly nervous at my tone. "What do you mean?"

I stepped beside him at the banister and slowly faced the yard. And Flynn turned, too, to get a better read on me. Both our backs were to the house, but I could still feel it—looming behind us like a mountainous shadow.

"I can't believe I'm saying this, but after seeing Rose, I think spirits *are* real," I said softly. "I think our house is actually haunted. And I think you are an actual medium."

"No. Not possible." On the verge of a core meltdown, Flynn squeezed his eyes shut. "I'm telling you, spirits *can't* be real."

I didn't understand how he could keep saying that after what happened with Rose.

But, then, he hadn't truly *seen* it, had he? During both séances, he'd blacked out. He'd seen the aftermaths—the cockroach, the floor carved with 13s. But he hadn't looked into those endless blue eyes. He hadn't watched the roses burst through the wallpaper and then vanish just as fast.

He needed to see something impossible, with his own eyes.

"Fine. I can't give you evidence of *spirits*—not the way you've done for me and Vivi—but." I marched down the steps to the flower beds lining the porch. Tried not to inhale the rosy stench as I grabbed a fist-sized rock from the border and carried it back to Flynn.

I wasn't positive this would work. I still wasn't sure how strong the beetle mask made me, and I was even more skittish to wear it after the rose mask had spasmed to life. But I *needed* Flynn to understand what strangeness lived on this property.

"How's this for paranormal?" I asked. I smoothed on my mask—held up the stone—and crushed it in my hand.

I was hoping it would crack. I figured that'd be enough to prove my point.

Instead, the whole stone crumbled in my fist. In a puff of powder, the rock was reduced to rubble.

"What the hell?" Flynn stepped toward me, reaching for my hand, the disintegrated remains of the rock—like a kid at a magic show.

"There," I said. I ripped my beetle mask off and shoved it back in my waistband. "Now *you've* seen something impossible, too."

Flynn was stunned, but apparently he was never too stunned to scowl.

"So tell me," I said. "Why can't spirits be real?"

Flynn paused, like he was fighting whether or not to tell me the truth, even now. But then, in the quietest voice, he admitted, "Libby, my dad believed in spirits."

He must've seen me snap to attention, because his eyes shot down to the porch boards. Away from mine. "Like I told you," he said, "my dad started doing séances here for the money, but then . . . he got obsessed with this place. With Ellen. He said her ghost was here and she spoke to him. He used to tell me all kinds of stuff, but Mom said not to listen." He shook his head. "He didn't know what was real. And I promised Mom, I promised myself, I would never . . . I can't be like him."

"Then why were you messing around with this house in the first place?" I asked. I knew I was digging into a freshly reopened wound, but I was done with Flynn's lies, even the ones he was telling himself. "I know your family needs the money. But there are other ways. It's gotta be more than that, doesn't it? Some part of you that—"

"Fine! Yes. Fine." Flynn held up a hand to stop the prodding. "When I first took over his séances, it wasn't just money. I figured if Dad was right about spirits, if he had died here . . . I thought maybe he'd answer me."

My heart sank. "But he never did?"

Flynn shook his head. He squeezed his jaw tight, fighting a pained tremble, and I understood—that was why he didn't want to believe in spirits.

If spirits were real, his dad could have answered him but chose not to.

"Well, maybe things are different now," I said. "Maybe you're a stronger medium. If you called him again, he might answer."

"No!" That burst from Flynn, hard and sharp, before he caught himself. "No," he said more quietly.

I understood. He didn't want to know. Didn't want to risk repeating his biggest heartbreak.

"Thanks, though," Flynn said, glancing at me with softening eyes. "Anyway, how did this happen? I dick you over, and you're trying to make me feel better? You're a good person, Libby. Maybe too good."

He sighed, jammed his hands in his pockets, and strode down the porch steps. "I'm sorry I lied to you."

He said it like a goodbye.

"Hey!" I ran down the steps after him. "You don't get to walk away like that. You're gonna leave my family here, with no real answers?"

Flynn turned back, eyebrows shooting up. "I just admitted I don't have real answers!"

"But you can help us get them."

He laughed, one sad, sharp bark. "I know you think I'm a medium, but for all we know, what happened at these last two séances had more to do with the spirits themselves. Or with you and Vivi being there. Look, I've done this enough times to know I'm not special. Truth be told, you're better off without me."

You're better off without me.

The exact calculation my suicidal brain had made about me, on Mom and Vivi's behalf.

He said it so flatly, so plainly, that I knew: He wasn't saying this to make a quick getaway—or because he was fishing for me to argue. This really was what he believed about himself.

My throat clenched. I didn't know if Flynn was suicidal, but, without a doubt, he had one of those nasty voices inside his own head, too—the same kind that had driven me headfirst into depression.

And voices like that didn't deserve to win.

"You're wrong," I said. "You screwed up here. You did. I haven't forgiven you yet. But I honestly believe that you are special. Not only because of the medium thing. Because you're the weirdest person I've ever met. And that might not sound like a compliment, but—"

"No, I know that's a compliment," Flynn said softly, with a lopsided smile.

"Look, you made some shitty choices," I said. "But instead of walking away, I'd rather you made up for it."

We stood on the path, staring at each other, my heart pounding. Flynn and the yellow print of his shirt bruised with blue ink.

"How do I make up for it?" he asked. "What do you want?"

"I want . . ." I swallowed hard. There were a lot of ways to answer that question, especially when Flynn was the one asking. Of all the possibilities, I couldn't believe I had to say: "I want another séance. With Ellen, this time."

Clearly not what Flynn had been hoping for. Under his freckles, his face paled. "A séance with Ellen?"

"Your dad said she was here, right? That he talked to her? Maybe she knows what happened to him. To everyone. Maybe she knows how to stop it from happening again."

Flynn huffed indecisively, rubbing his neck. He almost looked wistful, like he wished he could give me what I wanted. But he shook his head. "Libby, I told you I was only pretending to be a medium—"

"Then keep pretending! Whatever we're doing is working, right? Enough to call the spirits," I pointed out. "One last séance. Try calling Ellen for us. And that's it, okay? Whatever happens, I'll consider us even."

Flynn seemed doubtful. "If that's really what you want," he said finally.

"It is—thank you!" I was so relieved I grabbed his arm and hugged it.

Then we both got quiet.

And he looked down at my hand, still clutching his arm.

I hadn't even realized.

I jumped back, clasping my hands behind my back. "Sorry. I—"

"No, I don't mind." Either that was a sunburn I hadn't noticed, or the tips of his ears had gone red. "I mean, whatever." He cleared his throat. "But I outright told you I'm a fraud, so don't blame me if this séance doesn't work."

"I won't." I nodded. "In that case, should we . . ." Oh God, my mouth had started this one without my brain's permission. I tried to keep it chill. "Should we trade numbers? For logistics?"

Flynn had been gradually inching toward the fence, toward the nonhaunted sidewalk waiting on the other side. My proposition, however, put him on pause.

I made myself meet his sharp green eyes.

He was smiling. His usual version—that tilt to the corner of his lip.

"Well. If you think it's a good idea," he said, making no effort to bury his smirk. "For logistics."

"I figured it might be easier than showing up uninvited to

each other's houses." I shrugged, raising my chin, and pulled myself back together. "But if you'd rather—"

"No. Nope. Numbers are good." Flynn passed me his phone. "Plug yours in."

I did and passed it back.

"I'll text you," he said. "And I guess I better not wait too long, or you'll show up literally *inside* my house again." But his tone was light, and even as he turned away, I could hear the smile in his voice.

"Hey, I'm not the creeper here, creeper," I reminded him.

"Yeah, yeah." He tossed a wave back to me over his shoulder. "I'll text you," he said again.

I really liked it, that he said it twice.

He did text me.

We set up our next séance for the following night—late. After Mom was sleeping. And Vivi and I spent the rest of the day stewing in the aftermath of what Rose had done.

We tried to guess what she meant with those violent 13s. Maybe it was her age when she'd died. Some reference to the number of masks?

While Mom was still out getting groceries, we cleaned her room the best we could. We gathered the shredded paper and wiped up the ink, but there was no buffing such deep scratches out of the floor. In the end, we had to settle for dragging her bedroom rug a couple feet over to cover the mess.

And we hoped she wouldn't notice.

Meanwhile, the masks themselves remained a troubling mystery. Since my desperate rock-crushing demonstration for Flynn,

I kept mine slotted in my window, and begged Vivi to do the same with hers. We left the ant mask in the kitchen floor. Without understanding exactly what had happened with the rose mask, caution seemed warranted.

Vivi didn't see things the way I did, but I promised her we'd ask Ellen. And she agreed to leave her butterfly mask alone, at least temporarily.

I hoped she really did. In my room, I found myself hyperaware of the beetle mask's presence. What felt like eyes drilling into me.

The night of the séance, we'd planned to meet at the table in the yard, but nature conspired against us. A hot smog of a thunderstorm. Rumbling booms growling from a distance. The storm never came close enough for us to spot the lightning. But rain soaked the white stone of the séance table and all thirteen chairs.

We would have to meet inside. Ellen's old parlor—the one where that photo of her was taken—seemed fitting. It was on the main floor, tucked behind the living room, on the opposite side of the house from Mom's bedroom upstairs. So hopefully, she would sleep through any spirit summoning. The odds were in our favor. She was increasingly in a world of her own.

At one in the morning, I unlocked the kitchen door for a very soggy Flynn and his dripping duffel bag of séance gear. "Why didn't you bring an umbrella?" I asked as a puddle pooled under him.

"I thought the hoodie would be enough." Flynn pulled back his soaked hood, raking his sopping bangs from his forehead. "Spoiler alert—it was not."

He stripped off his sweatshirt, and I tried not to stare. The rain had soaked through to his pale-gray shirt underneath, plastering it across his chest.

"Could I, uh, have a towel?" Flynn asked.

"Right. Towel! Yes."

My chest lit on fire. What was *wrong* with me? I'd sworn off crushes. At least until my moods were under control. It was too much of a potential trigger. For highs and lows.

And what were the odds Flynn genuinely liked me? That I wasn't a means to an easy ego boost? My gut twisted with a flashback to the party last spring. To Mason. Even if I'd suspected he was more into Gemma than me, he had strung me along during *Romeo and Juliet* rehearsals, feeding me enough hope to keep me on the hook.

So, yeah, maybe there was a spark with Flynn—but I should know better than to trust it.

I got him a towel.

Once he'd dried off and stopped his teeth from chattering, we slipped into the parlor, where Vivi was waiting.

It was a small room, complete with furnishings fusty enough to be original. A gramophone sat in the back corner, its brassy trumpet dull with age. A circular table, decked in an ornate tasseled tablecloth, stood at the center, surrounded by brocade armchairs.

The stained-glass window was an ode to soft gray moths, a faceless figure leaning too close to a celestial golden light. Like the other windows, there was a flat sheet of blue glass where the face should be, and tiny hooks around its edges.

Another long-gone mask.

We took our seats beside Vivi at the table. The chair's springs screamed under me, and the cushion gasped out a puff of dust.

I wished I could spit out the taste of this place.

From his bag, Flynn unpacked long white candles and a spirit board. We didn't have access to Ellen's original crystal ball, unfortunately, since it was built into the séance table outside. But, then, we hadn't needed one to summon Rose's spirit.

We lit the candles and turned off the lights. And Flynn unpacked one more thing from his bag—a long bolt of white mesh. He draped it over his head, blurring his features behind the makeshift veil.

Between the dim candlelight and the paleness of his skin and shirt, he looked half-dead. A ghost already sitting at the table between me and Vivi.

She beat me to the question: "What are you doing?" she whispered.

Mom was all the way upstairs and across the house, but it always felt—always, always, always—like something in these walls was listening.

Flynn must've felt it, too, because his voice was just as low when he answered. "Some spiritualists used to wear veils. Traditionally, black, to help them blend into dark rooms and to hide any illusions they wanted to pull off, like 'coughing up' fake ectoplasm. But Ellen used a white veil—the one attached to that rose mask. You know how she insisted on holding séances outdoors, to prove she and Joseph weren't faking anything with trick cabinets? The white would've made her *more* visible, making it harder for her to sneak in any sleight of hand. In theory," he said, "more trustworthy."

"Uh-huh," Vivi said. "And *you're* wearing it because . . . ?"

He shrugged sheepishly. "If you really want to summon Ellen—which, by the way, I don't know is possible—then I figured it wouldn't hurt to butter her up. Give a nod to her own séance methods."

Even if Flynn was clearly hoping this didn't work after the

trauma he'd endured with the rose mask, I appreciated that he was giving it his best shot.

The three of us held hands, or rather, rested palms on palms. And I was too aware, yet again, of Flynn's skin touching mine. No wonder he was always in long sleeves. He really did run cooler than most people. The more we touched, the more I noticed.

Flynn began, "We call on the spirit of Ellen Clery to bless us with her presence."

Vivi and I whispered it back.

Words like this felt heavy after what had happened last time, with Rose.

I thought again of her endless blue eyes. Did death really change a person that much? Into something so inhuman?

"If you are here, Ellen Clery, please give us a sign," Flynn said.

Vivi and I repeated that, too.

In the shadowy corner, over Vivi's shoulder, something moved.

The gramophone.

With a scraping wheeze, its handle began to crank—in slow, insistent circles.

The needle bent its neck down onto the old record waiting on the turntable.

At the hissing static, a slew of nesting moths flapped free from the trumpet's mouth, to take refuge in the curtains.

And an old song, tinny and distant, crackled through the room:

Say au revoir, but not goodbye,
For parting brings a bitter sigh;
The past is gone, tho' mem'ry lives,
One clinging thought, the future gives . . .

At the center of the table, the candles flared brighter.

"It's happening!" Vivi squealed. "She's here!"

Flynn's hand squeezed mine. But he stayed where he was, stiff in his chair, as a cloudy mist trickled up from under the table.

I knew he wasn't faking séances anymore, but I still caught myself scouring for dry ice. Some ordinary explanation.

There was nothing ordinary about this.

The thin icy mist curled around the three of us, and I stopped breathing, afraid I'd suck it in. It skimmed my neck, trickling down my bare arms, pushing up goose bumps.

Like it was taking a good hard look at us.

Then, slowly, it gathered around Flynn, thickening into a cloud.

"Ellen Clery?" he choked out. The room was suddenly so cold that his breath brushed visibly against his veil.

The candles flickered.

As if in answer.

He flinched but steeled his jaw and spoke the last line: "Accept this body as your vessel."

I hated to repeat that. But Vivi and I closed out the call-and-response invocation: "Accept this body as your vessel."

The fog seeped into Flynn's skin.

The record scratched into silence. And the candles snuffed out.

The room plunged into darkness.

Beside me, faint noises stirred in Flynn's throat. A ragged breath. A low moan.

"Flynn?" I whispered.

His hand went limp.

"Flynn!" I squeezed.

But he didn't squeeze back.

"Vivi! The lighter!" I broke contact with her to grab at the mockingly empty velvet tablecloth, groping to find it. "Get the lighter!"

We bumped frantic fingers as she groped, too. "I don't see it! Where did it—"

A round floating light, ghostly pale, popped on near my head.

Then a second.

I gasped and pulled back. It was at eye level, between my chair and Vivi's, right where Flynn was supposed to be sitting.

Where Flynn *was* sitting.

Those were his eyes. They'd rolled back in his head—only whites. Lined with pale-pink veins. Softly glowing through the veil.

"My, how you girls are shaking." A voice croaked in the dark. From Flynn's throat.

Only it wasn't his.

It was a woman's voice—scratchy and ragged and hollow—followed by the trace of an echo. Two speaking at once, almost in sync. But not quite.

"What's the matter?" she asked us. *"Never held hands with a ghost before?"*

CHAPTER SEVENTEEN

IN THE DARK, THE GHOST'S WHITE eyes blinked. *"Forgive me for the song, won't you? I never could resist a good entrance."*

I focused on the scrap of Flynn's whisper, buried under the crackle of her voice. It was a small comfort, knowing he was still here. Somewhere.

"Ellen . . . ?" Vivi dared to ask.

I was impressed she managed to speak. My breath came so shallowly.

Again, this was something Flynn could not be faking. But it was one thing to believe this was possible and another to, as Ellen put it, hold hands with a ghost.

"In such circumstances, I generally prefer Madame Clery," she said. *"But you younger generations, so informal. I'll allow Ellen. I know all about you two: the young Miss Feldmans. About time we were introduced."*

"H-how do you know about us?" Vivi stammered.

"Oh, dear heart," she said to Vivi, *"I know nearly everything*

that happens in my house. And I know you have many questions. Shall we start at the beginning?"

Wow, the spirit board was completely redundant. Ellen, unlike our past visitors, was shockingly articulate.

My throat finally unclenched enough to eke out, "Do you mind if I relight the candle first?"

A pause. A sigh.

"If that would make you more comfortable," said the glowing eyes in the dark.

"Yes," I replied in a mild Mom voice. "I think it would."

Funny how quickly it had flipped from our séance, our house, to Ellen's séance, Ellen's house. Now I felt very much like *her* awkward guest.

"Go on, then."

I fumbled for the lighter under those watchful glowing orbs, until I found it and sparked the candle back to life.

"Well, do you feel better?" Ellen asked wryly—through Flynn's lips.

Orange candlelight played across the white veil, twisting shadows over the sharp planes of Flynn's face. And Ellen's mannerisms puppeteered his familiar form into a stranger's. She sat taller, stiffer, held her chin higher. She commandeered Flynn's resting scowl face into her Mona Lisa smile, a smug portrait of unspoken secrets.

And his forest-green eyes had been swallowed whole, into that relentless white glow.

No, I didn't feel better at all. As Ellen had clearly predicted.

"Don't get too shy, dear." She grabbed my hand with Flynn's, and latched on. *"Reestablish the circle, please. I need your electricity to manifest. Otherwise, I'll have to draw on the young Mr. Driscoll's*

energy even more, and I doubt he'd appreciate that." She inclined his head slightly. *"Indeed, he says he would not."*

I'd thought the medium was supposed to translate for the ghost, not the other way around.

Vivi and I uncertainly relocked hands with each other, too. So the circle was again unbroken. "Flynn can hear us?" I asked.

"Yes, I'm taking pains to allow him to stay present with us, unlike some *spirits. I can hardly believe you three made the mistake of approaching Rose before myself. I really can't advise encouraging her."*

Encouraging her?

My brain was fighting to keep up. Of all things, I blurted out: "Why are your eyes white?"

"Hmm?" Flynn's neck cricked as Ellen regarded me.

"Rose's glowed blue. Yours glow white."

Yes, Ellen's eyes were chilling—like distant lanterns one puff away from losing the last of their light. Sitting here with her felt wrong. But sitting with Rose had felt impossible. When I'd looked into those blue eyes, so hungry and consuming, it felt like she and I inhabited two separate worlds that should *never* have collided.

"Ah, yes. A keener observation than perhaps you realize." Ellen scoffed, a softer version of Flynn's laugh-bark. *"I told you I'd start at the beginning, didn't I? It's easiest to show you."*

Flynn's hand, bitter-cold, clutched mine. Ellen's influence seeped deeper into his body and zipped through me, an icy shiver that zinged from my hand to my brain.

The dark of the parlor faded. And a whole new vision unfolded before me.

A fresh new start. A fresh new house.

This house. But smaller, free of dizzying rooflines and turrets, with walls that weren't blue on blue on blue. The wallpaper was fresh and floral and friendly. The windows were clear.

This house, the day Ellen and Joseph moved in.

"Dreadfully dull, wasn't it?" Ellen remarked. Her words trickled into my mind, like a voice-over. I couldn't see Flynn or Vivi sitting beside me anymore, only the images she funneled to me.

In the earliest days of this house, where Ellen saw dull, I saw a time before stained glass reigned over every room, forcing even the sunlight to pretend to be something it wasn't.

The parlor was the first room she'd set up. *"In those first years after the earthquake that claimed so many lives, I was able to turn sufficient profit by performing ordinary séances. But as more mediums trickled into the area, demand thinned, and my act required more than ordinary offerings."*

That's when Ellen decided to become better acquainted with her new neighbors—and not the kind that lived next door.

One night, she sat alone in the dark in this very parlor—at this same circular table, decked in fresher velvet and fringe. At the center was one flickering candle and her most prized possession: a crystal ball encasing a blue velvet rose.

The crystal ball from the backyard séance table.

"My conduit," Ellen told us. *"The object used to channel my spiritual invitations. Bold of you, by the by, to attempt this séance without one. I hope you know your calls only worked on me and Rose because we're already tethered to this site. Me from the manner of my death. And Rose because . . . Well, I'm getting ahead of myself. . . ."*

In the vision Ellen imparted to us, her crystal ball began to flicker—shimmering with strange lights and stranger shadows.

The Ellen of the past sat with her candle and conduit and spirit board, fingers twitching on the planchette. Waiting, waiting, for someone to come calling. Over and over, she whispered: "Is anyone there?"

And then came a bite on the line. A pull so hard and so sudden the planchette nearly ripped from Ellen's hands.

It swung to YES.

The spirit was eager to say hello. But not to answer questions.

Instead, the spirit preferred to wander the parlor, taking measure of the place, of Ellen. Opening and slamming the doors of the cabinet along the wall. Blowing out the candle—several times. Touching Ellen. Even tugging her hair.

"A test," Ellen said. *"To see if I would startle. But I would've made a poor medium indeed if I'd been afraid of the dark, or the brush of cold fingers, even ones strong as these."*

Her answer was always the same: To calmly relight the candle. To inform the spirit that ill manners would not be tolerated.

At last, the chair beside her creaked. The spirit settled in. And, question by question, letter by letter, spelled out an answer or two on her spirit board.

She was a young girl, the spirit said, a victim of the earthquake.

Several times, Ellen asked for the girl's name.

Finally, an answer: R-O-S-E.

"My middle name," Ellen told us. *"My favorite flower. The center, in fact, of my crystal ball, the conduit used to summon this spirit forth."*

I said, "Well, that's . . . quite a coincidence."

"No." Ellen laughed. *"No coincidence at all."*

She'd known, from the start, that "Rose" was lying.

Rose was not a little girl.

She was not a she.

She was an *it*.

But an *it*, truly, was what Ellen needed. A powerful spirit, one she hoped could be groomed to entertain séance guests. So Ellen encouraged Rose's visits—courted her with gifts, tin horses and teacups, items too delicate to survive the spirit's curiosity.

One night, Ellen invited Rose to stay, to settle into the house.

And Rose accepted.

I jolted in my dusty armchair. "You *invited* Rose into this house?" I demanded. "You knew what she was, and you invited her to stay?"

The parlor of the past melted into the parlor of the present. And I shivered. Flynn's hand, in mine, was icier and icier, stiffer and stiffer.

Like a corpse's.

A fine foggy mist curled out from his mouth with each breath, filtering down to dance with the candle flame on the table.

Vivi's hand in mine shivered, too.

Only Ellen seemed unbothered. She curved Flynn's mouth into a smirk. *"I was no amateur, Miss Feldman. You might say, I fancied myself something of a lion tamer. Believed I could tame the most ferocious of beasts."* Her smile faded. *"No one likes admitting they overestimated their own abilities."*

At first, Rose helped with the séances as Ellen had hoped, but the spirit soon lost interest in aiding with parlor tricks. Instead, Rose seized control of Joseph, Ellen's husband. Then Rose had the audacity to refuse to come out.

Rose had proven herself a most unruly houseguest, and hadn't Ellen warned her, from the outset, ill manners would not be tolerated?

"So you see"—Ellen's voice picked up a hot edge of ire—*"it was her own bad behavior that forced me to do what I did."*

To bring out the first mask.

A perfectly ordinary mask—white, with blue rose detailing. One Joseph had crafted for her in their younger days, when Ellen had assisted his illusionist performances.

The spirit wanted to pretend it meant no harm? That it was an innocent girl named Rose? Then wasn't it fitting to channel Rose out of Joseph and trap her inside that sweet doll-faced mask?

Ellen found it a superior arrangement, to access Rose and her power when—and *only* when—she saw fit. She could don the rose mask for séance performances and then, at the end, tuck Rose safe and sound on a little shelf.

Rose raged at her confinement but eventually gave up on her futile pleas to be released.

Instead, she made a different request. A lonely wish for the company of other spirits.

Ellen agreed. She merely neglected to mention she would be caging the new spirits upon arrival.

While Rose was proving an excellent main séance attraction, no séance was complete without a good story. And Ellen was partial to Myers's allegory "The Caterpillar and the Cabbage Leaf."

"Making it a rose leaf was much more whimsical, don't you agree? Besides, we already had the rose mask."

To match the story, Ellen tasked Joseph with constructing a butterfly mask.

The next spirit Ellen summoned, she channeled directly into this mask.

She was not interested in discerning the new spirit's actual identity, whoever or whatever they'd been before. So Ellen gave the spirit a new name, a new assigned role: the Butterfly.

My stomach dropped. The story of House of Masks was clicking into place for me. And suddenly, I wished I hadn't heard it.

"The Butterfly? You mean . . ." Vivi's voice came out very high.

I must've looked as terrified as Vivi, because Ellen patted both of our hands. *"Don't be alarmed, dears,"* she said. *"Yes, every mask in this house is home to a trapped spirit. But like people, some spirits are better influences than others. You two have chosen excellent company. Truly, it warms my heart to see how much you've gained from your communions with the Butterfly and the Beetle."*

"Communions?" I asked weakly.

"Certainly. You channel them every time you wear their masks. How else did you think you were acquiring that sudden strength? The ability to levitate? The spirits are acting through you, as I am now." She nodded down at Flynn's body.

But obviously it wasn't quite the same. "They don't move our bodies for us," I said, confused. "And they don't talk either."

"Well, you're not mediums, and they're here to help you, dear—not to turn you into puppets by force." Ellen hitched Flynn's eyebrow even higher than I'd seen him manage. *"But really? You've never heard a voice in your head when you wear the Beetle's mask?"*

A voice in my head . . . ?

Something *had* spoken to me. When I'd been terrified by what turned out to be Vivi's wild laughter, it told me:

You are not broken.

You are strong. brave. enough.

When I'd choked at the bottom of the hidden stairs behind my closet door, it had told me again:

You are strong.

But it had spoken in what sounded like *my* voice. I'd been so sure I was finally learning to advocate for myself. To trust myself.

Instead, it was the Beetle?

"But it made me think . . ." My cheeks burned. "It spoke in *my* voice! Why would it trick me if it's a good spirit like you say?"

"It spoke in your voice?" Dots were connecting for Vivi, her eyes widening. "The Butterfly has been talking to me, too! In *my* voice. Were they tricking us on purpose?"

Ellen shook Flynn's head, with wry amusement. *"Oh, don't take it personally. They're only borrowing your voices because they don't remember their own. Once I pinned the spirits inside those masks, assigned them new identities, they all but forgot themselves. The Beetle forgot it was anything but strong. The Butterfly forgot it was anything but light. Trust me, it's for the best that the rest of their powers have been stripped away. It's wise to keep strong spirits neutered."*

Neutered. As if they were pets.

I frowned. "But the other twelve spirits you summoned, you said they're strong. But they're not . . . inhuman, like Rose?"

Ellen laughed and waved off my concern. *"Don't panic, dear. They're not like Rose."*

But, then, did Ellen mean the other spirits she'd trapped had once been *human*?

"Are you saying the spirits didn't originally have anything to do with bugs?" I asked, a bad taste working its way into my mouth. "Those were just shapes you assigned to them?"

"Correct. And, of course, their real names were never the Butterfly or the Beetle, for instance. But those are honorifics! Insects metamorphose—transform from one shape to the next—as a natural part of their life cycle. To my mind, that makes them the most sacred creatures on Earth.

"You see, we are born as lowly caterpillars, who dream of the sky but cannot reach it. These spirits have the wings we long for. And with the right human, they don't mind sharing. Raising us up."

Did they really not mind? Ellen seemed awfully firm in her conviction.

The words painted inside the trunk in the attic echoed in my mind: *Metamorphose. Ascend to Glory!*

"An ascension," I said.

"Precisely!" Ellen squeezed my hand with Flynn's. It was so cold I was getting scared for him. It was taking a toll, allowing someone dead to wear his body. *"I had to make the spirits accessible to us, so that they could help us grow. But, I must confess, it's pathetic to see what being trapped in these limited forms has done to them. The poor dears can barely express themselves outside of the form and materials of their masks. Can you imagine—expressing yourself through animated projections of feathers and lace?"*

Vivi and I shared a disturbed look. "You mean the butterflies themselves?" she demanded. "That's part of the spirit?"

"Extensions of the Butterfly, yes."

"Then you're saying the beetles *are* the Beetle?" I asked. "The roses *are* Rose?"

At Ellen's nod, an even worse thought hit me. "When Mom is drinking that tea, is she drinking . . . ?" I remembered the electric tang of it sliding down my throat, and I had to stop myself from gagging all over again.

Again, Ellen nodded. *"Yes, your mother, perhaps unknowingly, has been feeding off Rose, and I'm afraid Rose has been feeding off your mother."*

Under the table, my toes curled in my shoes. Then it was no coincidence Mom had finished that mosaic floor to match Rose's designs without ever seeing them. Rose's designs were already in her head because Rose, to some extent, was in her head, too.

"Rose has had her eye on your mother since she was a baby. How Rose hated when she managed to escape this house as a child. She never gave up on her, of course.

"Several weeks ago, your mother visited this property. Something

about her energy was different—very unbalanced, very vulnerable. And perhaps that's why Rose was finally able to sink in her hooks. It wasn't much at first, just enough to convince her to bring you all here. But your mother was still off-kilter enough when you moved in that Rose managed to influence her very quickly. I know that you've noticed, even if you didn't know what to call it."

I wanted to nod, to ask a million more questions. This, after all, was the main reason I'd wanted this séance in the first place. To understand what was happening to Mom. To try and stop it. But what Ellen was saying, that Rose had been able to gain power over Mom because she was so unstable . . .

In the kitchen, when I'd asked why Mom had brought us here, she'd told me about visiting the house while I was in the psych ward. How she'd reconnected with the blue roses: *It was a difficult time. I needed something—anything—beautiful in my life. And those roses. When I saw them and smelled them, they touched me in a way I hadn't felt before.*

My suicide attempt was the reason. Why Mom had been in such a difficult place. As Ellen put it—so unbalanced, vulnerable, off-kilter.

I was the reason.

My tongue was achingly hard. I fought to swallow. To blink back tears.

"Are you quite all right, dear?" Ellen regarded me curiously, like heartfelt emotion was a novelty she'd long forgotten. Then she seemed to catch herself. *"It's upsetting, to be sure. I can commiserate, as Rose's first victim."*

"Victim?" I choked out. "Rose is the reason you died?"

Ellen was quiet for a moment. *"Well, even many renowned lion tamers in the end lose their lives to a lion."*

Vivi's eyes, glistening in the candlelight, were wider than I'd ever seen them. "Then is Rose behind *all* the disappearances?" she asked.

Ellen frowned at Vivi like she'd said something sour. *"I'm afraid Rose is the largest part of a larger problem. There are benevolent spirits on this property, but others besides Rose have grown restless and angry. Together, they have been wreaking havoc on this house and its inhabitants for over a century."*

Flynn's body tensed. And this time, I didn't think it was Ellen moving on his behalf.

"That's correct, dear," Ellen said, responding to a question only she could hear—one Flynn must've spoken in his mind. *"Your father got tangled up with the wrong spirit, too, I'm afraid."*

Ellen rushed past our growing gloom—mine and Vivi's, and no doubt Flynn's, too—to her main point: *"I know we would all like to prevent that sort of tragedy from reoccurring."* She turned to me and to Vivi. *"Your grandmother tried to warn you, I believe, but your mother doesn't have much time."*

"Is there anything we can do?" I asked.

"Yes, that's the good news!" Ellen assured me. *"We must exorcise Rose, and the other worrisome spirits, before it's too late."*

I nearly collapsed in relief.

An exorcism. That sounded good. That sounded great.

"I can take care of the trickiest part," Ellen said. *"What I need from you is relatively simple: hold a séance at the stone table, with as many attendees as possible—ideally thirteen, one for each chair."*

I hesitated. "A séance? Isn't that the opposite of an exorcism?"

Ellen nodded at me, even as impatience clipped through her tone: *"I know it may seem counterintuitive, but I'm an old ghost, dear, with limited power."* She twisted Flynn's lips as if it pained her to acknowledge the limitation. *"To exorcise a spirit as strong as Rose, we'll first require a great deal of spiritual energy, which we can harness both from the living and from any benevolent spirits willing to aid us. To that end, all three of you should wear your masks, inviting the Butterfly, the Beetle, and the Ant to join our cause.*

"And it wouldn't hurt to put in some extra bonding time beforehand, particularly for Flynn, since he and the Ant remain unacquainted. Despite the Ant's best efforts. That poor spirit has been sending feelers to Flynn since he was a boy—a medium, no less, who should surely recognize such signs!

"Even a few hours of communion could help the Ant feel less disoriented. Especially considering I would need to hop into this body again, in order to conduct the séance."

Vivi was nodding, like this pseudoscience made sense, but my fingers twitched with the impulse to tear at my nails. "You want us to put on our masks again," I asked, "knowing there are spirits inside?"

Ellen stiffened, clearing her throat in an offended manner. *"I know spirits like Rose can be frightening, but has the Beetle given you any indication that it means you harm? The right spirits can be a great help to us. Truly, we cannot exorcise Rose without them."*

I hesitated. "If we did this," I asked, "Mom would be safe from Rose?"

"That would be the aim."

"Well, we'd have to . . . we'd have to ask Flynn," I said.

"Of course," Ellen said. *"Discuss. Consider. Only for your mother's sake, I suggest you act . . . well, sooner rather than later."*

With that, the ghostly glow dimmed from Flynn's eyes until they were nothing but rolled-back whites, with a few popped, veiny blood vessels streaking through. He exhaled a shivering cloud of smoke. It leaked out from behind his eyes, from his skin, from everywhere. All the fog that had poured into him leached out into the dark parlor. And faded away.

Ellen was gone.

Flynn's eyes rolled forward, his usual green snapping into place. And he came back to himself with a sharp stab of breath. He ripped his icy hand from me and Vivi and tore the white mesh from his face, gulping air.

"Flynn! Are you okay?" I asked.

His teeth were chattering, but this time it had nothing to do with the rain. Under his freckles, his face was whiter than those ghostly eyes had been. His own voice came out raw, croaking: "Worms."

Vivi snapped to attention. "Worms?"

"I don't know where Ellen's body is, but . . . worms found their way inside. There can't be anything left for them to eat by now, but I could feel them anyway, like they were in my own body—in my stomach, in the muscles of my thighs, wriggling." He ran his trembling hands up and down his legs. "The whole time you three were talking."

"I'm so sorry, Flynn." I wanted to touch him, to give him something solid to latch on to, but I wasn't sure if that's what he wanted.

He looked so lost. Alone. His chest was heaving.

"If it helps," I said, "the séance worked. And you heard Ellen, right? She said you *are* a medium." My doubts about that were long gone, but I thought Flynn might still need the confirmation.

"Lucky me." Flynn blinked his green eyes into focus. "Yeah, I heard the whole conversation. From far away. But I think I understood."

"We have to do it, right?" Vivi said. "Ellen's séance. If Mom is . . ."

I guess she didn't have the words. For what Mom was now.

But Flynn pushed up from his chair. "I . . . I don't . . ." He paced the parlor, in and out of the tiny circle of candlelight. Rubbing his thighs, touching his stomach. "She wants me to put on the ant mask? To let her back in my body, for even longer next time?"

He stopped abruptly, facing me. "I don't want to feel that again," he said softly. Almost ashamed.

I understood. I did. I'd promised him I'd never ask for another séance after this one with Ellen. But.

"We can't do it without you," I said.

"I know." He started pacing again.

"And Mom is . . . ," I started. But Vivi had been right—there weren't good words for it. "If people have died in this house before from getting involved with the wrong spirit . . ."

"Yeah, including my dad, apparently." Flynn scowled miserably. Sick and shivering.

I wanted to ask again if he was okay, but he didn't leave an opening. "Maybe I'm only freaked-out because I spent the past twenty minutes getting gnawed on by worms," he muttered. "I just have such a bad feeling."

"But what else are we supposed to do?" Vivi asked.

No one had an answer.

"Libby." Flynn locked eyes with me. "Do you really want to go ahead with this?"

In many ways, of course not. I was losing my appetite for séances in a hurry. But I nodded. "There's a chance this will save Mom. So yeah. I think we have to."

"Exactly," Vivi agreed. "Besides, what's the worst that can—"

"Nope," Flynn said. "You have got to stop saying that." He sighed and rubbed his forehead, mulling it over. "Okay," he said finally. "I'll do it. But if Ellen needs all the chairs at the table filled, it'll take me a few days to round up guests."

Vivi and I nodded.

A few days.

We just had to hang on until then. *Mom* had to hang on until then.

CHAPTER EIGHTEEN

AFTER FLYNN PACKED UP HIS THINGS and headed back out into the rain, I knew I should sleep. It was past three in the morning. Instead, I found myself pacing in my creaky bedroom. Watching the beetle mask in the window as much as it might have been watching me.

I licked the sweat from my upper lip. I tasted as stale as this house smelled. It kept me wrapped tight in its musty arms. Smothering me with its humid haze of roses and mildew.

Questions tore at my mind as I reconsidered the conversation. Ellen Clery had turned this place into some nightmarish Victorian spirit zoo. She'd made the mistake of *inviting* Rose, a spirit stronger than she could control, into this house. After Rose had betrayed her, she'd summoned twelve weaker spirits—human spirits, apparently—and unrepentantly shoved them straight into masks. Into molds of her own choosing, for the sake of some spiritualist parable. She was obsessed with a metaphor involving bugs—the concept of spiritual metamorphosis—and she'd wanted her séances to match a theme: The Caterpillar and the Rose Leaf.

No wonder so many spirits here were restless and angry. It was a wonder they *all* weren't.

Ellen had freely admitted that she hadn't bothered to learn who these spirits were before shoving them into insect masks. That even the spirits, forced into strange new roles, had forgotten their true identities. Could that be true?

It sounded crushingly lonely.

I hadn't touched my beetle mask, not since my demonstration for Flynn, following the Rose séance. But now, pity began to outweigh my fear.

I lifted the beetle mask away from the stained glass, extra-gingerly this time, and slouched into the window seat, staring at the molded glass in my hands.

I traced the widow's peak that matched my own, and the blossoming blue veins under its surface. The more I engaged with the mask, the more it came alive.

As I ran my fingers along its warm edges, the mask stuck ever so lightly to each one, like a nibbling fish. I winced, long-ingrained logic insisting that this should be an *inanimate* object. But I fought the urge to pull back. With each nibble came a tiny whisper of calm, of strength.

I wanted to believe the Beetle spirit was benevolent. That wearing the mask didn't just feel good—it *was* good.

Ellen was right that the Beetle had never done anything to hurt me. On the contrary, it had reassured me when I needed it most. Advocated for me when I didn't know how to advocate for myself.

But, then, Ellen said the Butterfly was benevolent, too.

I couldn't shake the night I'd heard Vivi's laugh, too shrill and shrieking and out of control. Vivi insisted she'd been having a wonderful dream, but in reality she'd been huddled on the ceiling, swarmed by bugs.

At Ellen's direction, Vivi was probably across the hall now, snuggling up to the Butterfly mask.

I wrestled with the uneasy squirm in my gut.

Still, I knew we had to move forward with the exorcism. And if Ellen was telling the truth, then bonding with our masks was important. We needed their help to save Mom from Rose.

I pressed the beetle mask on, soaking in the accompanying rush of relief. It locked on almost magnetically, like it was meant to be part of me and it was glad I'd finally noticed.

Glowing dots flared to life around my room—huddling above me in the stained-glass window, spotting the walls and floors. Beetles. Suddenly impossible to miss through the eyes of this mask. I hadn't realized how many were crawling around in here. I winced at the sight of them all.

And I sat, waiting for something to happen. Now that I knew the mask's secret. Now that I knew, when I put it on, that I wasn't alone.

"H-hello?" I finally whispered. Feeling ridiculous.

And even more ridiculous when nothing answered.

I tried again. "Is anyone there?"

My propped bedroom door shivered, rattling softly against the knee-high metal trash can.

I squinted at it from across the room, wondering if I'd imagined it. If—

The rattle intensified. The trash can tipped. And the door swung closed.

My heart pounded harder, but the signals from my mask were

soothing. Gentle. Unclenching the nervous muscles in my jaw as fast as I could clench them.

As if reassuring me that this was only the spirit's way of letting me know it was here. It was listening.

I swallowed. "That was you, wasn't it? You're the one who's been moving my door?"

Nothing.

If the Beetle really could talk, I'd much rather it communicated in my head than by spilling trash all over my floor.

Guess I'd have to be more explicit.

I tried again: "Well, uh, we spoke to Ellen tonight, and she told us a little bit about you. She said you can hear me. That you can talk, too, if you borrow my voice?"

can hear can talk

An echo inside my skull answered—my own voice, caught like a ball and lobbed back to me.

And I jumped, knowing this time it hadn't come from me.

I gripped the window seat. To tether myself to some vestige of reality. I'd spent my whole life certain that spirits weren't real. And in the last couple days, I'd now spoken to three of them. I kept expecting to wake up, for reality to shift back into its expected shape. But it only distorted more and more.

I clutched the solid wooden seat, breathed in and out. "So it is true," I said to the Beetle. The spirit that I couldn't see but was here with me—in this mask and in my head. "You've talked to me all along. But you can only repeat words I've said? You don't have any of your own?"

true. only repeat

A rearrangement of the words I'd used, in the same tones in which I'd spoken them.

I couldn't believe how much Ellen had stripped away from

whoever this spirit had once been. The horror of it stabbed dully at my chest.

"I'm sorry. Ellen shouldn't have done this to you. To any of you." I sighed, glancing out the window beside us. I could barely see through the heavily tinted glass—to the storm outside painting the world shiny and black. "You must be scared. Lonely. You must feel trapped."

trapped. all along. trapped. trapped. scared. Lonely.

I nodded. Maybe the Beetle could feel it when I moved my head. I had no idea how it perceived anything. "And even though no one has helped you all this time, you've been helping me? On purpose? Making me stronger and taking my bad feelings away?"

true.

True. Simple as that. "But why?"

If I were in this spirit's position, I'd like to believe I'd be selfless, too. Not furious. But it had to be an awfully rare person who could meet a situation as unfair as the Beetle's with grace.

No answer.

I must not have given the Beetle the right words to speak back. I frowned.

Maybe Ellen was right, that certain spirits could be hugely beneficial to the living. Could inspire us to be better ourselves.

Maybe the Beetle really didn't mind helping. "I hate to ask you for more," I said, "but my mom is in trouble, and we have to get Rose away from her."

Silence.

I continued. "So, uh, Ellen says we need your help to hold a séance. Something about gathering spiritual energy to exorcise Rose and the other restless spirits—you probably understand better than I do. If I wear this mask, will you help us?"

wear this mask, will help you

I sagged against the window seat with gratitude. "Thank you." The help was so freely and easily offered, but it felt like I was taking advantage of the spirit. "Is there anything I can do for you to return the favor?"

wear this mask

"That's it?" A strange request.

I'd expected more—a plea for freedom, maybe. But the Beetle had admitted to being lonely. Mitigating that was truly the least I could do.

"I can wear the mask more often. Stay with you a little more," I said. "I don't know why, but you've been something of a friend to me. I hope I can be a friend to you, too."

friend

In a glowing flash, a beetle whirred down from the window and landed on my knee. I tried not to startle.

Ellen had told us that these beetles were part of the Beetle, too. An extension of the spirit.

Another beetle flew down from the window, and another, and another. They landed on my knee to join the first. Two more landed on my fingers, their tiny legs hooking into my skin, nestling in, getting comfortable.

I stifled the urge to swat them away.

I shouldn't be scared. The Beetle didn't mean me harm. The Beetle was helping me. And now I was helping the Beetle.

So I left them alone.

I let them crawl.

With the mask on my face and the Beetle's fresh promise to help me, I climbed into bed. The mattress was comfortable, even welcoming, as I snuggled into it. From inside the shield of my mask, the oppressive heat of this house couldn't touch me. The scratching overhead meant nothing to me.

The beetles followed, too. They crawled through my hair on the pillow. Even a few minutes ago, the tiny stirrings and tugs on my scalp might've been too much for me to bear. But my mask was steeping me full of delicious calm. So I relaxed into the sensation.

I let my eyes close and started counting my breaths, to drift off to sleep.

Then, behind my closed eyes, something flickered.

A faint swirl of blue.

Once or twice before, when I'd tried to meditate at Dr. Glaser's recommendation, colorless light had danced behind my eyes. But this was unmistakably the rich, intoxicating blue of the roses. Of the beetles.

The swirl intensified, branched out in six directions, crashed in together, then separated again, twinkling into little stars. A whole sky of stars. Stars with too many points. Thirteen points. Glowing in a throbbing blue neon. Like the inside of the secret stairwell.

Now, the stars painted the backs of my eyelids. And they danced, just for me.

I was at peace, one relaxed breath after another carrying me toward sleep.

Until the knob on my bedroom door turned.

My eyes flew open as, across the room, the door opened. Revealing a wide, dim gash of hallway.

I rocketed upright, clutching the blankets, beetles tumbling from my hair. "Who's there?"

"Knock, knock." Mom's soft voice drifted through the dark.

Her tall silhouette clogged the doorframe. "Libby, why was this door closed?"

My heart thumped hard. Why was Mom awake at this hour? She hadn't heard us downstairs earlier, had she?

I hated to lose the strength and comfort of my beetle mask—but she had made her feelings about the masks clear. I tore it off and shoved it under my pillow. The beetles in my bed took the hint and followed, scurrying out of sight.

I reached over and clicked on the lamp. "Sorry, Mom. I told you that door is a little loose on its hinges. It knocked the trash can over again." My voice came out thin. "I tried to leave it open."

"Is that right?" Her curls lay greasy and flat against her skull. She was ghostly pale. Her veins were so blue—in her neck, her forehead, the back of her hands. She shuffled toward me. "I came to check on you."

When I was little, when I'd been sick, she used to come check on me. Back then, her soft shadow made me feel safe. And if I couldn't sleep, she'd bring me hot water with lemon, or once, when my throat was achingly sore, a mug of vanilla ice cream. *Don't tell your mother you're eating ice cream after midnight,* she'd said with a little wink.

But now . . .

It was past four.

And her hands were empty, curled tight as talons, as she stepped toward my bed.

Acid rose in my throat. I pressed against the headboard, the way Mom had the night she'd had that nightmare—had thought she'd seen a monster.

After what Ellen had said, I wasn't exactly sure if I was seeing one now. But I scooted over to make room for her.

The old bed groaned, its springs shrieking, as she sat down beside me. "I'm worried about you, Libby."

She smelled like sweat and something sickly and metallic. The drunken potpourri of the blue roses seeped from her pores.

The fumes made my head spin, practically giving me a contact high.

"Worried about me?" I croaked out.

She nodded and reached toward my face.

I flinched.

She saw. And her hand froze as she gave a pained wince of her own. But we both pretended it hadn't happened, and I pretended not to notice that the pads of her fingers were stained blue from chopping petals.

She touched my forehead, tucked a stray curl behind my ear.

Then she leaned in. So quiet, so close, she asked: "Why did you carve thirteens all over my floor?"

I stopped breathing.

She had noticed. We'd been counting on her not noticing.

Oh, this was bad. This was so bad.

"Th-thirteens?" I choked out.

She nodded. Her face was placid, placid, placid. Her tone oh-so-mild. "Why did you steal my mother's locket?" She tugged the chain now hanging around her neck, trailing under her bathrobe.

Carrying a reminder of her parents, acknowledging her loss, *could* have been positive. But nothing about this felt positive. Mom wore her trauma like a sinking anchor, one that was dragging her down to drown.

I struggled to swallow.

"And why," she asked, her breath reeking of roses, "did you put that baby blanket on my bed?"

"Mom, I . . ." I ripped at my nails under the comforter. "I . . . I, uh . . ." My brain wasn't working fast enough.

Most of all, I needed some plausible excuse for the 13s, but the stench of roses and iron was choking me.

It didn't matter, did it? No way she'd believe anything I said.

Something wet brushed my arm. Her bathrobe. A stain, red and fresh, seeping through the sleeve. A drop ran down her wrist, her finger, and splattered onto the white of my comforter.

And something thicker fell from her sleeve, too. Writhing like a worm. A worm with legs.

A centipede. Half slick with blood.

It flailed against my comforter and then dove for Mom's trailing bathrobe again. Tucked itself inside.

We both watched it.

She didn't move. She didn't shriek. She didn't recoil. Instead, she glared—with hardened, hooded eyes. Daring me to say something.

I pressed back harder against the headboard, away from her, and my hand smashed down, accidentally, on one of the beetles that had squirmed under my pillow for shelter.

It cracked and shattered like glass under my palm—tiny shards grinding into my skin.

I bit down on my cheek with a swallowed cry.

I didn't want to call any attention to the beetles or the mask under my pillow, the one missing from my window.

But now, I was bleeding, too. And all I could do was squeeze my hand into the sheet and hope it would stop.

This woman on my bed, she wasn't . . .

This wasn't my mother.

What was Rose doing to her?

"Don't cry, sweetie. It's okay," she said. But a dangerous undercurrent snaked through her face, a blue vein bulging in her temple. "I'm just worried about you," she continued. "If behavior like this continues, I might need to make a call to Dr. Glaser. See if there's somewhere that could provide you with better care than I can."

The blood in my chest curdled.

The threat was more explicit than ever. She would send me away.

Away from her. Away from Vivi.

Oh God. Vivi.

With me gone, Vivi would be left alone with Mom.

I couldn't let that happen.

"Mom! It's not what you think, I promise. I'm okay." My heart was pounding so hard I could barely hear myself over it. "Please, I'll prove to you that I'm okay. I'm not trying to cause trouble."

Mom shook her head and stood. "But you *are* causing trouble. Aren't you?"

"I . . ." I choked with the start of a sob.

My mom was the one losing perspective, spiraling out of control. And I could tell Dr. Glaser that, but even if she did believe me—big *if*—I might still be sent away.

"You know I only want what's best for you, sweetie," Mom said. "And what's best for me and Vivi, too."

It was like she was drunk—both here and not here. She couldn't see straight.

"But . . . but . . ." I stumbled for words, but nothing was coming and—

"It was me." Vivi stood in the doorway, eyes wide and panic-stricken, in her oversized T-shirt and nightcap, with her tiny shorts and skinny legs. "All of it, Mom. I'm the one who did the pranks."

Vivi . . . ?

I made a questioning face behind Mom's back, but she shook her head at me. This was something she'd decided. She was committing.

"*I* put the blanket on your bed," she said. "It was my idea to break into the locked room. *I* carved the thirteens in your floor."

Mom stood by my bed, shocked into place. "Baby, why would you do that?"

Vivi didn't answer. She broke down sobbing. She was a terrible liar, but the sobbing—that came from someplace real. "I'll stop. I promise."

The truth of Vivi's hurt was real enough to make Mom believe. When she turned back to me, for a second, she looked like herself again. And so jarred, so confused—almost like she'd been sleepwalking through our entire encounter and was just waking up. "Libby, I don't know what to say. I'm so sorry."

I didn't know how Rose's influence worked. If she was feeding Mom thoughts or feelings. But one way or another, Rose was breaking her brain.

"It's fine," I mumbled.

She turned back to Vivi. "You and I, we'll need to talk about this."

Vivi nodded, staring down at her sparkly polished toes.

Once Mom left and her shuffling footsteps creaked away down the hall, I shook my head at Vivi. "What did you do that for?" I whispered. "Now you're the one in trouble."

"I don't care." Vivi rushed over to me and jumped into my bed, snuggling into me like she used to do after her worst nightmares. "Don't leave. Please stay with me. Please."

"Vivi . . ." I wrapped my arm around her shoulders.

"I dream about that all the time, you know. That you're dead or you're missing. You're gone." She sniffled against my chest, pressing her head into my heart.

I held her, as firmly as I could. "I'm not going anywhere," I promised.

And I realized I meant it.

In that moment, there was no part of me that wanted to erase myself. To make myself disappear.

I wasn't even wearing the beetle mask, so that inner strength, that inner trust, it came from me this time.

From me—and from Vivi, too.

After a few more sniffles, she released me. "I didn't mean what I said, about you going to college and that being the end of us. I don't want that. Not at all."

"Me neither."

"I want it to stay like this."

"Me too."

I knew nights like this wouldn't last forever, when she was still small enough to come to me for comfort—cuddling arms, cold feet, and all. The two of us together were already getting a little big for this bed.

"Thank you for . . ." I gestured to the empty doorway, as if Mom were still standing there. "You did completely save my ass."

Vivi grimaced, with a sour sadness she didn't used to carry. "Mom's in bad shape."

The wriggling, bloody stain from the centipede marred my white comforter. And I flinched all over again. "I know," I said. "I'll talk to Flynn. See if he can get guests faster."

I shifted, to free my bloody hand, the one that had smashed the beetle. I hadn't gotten a look at the damage yet.

Sharp pebbles of blue glass were embedded in my palm. A gold antenna still clinging.

Vivi grabbed my hand, peering at the wound. "What happened? Is this—?"

"I accidentally smashed a beetle. They really are made of glass, like the mask." I waved away the worry in Vivi's face. "I'm fine. Pass me a tissue?"

"I can help," she said, almost hopeful. "If you want."

I let her pick out the glass, collect it in the tissue. Wipe gently at the smeared blood. It wasn't coming off. Without thinking, she dabbed her tongue on the tissue and moved it back to my palm.

"Okay, maybe don't spit in my open wounds, though."

"Sorry." Vivi laughed. "Although some scientists think saliva is beneficial for—"

"Oh my God, shut up. I'll use hydrogen peroxide, thanks."

In some ways, it was the most normal exchange we'd had since I'd been back from the hospital.

Weird as that was.

"Hey. Um." Vivi stared at the tissue in her hand—the fractured beetle, smeared with blood. "Ellen said the bugs are extensions of each spirit, right? And that the spirits live inside the masks. So it makes sense that we've been seeing beetles and butterflies and ants. But . . ." She shook her head and set the crushed beetle on my nightstand.

"What are you thinking?" I prodded. "You can tell me."

"Well, how come there are still cockroaches running around if the cockroach mask is gone? I've seen wasps and mosquitoes and every kind of bug that has a seat at that table. How come those bugs are still here if the masks aren't?"

I hadn't considered that. "You mean, you think the other masks are still here? Somewhere on the property?"

"They'd have to be, wouldn't they?"

I nodded slowly. "There are a lot of questions Ellen didn't really answer tonight."

"Do you trust her?" Vivi asked.

Ellen clearly viewed herself as on our side. She was more than willing to answer our call, to offer a solution. I was grateful for that, but so much of what had happened in this house was her fault.

And she hadn't come across to me as all that sorry. Like she was really taking responsibility for what she'd done.

Maybe that was why she was so eager to conduct the exorcism. To release the restless spirits, once and for all.

I *hoped* that was why she was so eager to conduct the exorcism.

"I don't know if I trust her," I admitted to Vivi.

But I glanced down at my bed, at the blood Mom had smeared on my comforter.

I guess all that really mattered was, I trusted Ellen a hell of a lot more than I trusted Rose.

CHAPTER NINETEEN

FOR ELLEN'S BIG SÉANCE, WE NEEDED ten more bodies. She wanted every chair at the white stone table filled, and Flynn and Vivi and I only covered three.

I texted him in the morning: *Can you find guests any faster? Mom is in worse shape than we knew*

Flynn had said it would take him a few days to gather our audience. He'd explained that he usually posted notice of his séances on dark tourism threads and had some other contacts. I didn't know how much he could speed along the process. I braced myself to convince him of the urgency. To volunteer whatever it took to help.

But he texted back right away: *on it. just take care of yourself and Vivi. i'll send updates asap*

I melted with gratitude. And he was good to his word. To my surprise, after dinner he sent: *i got a big group. we're good for tomorrow at midnight*

He must have *hustled*—that was sooner than I'd dared to hope for.

We also needed an excuse for him to come over early, so he could try on the ant mask. Ellen had said he needed to spend time bonding with it. But that meant he'd need to hang around wearing it, and we needed Mom not to walk in on that.

Flynn was the one who suggested: *is it better if your mom thinks it's a date? like will she leave us alone?*

I froze, fingers hovering over my screen. I couldn't tell if all the blood was draining from my face or flushing into it.

I reread the text a thousand times, my brain blaring a panicked alarm: *if she* thinks *it's a date.* He wasn't asking for an actual date.

But why did he bring it up at all?

I waited so long that he texted again: *no big deal. it's just pretend right?*

The breath slumped out of me. Just pretend. A calculated ploy to get Mom off our backs.

With weak fingers, I wrote back: *Obviously. Yeah that's smart*

I was on edge approaching her about anything, unsure which Mom I was going to get. Since her nightmarish visit to my room, she'd been in a dreamier phase, sweating the day away in the garden. She hadn't punished Vivi for confessing to those "pranks," either. It was almost like she'd forgotten the whole thing. Which was impossible, given her floorboards were carved up with a million 13s.

But the idea that I was making a friend—or more than a friend—had been the one thing, other than the roses, that had made Mom consistently happy, no matter how far gone she seemed. When I asked if Flynn could come over tomorrow for a movie night, she looked up from the fresh batch of roses she was chopping for tea. Her eyes swam with way too much joy. She bit her lip. "Like a *date* movie night?"

I nodded. Didn't have to fake the blush.

"That's fine, sweetie," she said, as mildly as possible. "You don't have to worry about me. I'll stay in my room, okay?"

And I felt like shit that one definite piece of Mom was still here, rooting for me, and here I was, lying to her.

The only advantage to Mom's far-off haze was that it allowed me and Vivi to focus on bonding with our masks. The night and day that followed, we both wore them as much as we could.

When Vivi didn't have hers on, she was dragging. Worn-out. But she said that was only because the Butterfly was helping her practice ballet. She showed me. Hopped into the air and hovered, suspended in a fully extended arabesque—the most graceful I'd ever seen her pull off.

It had to be a good sign that she was dancing again.

And she'd opened up all the jars and boxes in her room and set the bugs free. She figured it wasn't right to trap pieces of the spirits. So there were no more shoeboxes, no more jars. Her room was simply a mess of flapping lace butterflies.

Mine glittered with glass beetles.

When I took off my mask, I was weak. Unsteady. Faintly nauseous. There was the slightest shake in my hands.

I couldn't tell if it was some kind of strange withdrawal effect or if the beetle mask was working *that* hard—managing to make me feel so good, when the reality was that I should've been a trembling ball of nerves.

I didn't bother trying to sleep without it—my mask-shaped security blanket.

Noises grated from the attic overhead, but behind my eyelids, those blue stars danced. Swirls of light crashed together, broke apart, crashed back together. And then there was gold, too. The colors kaleidoscoped into a rectangle. A wall. It grew taller and wider. Thinner. Transparent, like stained glass. More rectangles sprouted from it, building bigger shapes. Rooms. It was a house of glass, knitting itself together, behind my closed eyes.

It gave me something gentle to focus on. Lulled me to sleep.

My mask kept me sane.

And finally, we made it to séance night.

I spent the early evening agonizing about my not-a-date, which was marginally less terrifying to fixate on than the prospect of the séance waiting for us at the end of the night.

But Ellen would mostly take care of that. This part was on me. Ready or not, Flynn would arrive at eight.

I had to pick an outfit that Mom would recognize as a date look, without Flynn getting the idea that I actually liked him.

Of course, I *did* actually like him. But if he didn't like me, I didn't want him to know that I liked him. At the same time, if this outfit could nudge him in the direction of liking me back, that would be ideal.

It was all very complicated.

I finally landed on a sleeveless black top with a decent plunge to its neckline. It had a little ruffle action, a little flounce. Platform sandals. And my favorite cropped jeans, which were perfectly tight in the butt.

It'd been months since I bothered with makeup beyond concealer. Flynn hadn't seen me in any. I threw on some eyeliner, mascara, a rosy smidge of blush, a touch of eyebrow pencil and highlighter. . . .

It kept snowballing until Vivi ducked her head into the bathroom and grinned. "You sure this is a fake date?"

"Shh," I hissed. Mom was in the kitchen, out of hearing range, but come on.

"Just sayin'." Vivi's giggle trickled down the hall.

At 8:00 on the dot, the doorbell rang.

"I'll get it!" I called.

To no avail.

Even as I clattered in my sandals down the staircase, Mom crossed into the foyer. She swung the door open wide—though not half as wide as her stained grin. "Oh, hi, Flynn! So nice to see you again."

"You too, Mrs. Feldman." Flynn managed to make that sound polite. He must've had a deep-buried reserve of manners, exclusively drawn upon for grown-ups.

I paused on the bottom step.

Flynn's eyes met mine with a spark, and I flushed with satisfaction as he did a double take.

He was wearing an open black button-down, black T-shirt underneath. A little dressy for Flynn.

Dressy looked good on him. Everything looked good on him.

He cleared his throat. "Hi. Brought you something." He hit me with a sly—bordering on evil—grin as he yanked out something from behind his back.

Oh my God, flowers.

They weren't fancy, not even the cheap-fancy kind you could get at a grocery store. They were raw and fresh. I almost expected them to be the blue roses from our own garden. Seemed like a very Flynn move, to pick our own flowers and gift them back.

"Bluebells," Flynn said. "From our yard."

First, I got choked up.

Then I remembered his text: *it's just pretend right?*

What the hell was he playing at?

I ground my teeth as Mom watched with dewy eyes. I knew romance wasn't her personal jam, but if there was any way to her heart, it *would* be with plants.

"Wow," I said. "How thoughtful."

"Isn't that nice, Libby?" Mom collected the flowers from Flynn. "I'll get these in a vase."

"Mom, I thought you had some stuff to do. You know . . ." I nodded toward the upstairs. She had, after all, promised to stay out of the way. That was the whole point of this humiliating venture.

"Oh. Yes. I'll get the vase, and then I'll be off to . . . do that." With a tight smile, she slipped away to rattle around in the kitchen cupboards.

As soon as she was out of sight, Flynn burst into one of his sharp, laughing barks. "You should've seen your face."

I stomped down to meet him head-on in the foyer. "What do you think you're doing?"

Flynn sobered, acting innocent. "Playing the part."

"A little over the top, if you ask me."

"Come on, it was a joke."

Not a funny one.

I felt the shame from Mason all over again—smiling reassuringly at me one second, laughing with his friends about my transparent crush the next.

"Stop screwing around." I pushed past him, toward the front entrance. "Let's go outside."

The evening was sweltering, the air sticky-thick. I was going to sweat through the armpits of this shirt in no time, but guess it didn't matter.

I charged around the house through the side yard.

Unfortunately, it didn't take Flynn long to catch up, not on those long legs. "Hey, slow down. . . ."

I pretended not to hear him. Made him follow me into the heart of the backyard, to the stone table surrounded by rosebushes.

There. This was better. This was business.

"So," I said. "Your mask." We'd stashed it on the seat of the ant chair. I grabbed it.

He held out his hand.

Instead, I plunked the mask down on the table. "Have at. Like Ellen said, it took you long enough, so let's get this over with."

Flynn didn't reach for it. He crossed his arms and leaned back on his heels, staring at me.

Crickets chirped from the rosebushes.

I turned away so he couldn't see the blush flaming over my skin. My tongue was getting heavier in my mouth. My body felt like it was carrying extra weight—not in the powerful way of the Beetle, in the crushing way of an oncoming low.

Really, brain? Now?

After everything I'd been through, this—*this*—was the thing that my body decided was worth crashing into a low over?

The beetle mask could make this go away. The beetle mask could save me.

I reached for it in the back of my waistband. But these jeans were tighter than my usual shorts. I forgot that I'd left my mask upstairs, in the window.

That's how delusional I'd been about this fake date—I'd thought I wouldn't need my armor until the actual séance.

And here came the hot rush of water to my eyes, not even remotely proportionate to anything that had happened tonight.

God, Flynn hadn't signed up for this.

"Listen, um, try on your mask, and I'll be right back." I fumbled for any excuse to disappear. "I need my mask. And Vivi. So we can plan." I turned to dart into the house.

Flynn stepped in my path. "Libby."

I hesitated, glancing up through my moistening lashes.

He stood framed by two columns winding with vines and roses. His coppery hair shone like candle fire under the setting sun. He didn't look angry. His normally sharp eyebrows had softened. His hard eyes, too. "Is this about the flowers?"

"No. No!" I shook my head. "It's . . ." Dammit. The only thing I'd find more embarrassing than explaining my mood disorder would be letting him think this was purely about fake-date flowers.

I spat it out: "On top of everything else, I have cyclothymia. It's a type of bipolar disorder. Sometimes I get lows. There's nothing rational about them."

"Okay." Flynn took that in stride more than I'd expected. "But they can happen because of triggers, right?"

Curse him for knowing that.

In fact, Dr. Glaser had identified disappointed expectations as my number one low trigger.

Flynn frowned, burying his hands in his pockets. "See, when I first got here tonight, you looked like you were in a really *good* mood." He scuffed a shoe at the mossy stone beneath us. "And then . . ."

I'd given him an out. Why was he still picking at this?

I stared down at my misguided date-night platform sandals. The tiny streaks of blue polish I hadn't quite managed to wipe off surrounding the nail on my big toe. I must seem so desperate.

"I get the joke, okay?" I mumbled. "The flowers. Obviously, no one would actually want to go out with me. I already know. I don't need you to make funny little points about it."

I couldn't look him in the face, but even staring at his Chucks, it was obvious—his full body flinched. "That's what you thought I meant?"

I met his eyes with a full-on glare. "I know when people are making fun of me. Plenty of experience in that arena, trust me."

Flynn shook his head. "That wasn't the joke."

"What was the joke, then?" I crossed my arms over my chest, my nails digging into my elbows with merciless fury.

Flynn cleared his throat. "Look," he finally said. "I know you're new around here, but I'm . . . I'm the outcast séance kid. If anything, I was making that joke in the opposite direction."

There went the crickets again, punctuating our silence.

"You thought it was funny that *I* would go out with *you*?" I blinked, stunned. "Maybe we're both outcasts, but at least you're hot!"

Flynn laughed. "Uh, Libby, don't know how to break this to you, but you're the one who's been running around in the shortest shorts known to humankind, murdering me."

Well. I guess this was a stalemate I didn't mind. With all the pretense stripped away, there was nothing real to fight about.

And Flynn smiled. Raw and open. "Then I guess those flowers aren't a joke after all," he said. Apparently, he'd never wanted them to be.

He held out a hand to me, and it was stunningly automatic the way my fingers threaded through his.

So many people had been treating me like I was made of glass, like I was breakable. He touched me like I was precious—not fragile. There was a difference. One that was slight, but meant the entire world.

He tugged me closer, his free hand brushing one of my curls before settling at the back of my neck. My hands fell on his chest, against the hard beat of his heart. He leaned down. I leaned up.

Our lips met in the middle.

And he tasted like oranges and smelled like boy, and it was perfect. He was perfect.

I squeezed his hand, and he squeezed back, and I clutched his shirt, deepened the kiss. Flynn let out the lowest moan and weaved his fingers into my hair.

The heaviness in my body was melting away, overpowered by the happy shock of this kiss.

But then, with a stab of horror, I pulled back. A clammy shake rippled through me.

"You okay?" Flynn scanned me like he was inventorying for injuries. "Did I do something wrong?"

I shook my head, my fingers tracing my lips. Tingling and alive with every atom Flynn's mouth had touched. "I just realized . . . I could've missed this."

I'd tried to. I'd tried to miss this. I'd tried to miss everything.

Fan-freaking-tastic. I was crying again. I leaned my head against his collarbone. "Sorry, you were probably hoping for a nice, normal first date. A nice, normal first kiss. And here I am, sobbing all over everything."

Flynn shook his head. His hands rested on my lower back, and he only pulled me closer. "I don't think I've ever wished for a nice, normal anything. Normal is . . . It feels like a lie to me, I guess. But this feels true."

"It is." I could've kissed him all over again.

Unfortunately, Flynn and I had a séance to prep for.

A haunting to face.

It was time.

CHAPTER TWENTY

FOR OUR FIRST SÉANCE OF THE evening, the three of us—including Vivi, who'd arrived shortly after with the butterfly and beetle masks—called Ellen, so that she could help us plan for the main event. Flynn let her climb back into his skin, glowing eyes and all.

And she was not pleased that Flynn and I had been distracted from our preparations: *"In a sacred space, too."* Ellen shook Flynn's head and tutted. *"He's supposed to be bonding with the Ant—not you, Miss Feldman—and he still hasn't tried on the mask!"*

She grabbed it from the table. *"I'll put it on now, yes?"* Ellen paused, the mask halfway to Flynn's face, and sighed impatiently. *"You have to agree,"* she said aloud, although she must've been talking to Flynn. *"This kind of spiritual connection is a sacred union. For a true bond to form, you must choose the Ant, and it must choose you, too. So say yes."*

After a moment, she nodded. *"There. Was that so difficult?"*

I couldn't blame Flynn for being hesitant, not after he'd lost himself in the rose mask. Whether that had been because Flynn was a medium or Rose was so powerful or both, it was hard not to flinch as Ellen lifted the ant mask to his face.

It bonded effortlessly.

The ant mask, a half mask like Vivi's, left his dimpled chin exposed. But I was positive that the pleased-as-punch smile showing through was Ellen's, not Flynn's.

"Ah. It's been a long time, but I remember this mask fondly," Ellen said. *"Before the masks began to insist on bonding with one person at a time, I took turns wearing them during my séances. I designed each mask to carry off a popular séance trick, but the Ant's was among the most impressive feats."*

"What was it?" Vivi always took the bait.

Hello, dears. Ellen's voice. But not aloud. It jumped straight into my mind, without the filter of Flynn's throat.

I jumped. "Whoa! Did you—?"

"An open line of communication. Not only can I project thoughts, I can receive them—even if you don't want me to. A sort of collective intelligence inspiration," she explained, tapping the mask. *"Get it? The Ant?"*

"But real ants don't read each other's minds." Vivi had adopted her *Um, actually* voice. "They react to each other's pheromones."

Of course, entomology would be Vivi's concern—not that Ellen, and maybe Flynn, too—could overhear our thoughts.

Ellen sighed. *"Well, scientific accuracy wasn't especially the point. Was it, dear?"*

"It could've been," Vivi mumbled sullenly.

Ellen moved right along. *"Have you been bonding with the Butterfly and the Beetle?"*

We nodded.

"Put on your masks, then. Let me have a look at you."

As I pressed the beetle mask over my face, the world glowed to life around me, and I gasped. I'd known that the bugs glowed, had seen the roses that Vivi had stuffed inside jars glowing, too—but I'd never worn my mask outside. Or looked directly at the backyard while wearing it.

The night was suddenly so bright—as every rosebush, the entire hedge maze, blazed with eerie blue. Even the stone table and chairs. All like fluorescent stains under black light.

Ellen's eyes burned even brighter, as did Flynn's every exhale—a slow leak of glowing smoke. She stepped toward me and tapped my dropped jaw. *"Mind yourself, dear, or you'll start catching bugs in that trap."*

I snapped my mouth shut and tried not to shiver as she ran Flynn's rapidly cooling fingers along the seam across my forehead. She frowned. *"You and the Beetle need more time. A pity, but it'll do for now."*

What does she mean, I asked the Beetle in my mind, *that we need more time?*

Before the Beetle could answer, Ellen did, responding to my literal thought: *"Only that you haven't reached your full potential together, dear. Don't worry. You'll be plenty strong for the Beetle's primary purpose during séances. You're the table lifter."*

This mind-reading thing is already getting old, I thought.

I didn't care that she'd heard that, and I was certain she did, because she made Flynn's face frown at me.

"The table lifter?" I asked.

"We'll rehearse. I'll show you."

Ellen touched Vivi in the same spot. *"Oh, I see you and the Butterfly have been spending a great deal of time together. Excellent!"*

Vivi, no question, had bonded with her mask more than I had. She'd had a big head start, after all. Now, the glow in the back of her eyes was deeper and brighter than ever, and the butterfly mask had truly metamorphized from the dusty delicate relic we'd found in her window.

The lace stretching across Vivi's forehead and cheeks was as lumpy as tumorous tissue. The pus-colored surface had developed visible veins like my mask had, only the ones on hers were thicker—softly pulsing with their own quiet life. The feathers lining the mask's nose were too sharp, too hard. And the interwoven tiny beads glinted with a sickly sheen, like the sweat of someone diseased.

Honestly, just looking at it made me feel a little sick.

But Ellen beamed at Vivi. *"You, dear, can be the star of the show,"* she said, winking one of the glowing orbs that passed for her eyes. *"Levitation always plays so well anyway. It's no surprise that the Butterfly was among our most popular spirits."*

"I don't understand," I said. "Why are we doing these weird tricks? Isn't this séance about gathering the energy you need to exorcise Rose? When does the exorcism happen anyway? Right afterward, or—?"

"One thing at a time, dear. Of course, the exorcism is the most important thing, and we'll get to that straight after the séance," Ellen assured me. *"But these 'weird tricks' are precisely how we'll gather the spiritual energy we need."*

I stared at her.

And Ellen sighed, like my ignorance was shocking. *"High emotions carry spiritual energy. That's why we need a full table of séance guests and the biggest responses we can muster from them. All of it is fuel. And the more fuel the better, especially to power the exorcism of a spirit as strong as Rose. So indulge me and my weird tricks for one séance, won't you?"*

I guess Ellen was the expert. I frowned but nodded.

So we rehearsed. For hours.

Every second woke Ellen up more. She'd clearly lived for shows like these. And I could relate—I craved that onstage rush, too. Even if I had to settle for a séance instead of a play.

But as she made me practice lifting the table and I drew on the Beetle's strength again and again, I had this uncomfortable wrenching sensation—like a muscle being twisted the wrong way. Not one in my arms or back. Something deeper. Something I couldn't put my finger on.

Finally, at eleven-forty-five, Ellen released Flynn. The show was at midnight, and she had to leave his body, at least for the moment, so he could meet the guests in the back alley without terrifying them with glowing eyes.

He desperately needed the breather.

The second she was out, Flynn ripped off the ant mask and half collapsed against a nearby column for support. His face had paled to gray, his freckles bold like blood spatter. He looked like he'd clawed his way out of a frozen lake.

The night was warm, but he was so shivery. When I took his hand, his skin was sticky and clammy, his fingers stiff.

"Do you need a blanket? A sweatshirt?" I asked.

"W-won't help," he forced out through his shuddering jaw.

Stiffness had locked into his arms, through his elbows, crawling up toward his shoulders. And he had to shake and shake to get his joints moving again.

But in a few minutes, his breathing did return to a normal rate, and he pushed himself fully upright. "I have to go meet the guests."

"Wait. Will you be okay?" I asked. "Channeling Ellen again?"

"Another hour or so max, right? Let's get this over with." Before he left, he touched my arm. "Good luck tonight."

"You'll be here with us," I reminded him.

Flynn smiled tightly. "Between the Ant and Ellen, I'm not sure how much I *will* be. I'm anticipating another thrilling hour of spiraling in the void and being gnawed on by worms. Not sure where the balance will land."

"Is that what it's like for you wearing the Ant mask—a spiraling void?"

"It's not as bad as the rose mask, but yeah. It's . . . dizzying. Like I've lost touch with the ground."

As a medium, wearing one of these masks must've been a more intense experience than it was for me and Vivi, not to mention that he was channeling Ellen, too. It wasn't fair that he had to make that sacrifice. I wished I could do it for him. But I had the Cragg genes, not the Clery genes. "Thank you for doing this," I said.

"It's the right thing to do. Maybe it's too late for my dad, but we can't let that happen again. Not to your mom." He picked up the ant mask. "One last time. And then no more spirits?"

"No more spirits."

He nodded and put on the mask.

At midnight, Vivi and I waited at the table while Flynn waited in the alley to collect our guests. *All that fresh living electricity!* as Ellen had so disconcertingly called them during our rehearsal.

The crystal ball sparkled on the table. The sky overhead was clear. The moon was on full display, and the stone table gleamed ghostly white. Flynn had brought fat white pillar candles, and, at Ellen's direction, we'd set them on the table in a long slithering line. We'd plucked the biggest roses from the bushes winding between the columns and scattered their petals, bright as flakes of cobalt. Glowing cobalt, through the eyes of my beetle mask.

The air felt dead. Balmy, windless. Like breathing through a thick blanket. Or a thick mask.

The stench of fermenting grapes was almost choking.

As Vivi and I waited, sweat trickled down my low back. Not only had Flynn given us cloaks to wear, but the chairs themselves were warm tonight. The stone felt slightly sticky in the same way the masks did. Yet it wasn't uncomfortable. More like the cushiest couch, one I wished I could melt into.

But I forced my spine straight. Locked my jaw against the would-be yawns.

At ten past midnight, Flynn returned, leading a shuffling group to the table. And suddenly, I was wide awake. My fingers gripped the arms of the beetle chair as he gestured for everyone to pick their seats, maintaining an eerie pre-séance silence.

Some of the guests seemed around our age, and I wondered if any were my future classmates. What a wild first encounter. I took some comfort in the shield of my mask. Between the blue glass and the dim candlelight, I doubted they would recognize me later.

Flynn waited until everyone was settled before tapping his ant mask and pointing to the cheap masks we'd laid out at the empty seats.

We filled the whole table—a body for every chair, like Ellen had requested.

As everyone covered their faces, became a circle of silent white plastic punctuated by our three overly adorned insect faces, a high titter escaped from Vivi. Not planned, but definitely creepy enough to belong at a séance.

At Flynn's glare, the giggle cut off abruptly. Vivi clapped a hand over her mouth, as if she hadn't realized she was making the sound.

Flynn nodded and slid into the ant chair beside her. He hadn't even gotten that white mesh over his head, didn't even have a chance to reach for it, before glowing fog curled up from under his chair.

Guess Ellen didn't care about bothering with veils tonight.

Flynn sucked in a deep breath, the last he'd get to take of his own volition for some time, and then gave the fog a slight nod. Instantly, it seeped into his skin.

He pressed his eyes closed. And when they opened, there it was again: that ghastly white glow.

Our guests gasped and nudged each other. They'd seen the fog, too, I'm sure, but smoke was easier to fake. "How are you doing that?" one demanded.

Flynn—or, now Ellen, really—held a finger to his lips, which curled in a slow smile. She surveyed each of us at the table, Flynn's chin held especially high. Candlelight flickered off the red of his ant mask.

The soft crackles of burning wicks ate into the silence. And the newcomers shifted in their seats, fiddled with their elastic mask straps.

"Welcome." Flynn finally spoke, in a voice halfway between his own and that tinny rasp of Ellen's. She was trying to sound more like him, I think. To stop the guests from spooking and immediately abandoning the table.

Some of them still looked close to fleeing, and I couldn't blame them.

"Tonight," Ellen spoke through Flynn, *"we've gathered to call forth spirits. Please know, everything you will see is natural and ordinary. Merely* super*natural.* Extra*ordinary. If anything, it*

is our understanding of what is natural, what is ordinary, that is mistaken. Tonight, we take a crucial step toward realigning those definitions."

From there, Ellen jumped into a spiel similar to the séance script Vivi and I had found in the attic: *"Knowledge of the future may be gained by scrutinizing the past. In fact, Frederic W. H. Myers compared a living human to a caterpillar. . . ."*

She told the story of the caterpillar on the rose leaf, who believed it was meant for more, who saw a butterfly and knew that it was meant to become one. All the while, Flynn's body moved with the gestures of a stranger—larger and rounder, dramatic in a practiced way. Ellen must have performed these words, every accompanying pause and sweep of her hand, a hundred times. Or more.

She wrapped up her parable with: *"There is an undeniable similarity of structure between our own intelligence and an invisible intelligence. Or, rather, should I say, invisible to you, my dear guests? I need but don this mask . . ."* Ellen made Flynn point to his ant mask.

That was the last line before the script in the attic had cut off. But, of course, Ellen knew it by heart. She continued, *"And here is an invisible presence within me. You may notice that these masks depict no larvae—all fully evolved insects."* She gestured to me and Vivi. *"You see,* we *are the larvae."*

Vivi stared at her, enraptured. Starry-eyed. Giddy on the high of her mask.

"Of course, most of us will not become butterflies," Ellen said. *"We merely hope to bear witness as one flits by. This is how we learn about our own untapped potential, and the future that may await us—should we be found fitting.*

"And so, without further ado, we shall call forth the spirits within this house. Please join hands. . . ."

With the extra strength that the beetle mask gave me, I'd have to try not to crush the hands of the people on either side of me. I took the hand of the girl to my left, then the guy to my right. His palms were even sweatier than mine.

"And bow your heads. . . ."

I stared down at the edge of the table, carved with scrolling rose vines and crawling bugs.

"Repeat after me: We call forth the spirits in this House of Masks. We offer our presence. We offer our energy. To help you manifest."

"We call forth the spirits in this House of Masks . . ." My voice scraped nervously from my throat, along with the other half-halting whispers, finishing with: "To help you manifest."

"Very good," Ellen said. *"Open your eyes."*

To most of our guests, it probably seemed like nothing had changed. But through the beetle mask, there was a definite shift. The dull glow of the table and chairs was brightening, intensifying, wherever our bodies touched the stone. That feeling of warmth, of strangely sticky softness, was stronger. I peeled my thigh from my seat, to prove I still could, and when I set it back down, the glow shifted with me. Some kind of spiritual interaction was taking place.

Vivi clocked it, too, grinning with wonder as she lifted her hand from her chair to dim the glow and then brightened it again with her touch.

Judging by Ellen's widening smile, this was what she wanted. We must've been collecting the spiritual energy she was so hungry for.

"Unlink hands," she commanded everyone.

My cue was coming, and we had to drop the hand-holding for it.

I slipped mine into my lap, scooting close to the table.

"Spirits, if you are here, please give us a sign."

Everyone echoed that, too, and then we stopped and waited.

Breath paused around the table. The humid air hung in a rose-thick cloud. Sweet, like overripe fruit. Bitter on my tongue.

My mask was extra-warm. Especially where it met my hairline. Like it was picking up a static charge. Electricity buzzed through my veins, trickling into my muscles. It felt like I really could lift an elephant.

But I didn't have to lift an elephant. Just this stone table.

I clutched the rest of me as still as possible—holding my face blank behind my mask—and pushed up on the stone with both hands.

The table trembled. Then wobbled.

Gasps chorused from our guests.

With a shift and a groan, a stirring of the old stone beneath our feet, the table rose.

An inch. Two. Three.

Someone shrieked.

Deep inside me, there was that feeling again—something bending the wrong way.

I dropped the table. With an earth-shaking thud. One I desperately hoped Mom wouldn't hear all the way in her bedroom.

Guests squealed with shock. A couple leaped to their feet.

"Please. Remain in your seats," Ellen said, owning the ant chair like it was a throne. *"This is what you came to see, isn't it?"*

They exchanged uncertain looks but tiptoed back to the

table. One, who'd ripped off his white mask, held it to his face and peeked around it, not putting it all the way on.

"So there must be at least one spirit here with us," Ellen said. *"But perhaps there are more."* She turned to Vivi. *"As a resident of the house, you have a stronger connection than most with the spirits who dwell here. Would you be willing to volunteer? To climb up on this table for us?"*

We'd been careful to leave a space for her so she wouldn't knock over the candles.

Vivi stepped up, her movements more spritelike than usual. She really was perfect for this.

She lay down, arms folded solemnly across her chest, like she was playing dead in a coffin.

Ellen hadn't given that instruction yet; Vivi might've given away that this was rehearsed. But Ellen mostly swallowed an annoyed huff. *"Yes. Like that. Good."*

Honestly, the guests were so stuck on the table-lifting incident that they didn't seem to be paying much attention to Ellen and Vivi's setup. Some were eyeing the table, afraid it might lift again. One girl finally had the bright idea to glance underneath, to see if we had any special machinery rigged up.

Ellen held up a hand. *"Silence around the table."* She flashed Flynn's white teeth into a wolfish grin. *"It will take all of us to pull this off. Again, I need you to repeat after me."*

The table hushed. The shifting ceased. All eyes flicked between Vivi's prone body and Flynn.

"O spirits of this house, we know you are here. We command you to wake up. We command the spirits at this table to unite with us, and to help this girl ascend."

Ellen was probably getting swept up in the drama of the

show—trying to impress the guests—but commanding the spirits of the house to wake up sounded like the *opposite* of an exorcism. I choked on the words, couldn't quite get them out, but everyone else did.

The beetle mask squeezed the edges of my face.

The stone touching us brightened. The carved faces at the top of each chair—the ones that must have matched the masks—alit like tiny supernovas. Every single one.

The ground under us lurched—so sudden, so quick, I would've sworn I'd imagined it. Except I wasn't the only one who gasped, who grabbed the arms of their chair to stay steady.

I started to ask Ellen, "What was—?"

But she tapped a finger to Flynn's lips. As if to assure me: this was all still on track, all part of our plan. Then she pointed at the center of the table.

At Vivi.

My sister stiffened, head to toe, rigid as a corpse.

The guests, eyes wide through the holes in their masks, stared, riveted to her every move.

Vivi's back lifted from the table, then her legs, her whole body, top to bottom. Air collected between her and the tabletop. Clear, empty air.

Even I gasped a little. It wasn't something I could get used to, my little sister learning to fly.

She hovered a half foot from the table and kept floating, inch by inch, even higher.

She lifted above our heads, giving me an unobstructed view of the girl across from me, horrified behind her mask as she gaped up at Vivi.

I'd told Vivi, in no uncertain terms, I didn't want her getting too far from the table. That thing was hard stone. If she lost control and dropped . . .

The actor part of my brain insisted that the show must go on, but it was getting harder not to interrupt. Vivi was still rising, higher than she'd gone in rehearsal. At this height, I could still stand up and reach her, but not if she went much higher.

I turned a panicked glance to Ellen. She nodded at me, like everything was in order.

The Beetle was sending me its most soothing signals.

But my anxiety was splintering through its mood-dampening effect.

It didn't feel like everything was in order. Not to me.

Flynn wasn't here to weigh in—not really. Vivi was completely consumed. It was only me. Me and the Beetle and Ellen, making the call.

I dug my fingers harder and harder into the arms of my chair. With a small crack, the stone under my fingertips crumbled, raining tiny chunks down to the grass below.

Vivi was reaching five feet, six feet, seven feet, and I was reaching the limit of how high I could tolerate.

Luckily, she stopped there. Hovering.

The guests were gushing disbelief. Some even started applauding.

Vivi had to be eating it up. She wasn't coming down.

Soft fluttering stirred around us, from the rosebushes surrounding the table. A glowing cloud rose up. Light and lacy. Butterflies. They rippled through the still night air to join Vivi's levitating form.

No one said a word. Not even Ellen, though she didn't seem surprised.

I was no bug expert, but it was *impossible* to tune out all of Vivi's scientific babbling, so I knew butterflies didn't come out at night. Only moths. But, then, these weren't real butterflies.

These were extensions of *the* Butterfly. Who, apparently, was as excited as Ellen to be part of the show.

One alit on the thigh of Vivi's jeans. Another on the toe of her sneaker. And then more: one on her shoulder, on the forehead of her mask, her chest, her stomach. They kept landing. Featherlight. Flapping like white bats under the pale moonshine. Wings pulsing and glittering.

God, I hoped Vivi's concentration didn't snap. It flashed into my mind, the unbidden nightmare of my little sister's skull cracking against the table. Mask lying askew over her brain-dead face.

She didn't seem to notice the butterflies. She was frozen.

She still wasn't coming down.

The metallic taste of panic gummed up my throat. Ever since I took all those pills, that's where panic hit me, right in the esophagus.

You must be scared.

but not bad

The show must go on.

The Beetle remixed my past words and thoughts, playing them back, trying to soothe me.

But I didn't care about the show anymore—not more than Vivi.

My desperate whisper pushed free: "Vivi, you can come down now."

A spasm ripped through her floating body, from the top of her lacy mask to her butterfly-covered toes. Except the butterflies didn't startle. They stayed exactly where they were.

She started to rotate in the air, her head pointing up, her feet pointing down.

I sighed, relieved. Okay, she was landing. She was—

No. She stopped. Standing in midair.

And then she extended her arms into third position, out to the side and overhead. She lifted a graceful leg and began to twirl. As close to en pointe as one could get in pink sneakers, across an invisible stage above our heads. Her eyes were closed, like a sleepwalker's. Her hands swished breezily, soft and pretty, like she'd been trained, as she spun one way and then the other.

She wore jeans and a tank top, no sequins or tulle, nothing fancy except for her cloak. And her mask. But her grin was radiant—pure sunshine—like she was dreaming an especially sugarplum-dusted fairy tale.

This was Vivi's dream—the one I'd ripped away from her. To be the star of the show.

And she was utterly mesmerizing.

The butterflies danced with her. Her fluttering hands swooped around them, like she knew precisely which way they would move, or they knew precisely which way she would move.

Around the table, some people leaned back, some leaned in, all glued to Vivi's every gesture.

Midmove, she and the butterflies paused.

Vivi lifted an ear as though another dancer had entered her invisible stage.

She turned and bowed deeply. Outstretched a hand as if reaching for someone.

Her grin was as wide as ever, like she was greeting her very best friend. I was almost jealous—she looked happier to see this imaginary friend than she ever looked to see me.

Of course, there was no one there, seven feet up in the air.

But then, Vivi jerked, her arm tugged forward as if a duet

partner really had taken her hand. And then pulled her into a lift, a spin.

She dropped into a backbend as sudden as a trust fall.

I gasped.

But the air caught her. Like she was supported by invisible arms.

Vivi bounced back up. She whirled faster and faster, her chest heaving with harder pants, as she threw herself into fearless dips and twirls and leaps. And suddenly, I thought of the clockwork ballerina in that thrifted windup jewelry box Mom had found for her years ago. The tiny ballerina, with her stiff slippers and outstretched arms, suspended on a spring that sagged with age. Her spinning went from prim and perfect to leaning to lurching. Her dangling plastic legs sputtered in their sockets.

Finally, the music box had broken. And every time Vivi opened the lid, the tiny ballerina would topple, to nothing but a whirring, sputtering click.

There was no music now either, and Vivi's breaths rasped louder, ragged. She swirled and swooped with the butterflies. With her invisible partner. Sweat slipped down her neck. A butterfly lapped at it as more swarmed around her. There were so many they weaved like fog through her dancing limbs.

The whole table was cheering her on.

But her eyes wouldn't open, and her grin was getting strained.

Something was wrong.

"Vivi!" I cried.

Ellen reached a hand toward me. *"Libby, dear, please don't interfere!"*

"No, this trick is over!" I peeled away from my sticky chair and leaped up, standing on the seat to reach out to Vivi. "Stop! Come down *now*!"

Vivi stopped.

The butterflies stopped, too.

The whole dance lurched to a standstill. And the butterflies settled on her, all at once. Most landed along her shoulders and arms, the back of her cloak, like living wings.

I'd committed the greatest sin of live performance—interrupting an unforgettable show—and some of the guests booed.

But Vivi was finally descending, and that's all that mattered. She lowered until her feet hovered inches from the table.

Then she turned to face me.

Behind her butterfly mask, Vivi's eyes were gone.

All that filled the holes were blue wells. Glowing ocean-deep shadows from corner to corner. Screening over where her eyes should have been.

They weren't white like Ellen's.

They were blue like Rose's.

Like the murals . . . the mosaics in the floor. Those baby rabbits munching on meat, blood staining their tufted chins. Their eyes looked like this.

Exactly like this.

CHAPTER TWENTY-ONE

WITH THOSE FLAT-OCEAN EYES, VIVI SMILED at me. Way too wide. Her lips stretching and stretching and stretching until they started to split. A bead of blood welled from the center of her bottom lip and dripped down her chin. Her giggle bubbled into the air, sickly sweet, her shoulders bouncing too violently for such an angelic sound.

I thought of Flynn in our kitchen, studying our mural. All the blood-dripping prey turned predators. What he'd imagined it meant: the corruption of the innocent, betrayal, a tongue-in-cheek joke. *Maybe we don't know the punch line yet,* he'd said.

This was it, wasn't it? The punch line.

According to the drawing we'd found in the attic, Rose had titled that mosaic "The Feast."

We hadn't realized: *we* were the feast.

I whipped around to Ellen. "What's happening to her? Something went wrong!"

"No, no," Ellen assured me. *"Please don't be alarmed. This is what we want."*

"What?" I gaped at her. I gaped at Vivi.

friend

In the back of my mind, the Beetle spoke in my voice.

Friend? What the hell did that mean—friend?

Vivi couldn't stop laughing. Shriller. Wilder. Eardrum-skewering stabs.

It was so sudden. Like she'd inhaled an entire canister of laughing gas. Like she was OD'ing.

She raised a finger and pointed at the house.

I turned to look. The round attic window glowed with the ethereal light of all those blue stars. And something was there. A hulking silhouette, half blocking the light.

Mom was the only one in the house. What *was* that?

friend

The Beetle spoke again.

The blood around my heart throbbed, constricted. The air felt too thin in my lungs.

Shrieks erupted around the table. Guests leaped from their seats—or tried. Some of the chairs had become stickier than others. The guy beside me fought so hard to free his jeans that they tore. But even he managed to break free. The guests stripped off their white masks, littering them over the ground as they all ran.

Let them run. They should. I would if I could.

"Vivi." I stepped up on the table beside her. With shaking fingers, I reached out to touch her shoulder.

"Oh, no," Ellen said. *"Dear, I wouldn't advise touching—"*

Vivi spun to face me. Masked in quivering fleshlike lace and feathers, swarming with butterflies. Her eyes blue and hollow.

I grabbed for her mask, hoping to catch her off guard.

She snatched my hand and crushed it in hers.

She wasn't laughing anymore.

My beetle mask dulled the pain, but her nails dug into my skin. Piercing. Merciless. This was nothing like our fights as kids, when she'd scratched harder than she'd meant.

Either she didn't realize what she was doing, or she did—and she was trying to hurt me on purpose.

She shoved me, brutal and sudden, and my shocked knees buckled. I collapsed to the tabletop, smashing down into rose petals and worse—much worse—lit candles.

Burns seared into my back, my thighs, as the candles rolled and smashed beneath me. Molten wax sprayed, catching one or two of the guests who were still nearby. I heard their pained cries.

Before I could pull myself up, Vivi was on top. Straddling me, holding my shoulders down.

"Vivi! Stop!" I squirmed, afraid to fight back while wearing the beetle mask. I'd cracked those chair arms without trying. I didn't want to know what I could accidentally do to my sister. But my shirt had ridden up and hot wax pooled under my back, scalding the skin into blisters.

Vivi was in the hot wax, too. It puddled under her knees—but she didn't react, fixated on holding me down. She grinned. Blood had spilled from her split lip into her smile, stuck between the cracks of her front teeth. She reached for my face.

I thought she wanted to rip away my mask, to steal my strength before I worked up the nerve to use it.

But she didn't pull my mask off.

She *pushed.* She smashed it against my face, as if she could press it permanently into place.

Solid inch-thick glass crushed into the bridge of my nose. Hotter and stickier than ever.

I gasped to cry out, but my mask's lips wouldn't open. The

scream got trapped inside, echoing in my head as it bounced against glass.

be a friend to me too.

The mask's edges burned hot, hotter than the wax—melting into my skin.

"Good, that's good!" Flynn's body stood beside us, leering down with Ellen's cold white eyes. *"Don't let her take that mask off—the Beetle needs time to finish bonding. We may need to tie her or—"*

Vivi raised her head to growl at Ellen.

"Resent me all you want," Ellen snarled back, *"but I'm trying to help you, you miserable monster!"*

Ellen wasn't on our side at all, was she? She clearly wanted the Butterfly and the Beetle to take over our bodies. I had no idea what was in it for her, but she was happy to throw us under the bus to get it.

I tried to call out to Flynn, even if he might not hear me, but my lips were sealed, my face numbed. The world dimmed: My view of Vivi, her looming fleshy mask. Butterflies circling her head like a halo.

Then she fuzzed out of view entirely, and all I could see was darkness broken by kaleidoscopic colors.

Blue and gold.

The same swirling blue and gold my mask had revealed before if I'd kept my eyes closed. Except this time, my eyes were open.

And still, all I could see were those blue and gold shapes. Now they were rectangles, stacking like walls.

Pressing in around me.

Crushing me.

A tingling burn flamed across my scalp, down my neck. My spine.

Something crawled over my hand. Skittering legs. Into my sleeve. Another something. Many somethings.

I needed to get my mask off *now.*

I shoved Vivi, as hard as I dared.

Light as a bird, she flew backward, releasing me.

The clutch of my mask eased. The darkness and shapes faded from my vision.

"No! Wait!" Ellen reached out to grab me, Flynn's frozen fingers latching on to my arm. *"Dear, I know it's a scary process, but communion with the Beetle is what's best for you! An ascension! Remember? Even you said—"*

I didn't want to, but I had to—I punched Flynn in the face.

In the cheek of the ant mask, which I prayed would cushion the blow.

The mask flew from his face, and he reeled back, coughing cloudy fog. His eyes rolled forward, from glowing white to human green, and he collapsed.

I scrambled from the table, sloshing through burning wax, scraping my palms against the stone, tearing holes in my jeans. I shook my arms against the itchy onslaught of crawling legs.

Blue beetles tumbled from my clothes, shattered against the hard ground. But not all of them. Some lit into flight, tickling my scalp as they landed on my head.

I shrieked, swiping and swatting them off.

I dug my fingers into the glass lip around my hairline. The mask really was melting into my skin, the line starting to vanish. I'd bitten off most of my nails and had to scramble for one long enough to hook under the thinning rim.

Stop! Stay Stop!

I tore the edge back from my face.

Cool air rushed into the gap. But the rest clung like glue as I ripped at it, tugging and tugging. My skin sticking. Catching on the mask.

Every survival instinct in my animal gut told me I couldn't stop tugging, no matter what. Even if it did take half my skin with it.

I pulled and peeled harder.

Stay Stay Stay Stay

With a stinging yank, at last the mask came free in my hand.

I hurled it at the stone table with vengeful relish. But it didn't break. It bounced.

Glass wasn't supposed to bounce. Even the beetles broke. But nothing about these masks worked like it should.

I gulped down air by the mouthful. My hands flew to my face, touching to make sure that there were no dripping gouged pockets of blood. Or exposed muscle, sinew.

No, the skin was raw, but it was all still there.

Fluttering behind me made me whip back around.

Vivi had landed where my mask had fallen. The shadows of this yard played tricks—made her flapping cloak look like big, wide wings.

She scooped up the beetle mask like it was precious to her. A friend.

And those blue voids of her eyes landed again—on me.

"Vivi. No." I backed away.

Without the Beetle's extra strength, I wasn't sure I could fight her off. But if I let her put the mask back on me . . .

The all-time worst catch-22.

She stepped toward me.

And Flynn tackled her from behind, knocking her into the grass. The beetle mask dropped from her hands.

I charged after them. With a desperate leap, I pinned Vivi under me.

A low, strange growl came from past Vivi's bloody teeth. She was stronger than she should be. She ripped one hand free and tore into my arm with her nails.

"Flynn! Help me!"

He held her down by the shoulders. "Get that thing off her!" he shouted.

I wrestled Vivi like her life depended on it, gritting my teeth through the taste of my salty sweat, the bloody sting of the wound she'd scratched in my arm. I dug my fingers into the vanishing seam by her temple.

To get this thing off, I needed to be powerful. Decisive.

I pleaded with the universe, *Please don't tear her skin, please don't tear her skin—*

In one fierce tug, I ripped her mask off.

It came away in my hands, and her face was whole underneath, and I could've collapsed with relief then and there. But the butterfly mask was searing my fingertips, in a way that felt deliberate. Spiteful.

I threw the damn thing. As far from my sister as I could.

Vivi gasped, as if resurfacing from deep waters. Where her mask had tried to bind, a raw red line encircled her forehead and cut across her cheeks.

The edge of my own face burned, the wind too cold against it.

Her huge brown eyes flickered with panic, darting to find the danger she still sensed, but couldn't see. Then they found me. "Libby?"

She threw her arms around my neck and started to cry.

* * *

"You're safe," I said. And I couldn't stop saying it—"You're safe"—over and over.

I clung to every sign that my sister was here with me. Really here. Really *her.* I pressed my cheek against the top of her head and breathed in her green-apple conditioner. I'd never loved fake green apples as much as I did in that moment, squeezing Vivi's bony back.

"Okay, look at me." I pushed Vivi back, holding her by the shoulders, so I could scan her for injuries, like Flynn had done to me earlier. "Are you hurt?"

Her brown skin was ashy. Her chin was trembling, and her bottom lip was puffy from splitting—a congealed crack ran down the center.

"I'm fine," she lied. "But, Lib . . ." She ran light fingers up my arm, stopping before the bloody gouges her nails had left behind. "Oh God, *I* did that, didn't I?"

"No. You didn't." Her body. But not her.

She looked me up and down, wincing at my battered arms and knees. Honestly, the pain was worse on my lower back, where the hot wax had seeped. I was worried about her knees, her shins. That mask had made her crouch in molten wax, too. And it hadn't cared how much that would damage either of us.

Flynn knelt beside us, gasping for breath. His cheek was already bruising, cut from my punch.

The remnants of our séance lay scattered around us. Dripping wax pooled over the patio. Only a few sputtering candles remained, strewn across the stone tabletop.

The ant mask lay by Flynn's chair, where it had fallen.

Mine and Vivi's were abandoned, face up in the grass.

"What the hell . . . ?" Flynn surveyed the scene like he was trying to remember a dream. Or, more accurately, to shake off a nightmare. "You two okay?"

At my nod, he exhaled in relief. And then touched his swelling cheek. "Also, did someone punch me? It really hurts."

I winced. I really hoped I hadn't broken anything. "I'm so sorry. Ellen was attacking me, and I didn't know how to wake you up." With a bolstering touch to Vivi's shoulder, I released her to take a closer look at Flynn's face. The skin was red and angry, blood seeping from a gash left by the ant mask. I hated that I was the one who'd done that to him. But his cheekbone wasn't caved in or sagging or pressed up toward his eye. "I think you're okay," I told him.

"Did you . . . ?" Flynn rubbed his scalp, as if he could thaw his brain. He was several steps behind, blinking and disoriented. "Did you say Ellen *attacked* you?" Then, with dawning horror: "You mean, *I* attacked you?"

"Don't worry, she didn't get far. But yes," I said, steaming with fresh rage. "She lied about everything. This was never about helping Mom. She was trying to get those masks to take over our bodies. And Vivi's nearly did."

"She tricked us." Vivi tore at a blade of grass in her lap. Like Flynn, she was still shivering. "And the Butterfly tricked me, too," she said. So softly. So ashamed. "I thought . . ." Her eyes teared, and she shook her head.

She'd probably thought she and the Butterfly were friends.

"I thought the Beetle and I were friends, too," I confessed.

She nodded gratefully.

And it was true. I had *wanted* to believe the Beetle. That it could save me from my own brain. And I'd wanted to believe Ellen, too—that she could save Mom.

Flynn went rigid. "My dad . . . Before he vanished, he said he was talking to Ellen. Holy shit." Miserable, he rubbed a hand through his hair. "Did she trick him, too? What did she *do* to him?"

My stomach dropped. "We'll find out," I promised. "If it's at all possible, we'll find out what happened."

"But how?" Vivi asked. "And now what do we do? About Mom? About anything?"

They both looked at me.

To be fair, I'd been the most conscious during the recent debacle.

"I—I don't know," I said. "First of all, we have to get Mom out of this house. We *all* have to get out of this house."

"You know she won't go," Vivi said. "No way."

"Well, we'll tell her . . . I got burned." My lower back and thighs were screaming. "And you did, too, right?" I pointed to Vivi's knees. "We'll say we need to go to the hospital. Once she's out of the house, it might be easier to get her to listen."

"Do you want me to come with you?" Flynn asked.

I hesitated. I did want him to come—he made me feel safer. But he'd already taken a physical and spiritual beating tonight. His eyes carried an exhausted glaze. Cold quaked through his shoulders. "That's okay," I told him. "She might respond better if it's just us. As long as you'll be all right on your own."

He waved the concern away. "I'll be fine. Do what you need to do." He pulled himself up from the grass and shook out his arms, glancing bleakly at the stone table like he was wondering if he should try to clean it up.

But candles and trampled petals had spilled everywhere. Fleeing footprints tracked through grass and mud. A wayward cloak fluttered, snagged on the hedge maze.

It wasn't just the table. We'd trashed the whole yard.

"Forget it," I said. Truly, the least of our collective worries.

Flynn nodded. He zipped up his bag and hoisted it onto his shoulder. "Libby," he said uneasily, "if you do get her to leave, where will you go?"

I bit my cheek. Our old apartment was an hour away, at least. "Wherever it is, you and I, we can figure this out, right?"

"Sure," Flynn said. But he looked so sad.

True, long-distance was hard, and Flynn and I had only just gotten started, but . . .

"Maybe we'll find someplace close," I said.

"Maybe you will."

For someone so used to lying, Flynn should've been more convincing. But his hands were buried in his pockets, and he was staring at the ground. He shook it off. "Go on. Take care of your mom."

With one last squeeze of my hand, he grabbed his duffel bag. "Text me, okay?"

"I will."

I wanted to say it twice, like he'd done for me after we traded numbers, but something in my throat felt too thick.

And he left. Slipped away through the crack in our back fence.

I was suddenly painfully aware of my outfit, the fake-date top, now stained and ripped.

Destroyed, like everything else.

Then Vivi slid her hand into mine and squeezed, and I came back into my body.

Right.

Keep it together, Libby.

I managed a wobbly smile. She wobbled one back. Funny how those fake smiles, those faulty reassurances, had become so second-nature to my family, especially in the past few weeks. They'd always felt like lies to me.

This time, it didn't feel like a lie.

Suddenly, I wondered if that's what Mom had meant all along by her watery smiles. That it didn't matter how much I'd cost her in hospital bills or pain, even agonizing trauma. To her, it was always worth it.

I was worth it.

I swallowed the lump in my throat. "This damn house. These damn masks."

I grabbed the ant mask next to Flynn's chair. And the beetle and butterfly masks from the grass. Pinched them between my forefingers like they were the nastiest bugs of all. They were squishy and sticky. Still warm—Vivi's especially. It didn't have enough heat to burn me this time, but I did have to shake my finger free from its forehead.

I dumped the butterfly mask and the ant mask in a bush near the table.

My fingers trembled against my plan to do the same with my beetle mask. Some latent longing urged me to keep it—to hold on to our promise of friendship.

But that desperate echo of *Stay,* over and over, in my voice. The searing burn against my hairline.

The indentations of the mask's eyes stared up at me. They looked round. Softer. Pleading.

"I'm sorry," I whispered. "Goodbye."

I made myself chuck it into the bush, too.

Together, Vivi and I trudged toward the house, my arms wrapped around her shoulders to guide her, as if she'd forgotten how to walk. She might as well have. She was stumbling over her toes. Weak. Like something big had been drained away.

She kept glancing back toward the séance table and the bushes where I'd stashed our masks.

"Lib," she whispered, in the tiniest voice. "I'm afraid I'll miss it. I know I shouldn't, but the world's different from inside there. I don't have to feel heavy like this. It's the only time I can forget. . . ."

"I know. Me too," I confessed. The beetle mask was pure relief. It let me be someone I didn't hate. Someone I could be proud of. Strong and resilient. Everything I wasn't. It was a beautiful fantasy. Wrapped in horrific bug-shaped packaging, but still . . .

Vivi nodded, swallowing a dry sob.

"We'll do it together, okay?" I said. And, God, I hoped I could.

I kept wondering how long I could get away with wearing mine before it got dangerous. Whether it might be safe in five-minute intervals. One-minute intervals?

It wasn't worth it.

I should never want to touch that thing again. And yet . . . I was so hyperaware of the distance between me and those bushes, like I was leaving part of myself behind. The best part of myself.

"It'll be better this way," I told Vivi, even as I wasn't sure I believed it.

We stepped inside, into the shadowed kitchen. I reached for the light.

Then I saw the figure hunched over the island.

Mom.

In her robe.

Sitting, waiting for us.

My heart stopped.

"Mom!" Vivi raced to her side. "I thought you were in bed."

I flicked on the light as Mom turned to face us. Illuminating what wasn't her face at all.

A mask.

White. Topped with a metal crown, twisted as old teeth. A snowy veil trailed down over Mom's dark curls. And there was no longer only an outline of a flower on the left side of the face. Now, the mask was blooming—velvety blue flowers blossoming through porcelain.

Rose.

But behind the mask were Mom's desperate brown eyes.

"Girls . . ." She spoke through those shimmering rosebud lips. "Please . . . I need your help."

"Mom," I choked out, "how long have you been wearing that mask?"

Mom's neck bowed under the ivory veil that lay limp against her neck, like the gauzy fabric weighed a thousand pounds. "Since the second night we moved in. When I realized it could pop out of the window."

The second night? This house had wasted no time digging its claws into her.

She curled in on herself like a flower out of water. Slouched on her stool, slumped on the counter. Laid her head down between a rose in a vase and a drained blue-stained teacup. "I can't get it off."

"Get what off?" Vivi backed up. "The mask . . . ?"

"Libby, sweetie, could you make me some more tea?" She nudged the cup toward me with weak knuckles, without lifting her head from the counter. "It's the only thing that makes me feel better. . . ."

Her lips were blue. Her teeth were blue. Her tongue was blue.

"Mom. No." It felt like I was denying a dying person water,

but rose tea was the last thing she needed. "Why don't you try some water?"

I grabbed her teacup and filled it at the sink. Set it back in front of her.

But she didn't touch it.

"The truth is," she mumbled, "the blue roses and this face, those are the best things I remember from my time here when I was little. It sounds silly, but I always felt like this mask was watching over me. When I wear it, I feel . . . well, in control. I've needed that. A moment each day to feel that way."

Of course. It was suddenly transparent to me. Each of these masks, they lured us with the thing we craved most: For me—resilience. For Vivi—joy. For Mom—control.

Vivi's split lip was clear proof that these temptations could go too far. Way too far.

And on the inside, Mom may have *felt* in control, but she definitely hadn't seemed that way to me or Vivi. Least of all now.

She was limp and shivery, panic in her glassy eyes. "You won't believe this, but the mask gives me these abilities to . . . Well, look."

She pulled herself up, then reached out and pricked her finger on a thorn from the vase's rose.

"Mom!" Vivi reached out to stop her.

"Shh. Watch." Mom squeezed a drop into the water. And the rose squirmed with sudden life, a sleeping snake poked awake. The bloom swelled, bigger, wider. Its red-tipped thorns sharpened. The stem lengthened, curled, twisted as it flopped over the side and toppled the vase to the counter, glass cracking, water sloshing down the sides to the cabinets, the writhing flower wriggling out.

It flopped like a wet fish for a few seconds more. Then lay there in a pool of water and broken glass.

"If I give it more, it keeps growing," Mom said. Strangely proud.

Vivi was as horrified as I was.

And Mom caved in on herself when she saw the way we were looking at her. "It felt so good," she said softly, "to make something beautiful grow. But I gave those roses more and more of myself. I didn't even notice how far I'd gone." She pulled up the stained sleeves of her bathrobe. Underneath was a tangled ruin, worse than I'd feared. Bloody gashes carved deep into the tender skin of her forearms—some thin, some thick.

Three houseflies had been tucked up her sleeve, sipping at the seeping wound near her elbow. More tiny, wiry mosquitoes than I could count, their bellies bulging with blood.

I gagged.

With a gasp, Vivi shooed them away. But they only buzzed into the air and landed in the same spot. Sucking away.

And Mom didn't have the energy to fight them off. "I'm not fit to take care of anything," she said, through the clutch of a sob. "I love my job, but the thing I wanted most was to be a mother. It gave me purpose. It felt like everything. But I can't even take care of *myself,* let alone . . ." She turned to me. "Of course I wasn't able to give you the happy life you deserve. Of course it was Vivi, not me, who was there to save you. By the time I got home, you would've been dead." It ripped from her so painfully, dredged from some secret, gnarled place.

And it stunned me. This must have been haunting her this whole time. It hadn't even occurred to me—that maybe there was more to her insisting I not know the truth about who found me.

She'd *wanted* it to be her. She'd wanted to be able to give me at least that much. Protect me from myself. Protect Vivi, too.

"Mom, no!" I said. "That was my fault, not yours—"

"No. The fact that you even think that . . ." Mom shook her head. "You were sick, baby. It's not your fault."

It's not your fault. In spite of everything, hearing her say that nearly made me crumple me with relief. With a longing I didn't know I'd even had.

"It's not your job to make me feel better, girls. I'm so sorry to ask this, but"—Mom buried her masked face in her hands—"can you help me get this mask off?"

My chest squeezed tight, but I'd done this once tonight for Vivi. I could do it again.

I stepped around the island to her side. "Mom, this might hurt. Let me know if it's too much, okay?"

She nodded, turned her mask to me. She held her breath the same way I'd done when she'd taken me to get my ears pierced, waiting for the stab of the gun. This would be prescribed pain—a means to an end.

I ran my fingers along her cheeks, searching for an edge. But . . . there was no lip left. Not even the thinnest one, like there'd been on Vivi.

I couldn't find the line where the mask ended and my mom began.

"What's wrong?" Mom asked, her voice breaking brittle. "What is it?"

"Nothing. It's nothing," I said, trying to reassure her like she would've done for me. I traced desperately down the sides of her face. No edge there either. Maybe under the chin?

Yes! The tiniest ridge under her jaw.

With a surge of relief, I worked my finger under it. Mom's skin was hot, soft, sweaty.

This had to be hard and fast, like a Band-Aid. That's what had worked on Vivi. I just had to summon the guts to do it again. "I'm gonna pull," I warned her.

"Yes, do it."

I pulled.

It jerked up. Just the edge.

Mom hissed a pained breath, clutched her hands in her lap to stop herself from interfering. "Keep going."

I pulled harder. It ripped back a full centimeter and—

Something wet ran down my fingers.

Blood.

I cried out.

The skin had pulled back from her jaw like paper. So close to her throat, to the pulse of her jugular.

Mom strangled her yelp, but behind her mask, her deep-brown eyes—the ones she'd given to me and Vivi—were crushed with pain. Her hand flew to her jaw, clapping over the wound.

"I'm okay, sweetie," she stammered out. Blood welled between the cracks of her trembling fingers, and—damn her—she smiled at me with her mask's porcelain lips. A fleeting, tiny twitch. "Keep going. It's okay."

I'd nearly ripped out her throat, and she was still trying to reassure me.

"No, Mom, it's *not* okay!" I tore paper towels from the dispenser and shoved them at her.

She pushed them against the wound, and the red blossomed instantly, devouring the dimpled white.

A sob seized me. I didn't know what to do with my bloody

hands. My mom's bloody, hidden face. Anything. "I can't, Mom. I can't take it off."

"Okay." The more upset I got, the calmer she pretended to be. "Don't worry. The cut's not deep. Here's what we'll do. I'll bandage this up for the night. Tomorrow, I'll see the doctor. This is humiliating, and I can't believe I've done this to myself, but they must have some way of dealing with an accident like this—a solution that can dissolve the bond."

She stood and stumbled.

"Mom!" I caught her arm to hold her up.

But she pulled back. "I'm fine. I am. It's just, truthfully, it's been stuck like this for a few hours now. I'm a little worn-out."

Her voice was changing, growing both harder and fainter.

She grabbed a fresh wad of paper towels and shoved them over the ones that had bled through. Like those hidden mirrored doors this house's owners had built new closets on top of: slap the new over the old, pretend the old was never there.

But the new towels were already staining, too, and Mom was backing away from me and Vivi. Retreating from the lemony glaze of the kitchen light into the recessed blue shadows by the stairs.

If she went up those stairs, if she vanished into the house alone, would it really be her that came back?

My gut lurched.

"Wait!" I charged after her and grabbed her hand, catching her only a few steps up. "I don't think the masks work outside of our property. Real quick, let's try walking past the fence and see if it falls off on its own."

She stared at me vacantly, concealed by unfeeling porcelain perfection. A hard-pointed nose, the white brow cutting cruelly over the shimmery blue-lined eyeholes. Velvet roses eating up the left side of her face. Had she even heard me?

"Mom, please," Vivi begged from the foyer below us.

"Oh," Mom said. And her doll mouth relaxed into one of her thin smiles. "Yes. Let's try that."

I let out my stale, clamped breath in a whoosh.

She took one step down toward me.

And then her hand in mine spasmed. A yelp burst from her, sudden and twisted as a stab in the back.

"It burns!" She dropped the bloody paper towels to the stairs with a limp, wet plop. Grabbed her face. "It's burning me!" The cry flew out in piercing animal panic. Naked and raw.

She pulled at her mask, tugged and tore.

Was this because of me, because I'd tried to make her leave the property and she'd tried to agree?

"Mom!" I tried to hold her up.

But she shuddered and writhed with sobbing shrieks. "Libby, get it off me! *Get it off!*" I'd never heard Mom scream like this, a cracking, tearing sound like she was ripping in two.

There was a smell, a stench, like steak on the grill.

Cooking meat.

But it was coming from Mom.

She crashed down, with a hard thud, on the step above me. Her head smacked against the wall, spraying little red dots over the wallpaper. From what? Her throat? A new wound in her scalp? She didn't even seem to notice it.

Pulling and prying her mask wasn't working. Mom clawed along the sides of her cheeks, in front of her ears, where the line of the mask should have been—if it hadn't melted into her. She dug in her nails.

Something wet and warm splattered against my arms. Blood.

"Mom! No!"

But the pain had to be searing, white-hot. The charring stench of her skin, where was it coming from? Her whole face? Only the edges, where the butterfly and the beetle masks had started to burn Vivi and me? She had to think she couldn't survive the mask staying on, but I wasn't sure she could survive it coming off either.

Every cell in my body begged me to stop her, but I didn't know if I could—if I should.

She split into her own skin, raking it pulpy and puckered. A strip tore and caught under her thumbnail, the wispy baby hairs from in front of her ear still attached.

She pitched forward, keening against her knees. Red dribbled down her calves, leaked into her socks and slippers. It ran over the pale wood of the stairs, spattered onto my jeans. As she rocked herself and kept clawing at the mask. At her face.

"Mom . . ." At the bottom of the steps, Vivi stood, shell-shocked. White visible all the way around her watering eyes. As if she were watching someone tear the entire world apart, right in front of her.

Is that how she'd looked at me when she'd found my body in the bathroom, collapsed in the stink of my own vomit?

First me, now Mom.

That slammed the breath back into me.

"Mom, you have to stop!" I snatched one of her hands around the wrist. *"Stop!"*

She did. She stopped.

She went silent.

And then came a slight pop. A strange little suck, like a vacuum seal breaking.

Something fell into her suddenly limp hand.

The mask.

It was off.

I couldn't understand how the crown and veil hadn't fallen off with it—the gauzy lace hung like a thin curtain between us, streaked and splattered with blood, and a hunk or two of something thicker. But Mom wasn't screaming anymore, and I seized on that. Her ragged breaths, which had been hard as dying gasps, were slowing. Losing their rough edges.

My own breaths slowed with hers. That screaming panic in my chest blunted into a duller stab.

She held out the discarded mask to me, face down, like she didn't want to touch it anymore.

The back was slick with dark red. Blood that somehow already seemed to be drying, hardening shiny and smooth as lacquer, like some sick magic trick.

I didn't want to touch it either, but I let her give it to me.

"Mom?" I whispered.

The veil turned toward me.

And my brain couldn't understand what it was seeing.

From Mom's body, blossoming porcelain stared back at me, with blank arched brows, tiny, prim lips.

But how could she still be wearing the rose mask? I'd seen it fall off. I was holding it now.

Wasn't I?

I flipped over the mask in my hands.

The face was locked into a dropped-jaw scream. It was so realistic, down to the pores in her cheeks, the crow's-feet around the eyeholes.

No, it wasn't the rose mask I was holding.

I was holding a mask of Mom's face.

CHAPTER TWENTY-TWO

ROSE. ROSE WAS HERE.

And now Mom wasn't.

I clutched her fallen face to my chest, against my pounding heart. It was the only part of her that we had left. Because this body . . .

Where Mom's eyes should be were those sky-wide blue voids. The ones Flynn had worn when Rose had grabbed hold of him during the séance.

And they were fixed, intent. On me.

The gaze coated my body like ice. The stench of wine-drunk roses rolled off her. It was choking, fogging down my throat.

I thought of the way she'd plunged that pen into Mom's floorboards, the stabbing violence of those 13s.

Run. I had to run.

I staggered on the stairs.

But she grabbed me, her stinging nails digging into my hand. This wasn't Mom's strength. It was something else entirely. Immovable as an ancient stone.

She rose to her feet, holding me fast as she loomed over me, her pointed crown spearing up into the shadows of the staircase.

And under the skin of Mom's carved-up forearm, something wriggled. Poked through the largest of her wounds, with a fresh gush of blood. Green and slithering toward me. A snake head?

No. Thorns skewered the skin open wider. And with a wet suck, they pushed through.

A vine.

It ruptured free from her arm, wrapped around my wrist, and *squeezed.* Thorns punctured my skin in stinging bursts, latching into me like leeches.

"Vivi!" I screamed. She was frozen in the foyer. "Run!"

Vivi sprang into action—in the exact wrong direction. "Libby!" She charged toward us and wrapped her arms around my waist, trying to pull me free.

But even if she succeeded, I wasn't sure how much of my wrist would tear away with me. The thorns throbbed deep. Past the pain, my hand was going weak and tingly and numb.

The vine wasn't just cutting into me, it was feeding on me. Rippling and swallowing like an esophagus, siphoning the blood from my body to Mom's.

I couldn't look anymore—if I looked, I was going to faint. "Stop! Please! Rose, tell us: What do you want? Thirteen?"

The vine didn't stop. But its pulse against my wrist slowed.

The white mask tilted, regarding me.

"What's thirteen?" Vivi jumped in. "Tell us! You can tell us, and we'll—"

A creak pierced the chaos. From the kitchen.

The patio doors. They had opened.

Someone was in the house.

Flynn? Was there any chance he'd come back? If he hadn't left the alley behind our house, he could've heard us yelling.

"Flynn!" I screamed. "Help! Rose has Mom! She's—"

Rose's stranglehold on my wrist—without warning, it released.

Vivi and I toppled backward on the stairs.

We fell in a bruising tangle of thrashing limbs. Vivi's phone bounced from her pocket, and mine cracked under my butt, a chorus of shattering screens.

But I'd managed to hold on to the most precious thing—that mask of Mom's face.

Something ran across my arm. A cockroach. Several. A whole horde—they flowed in from the dining room, to swarm me and Vivi, still on the floor. A praying mantis landed on my cheek, its spiny pincers millimeters from my eye. And more mantises kept flitting in—a glittering cloud of green wings settling in the foyer. Perching on me, Vivi, the walls, the lower stairs.

I'd never seen so many. Where were they coming from?

I shrieked, batting them away.

Just in time, footsteps pounded through the kitchen, the dining room—someone running quick to join us.

But when I looked up, I saw . . . it wasn't Flynn.

The thing staring back at us, it was impossible. Tall as me and a half.

Nothing about it was right.

The face was smooth and shiny. A mask. Carved from polished caramel wood.

The missing cockroach mask. It had to be.

But the mask had taken on a life of its own. Its jutting antennae moved of their own accord, flicking the air like whips. The eyeholes—shining with that same gaping blue—were set wide in its head. Wider than human eyes were meant to sit. Mandibles dangled down the cheeks.

And they framed a withered and torn human chin. White bone, teeth, protruding from shriveled lips.

Lips that looked so very long dead.

A limp brown curl spilled over the masked forehead. Embedded in the wooden plating that had grown over the chest was a flash of gold: A chain, an orange pendant. A five-petaled flower.

I'd seen that jewelry before. In the picture of my grandparents from the locket.

The saliva dried in my mouth. I couldn't move. I couldn't breathe. I lay petrified where I'd fallen, swarmed by cockroaches and praying mantises, the mask of Mom's face clutched to my chest, Vivi half under me. My hip throbbing. My brain stopping.

What had been Margaret Feldman was the Cockroach now. And it had twisted her body into a nightmare—a lurching mash-up of bug and human.

The missing people. Was this what had happened to *all* of them?

Capelike brown wings hung from the creature's shoulders. Its arms distended from its sides, elbows breaking in the wrong direction, sharp bristles extending from a wooden shell that encased its whole body. Its legs turned out in a permanent squat. Two thin extra legs—bug legs—spindly and crunchy, jointed out from under its armpits. They wiggled at the air, reaching, as if deciding where to scuttle next.

That "costume" we'd seen in the attic. It *had* been an exoskeleton.

The Cockroach took a tottering step toward us. Its jaw hung

by a stretched tendon, sagging with rot. Before much longer, the human jaw would drop off entirely, leaving only wooden insect parts behind.

A stench seeped out from under its shell—decay. The same sour reek from the attic.

It was only then that I processed that the Cockroach was carrying something.

Our masks—mine and Vivi's.

The beetle and the butterfly.

Holy shit. This had to be what Ellen was trying to do to me and Vivi. *This* was Ellen's idea of ascension? Turning us into monsters like this one?

Nothing about this union was holy.

Something else staggered into the foyer. Peering out from behind one of the Cockroach's wide shoulders.

Another masked face. A green triangle made of hard-lacquered leaves, its eyes those same gaping blue holes.

The Praying Mantis. The second mask missing from my grandparents' room.

The mask was supported by a human neck—one that was tearing and peeling like parchment paper to reveal the muscle underneath. Mealy, grayer than pink. Thick leafy plating was growing up from its collarbone but hadn't yet covered the gap.

Its formerly human arms had stretched hideously. From the wrist joints, instead of hands, a skinny growth extended, like two extra-long fingers, fused together, ridged with teeth. Its legs splayed wide like the Cockroach's, supporting a torso permanently curved in an impossible backbend, an extra set of thin green legs sprouting from its hips to hold it up.

Something silver gleamed from what used to be one of those wrist joints.

My grandfather's watch.

Vivi had been right—the other masks had been here all along. Hiding, maybe half slumbering, until Ellen had used our séance to wake them up.

If these monsters got hold of me. Of Vivi . . .

I was a throbbing knot of pain, but I scooted back from the towering monsters.

Vivi scrambled out from under me. She tried to stand but staggered on an ankle injured by our fall.

On the staircase above, Mom's body stood—crowned in glimmering metal spikes. Her white veil hung like a splattered ghost. Her own blood trailed down her face, her neck, dripped from her fingertips. The thorny vine hung limp from her arm, so long now it nearly dangled to the stair below.

Rose didn't chase. She watched. As if she were the queen at the back of a chessboard, merely assessing if she would need to move.

The bugs weren't advancing. Not yet.

The Cockroach held our masks out to us.

An invitation.

The front door was fifteen feet away. Within range of a frantic dash. If we could get off the property before these things grabbed us, we might have a chance.

"Vivi," I whispered. I must've bitten my tongue falling down the stairs. All I could taste was the sickly iron of blood. "Front door."

"When?" she whispered back—the tiniest scrape of sound from her lips.

"Now."

It was our only chance, one tiny window to surprise them.

I leaped up and shoved Vivi ahead of me. "Go!"

She stumbled, gritting her teeth, charging for the door as best she could.

The Cockroach and the Mantis burst into slithering motion, squirming their overgrown bodies after us. I crammed Mom's mask into my tight waistband and looked for any possible weapon to hold them back. The coatrack was within reach.

I shook off our raincoats, the hanging umbrellas, and swung its unbalanced weight at the charging Cockroach.

The coatrack smacked against its segmented, shiny gut.

It let out a hair-raising hiss, scrabbling at me with its long front legs. Moldy gray jelly oozed from between its wooden armored plates.

A thorny bristle grazed my bare arm. Its waving antennae whipped my cheek.

I shrieked. I squeezed my eyes shut and kept whacking. Like I was chopping a tree.

The sickening thuds and spitting hisses kept coming. Getting louder. Practically on top of me.

Vivi fumbled with the front door locks, tugging at the chain.

My coatrack caught in midair, stuck.

The Mantis.

It had snared the wooden rod between a long saw-toothed finger and forearm.

I tugged to free it, digging my heels into the foyer rug.

The coatrack hardly moved. Stuck fast.

Crack.

As the Mantis's grip tightened, the coatrack splintered.

And fell to the ground, split in two.

The Cockroach grazed my sides with groping arms.

No, no, no—

The front door flew open with a cool blast of night air, and I bolted for the outdoors.

But a ragged shriek tore from Vivi's throat. She stopped, trapping me behind her in the foyer.

Something enormous was blocking the doorway. It shoved Vivi so hard that she hit the wall across from the door. And nearly took me down with her.

A pulsing hum vibrated through the floor and the walls as the creature pushed into the cramped foyer.

A screaming-yellow mask: brass. Enormous mandibles as long as half my arm.

The Wasp.

The thing was seven feet tall. Brass had grown over its neck and shoulders and plated its hands. But an expanse of arm, past a torn, moldy sleeve, was visible. Skin peeling away from rotting bone.

Freckled skin.

And behind the brass mask, the human hair clinging to its scalp was coppery orange.

Oh God, no. Those looked like Clery genes. And that body looked fresher than the Cockroach or the Mantis. There was only one person who'd disappeared more recently than my grandparents. . . .

Though the Wasp remained more human than the others, its skeletal knees bent backward and a bulbous abdomen protruded from its back like a throbbing tumor—wielding a red stinger as long as a knife. Its transparent wings fanned out to bar our way.

We were surrounded. Totally. Utterly.

The mail table knocked against my lower back. I had run out

of space to retreat. Vivi, hiding under the table, hugged my calf. Her heart pounded against the back of my knee.

I wanted to be brave like the Beetle.

But I wasn't the Beetle. I trembled, weak as water.

Three pairs of swirling cosmic-blue eyes stared down at us. I shrank under them, my shoulders caving. When these misshapen goliaths held still, they were completely still. No rise and fall of lungs or air sacs. That'd been my one comfort with Mom—her body was still breathing.

These weren't.

The Cockroach held out our masks again.

They wanted us to join them. To let these masks eat our real faces, to wrench and bloat our decaying bodies into monstrous shapes.

The Cockroach was a little too similar to a beetle.

I stared up at its ribbed plating, streaked with dribbling goo, its spiny appendages and antennae.

Over its shoulder, the Praying Mantis watched, its serrated arms held aloft. Any second, it could swing them down like scythes.

The Wasp in the doorway clicked its sharp mandibles in deliberate scissoring snips. The moonlight spilled in behind it, tipping its wings and stinger in silver.

"Okay." Vivi broke the silent standoff. She let go of my leg and crawled out from under the table.

Lifted her hands in peaceful surrender, like that would mean anything to these monsters.

"What are you doing?" I hissed.

Vivi straightened to her full four-foot-eleven-inch height. Fear vibrated from her skinny back—or maybe that was the buzz of the Wasp, rippling through the floor and up through our too-breakable bones.

Vivi offered her cupped hands, gently, to the Cockroach.

"Okay," she said again.

The butterfly mask fell into her waiting hands, and I couldn't tell if the Cockroach had dropped it there, or if the mask had been drawn magnetically.

Vivi gulped—a thick, sick sound. She traced the lace wings, the tufted feathers of its forehead and nose.

"Don't." I clutched the back of her shirt. "You know it won't come off."

"I know," she said.

She flipped it, staring at the sticky back. Centimeter by centimeter, she raised it toward her face.

"Vivi!" I gripped her shirt tighter. *"No!"*

It was one fraction from her face. I was one second from snatching it out of her hands.

When she punched the butterfly mask into the Wasp's staring eye.

The Wasp reared back, slapping at its face.

"Libby, come on!" Vivi dove under the Wasp's belly, crawling for the open door.

The Wasp's buzz rocketed to fever pitch, shaking the floor under my sandals. Vivi was risking everything to sneak past that stinger.

But we didn't have a choice.

I dove after her, shoving the Wasp's swollen abdomen to knock it off-balance. Its body was thick and clammy—its slick metal shell sliding under my palm—as I squirmed underneath.

But something caught my ankle.

Hot pain seared through my leg, jangling all my nerves.

The Mantis. Crushing like a vise.

It caught me like it had caught the coatrack—and could

shatter me, too, with one hard snip of its saw-toothed arm. If I kept going forward, my foot was going to stay behind.

With my free leg, I kicked at the Mantis and lost my grip on the carpet.

It dragged me back into the foyer, away from the open door. Away from Vivi.

The Mantis hoisted me into the air, dangling by the ankle, and I cried out against the impossible pain.

Mom's mask slipped from my waistband and tumbled to the foyer rug. Face up, locked in a scream that mimicked mine. I reached for it, thrashed for a grip on anything, but my hands brushed uselessly against the lacquered plating of the Mantis's deformed legs.

The monster stared at me like it was a dead thing or I was a dead thing. Or both.

And it dawned on me: *I'm not going to make it.*

Mom was going to die, if she wasn't done for already. I was going to die.

But Vivi was going to survive.

If only one of us could, I needed it to be her. There she went, flying over the front walkway, faster and smarter than these monsters—than me and Mom, too.

Yes. Don't stop. Go, Vivi, go.

I thought all the things at her fleeing back that I'd never get the chance to say, like: *I love you, and you're going to find a new family—one that can make you so much happier than we did. I held you back. But that won't be your story anymore. Three steps to the gate, and you're out. Be the star you were born to be. Go be the swan, be the lake, be the whole damn show.*

But then she stopped.

She turned. And she saw me, in the Mantis's grip.

I'd thought she already knew I was trapped, but panic boomed through her face and it was clear: she'd thought I was right behind her.

"Go!" I screamed at her.

She just stood there. Paralyzed.

With an icy breeze, a burst of oversweet roses, Mom's legs swept past me. Rose had descended from the stairs, and the Cockroach and the Wasp scrambled out of her way. She kicked the mask of Mom's face aside, like it was trash. Then, with tender care, she plucked the butterfly mask from the Cockroach's grip. Cradling it, she strode out onto the porch and stopped.

She held up Vivi's mask for her to see. Then she turned to me and the Mantis.

The Mantis stepped forward, framing us in the doorway. It squeezed my ankle, digging its saw-toothed grip deeper. I shrieked. Blood trickled down my upside-down leg, running into the cuff of my jeans, warm and wet against my calf.

Rose held up a hand to pause the Mantis.

She turned back to Vivi. Bounced the butterfly mask in her hand.

She didn't need to speak. The either-or was deadly clear: *Come back and put on this mask or look what we'll do to your sister.*

Vivi was so close to the fence that yellow light from the streetlamps spilled over her. The sleepy neighborhood around us suddenly felt so out of place. So achingly ordinary.

But Vivi wasn't looking at the neighborhood on the other side of our gate. Her eyes were locked on me.

"Keep going," I screamed. "They want me to wear the beetle mask. They won't kill me!"

I didn't know if that was true. But they already had me. Vivi could still make it out. They knew she could. That's why they were trying to blackmail her.

The Mantis shook me by the ankle, a predator thrashing its prey. Its teeth sawed my skin, and I cried out again—I didn't mean to, but I did.

Vivi's head drooped.

She took a step back toward us.

Then another. And another.

"No, no, don't!" All my hopes for her future were avalanching down. "I'm not worth it! Vivi, go!"

Vivi kept trudging toward the house. She creaked up the porch steps as she walked back to Mom's body. And held out her hand for the butterfly mask. "You never think you're worth anything, Libby." She smiled at me, wobbly, tearfully. She'd learned Mom's smile too well. "But you'd do this for me. You're doing it now."

Her shoulders slumped in resignation as she lifted the mask to her face.

"No, Vivi! *Vivi!*" I kept screaming her name, like that could keep her here with me.

But then came that manic butterfly laugh.

Vivi was gone, too. Just like Mom.

And now, all the masks turned—to look at me.

CHAPTER TWENTY-THREE

THE MANTIS DROPPED ME IN THE foyer with a teeth-chattering thud. The Cockroach laid the beetle mask in front of my collapsed body.

Behind them, at the foot of the stairs, more monsters had gathered. The older the body, the more pinched and gray and decayed, the less human each creature had become. Warped exoskeletons, made of inorganic materials like metal or lumpy rope, had advanced over peeling flesh that was stretched too tall, too wide. Spindly appendages erupted from torsos, antennae from heads.

Glimmering glassy hairs bristled from the body of the Cicada, crystal wings dragging down from its shoulder blades. The Mosquito's human legs were impossibly thin, elongated, but the tottering beast was so hunched and bent that it looked like it would break any second. Its wiry proboscis, encrusted with blackened blood, was so long that it scratched across the floorboards. The Centipede was an overstretched wreck. Practically one enormous spine, wriggling with cherrywood legs.

The rot was suffocating.

I fought the stomach acid burning my throat. My heart pounded against my lungs, and I sucked shallow gulps as fast as they would come.

I made myself count the number of masks.

Eleven. Now that Mom was Rose and Vivi was the Butterfly.

I was viciously outnumbered.

Every masked monster peered down, waiting for me to put on the beetle mask.

I was hemmed in by open pincers, gnashing mandibles, pulsing stingers. My shredded ankle throbbed with the reminder that the Mantis could have already sawed off my foot if it had wanted to.

But the most heart-stopping prospect wasn't the damage they could do to me, here and now. It was becoming the Beetle—becoming *one of them.*

Mom's foot nudged me.

I gritted my teeth. "No."

Rose grabbed my mask from the floor. I was sure she'd crush it onto my face. Instead, she smashed me over the head with it.

The foyer dimmed. Those leering masks blurred. Most hauntingly, Rose and the Butterfly. A grin stretched Vivi's bottom lip until the split made during the séance reopened and blood welled up all over again.

In the nearest corner, Mom's face lay abandoned, frozen in silent agony.

I thought, *That's it. My sister's bloody lip. My mom's face, tangled in spiderwebs. These are the last things I'll ever see.*

But.

I woke up.

Alone.

In the dark. Some small, enclosed space. A strip of light filtered in under a door.

Something heavy sat in my hand. Warm. I shot upright and dropped it with a clatter.

I winced and froze, straining my ears.

The house's distant groans answered. Above me, the sounds of scuttling—creeping and crawling.

Is that where the masked spirits and their hijacked bodies had been hiding all along—in the attic? Those lumbering monsters stuffed under sheets, pretending to be furniture.

We'd been standing right next to them. If Vivi had pulled off one or two more sheets . . .

Would finding them earlier have saved us? Before Ellen had fully awakened them, channeled more spiritual energy into them from our big séance? I'd heard those sounds since our first night here, so clearly, at least some of them had been partially awake. Probably awake enough to make mincemeat of us, if that's what they'd wanted.

But instead, they wanted something so much worse.

My breath huffed shallow; my heart thudded. But the house, for the most part, remained eerily quiet.

No one seemed to be coming for me. Not yet.

Every part of me ached: my bruised head, my burned back, my smashed hip. . . . My hand and arm were caked in dry blood, damaged first by Vivi's nails and then by Rose's coiling vine. My wrist was a mess of ruined flesh. But my ankle throbbed worst of all.

I touched it with quivering fingers. It was warm and swollen, gashed over the anklebone, the skin around the wound's edges ragged. But it wasn't as deep as it could've been. The Mantis had dug in only hard enough to make a show of my pain. So maybe these monsters did want me intact, if possible.

I cast my fingers over the floorboards, searching for whatever I'd dropped.

They knocked against glass.

The beetle mask.

They'd left it with me, but in my hand—not on my face. I'd been so sure I'd wake up wearing it, if I woke up at all.

Why hadn't they put it on me? Unless . . .

Before Ellen had placed the ant mask on Flynn, she'd needed him to agree: *"You must choose the Ant, and it must choose you, too."*

I had to choose the Beetle. They needed me to put that mask on myself.

Mom, they'd tricked. She'd slipped on her own mask earlier tonight, before we knew the truth. Vivi, they'd blackmailed. As for me . . . ?

They'd left me here, wherever *here* was, waiting for me to break.

They thought I was weak.

And maybe they were right.

I hadn't been able to save Vivi. Or Mom. The one piece I'd had of her, I'd lost.

If I wanted to wax wildly optimistic, I could imagine there was some way to bring them back. Vivi still had her own face under that mask, as far as I knew. Even Mom was still breathing. If I could recover that mask of her face, then maybe . . .

Ellen had said the spirits of Rose and the Beetle and the Butterfly "resided" in their masks. There was a chance Mom's spirit was trapped inside hers, too.

Even supposing that was true, I didn't know if it was possible to get her spirit back into her body. If, underneath that rose mask, there was anything left to save.

I felt so hollow. So dead inside.

The same way I'd felt weeks ago, when I'd sunk onto the bathroom tile. My knees had thudded down too hard, and even as I'd felt the bruise start, I'd thought, *Not my problem. Not anymore.* My head had been swimming, my stomach churning against all the pills. Acid heaved up my throat and burned my tongue and teeth as it spilled from my dribbling lips. I was vomiting the warmth out of my body. And in its place, something cold oozed from the deepest part of my gut. Something that had been waiting for me. A chill that clutched at my intestines, squirmed through my spasming stomach, wormed its frigid fingers through my rib cage. Toward my heart.

Dying hadn't felt like the relief I'd thought it would.

Instead, it felt like consuming terror. An icy void.

Like looking into Rose's eyes.

And, like Ellen, I was the one who'd invited it in. I'd dug my clenching fingers into my scalp, pressing my skull in one last illogical fit to keep hold of my mind. Brain racing, body slowing, breath stalling.

You've done it now, I'd thought. *Be careful what you wish for.*

If Vivi hadn't found me, I would've died in that puddle of my own puke.

Ever since, I'd been too aware of the ice hiding in my gut, waiting to claim me. I could feel it now, touching frigid tremors up my spine, as I sat alone in the dark with the beetle mask.

That cold was waiting.

It would be easier to let it win. This was what I'd wanted: to die.

And I had every reason now to do just that.

Mom and Vivi were gone. Almost as good as dead. And I was,

too. All I had to do was put on the mask. And it would take care of the rest. End all this suffering once and for—

No.

I couldn't afford this drowning thought spiral.

Just keep moving, I told myself. *Keep moving.*

I had to. Because my body was getting heavier.

A catatonic low. If it dug in its heavy fingers, I'd never get out of here. Depression had nearly killed me before. It could do it again, as sure as this mask.

Keep moving. Keep moving, Libby.

I needed to figure out where in this house they were keeping me. I reached my hands up, assessing the space. Something brushed against my fingertips. Soft as moth wings—

I squealed and yanked back. Something was overhead. Now swaying.

I ducked, as low and flat as I could get, my lungs heaving panicked gasps against the floorboards.

Nothing.

Nothing happened.

The sway above me slowed and stilled.

I peeled open a terrified eye. Through the crack of light under the door, I couldn't make out much. A room. A rug. A blue rug, with teal and pink swirls. Not the house's typical fussy-grandma patterns.

It was my rug.

My room.

There was the foot of my shabby white dresser. Directly across from me, a door opened into the shadowed hallway.

I was in the closet. My closet.

I reached overhead, more certainly this time. My fingers latched into that soft, swaying thing. My sweater.

But just because I hadn't seen anyone in my room, that didn't mean they weren't lurking out of sight.

As quietly as I could, I worked my hand up to find the cool touch of the doorknob.

It wouldn't turn. It was stuck fast. Jammed.

From behind me: A click. A groan.

The mirrored door at the back of the closet cracked open. Without my mask, there were no stars waiting. Only darkness.

All the same, an invitation, just for me.

Nothing visible had pushed it open. Like it had opened on its own.

But I knew better. I glared at the beetle mask on the floor beside me.

A tendril of dusty, rose-thick air wafted from the opening.

No way I was going up there.

Keep moving. Keep moving. . . .

But the attic was a death wish, and the door to my bedroom wouldn't open.

On the floor, something crawled across my finger.

I seized back my hand. Small legs fought for purchase on my knuckle and lost. The creature fell with a hard clink, like shattering glass.

A beetle.

Another tickled over the lip of my sock, crawled across my stinging ankle.

I shook it off.

But already, with a soft whir of wings, another landed on my calf. It climbed toward my knee. I swatted that off, too.

One tickled above the waistband of my pants, squirming under my shirt.

I leaped to my feet, stamping at the ground and shaking my

arms, tugging at my clothes, but more scratching legs had already grasped on to me—the torn spots in my wax-splotched jeans, my bare arms.

"Stop! Make them stop," I cried to the mask.

But they didn't stop. They crawled in under the closed door—an army of marching glass. They burst into flight and latched on to me anywhere they could.

One landed next to my left eye, and I bit back a squeal. I flung it with a vengeful toss of my head.

Another landed on my neck. I reached for it, but another climbed up my chin. I slapped that off. And the one at my neck touched my earlobe.

I reached for it. It darted for the nearest opening—my ear hole.

"No," I cried, pinching its wriggling abdomen between my fingers. But it was made of glass. If I pinched too hard, shards would break off in my ear canal.

The beetle squirmed—digging in deeper. Pushing at the stretching hole of my ear, its antennae licking around inside my head. The rooting and rustling was explosive, roaring at my eardrum.

I pitched my head down to work gravity against it. My teeth ground against the pinching pain.

A warm wet trickle ran from my ear. Shit, shit, what kind of damage was it doing in there?

I twisted and tugged.

Crunch!

It boomed down my ear canal, vibrating through my skull.

I gasped, and ripped the back half free, its glass legs swimming frantically in the air. Until they stopped.

The front half clawed its way deeper, until it stopped, too. Plugging my ear.

But there was no time to do anything about it—beetles swarmed my entire body. Up my arms. Up my shirt, both front and back.

I clapped my hands defensively over my ears. My fingers were shaking, my throat seizing with clutching sobs.

I couldn't stay here.

The attic stairwell beckoned. A gaping cavern.

How awfully convenient the door had creaked open right before this onslaught. The Beetle was torturing me. Trying to force me to put on the mask. To flee to the attic, where who-knew-how-many monsters waited.

The Beetle—all the spirits—were *desperate* for me to wear my mask.

Well.

Ellen had said the Beetle and I hadn't bonded all the way. That we needed more time together.

How much time, I didn't know. But for a brief, precious window, I would be able to control my own mind *and* wield the Beetle's strength.

So they wanted me to put on the mask that badly?

Fine. Then I'd give them exactly what they wanted.

I grabbed my mask from the floor and shook off the beetles squirming over its surface. I pressed my face into its familiar hug. Heat flamed around my hairline, the sides of my cheeks and under my jaw, like the mask was branding into place.

Its grounding rush surged through me, the floor suddenly more solid under my feet.

With it came a balmy relief—the sense that this was good, that I'd done the right thing. And it would be an even better thing to walk past that mirrored door and up those suddenly starlit stairs.

That's what the Beetle wanted me to feel. But I knew now—it was a liar.

And I wasn't going to the attic.

With a deep gulp of breath, I stepped back from the closet door. I readied my good shoulder, one of the least bruised parts of me, and I rammed clean through.

In an explosion of shattering wood, I burst into my bedroom.

It hurt. But not as much as it should have. *Thanks, Beetle.*

Glass bugs rained from my clothes. I stomped across a whole line of their surging army.

My room was empty. For the moment. The fake moon hung proudly in my skylight, but the real moon was gone. The sky was melting from black to blue. Through the beetle window, tangerine whispered up from the horizon.

It would be morning soon.

I wanted to scream for Vivi, but she couldn't answer me.

Swallowing the metallic tang in my throat, I ran to my open doorway. My footsteps pounded the floor. The Beetle and its invisible spiritual exoskeleton made my teenage body boom louder, fall harder on the world around it. I hadn't realized that its shell wouldn't stay invisible. That the mask would eventually drown me in glass.

I leaned into the hall, scanning for movement. The corridor was its usual shadowy swirl of honeyed floorboards, the crushing blue embrace of overly decorated walls.

A flutter caught my eye. Lace wings. At Vivi's door.

The door was closed. Rose vines tangled over it like a spiderweb, woven quickly and thickly, burying the metal knob until it was a faint golden gleam. Around them, butterflies dipped from one cabbage-fat rose to another.

I tried not to wonder how much blood it had cost Mom's body to make those vines grow.

Vivi was behind that door. I just knew it.

The rose thorns glinted, with warning crimson tips.

But it would be harder to hurt me now.

I grabbed a knotted fistful from the center of the door and pulled. The thorns scratched, but the vines ripped back in my hand.

Stop!   don't

But I wasn't taking suggestions from the Beetle.

I tore the vines from the knob as butterflies flapped in protest and darted around my head like bats.

And I pushed the door open.

I braced for "Mom" and a fresh wave of vines to greet me. For "Vivi" to fly at my face, with that maniacal butterfly laugh.

Instead, silence.

In the center of the room, there was an enormous ivory mass.

Six or seven feet. Suspended from the ceiling by a wire-thin thread.

It swayed, ever so slightly, in the breeze I'd unleashed from the door. The dully rising light poured through the Butterfly's stained-glass portrait, glinting emerald and amethyst off its hard glaze.

A massive chrysalis.

Vivi had to be inside. Stewing. Trapped.

I froze, only a step into the room.

No. No, no, no.

I'd planned to swoop in and carry Vivi's body out by force. I'd been betting that if we crossed the property line, her mask would fall off on its own, and so would mine. Then Vivi would be back. And together, we could figure out what to do about Mom.

But I'd seen Vivi raise enough caterpillars. Once they stitched themselves into a cocoon or chrysalis, they did not come out the same.

I charged over to the structure. This close, it looked alive—pulsing. Fleshy as her mask had become, with thick, thumping veins.

A few times in Vivi's caterpillar rearing, something had gone wrong at this transformational stage. One deformed chrysalis had never fully closed. Worse, one had cracked open. *Worst,* one growing butterfly had fused to the inside wall and couldn't get the left half of its body free.

What they all had in common: the insect had died.

I pressed my hand against the shell. The interwoven silk was diamond-hard.

This was a bug question—if only Vivi were here to answer it: Was there any way, if I broke this thing open, that she wouldn't come out hideously wrong?

Something squeezed around my good ankle.

A vine. Red-spiked. Alive as a snake.

The door to Vivi's closet gaped wide, and Mom stood in the opening. Her white mask had erupted in velvet blooms like boils.

Vines slithered from the wounds in her arms. Surging past her ankles, over her feet, like a tide. All toward me.

Frantically, I kicked them away, crushing them under my shoes. The stems split, pouring out a watery iron red.

"Mom! Stop! Aren't you in there at all?" I cried, even though I knew the answer.

The rich blue of Rose's eyes hung like a curtain. No iris, no pupil. Just that same staring void.

This time, her vines dug into my injured ankle. Hard.

Even through the Beetle's armor, the thorns pinched and stung. Hot rage surged through my blood.

And then a sound came from the closet behind her.

Many sounds.

Scuttling and buzzing as the spirits from the attic joined us.

Behind me, shadows filled Vivi's bedroom doorway—the Cockroach and the Mantis.

Even with the Beetle's strength at my disposal, this was shaping into too big of a brawl. I didn't have time to debate breaking open that chrysalis. I couldn't help Vivi or Mom or anyone if I got swarmed now.

I would come back.

With a plan.

I pressed my hand to the chrysalis one last time, as a promise.

Then I ripped free from the vines and swiveled to face the Cockroach and the Mantis. Lowered my head, like a beetle ready to battle.

No don't

The Beetle didn't want me to fight the other spirits.

Too bad.

At the sight of my mask, the Mantis flinched. It knew I had the full power of the Beetle, and the Beetle didn't yet have full power over me.

But the Cockroach stood its ground, blocking the way.

"Move," I growled.

The Cockroach didn't move.

I charged it, head-on.

My shoulder cracked into the Cockroach's abdomen. Its wooden shell splintered with a burst of rot. Lukewarm pus sprayed down my arm. And into my mouth.

I gagged and choked, but there was no stopping now.

The Cockroach hissed, whirring and writhing, as I knocked it backward into the hallway. It tumbled against the opposite wall, smashing through paper to plaster. The Mantis scrambled out of our way, just in time for the Cockroach to stagger upright. It crawled up the wall and launched itself at me.

I beelined for the stairs.

But the Cockroach caught me in the ribs, knocking me off-balance. I grabbed for the railing. For anything. And caught the Cockroach's scrabbling leg, its splintery spines biting into my palm.

We tumbled down the stairs in a thrashing tangle. The Cockroach's antennae whipped my arms, my cheek. My back slapped against the wall, the stairs. Sharp blow after blow. My bones weren't snapping, but that must've been because I was wearing the beetle mask.

At the bottom, the Cockroach pinned me, snapped at me with dribbling mandibles—and with its off-kilter human jaw. Its cracking human teeth.

Blobs of its moldy spit splatted against my neck.

I landed a hard kick in its gut, knocking it off me and onto its back.

The Cockroach twisted and squirmed, trying to right itself. Its contorted front arms swiping at the air, middle and lower legs pawing at the floor. It spun on its slick shell, in a helpless circle.

I scrambled to my feet and grabbed the iron poker from beside the fireplace in the living room.

No No No No

I ignored the Beetle.

I stood over the writhing Cockroach and stabbed the metal into its gut with a juicy crunch. It wailed out a warbling, inhuman screech.

But the Cockroach grabbed the poker and squeezed it out inch by inch. Stinking white pus and liquefied guts leaked from the hole as the Cockroach got its legs back under it and slowly pushed itself upright. The monster staggered toward me, oozing fragments of bone. Crushed rib cage.

I fought down vomit. Sickening despair.

These things weren't killable. The human bodies inside were long dead. And the spirits just kept coming.

I tossed a frantic glance at the foyer corner, looking for Mom's face, discarded in dust and spiderwebs.

But it was gone.

They'd taken it. Or moved it. Destroyed it. There was no time to find out what they'd done.

The Cockroach was lumbering closer and closer, leaking guts and all. And the Beetle was searing the edges of its mask into me, fighting for control.

Before I lost the chance, I barreled for the exit.

CHAPTER TWENTY-FOUR

I BURST THROUGH THE WHITE METAL gate, breaching the fence that hemmed in our property.

The effect was instant. Something dropped from the hem of my shirt to the sidewalk. Glass shattered.

A clinging beetle, which had snapped from animate to inanimate.

That burning sear at my hairline started to mellow, ever so slightly.

I gasped in the fresh morning air, humid but clean—the dew cooling my heaving lungs—and glanced back at the house. The turrets and spires ate up the sky behind me.

A shadow crawled on the roofline. A flash of wings and slithering bony parts.

Whichever mask that was, I doubted it could reach me here, but I ran across the street to be safe, my busted platform sandals pounding the empty asphalt. The second I reached the opposite sidewalk, I tugged at my mask.

Pop.

The sticky vacuum seal broke. There was a lip now—a lifted edge at my temple. I kept pulling, and the mask stretched like overwarm taffy. Clung like glue that was more than half set.

But it did come free.

Unstuck.

There was hope. For Vivi. Maybe even Mom.

Slim, distant hope. But hope, nonetheless.

My knees buckled. Even my relief was heavy, the kind that wanted to crush me to the ground and keep me on the sidewalk, shivering in a ball. But no time for that.

The sun was peeking over the horizon, and I feasted on the dull orange glow. I hadn't known if I'd ever get to have this again. The sun. The sky. The robins and mourning doves calling out their songs.

My face was raw, the top layers of skin peeled away. Under my fingers, it felt buffed, smoother. Except the burned outer edges.

I examined the back of the beetle mask.

Well. That's why.

A silk-fine layer of my pasty complexion was stuck to the glass. It flaked under my touch, like drying papier-mâché. The Beetle had hooked deep.

And the mask wasn't the only beetle that had tried to burrow its way into me.

There was still half of a beetle buried in my ear canal.

I slammed a palm against the opposite side of my head and pushed everywhere around the ear I could reach—in front with my pinky, behind with my thumb.

After much wriggling and grunting and wincing, it finally dropped into my hand. Leaving a stinging slice behind, like a paper cut. Inside my ear.

I spiked the half beetle against the sidewalk and smiled when it shattered.

And then I looked at my mask.

When I'd thrown it at the table during our séance catastrophe, it had bounced harmlessly off the stone. But the mask wasn't magic here, off the property. Could it shatter, too, against this sidewalk?

God, it was tempting. My fingers itched for vengeance. How good it would feel to know it was gone.

But.

The beetle mask was the only reason I'd been able to fight my way out. The only reason that house hadn't swallowed me whole, like it had swallowed my family.

Vivi was trapped in that faintly pulsating chrysalis. Transforming.

Would *she* ever get to breathe this open air again? See the sun?

I swallowed, tears sticky in my throat. My heart pounded at my rib cage like it was locked behind bars—bursting to get back to my family. To hug them or hold them. To have any guarantee that I hadn't already done that for the last time.

I wanted my old life with Mom and Vivi back, imperfect as it was.

I wanted *life.*

The simple realization burst through me, warming my aching chest like sunshine.

How cruel that it took everything being stripped away to see that so clearly.

I had to believe I could get Mom and Vivi back. I had to. Otherwise, I would collapse.

And although the very thought prickled my skin like beetle

legs, I might need to put this mask back on. One last time. To get them out.

I tucked the beetle mask in my waistband, shuddering at its clammy touch. As it cooled, it deadened back to glass.

I couldn't just charge back into the house. Not yet. There were too many masks to fight.

If I borrowed a phone and called the police, they wouldn't believe me about those monsters. They *would* believe me if I said there were masked intruders in my house, holding my mom and my sister hostage. But what good were police and their guns? Their bullets would work too well on the still-living bodies of Mom and Vivi, but as for stopping the spirits themselves? I'd punched a hole clean through the Cockroach with a fireplace poker, to sickeningly little effect.

These monsters had physical forms, but they were spiritual in origin.

We needed a spiritual cure.

I glanced down the slowly brightening street.

I needed a plan.

And there was only one person who could help me.

I didn't have a phone anymore. I couldn't text. I couldn't call. Only one thing left to do.

I circled Flynn's house in the early dawn murk.

I passed the patch of bluebells in his flower bed with a bittersweet squeeze to my heart. The ones Flynn had given me sat abandoned in my kitchen, in the vase Mom had lovingly arranged for me just a few hours ago. It felt like years had passed.

I didn't want to ring the doorbell and wake up the whole

house, if I could help it. I stood on tiptoe, scanning for a room that might be Flynn's.

The smallest snatch of the front corner bedroom was visible through the cracked blinds, but the ceiling was overlaid with glow-in-the-dark constellations. I couldn't tell if that belonged to a younger sibling or was left over from Flynn's younger years. Then I made out the Nirvana poster.

I grabbed a rotting acorn from the ground and chucked it at the window.

"Flynn," I hissed. *"Flynn!"*

I tried another acorn. And another.

The sixth acorn was the charm. A lamp flashed on. Coppery hair stirred behind the blinds. Two exhausted green eyes blinked out at me.

He slid the window open with a sticky squeal, leaving a film of screen mesh between us. It reminded me of the veil he'd worn when he'd channeled Ellen, and I winced.

"Libby?" His voice was husky as he rubbed his eyes. "Wasn't this the reason we traded numbers—so we could stop stalking each other's houses at all hours? Is . . . everything okay?"

It was still dimmer around this side of the house, and clearly Flynn couldn't see me well. One good look at me, and he'd know—this was an emergency.

I opened my mouth to tell him, but nothing came out. I stood by the house's mildewed siding, choking on impossible words.

Flynn tilted his lamp toward me to get a better look. "Oh shit!"

There it was. Now he saw me.

"Stay there," he said. He squealed the window back into place, clicked off the lamp, and vanished.

I couldn't hold myself up anymore. I dragged myself over to the picnic table, where Flynn and I had sat with our powdered lemonade. A mockingbird danced on the branches of the over-hanging elm, eyeing me from every angle as I lay down on the bench and curled up on my side.

It almost felt like I was floating outside my own body. Like this was some deranged nightmare, and if I outwaited it, it would all melt away. Everything ached, my thoughts swirling in an end-less loop.

Mom. Vivi. Mom. Vivi.

What was happening to their bodies back in that house?

Please, nothing. Please let day be a time those monsters rested.

The sounds in the attic only started after dark. If nothing else, maybe they were less active when the sun was up.

I needed that to be true. I needed everything to pause, just for a minute.

Flynn rounded the corner of his house and came to kneel in the grass beside me. He cupped a hand to my cheek, poring over my face, my scalp, all the nicks and cuts and bruises and blood. "Lib . . ."

He'd never called me Lib before, the way Mom and Vivi did. It brought a longing burn to the back of my eyes. Longing for him. Longing for my family. Longing for anything to be okay so I could have those things again.

"What did they do to you?" Flynn's lip twisted with fury. "Was it Ellen? Because I'll kill her. I mean, she's already dead, but I'll—"

"It was Rose," I said. "And the Cockroach and the Praying Mantis and . . . all of them. They're awake. They have Mom and Vivi." I made myself tell him the rest, dredging up each painful word.

I kept wincing away from one crucial discovery, the one that would be the most personally painful for Flynn: the Wasp.

Orange hair and freckles, a body fresher than the Cockroach and the Mantis's.

But it wasn't fair not to tell him.

"Flynn . . ." I squeezed my eyes shut. I couldn't watch as the world fell apart for yet another person I cared about. "You were right, I think, about Ellen tricking your dad. He did die. And one of those things has his body."

Flynn's breath hitched. But he didn't move.

I opened an eyelid. I'd expected tears. I'd expected . . . something. But he was just kneeling beside me. Quiet for a long time.

Then he stood, hands clenched into fists.

"Ellen's a goddamn murderer," he said with venom. "I don't know what sick game she's playing, but this is *her* fault—that all these people died."

Flynn made himself unclench his fists, shake out his rage. "First things first, let's bandage you up." He'd brought the biggest first-aid kit I'd ever seen. His mom must've kept it on hand for day care.

And Flynn must've had plenty of experience. He treated me with creams and bandages. With hands that knew when to be soft and when to apply pressure. But he wasn't as skilled at hiding those low groans in the back of his throat, his pained hiss as he dabbed at the ruined flesh of my ankle.

I tried not to flinch too much.

"I'm sorry," Flynn said as he secured the last bandage. "I shouldn't have left you all there. I didn't realize . . ."

"None of us realized," I said dully. "But I can't let them die in that house, Flynn."

"Of course not. Okay, let's think this through. . . ." He paced through the whispering grass, moving for me when I couldn't bring my body to move. "If Ellen trapped the spirits inside those masks, there must be some way to untrap them, right? To actually exorcise them from the house."

I hoped so. "But how?" I said. "Ellen obviously isn't going to tell us the truth."

"We need another source. Someone who knows about House of Masks. Who we can trust."

The thought came to me slower, slogging through sludge, but it did come. "The people who disappeared." My jaw didn't want to move, but I forced it to keep going. "They're probably all tethered to the house by their deaths, like Ellen said she was. Grandma Margaret answered when you called, and she tried to warn us. So your dad . . ."

"My dad." Flynn stopped pacing. "You want me to call my dad?"

"He was a medium, right? Like you? You said he knew a lot about House of Masks."

"He didn't know enough not to get himself killed," Flynn muttered bitterly. "But maybe he put the pieces together too late. Maybe he *could* help us."

I knew how hesitant Flynn was to try calling him again, after his dad had failed to answer when he was young. A slight tremor was sneaking into his voice at the prospect. But he didn't argue, not in these circumstances.

"If he's tethered to the house, we should get back on the property to do this," he said. "Is that possible without being attacked?"

"I don't know. The house is overrun. The yard *might* be safer. Daylight *might* keep the spirits inside." But I couldn't pretend I knew that for a fact.

"Then we'd be risking everything on me pulling off this séance. *Fast.*" Flynn sighed. He sat on the end of the picnic table by my head. Slumped. Like he was exhausted.

I knew how he felt.

My body was getting heavy, sinking into the bench, the splintery old wood damp under my cheek. "You're a good medium, Flynn," I said. "I trust you. I think you should trust yourself."

"Trust myself." Flynn barked out the most bitter laugh. "I've gotta tell you, that's a foreign concept."

Above our heads, the mockingbird in the elm chirped and chittered all the birdcalls that it had stolen.

Flynn sighed up at it. "Maybe I should've told you before, but when I was nine, soon after my dad disappeared, I thought I *saw* Ellen. I'd come to the house looking for him. The hedge maze, I'd decided, for some reason. He had to be in the hedge maze. And instead, I turned a corner, and I saw"—he swallowed—"this foggy outline of a woman in a long lacy dress. She had her back to me. She called me closer, but then she turned around, and I *really* saw her. Libby, where Ellen's face should be, there's a caved-in hole."

That image shuddered through me. Ellen had told us she was Rose's first victim. Was that what Mom's body looked like now, underneath the rose mask?

But we didn't know if what had happened to Ellen was the same thing that had happened to Mom.

"Ellen scared me so bad that I told my mom what happened," Flynn continued.

I made myself listen. Made myself not think.

"*Big* mistake. She'd constantly called my dad 'crazy.' And after that, she decided I was, too. She sent me to a psychiatrist. Insisted they put me on meds."

"They thought you were hallucinating?" I couldn't bring myself to turn and look at him. Not because I didn't care. Because

I couldn't move anymore. I'd let myself get still on this bench. Curled on my side, facing the yard, the side of the house. I was so, so heavy.

"Yeah. I thought they were right," Flynn said. "I'm still on those fucking pills. And now, I don't think I need them at all. I don't think I ever needed them."

"I'm really sorry, Flynn."

And I was. Medicine was helping me, but I was increasingly sure my diagnosis was correct. Dr. Glaser was better equipped to help me deal with monsters in my head, not monsters in my house—but she was one of the good ones, I think. Her advice usually helped. When it didn't, she tried to adapt.

Given Flynn's awful experience, no wonder he'd been so twisted up about all this. This pain had followed him since he was a kid, festering in his skull. After everything he'd been through, he probably *could* benefit from good therapy. But that wasn't what he'd gotten.

"I see why you couldn't let yourself believe in spirits," I said. "But we know better now. No matter what they told you, or how often."

"Yeah," Flynn said quietly. Gratefully.

"What if you were onto something as a kid, when you imagined your dad in the hedge maze? When we were in the center together, you said you smelled something, too. Rot."

Right by that door in the ground. At the foot of Ellen's statue.

"True," Flynn admitted. "I always *felt* like something was down there. But that door is too heavy to budge."

"I can move it," I said, "if I wear the beetle mask."

Flynn jolted. He turned to look at me, a hard warning. "You're joking, right? You're gonna put that thing on your face, after—"

"Only for a second. Only when I have to." I'd already explained to him that my mask and its strength was the reason I'd escaped the house.

Flynn grunted. He did not like that idea. Not at all. But he didn't fight me.

"We should trust your instincts about the hedge maze—and the door," I said. "That's where we should go when we call your dad." Somewhere out of sight seemed safest, and that mysterious door was a lead. An idea. At a time when I had zero others.

"Okay. Then that's where we'll go."

Just like that, it was a plan. And it was really dawning on me—we'd agreed to go back to the infested property. Both of us, together.

But Flynn hadn't seen those monsters for himself. He had no idea what he was agreeing to.

"Flynn . . . ," I choked out.

He knelt back down beside me, facing me as I lay on the bench. "Yeah?"

I reached out a heavy hand and touched his cheek, near the bruise and the cut that my fist had left behind. The damage he'd already endured on my behalf.

He let me do it, his green eyes flicking questioningly over my face.

"This must hurt," I said softly.

Flynn shrugged. "It does. And I'll heal," he said. "The way I see it, Ellen was *way* overdue for a punch in the face. I'm glad you gave it to her, even if you had to go through me to do it."

In spite of everything, that pulled a weak laugh out of me. But I shook my head, cheek scraping the bench. "Flynn, those monsters are *dangerous.* I came here for advice. Not . . . I didn't mean to ask you to come with me."

"You didn't ask. But I'm the medium. It's not like you can talk to my dead dad without me. Besides, it's only right, isn't it?" Flynn said. "That house should've been half mine anyway."

His white teeth flashed in the dull light, his foxlike smile.

And my chest squeezed. With fond, aching warmth. With fear.

I couldn't bear the idea of the Mantis catching him like it had caught me. Or any of those monsters sinking their claws into him.

I'd let him go as far as the hedge maze, but no farther.

Even if that meant braving the rest alone to rescue Mom and Vivi. Assuming Flynn's dad could help us form a plan—that there *was* a way to rescue Mom and Vivi.

On my own, I gave myself maybe 10 percent odds of making it back out.

Or maybe five.

I sighed and stared at the green siding of Flynn's house. My watering eyes blurred it into a pale-green ocean. "I know we need to go. But I . . . can't make my body do it. Not yet."

"Don't, then," Flynn said. He sat beside me on the bench and helped me sit up. Clutched me to his chest.

I dropped my head to his shoulder and let myself be rocked. Breathed in the fresh laundry detergent of his shirt. Something clean.

I was anything but clean. I smeared blood and Cockroach ooze and clammy sweat all over him.

But he only gripped me tighter.

"Oh, your bandage." Flynn touched the loosening Band-Aids on my arm, covering the vicious nail tracks gouged by the Butterfly.

And now there was enough light that I saw that the vast majority of my Band-Aids were patterned with little sharks.

"Day care," Flynn reminded me. "It was sharks or teddy bears. I'll fix that one back up. Don't worry, I'm basically an EMT." In a lower voice, he added, "But after all this is over, you should definitely go to the hospital."

After all this is over. He said it like he believed this actually could be over. Like I'd still be standing on the other side.

It seemed like a waste, to bandage me up, to tend to a body that was only going to charge back onto that haunted property and get even more mauled in the process.

But I let him do it.

I wanted to believe it so much.

That this could be over. And it could end any way but bad.

CHAPTER TWENTY-FIVE

WE SLIPPED INTO THE BACKYARD THROUGH Flynn's usual gap in the fence.

And we held there, scanning for movement.

The house and the yard were quiet in the pale gold of morning. Dew sparkled on each blade of overgrown grass and glistened on the hedge maze. The blue roses were in proud bloom, petals fanning wide.

The house itself looked peaceful. Nothing moved past the dark windows. A sunlit glow shimmered over the rooflines, leaving fewer hiding spots for anything creepy and crawly to lurk.

But not spotting monsters was no guarantee they hadn't spotted *us*.

"Ready?" Flynn whispered. His skin was pale, with purple smudges under his eyes. But even as terrified as he had to be, he cut a stiff smile my way. A white-lie smile, offering false hope maybe—but still better than none.

I white-lie-smiled back. "Ready."

We raced for the maze, ducking low, in case that helped us stay undetected.

We pushed past the roses at the back entrance. The bushes were fuller than ever, their thorns longer and sharper. One scraped my bare neck, piercing as a bee sting.

The beetle mask nestled against my lower back. Once we'd stepped through the fence, it had started to wake up—an increasingly warm hug against my spine. My sweat slid down the glass of its nose and dribbled against my waistband.

The mask was my panic button. I wouldn't wear it, not unless it was *absolutely* necessary.

Two turns into the maze, I was already lost. But Flynn led us without hesitation, left and then right, and then right and then left.

At every rustle in the bushes, I whipped my head, expecting one of the rotting spirits to burst into view. But there was nothing. Only roses. Surrounding us like a slowly tightening chokehold.

"We're getting close," Flynn whispered. "The center is around the corner."

We turned the corner—and faced a dead end.

"No." Flynn gawked at the ten-foot wall of thorns. "This is the way. I'm positive."

My chest tightened. This was not the best time for Flynn to fumble navigation in the maze he knew so freakishly well.

The bushes around us rustled with what felt like more than wind. Some insect was singing—a scissoring whir—but I couldn't tell from where.

I took a deep breath and touched a calming hand to Flynn's shoulder. "There's more than one path to the center, right?"

"There is." Flynn turned on his heel. "Okay. We'll go this way."

Left, left, right, left.

The deeper we plunged into the maze, the louder the slithery rustling in the bushes. The leaves and vines quivered.

I couldn't feel any wind.

"One more turn, and we're there," Flynn announced.

We took one more turn.

Another dead end.

Flynn raked his fingers through his hair in bewilderment. "What the hell! Those are the only two paths to the center. I'm sure of it!"

We didn't have time for this. "Let's turn back," I said. "We'll try again."

With a frustrated groan, Flynn turned back the way we came. And stopped cold. "Oh shit, Libby."

I turned, too.

To get here, we'd walked through a passage of open grass. Now, it was gone. Pure vines. A new and very deliberate dead end.

Dead end ahead of us. Dead end behind us.

Ten-foot walls of roses hemmed us in on either side. The corridor was so narrow that I couldn't fully extend my arms.

We were trapped.

I backed up against Flynn, grabbing his hand.

The sunlight overhead dimmed. At first, I thought it must be passing clouds. Then I looked up.

The bushes surrounding us, curated into those straight high walls, were leaning in. Arching. Stretching toward each other, like twin tidal waves, to knit together over our heads. To seal us in.

Flynn's heart thudded against my back. "What's happening?" he asked.

Holy shit.

The roses *were* pieces of Rose. I'd seen them move, but I hadn't realized how much she could control them. Even if her mask was nowhere in sight.

We'd walked into the thick of these roses, following our only lead. And now Rose was squeezing us in her thorny fist.

The bushes beside us, they reached toward our bodies. Slowly, but inevitably, clawing closer.

Vines snagged my clothes—my ruined jeans, my wax-laden shirt.

Flynn's too. "We have to get out!" he shouted.

But the walls were *thick*. Too strong and sharp to run through.

Not without . . .

My beetle mask was still warm against my back. It could save us. But that could be why Rose was attacking in the first place. To force me to put on my mask.

Not yet. Not so soon.

But the maze was smothering us in a full-on thorny embrace. A vine slithered around Flynn's arm and punctured his skin. Started its leechlike suck. Flynn cried out. He tried to tear it away, but another caught his other hand.

I grabbed the vine feeding on him, and its thorns gored my palm. Blood streamed down my wrist. And I tried not to flinch. To get my fingers around it. To pull.

But another vine latched around my calf, dragging me away from Flynn. Down to my knees.

Flynn reached for me, and the vines yanked him back, too. Tearing us away from each other.

Rose had checkmated us.

My stomach twisted, but I had no choice. Before the vines could catch my arms, I grabbed the beetle mask and pressed it onto my face. It locked on instantly, melting into place. The line around the edge of my face burned white-hot. And the Beetle's strength surged through me.

I ripped my leg free and tore the vines from Flynn's arms. "Let's go!" I smashed the plant beside us and hacked through the wall, even as its vines squeezed us like constricting snakes. "Tell me the way."

He did. And I pulled him along.

Vines chased us, snatched at us. I stomped them flat, barreled through them.

And Flynn was right.

The hedge walls opened into the circular clearing at the heart of the maze.

By day, I could see the crumbling statue centerpiece more clearly. The long lacy dress. The curls of the hair. The weathered rose mask on the face.

Ellen Clery, wearing the mask that had once been hers. Communing with the spirit that was now trying to smother us with vines.

At her feet lay that flat square door. The heavy brass ring beckoned.

Flynn buried his mouth and nose under the neckline of his T-shirt. "God, that's rank." Standing next to it, he was choking back gags. His eyes streamed.

To me, it only smelled like roses.

I sucked in a deep breath, reached for the ring, and pulled.

The stone door scraped open with an ancient moan.

Now I smelled it.

From the dark below, a stench billowed up—earthy like the richest soil, sweet like rotting fruit, sour like mold. Decay.

But the vines were still groping after us. Snatching for skin and blood.

A wooden ladder reached down from the open door. And we scrambled to descend as the old steps creaked and buckled. I stepped down and down and down and down and down.

Until my feet hit the hard floor.

"Flynn! The door! Get the door!"

Vines were already reaching in.

He slammed it shut behind us, severing the wriggling vines. Sealing us in the dark.

The second we were safe from the vines, I grabbed my mask. Pulled.

No give at all.

The Beetle had seized its tiny window of opportunity. It had latched on to me deep and tight.

We'd outrun Rose's vines, but I was afraid she'd gotten what she really wanted.

The Cockroach flashed into my mind—its distended ribbed belly, the seeping pus, the extra legs that had burst out through the skin under its armpits.

If I didn't get off this property in time, that could be me. It *would* be me.

The timer had officially started.

We had to get Mom and Vivi out of this house—before I lost myself, too.

With the beetle mask anchored on, all I could do was take advantage of its strength, for as long as it was mine. At least the mask let me pretend to be brave. It erected a wall of fearlessness around me, kept my hammering heart at a distance.

The horrid smell in this place was thicker than sewage. And the cavelike darkness was the only thing thicker than the stench.

It was cool down here. Silent and still. But the slightest sour breeze stirred over the back of my neck. A prickling sensation, like there were eyes—eyes in the dark—watching me.

The ladder creaked as Flynn followed me down.

"God, what *is* that smell?" he whispered as he landed. His hand brushed my lower back, an instinctive promise of *I'll take care of you,* which was sweet and lovely. But I was the one wearing the beetle mask. As far as I was concerned, I was Flynn's bodyguard.

He jangled something in his pocket, and then a piercing white beam reached into the dark. His phone. I wished I still had mine.

It slanted onto swirling motes of dust. A stone floor at the base of the ladder, where severed vines wriggled limply, dribbling watery pink. The blood those roses had ripped from our own bodies, no doubt, leaking out onto the floor.

I could barely make out the low ceiling above, but I could feel the close crush of the walls around me.

This cellar was small, maybe ten by ten, the size of Mom's old storage unit. And I couldn't fathom what Ellen and Joseph would've used it for, until I remembered the article I'd found in my grandparents' room. The reporter had mentioned an unfinished attraction under the hedge maze.

A crypt.

Flynn swiveled his phone's flashlight over stone walls, a floor so dense with dust that it had accumulated like dirty snow.

A set of footprints tracked through it.

They looked human. Sneaker tracks. Small. Horizontal diamonds on the sole.

I knew those patterns.

These were Vivi's footprints.

And they were fresh. Extremely fresh. No dust sprinkled over them.

I couldn't speak. Just grabbed Flynn's arm and squeezed.

"Vivi?" he asked.

I nodded. But no telling if these tracks were from before or after the Butterfly bound her in that chrysalis. Either way, what the hell had she been doing down here?

Flynn followed the footprints with the light.

They led to the wall beside us, where the beam caught on a pale glint.

A face.

A man, his mouth dropped in a scream.

An answering shriek welled in my throat, but my mask helped me swallow it. I widened my stance, broadened my shoulders—in case we had to fight.

But the face wasn't moving.

It was a mask.

One that looked incredibly human, like Mom's.

The man was middle-aged, with saggy pockmarked cheeks, dark eyebrows, and a pencil-thin mustache. A mole on his chin.

Flynn ran his light down the wall. It caught mask after mask. Some full-faced, some only half.

Face after face, mounted in a line. Perfectly preserved. All their edges and empty eyeholes and nose holes were smooth and rounded. There was no trace of torn skin or blood. Nothing to prove these faces had ever been living.

Most were adults. A couple looked like they might be around my and Vivi's age. So many had features that resembled ours—the widow's peaks, dark eyebrows, deep-set eye sockets.

The world's most macabre wall of family portraits.

Our relatives had been pinned into masks. Collected like framed bugs in an entomologist's study.

Several masks down, there was a man and woman, maybe in their thirties. One of the woman's rich brown curls had tangled into the forehead of her mask. The man's eyebrows arched the same way as Mom's and mine and Vivi's.

My grandparents.

Who had become the Cockroach and the Mantis.

And beside them: the only face from a different family line. Freckles lined the bridge of a long, pointed nose. The mask's lips were pale pink and almost pouty. Painfully familiar.

Flynn sucked in a sharp breath, his flashlight trembling, just for a moment, before he refocused the beam.

"Your dad," I whispered.

"My dad."

Flynn's instincts about this place had been right. A horrific consolation. Still, I was desperate enough to hope that uncovering this crypt would benefit Flynn's efforts at a last-ditch séance.

But Vivi's sneaker prints trailed past his dad's mask. They stopped in front of the last two masks on the wall.

Mom.

And Vivi.

The gasp hit me deep in the throat.

Then Vivi had lost herself, too.

Her body had come here, but it had been piloted by the Butterfly. To seal her and Mom's real faces away in this vault.

I grabbed Vivi's mask with a choking sob. This piece of her matched the exact shape of the butterfly mask—her forehead to the bottoms of her cheeks. Her brow was crumpled in a way I recognized. How Vivi looked like right before she started to cry. Really cry. Full-throated-sob cry. She'd been so scared.

"I'll destroy them," I said. "I will break that house down brick by brick."

Flynn dropped a hand on my shoulder, and I realized how hard I'd tensed. Rage had activated my every fighting muscle. "Libby, is that really you talking?"

Shit. *Was* it me?

The impulse for justice, vengeance, had to be mine. Destroying this house couldn't be what the Beetle wanted. But the force of this rage, that couldn't be my own. Funny, the beetle mask had often made me feel so calm, so leveled out. But it had also made me feel strong. Overeager to use that strength.

The Beetle and I, we were tangling together, interweaving.

That couldn't be a good sign.

I released a shaky breath, trying to smooth the sharpest shards of this fury.

"We'll save her. We'll find a way," Flynn said.

I wasn't sure if he believed that, but those words were what I needed in order to function.

At least we'd found the masks of Mom and Vivi.

Then I noticed: "Flynn, there are two empty hooks on this wall."

Space for two more faces.

"I saw," Flynn muttered, not without disgust. He turned away.

On his next step, he stumbled. "What the hell?" He dropped the flashlight beam.

By his dusty sneaker lay a dustier mask, face down in the dirt.

He picked it up and flipped it over.

Another face.

Flynn brushed it off against his shirt, revealing a middle-aged woman with coppery eyebrows and splatters of freckles. She didn't look as purely terrified as the other masks did. Her lips were parted, but not dropped in a full scream. It looked like dread.

Like she knew exactly what was coming for her.

"Libby." Flynn's fingers flinched. "This is Ellen."

His flashlight touched the ground beside us and he full-on recoiled.

"Oh." The words squeezed from him in a whisper: "And I know what that smell is."

The beam fell on a ragged pile. Disintegrating scraps of lace. Of leather.

Of bone.

A body.

I reeled back, stumbling for distance between me and the corpse. Now that I could see the body, the rancid reek was absolutely choking. It shouldn't stink like this—the skin that remained was dry and papery, sunken, no tissue to speak of underneath. But, then, maybe there was a reason Flynn, a medium, had been the only one who could smell it from above. Why it might have taken the beetle mask for me to detect it, too.

The rot was supernaturally strong. Not a physical decay. A *spiritual* decay.

I swallowed a heave.

Flynn stayed exactly where he was. He had bypassed the survival options of fight or flight and jumped straight to freeze. "It's her."

Ellen.

His flashlight was locked on her crumbling rib cage, on the barest scraps of brown lace. Crusty stains dribbled and splattered over what was left of her chest, raining down from . . .

Flynn inched the light up the shriveled gray flesh clinging to her neck, to her sunken chin. To her face.

What should have been her face.

It was nothing but a gaping hole. A caved-in pit that began at her jaw and stopped short of her ears and the brittle frizz clinging to her slipping scalp. The light's beam touched through to yellow bone. Not the roundness of eye sockets or the triangular gaps of what had once been a nose. No teeth or jaw. Bones that were splintered, smashed, like the entire front structure had been stripped away.

A bloody puddle, long dried to powder, stained the earth beneath her head.

A cold tremor rippled in my gut. *Please* don't let this be all that was left under Mom and Vivi's masks. Mom was still breathing, after all.

I had to believe they were more intact than Ellen Clery.

Flynn stared at the mask in his hand, Ellen's face suspended in grimmest dread. "They threw her away," he said. "They took her face and didn't bother keeping her body. Why?"

"Maybe they hate her as much as we do," I said.

"Well. That's not too hard to imagine." He dropped her face where he'd found it, in the dirt. "I just don't understand why she's 'helping' them now, then."

"We need answers."

"We do," Flynn agreed. He walked back to the wall and lifted his dad's mask off its hook. He traced the edges of the mask, like he could absorb its secrets through his fingertips. "Let's give this a shot."

We found a bench built into the opposite wall and took our dusty seats. Flynn laid his phone flashlight-up in his lap, blinding us both. But the pocket of light it cast was small, the darkness of the cellar pressing in on us. I was grateful, actually, for the strength of that cold white beam.

It swelled our shadows up on the low-hanging ceiling. Made us a little bigger than we really were.

"The closest I've gotten to my dad in seven years is wearing his old T-shirts," Flynn said, "but here goes nothing."

He trembled as he lifted the mask of his dad's face and pressed it over his own.

He must've thought it would be like the other masks—that wearing his dad's face would provide spiritual access to him.

And the mask did stick, holding itself on. The light from Flynn's phone gleamed off his chin, striped sharp slices over the planes of his dad's final desperation. Before it was over, he must've realized his mistake in trusting Ellen.

But the mask wasn't remolding to fit Flynn.

It lay dead and static.

Flynn swallowed, his shoulders sagging. Maybe he'd been hoping his dad would recognize him right away, would know, instinctively, to hug tight.

"We should hold hands," Flynn said from under his dad's frozen lips. "I spent years telling guests that it helps to have an unbroken circle, and I guess it really does. Even if it's only the two of us."

In our séances, hand-holding only went as far as palms resting on palms. But I locked my fingers through Flynn's, and he gave me the slightest squeeze. Maybe he was thinking, like me, about our kiss, our hands intertwined the whole way through.

For the first time, his skin felt heated, not cool—slick with a sheen of nervous sweat.

But he began the invocation, in a mostly steady voice: "We call on the spirit of John Clery Driscoll to bless us with his presence."

I whispered it back, then echoed him as he continued the rest of the invocation.

Fog trickled from under the mask's forehead. This time, Flynn must've felt it.

His hands jumped in mine, his eyes widening under the mask.

He was calling, and his dad was answering.

Flynn pulled himself together, squaring his shoulders like he meant to be presentable, before speaking the final line: "Accept this body as your vessel."

The fog settled, and seeped into Flynn's skin. His eyelids fluttered and peeled back, first one, then the other.

Behind the holes of his dad's mask, there were only whites again, glowing like faint lanterns.

"Flynn?" It croaked from his throat, husky and cracked.

A broken voice piecing itself back together.

CHAPTER TWENTY-SIX

FLYNN'S FEATURES VANISHED BEHIND HIS DAD'S as the mask began to wake. The ghost blinked its white eyes, looking down at the body it inhabited, the hands it was holding—which were attached to me, wearing the beetle mask. *"What . . . What is . . . ?"*

The illusion was practically complete. John's face was older, his features slightly softer, his freckles in different spots. And his voice was cracked and broken from disuse, but so similar to his son's that Flynn's scratchy whisper underneath felt like an echo.

John seized Flynn's hands back from mine, breaking the circle, which I thought we weren't supposed to do. And then he did something even stranger—wrapped Flynn's arms around his shoulders and squeezed.

It took me a minute to recognize what was happening: Flynn's dad, after all this time, trying to give his son a hug.

Twin tear tracks ran from those white eyes, through the layer of grime that had settled over the mask's surface. And I had no idea if the tears belonged to Flynn or John or both.

"You look like a man," John said hoarsely.

Of course, last time he'd seen Flynn, Flynn had been nine.

Knowing Flynn, he'd probably been a scowling little menace. Or . . . maybe that attitude had come later. After his dad had died.

John nodded, smiled, at something Flynn must've said but that I couldn't hear.

This was a moment not to interrupt. I sat still, barely breathing, my hands half held out, in case John needed to take them again—borrow my electricity, as Ellen was fond of calling it.

"I don't know who you are, but my son is telling me to take your hands."

I glanced up from my lap to find John's glowing eyes fixed on me.

Benevolent or not, that undead white-eyed stare crawled under my skin.

"I don't mind doing that," John said, *"if you take off that mask. But I'm not holding hands with the Beetle."*

Flynn was probably explaining my situation silently in John's mind, but I couldn't hear what he was saying. So I'd have to explain over top of him.

"My mask is stuck," I admitted. "But, please, if you need the energy to stay, you can hold my hands anyway."

The ghost regarded me in silence.

"How do you know Flynn? Are you his . . . ?" He didn't know how to finish that question.

And I didn't know how to answer it.

I bit my glass lip.

But Flynn must've put me out of my misery and said *something,* because his dad chuckled. *"Well, all right. Good for you, kids."*

His tone was so paternal I ached all over again. I'd tried to imagine my own biological dad—wherever he was—but Flynn didn't have to imagine. He'd clearly had a real connection with his. Then it had been ripped away from him. That had to be worse.

"I'm glad to meet you, Libby." John took my hands. *"I hear you're someone special."*

He smiled, but as fragilely as Flynn had when he'd asked where my family would move when we left. Flynn's dad was scared for me. Hearing that I mattered to Flynn scared him even more.

"You really need to get that mask off," he said.

He had to be thinking about the Wasp.

What it had done to him.

"I know. But my family is trapped in that house. I can't leave without them."

"I saw the Butterfly with those new masks. So that's your family. . . . I understand. I do. But the two of you should go. Now. While you have the chance. I see the Beetle in you, more and more each second."

Right. John was a medium, like Flynn. And presumably a more practiced one.

"Can't you feel your time running out?"

I was, in fact, trying very hard not to notice the deepening burn around the edges of my face. The glass over my eyes was thickening, blurring the outside world behind a veil of blue. Slowly, though. Very slowly.

I still had time. Some.

"I need to know if there's any way to stop these spirits," I said.

John's mask stilled, so much that I thought it had lost its animation altogether.

But then his brow, his lips, so very like Flynn's, sagged in a portrait of defeat.

"There was *a way. Such a simple way. If any of us had realized it sooner."* He shook Flynn's head. *"Now, it's nearly impossible."*

"Tell me. Please."

John winced. *"Gently. On Flynn's hands."*

I'd gotten overeager and crushed down on Flynn without realizing it. "Oh, I'm sorry!" The Beetle made everything so very breakable.

"You've been talking to Ellen, so you know a little about what she's done here, right? How she trapped thirteen spirits in masks and turned this house into her own sick little spirit menagerie?"

I nodded. "I know the spirits got caught up in the identities of their masks and forgot who they were. And I know Rose—whatever she is—isn't human. Was never human."

John laughed. Weakly. Dryly. Darkly. *"The only* human *spirits in this house are the ones trapped in this vault."* He shrugged a shoulder toward the wall of my family's faces. *"On the other hand, that* thing *you're wearing . . ."*

Oh, I hated the way he said that. My stomach curdled. "You mean the Beetle was never human either?"

"Nothing Ellen summoned was human. They're just like Rose. A little weaker, sure. But monsters—every one of them."

Heat washed from my mask and surged through my scalp. The Beetle had stopped talking to me. But its rage, rising like a tide, simmered.

"The hands!"

I was squeezing again. "Sorry!"

"Maybe keep your palms flat," John suggested, increasingly wary. *"Whatever these monsters really are, Ellen calls them the Fallen*

Stars. They've never been alive, so they're not really dead. And they're more powerful than human ghosts, which is why she started summoning and trapping them in those masks in the first place."

The Fallen Stars.

I nodded, slowly. "Ellen told us she considered herself 'something of a lion tamer.'"

"Jesus Christ." John sighed.

"But she also admitted she had . . . been eaten by the lions."

"Oh, she was. When I was alive, she sucked me into her exciting lies. She's still playing the part of who she used to be. What she used to believe. She knows how to sell it, even though she knows better now. Only after death did I learn the true history of this place. From Joseph."

Joseph. As in Ellen's husband. As in . . . the first mask on the wall.

At least the spirits down here could communicate with each other. A tiny comfort—that meant Mom and Vivi weren't totally alone.

"But if it makes you feel any better—like it did for me—Ellen got exactly what was coming to her," John assured me.

"Rose was her mask. And it was Rose and the Moth, the mask Ellen's husband, Joseph, liked to wear, who first figured out that if they spent enough time with one face—only one face—they could bond with the body. And then they could steal it. Do what Ellen had done to them—trap the person's spirit inside a mask.

"The Moth got Joseph first. And when Ellen realized what Rose was about to do to her, before the bonding was complete, she tried to destroy the spirits. Instead"—he cricked Flynn's neck toward the faceless corpse, rotting in the dust—*"Rose destroyed her."*

"How did Ellen try to destroy them?" I demanded. If anyone

knew how, it had to be the person who'd brought them here in the first place.

"She was going to smash her crystal ball, her original conduit, the one that had opened a portal to these 'Fallen Stars' in the first place. Severing that portal while they're trapped here would destroy them."

"That's it?" I lit with hope. "Smash her crystal ball?" The one with the blue velvet rose at the center, from the white stone table. "Wait." Then came the rage. "That's all we ever had to do? And this would be over?"

"According to Joseph, yes."

"Then why the hell hasn't anyone destroyed it by now?" I demanded.

"No one knew the truth. And Ellen's ghost made sure to keep it that way. Joseph says that dying changed Ellen. She stopped wanting the Fallen Stars to be destroyed. She wanted, instead, to help them. So if anyone got close to thwarting the spirits, she led them astray."

Yeah, the leading-people-astray part felt familiar. "But what is she trying to help the Fallen Stars with? We asked Rose what she wanted, and she kept saying 'thirteen.' Thirteen *what*?"

"It's you," he said. *"You, your family, and Flynn. Thirteen bodies for thirteen masks. It's taken generations to round us up. But finally, Rose has eleven of us. You're the last two.*

"There's only one way for the spirits to be released from their masks without being destroyed—something Ellen calls the Rite of the Stars.

"To complete it, they need to sacrifice thirteen people. Or, more accurately, thirteen souls."

"Souls . . . ?" I choked a little on the word.

"Why do you think they've been collecting our masks down here?" John nodded toward the wall of hanging human faces. *"They're saving us for the Rite."*

"You're saying, if the spirits get all thirteen bodies, if they complete the Rite of the Stars like they want, every human soul they've trapped will be destroyed?"

He nodded Flynn's head.

"Doesn't that include Ellen's husband, Joseph?"

Again, John nodded. *"It's worth it to Ellen, because of how far she's fallen. When the monsters rip all our souls away, they'll tear them from the bodies that are still alive, too: you, your family, and Flynn. Your bodies will remain as living husks. And once a body is soul-free, Ellen can climb inside and live again.*

"Ellen, like these spirits, is after your bodies. That's the sad truth—there's increasingly little difference between her and the monsters she caged."

I should have been shocked, but Ellen's betrayal—the night she'd been so willing to sacrifice my thirteen-year-old sister—had already proven how corrupt she'd become.

And, in spite of everything, I wondered if a silver lining was buried in the reasoning behind Ellen's plan. "Then there's a way that a human soul, even if it's outside of a body, can permanently reenter one?" I asked. "Does that mean what's been done to my mom and Vivi can be reversed? That we could bring them back?"

John hesitated. *"I'm not sure that I should encourage you. I've already told you and Flynn to leave."*

He must've seen it in my eyes—there was no way I was going to leave. He sighed. *"Theoretically, restoring your mom's and Vivi's souls would be easier than what Ellen wants—to steal another's body. Souls know where they belong. If you got your mom's and sister's faces back on their bodies, I think they'd rebond."*

"Thank you for telling me," I said. I doubted he'd like this question, but I had to ask: "Is there anything that we can do for you?" My hopes weren't high—John's body, piloted by the

Wasp, hadn't been breathing. It was sickly mutated and riddled with rot.

John's laugh was the deadest sound. He shook his head, with a kind press on my hand. *"The spirits don't eat or drink. The Wasp killed my body within days. The most I could ask for would be reuniting my face with my corpse, finding some peace. But honestly, I gave up on that a long time ago. The last thing I want is for you to risk* anything *on my behalf."*

Reunite John's face with his body. He craved the peace Ellen had been so afraid of.

But he scowled, like he regretted telling me. *"Look. If you insist on facing the Fallen Stars, the only hope I can give you is that the oldest bodies are sapped. Frail. Scary as they look, they can't put up much of a fight. The more recent bodies are the ones to worry about—the Cockroach, the Mantis, the Wasp, the Butterfly, and, most of all, Rose."*

It was written all over his defeated tone: my odds were still horrifically slim.

He expected me to die.

He also knew he couldn't stop me.

"I won't waste more of the little time you have left. But please," John said, *"be careful. And please . . ."* He looked down at Flynn's body.

"I'll look after Flynn," I promised.

John nodded at me, a mix of pity and, possibly, admiration. *"Good luck, Libby."* He closed his white eyes. And he paused, so long I knew something silent was being shared between him and Flynn.

At last, fog leaked from behind his eyelids, around the edges of the mask.

And the mask popped free, seemingly of its own accord.

Flynn had to reach up fast to catch it. He stared at his dad's face in his hands. His jaw clenched. He was shivering again, so pale by the light of his phone.

Every time he held someone dead inside his skin, it took a toll.

I pressed on his hands—lightly, very, very lightly, mindful of the Beetle's strength—to remind him he wasn't alone.

His green eyes flicked to mine. But they caught on my mask. And he swallowed. "Libby, my dad couldn't stress enough how little time you have."

I tried to focus on Flynn. To ignore the faint, damning burn working itself into my skin.

"Then let's keep moving," I said.

First things first: we needed to test John's theory about the human masks being able to rebond with their bodies.

And I knew exactly who to test it on.

I grabbed Flynn's phone and shone it on Ellen. Her abandoned body. Her abandoned face.

Yes.

An extremely fitting guinea pig.

I grabbed her dusty mask and tried not to breathe in the rot as I leaned down toward her corpse.

The sour air stirred, an arctic fog steaming up from the mask of her face. It billowed into me, waking every goose bump I had.

Billowed past me.

"*W-wait.*" Flynn spoke from behind me.

But it wasn't his voice.

That awful, croaking crackle.

I turned.

Flynn had only just reclaimed himself from John, had been trying to warm up, bring the color back to his cheeks. Now, instead, he was stiff and trembling—his eyes rolled all the way back.

Another ghost.

From the proud hoist of his chin, the rigid spine, I knew right away: Ellen.

"Leave Flynn alone," I growled. "He didn't invite you in!"

Flynn's body resisted her. Quaking, almost seizing, fighting back. But Ellen hoisted him up from the bench, managed two choppy strides toward me. *"If you put that mask on me, I'll be gone."*

Sounded great to me.

But Flynn's body crashed to its knees on that cold stone floor. And Ellen clasped his hands. Literally begging me. *"Please don't. See reason."*

Rich. Very rich. "I thought you weren't afraid of death. You said it made us stronger—from lowly caterpillar to soaring butterfly, right?"

"I—"

"All that stuff about ascension, did you *ever* really believe that?"

"I did," Ellen insisted. *"All of us are born to die, and I truly believed once, from the bottom of my soul, that was our greatest gift. The height of what one can achieve. I devoted my whole life to death."*

This ghost on her knees staggered me more than I wanted to admit. But, in a very different way, I had also aspired to death. Or at least believed it was better than life.

Ellen saw my flicker of empathy and latched on to it. Desperately. *"You understand. I see that you do!"*

Flynn's body was turning against her, fighting to be free. Even as his knees buckled, knocking her down, Ellen refused to let go. She crawled, dragging Flynn's twitching body toward me.

"I expected to form a union with Rose. I expected death would make me greater. I expected to ascend. *But . . ."*

She laid Flynn's head down on the dirty stone and laughed. A sound jagged as broken glass.

Then she looked up at me, her white eyes shining through his muck-smeared face. *"Instead, I am this."*

She grinned wildly. Terribly. The brown-gray dirt of the crypt's floor streaked across Flynn's teeth.

"I know what I am," she said. *"I feel myself becoming less and less, running thinner and thinner. Not only my body, but my soul.*

"If you lay me to rest here, after what I've done—where does a spirit like me go? I've wandered from the path. I know I have."

She kept clawing Flynn's body toward me, even as he tried to pull back.

"If I could only try again—live the right way, die the right way—maybe it would be different. Maybe . . ."

"You had your chance. You don't get to take someone else's."

"But I'm not taking anything from you or your family. Not any-more." Her tinny voice crackled like a radio between stations. *"It's too late for you. You'll never escape this place. The Rite is inevitable. Can't at least one good thing come of it? I'll do better next time. In my second life, I'll—"*

"The Rite isn't inevitable. Not if I smash your conduit."

"You think you'll be able to reach it—you against them all?" Ellen's laugh was a well-honed stab. *"Tell me, Miss Feldman, why do you think the Beetle chose* you *as its host? Because you're strong, like it is?"*

I faltered. I hadn't really considered. I'd *like* to think that's why the Beetle chose me.

Ellen tutted, like she felt sorry for me. Like, dirt-streaked and begging as she was, *I* was the most piteous creature here. *"No, dear. No, no, no. The Beetle's strength would be such a problem for the other spirits if wielded against them. The Beetle never wanted a strong host, one that might run the risk of overpowering it. It wanted* you. *The weakest host it could find."*

Her words twisted into me, stabbed like a shard of glass in my gut.

"That's not true," I choked out.

"Stop deluding yourself, child. You might think you have the Beetle, but before long, the Beetle will have you."

Flynn's body pushed against Ellen. Convulsed with a furious shiver, clawing at stone.

Flynn was done with her.

I was done with her.

"Maybe I am weak," I said. "Good thing it doesn't require much to finish you. You've already finished yourself." I reached out to her corpse and dropped her mask over the pit that had once been her face.

"No!" Ellen wailed through Flynn's throat, the keen of something dying. Really dying. *"Take it off! Please. There's still time—"*

But there wasn't.

The edges of Ellen's mask began to melt. To fuse. With the gray, frayed flesh of her body. The torn seams stitching themselves back together.

Swirling fog coughed free from Flynn's body and was sucked back into Ellen's. Her mask, mummified in lacquered perfection, rejoined the reality of her body. It curled and shriveled into a leathery pucker—a corpse's face. Her rib cage collapsed. Her bones crumbled. Her whole body, face included, flaked into dust.

Until all that was left was her decimated dress. The lace fluttered like ash. The leather scraps of her shoes flopped limply to the ground.

She'd wondered where a spirit like her went.

Wherever it was, Ellen had gone. Or at least, she sure as hell wasn't here anymore.

And that was good enough for me.

If a corpse as withered as Ellen's had reknit her face and body together, there had to be hope for Mom and Vivi.

Flynn coughed, coming back to himself. "I can't feel her anymore," he gasped. "Thank God."

I helped him up, brushing at the dirt that clung to him and to the blood from his thorny scratches.

Since we'd set foot on this property, he'd endured one aching ordeal after another.

"Flynn . . . ," I said softly. "Thank you for coming with me. For braving all this. Your dad and Ellen . . ."

That snapped him out of his post-Ellen daze. "What's with that tone? Like you're saying goodbye."

"I need to get to the séance table. If I can smash the conduit, all this will be over."

"Right. And I'm going with you."

I shook my head. The table was in plain view of the house. It wasn't safe. And I wasn't sure how much longer it was safe for Flynn to be around me either. The second we were free from this hedge maze, Flynn needed to make a run for it. "Your dad warned us. I don't have much time left—"

"You expect me to walk out of here? Leave you like this?" He waved at my beetle mask.

"Flynn . . ."

"Stop saying my name like you're never going to see me again!" he snapped at me. "I'm not going to stand by and let you throw yourself away."

"That's not what I'm doing—"

"It *is* what you're doing! You know, martyring yourself is still killing yourself."

"Hey!" Angry heat collected behind my eyes. They blurred with unexpected tears. "I'm trying to do the right thing here! You think I want to face this bug-infested nightmare? *Alone?* You think I *want* to die?"

Flynn crossed his arms over his chest. "That's exactly what I think."

"Well, you're wrong! Honestly. You're wrong." Of all things, I laughed weakly, pressing a hand against my glass forehead, shaking my head. And the laugh made me think of Ellen, dragging in the dirt. Even if I hadn't already decided to live, how could I have witnessed that and still want to die?

"We'll get out of this maze together. But then you have to leave," I said. "*Please.* I promised your dad to help take care of you."

Flynn opened his mouth.

But then there came a stony rumble. A groan.

Above us, the door opened, and a square of sunlight seared down into the crypt, illuminating the ladder.

From the center of the hedge maze, masked silhouettes leered down at us.

I froze, terror icing my every muscle.

We'd used up too much time. And now we were going to pay for it.

The Butterfly giggled, contorting Vivi's lips into a too-wide grin. Enormous lacy wings extended from her back, flexing in the breeze.

Past her shoulder, Mom's body stood tall.

Rose. The worst of them all.

Something dropped from her hand, clattered at the foot of the ladder.

The ant mask.

I had no idea why they were giving it to us. Flynn was never going to put that on, not unless they were going to come down and make him.

Rose lifted Mom's hand in a queenly wave. A smug little farewell.

Then I understood.

They didn't intend to come down.

They didn't intend for Flynn or me to come up either.

"No!" I shouted, racing for the ladder.

If that door closed, I knew, *I knew*, it wasn't going to open again.

Too late.

With an unforgiving slam, the door sealed. The sunlight vanished.

Flynn and I were trapped.

CHAPTER TWENTY-SEVEN

I SCRAMBLED UP THE LADDER AND pounded at the closed door. Slammed my forearm, my elbow, my shoulder against it. Pain shocked my damaged body, and it only made me shove harder.

The ladder creaked ominously under my feet.

A feral growl burst out of me, sweat streaming from my glassy hairline.

"It's no use!" Flynn shouted up. "Stop!"

But desperation clawed like a rat at my rib cage. I couldn't stop. If I stopped, we were going to die down here. I pushed and pushed.

That sensation twinged deep inside me, the one that came the more I drew on the Beetle's strength—a muscle twisting the wrong way. A strength that didn't want to be used.

The door gave. Just an inch.

Wide enough to glimpse the sunlight. And to make out the vines. Rose vines coiling over top of the door, anchoring it down.

There were too many. An amassing mountain, burying us alive.

The door slammed down against my shoulder, and the rotting ladder step gave out from under me.

I toppled to the cold crypt floor.

Collapsed, in the dust.

Flynn was right. Ellen had been right, too. It was no use fighting. I was too weak to win.

"Libby!" Flynn crouched beside me, running his flashlight over my body. "Jesus, are you okay?"

I was intact, if that's what he meant. But only because of the beetle mask.

I grunted, which was meant to be reassuring. But I doubted it was.

Flynn set the flashlight beside us. It was our only little light source—and now I wondered how long his battery would last. He hauled me up to sitting, brushing the dust from my shoulders and back.

I glanced at the ant mask lying beside us. If only I'd fallen on it and crushed it. Although if my beetle mask was any indication, crushing the ant mask was impossible. "How long do they plan to leave us down here? Until you cave and put on the mask?"

Flynn flicked a hateful glance at it. "Probably."

"At least they didn't try to overpower us," I muttered. "Send down any of those monsters to threaten you."

Flynn swallowed thickly. "They didn't have to. One of them is already down here."

Oh.

Oh God.

My beetle mask.

Soon—maybe *very* soon—it would take over my body. Force me to turn on him.

I'd thought I'd understood the horror of our situation, but I hadn't. Not by half.

They'd caged Flynn in with a lion. And the lion was me.

"No." I tugged at my mask again, even though my skin so deeply tugged with it, I might as well have been trying to pull off my nose. "No, no, no. . . ."

If I used the Beetle's strength against myself, I could rip it off. All it would cost was a deep and bloody chunk of me. How deep, how bloody, I didn't know.

Almost definitely enough to kill me. To bleed me out all over this crypt.

And would even that be enough to save Flynn from these monsters?

He'd still be trapped. Unless he wanted to starve to death, he'd have to put on the ant mask eventually.

"Libby!" Flynn grabbed my hand, which was poised at the edge of my jaw—deciding whether or not to rip. "Hold on. Stop—"

He kept talking. His lips were moving, but . . .

Pain pinched hard into my temples, so hard I winced.

A white heat. The kind that could've come from fire or ice. So extreme that my body couldn't tell the difference—whether I was freezing, whether I was burning.

Either way, something was being stripped away.

Numbness spread across my forehead, washed down my nose and cheeks, dripped into my lips and chin.

A pressing heaviness. Like my lows, but stronger—so much stronger.

Crushing me.

A claustrophobic nightmare brought to life.

That white heat lit my entire scalp, surged down my spine and out through my veins. Into every part of me.

The Beetle.

I dropped my mouth. I tried to warn Flynn.

But it was like my throat, my whole chest, was packed solid with glass.

It didn't matter. All I wanted to tell him was to run. And there was nowhere for him to run to.

Rose and the Butterfly had seen to that.

The world dimmed, like a cloud passing in front of the sun. The beam from Flynn's flashlight was suddenly muted through my eyes.

The shapes were back. The blue and gold rectangles. Stacking around me, sure as the four walls of this crypt. Pressing in tighter and tighter—until they closed around me like a fist.

A me-sized cage of solid glass.

My view of the crypt, of Flynn, blurred. Everything streaked and distorted. My hearing, too. It echoed strangely, fragmented, broken into shards.

Flynn was calling my name. He sounded scared. He was looking for my eyes behind the mask and couldn't find me—his gaze kept darting like there was nothing to latch on to.

I knew exactly what my eyes must've looked like from the outside. That corner-to-corner blue I'd seen on Vivi. Mom.

I wanted to tell him I was still in here. And that I was sorry.

I couldn't help him, or reach him. I couldn't help Mom or Vivi. I couldn't help myself.

Because I was weak, like Ellen had told me.

The Beetle, on the other hand, who was seizing control of my frozen body . . . The Beetle could reach Flynn just fine.

A piercing white beam broke through to me, a snatch of Flynn's shout: "Libby, don't do this. You're still in there, right? You have to be—"

It strangled off into a yelp.

No. No. I couldn't tell what was happening. What this mask was making me do.

Flynn! I tried to scream. But nothing came out—the sound bounced back at me. Echoed in my mind.

I was encased. Buried. In my very own glass sarcophagus.

Flynn couldn't hear me. But, then, what about the Beetle? It was in here with me. My only hope, Flynn's only hope, was to reason with it.

Please don't do this, I begged. *You know I'm sorry about what Ellen did to you. You know I never wanted to hurt you. Not until you all started hurting us. And maybe there's another way, to free all of you without destroying all of us! Maybe we can figure one out if you . . .*

Nothing answered. Nothing at all.

Please? I tried again, one last time. *I thought once that we were friends.*

I'm sorry.

My voice echoed back to me. I recognized that particular whisper right away. The one I'd spoken to the beetle mask as the indents of its eyes stared up at me, round and pleading. Right before I'd thrown it away.

Goodbye.

No. We weren't friends. We'd never been friends. The Beetle's friends were inside that house. It was going to help *them,* not me.

And it wanted me to know that.

Flynn really was the only person left. One human against twelve spirits.

He didn't stand a chance. Not against all of them.

Not even against the Beetle.

An impact ricocheted through my right hand. Then my left. Like, through my armor, all ten of my knuckles had been smashed with a brick.

My stained-glass eyes barely made out the shadowy outlines—my pummeling fists, swinging after Flynn. He ducked and dodged, scrambling out of my lumbering path.

My body kept missing. Pounding into the walls. The floor.

Stone cracked. Chunks flew.

Come on, Flynn, I begged silently. *Be smarter than this thing. Be faster.*

I was hitting so hard. Crushing the crypt around us. Sooner or later, one of these blows would land.

Please don't! I knew the Beetle wasn't listening, but I couldn't stop pleading. *Stop. Not Flynn. Don't!*

This time, the Beetle didn't answer with my voice. It answered with an image: me, fireplace poker in hand, standing over the Cockroach as it writhed, belly-up.

Me stabbing the poker down.

Crunch.

Through my blue-glass prison, all the blood looked purple. New purple freckles that sprayed across Flynn's face, his throat.

He smacked into the wall. Fell to the floor.

I'd shattered his arm. I'd smashed the bone right out of his body.

It cut through his sleeve, stabbing into the open air like a brittle twig. His muffled moans filtered through to me.

And his broken cry: "Stop! You win!"

The Beetle handed him the ant mask.

It let me watch as Flynn put it on.

The glass that was crushing me was only getting thicker, but I glimpsed snatches of what came next.

The Beetle slung Flynn over my shoulder. Like he was nothing.

Carried him up the remaining steps of the ladder. Thumped hard at the door.

Rose seemed to know it was the Beetle, not me, in control. The door opened into sunlight that was warm and welcoming—and so very wrong. So disjointed from this dismal reality.

The Butterfly was delighted by Flynn's splintered arm, and those awful giggles lodged in my ears. All the worse because they came through Vivi's throat.

We were all back together: Mom and Vivi and me and Flynn. Everyone I cared about. Except the only one still in control of their own body was Flynn. And even through my armor, I could feel him shaking on my shoulder. Slipping into shock.

I thought the spirits might pilot us straight to the séance table. But no.

Séances were best performed at night. Maybe rites were, too. Or maybe it was true, after all, that the spirits weren't at their full strength during the day.

The Beetle followed Rose and the Butterfly back into the house. Hauling Flynn all the way.

When we reached the second story, Flynn tried to break free.

He didn't get far.

The Beetle made me squeeze his injured arm until he screamed.

We pushed through my closet and its secret door. Wound up the stairwell lit so prettily by glowing stars.

And I thought of the name Ellen had given these spirits: the Fallen Stars.

A pretty name, for something not pretty at all.

The attic looked empty at first glance. All those dusty white sheets draped over what had never been furniture.

The Beetle passed Flynn off to Rose, who bound him in vines in the attic corner. He lay there, limp and silent, wearing his ant mask, bleeding into the floor.

I lost sight of him as the Beetle turned to face the white sheets at the center of the room. Lifted the nearest corner and ducked under.

It wedged my body into a tangle of gigantic bugs, nestled under these sheets. This was where they'd been hiding, hunkering during the daylight hours.

The Beetle tucked me in among the repulsive bristled torso of the Housefly. The rusted cast-iron armor of the Cricket, which was stretched over a spindly, twisted body. The Butterfly slept draped over my back. Vivi and I had given the Butterfly and the Beetle the opportunity for recent quality time—maybe those spirits had taken a liking to each other. How touching.

The Beetle closed my eyes.

The attic went quiet. The spirits resting, as still as dead things.

Until a whisper scraped through, at the back of my mind: *Libby?*

Flynn.

The ant mask. I'd forgotten the ability Ellen gave it—or, more accurately, the trick Ellen made it perform.

I tried to answer. But my mind was encased in a slick, thick sheet of glass.

I couldn't even think back at him.

Libby . . . ? I don't know how to do this alone. Please tell me you're still in there.

I wanted to tell him that.

But I couldn't.

He whispered to me for a while, and he begged me to answer, and, finally, after I didn't and didn't and didn't . . .

Flynn gave up.

For a time, there was nothing to see. To hear.

Not until the Beetle finally stirred.

The first thing I caught was the attic, glowing bright blue by night, all those shining stars with their thirteen points.

Insect feet scuffled. White sheets were ripped back.

The spirits were trundling out of the attic, single file. Marching down the stairwell, through the house, toward the yard. Like some grim procession.

The Cockroach carried Flynn outside. He looked half-dead in its arms.

How much blood had he lost?

Damn these glass walls the Beetle had built around me—stained and rippled, giving me a clear view of absolutely nothing.

The spirits walked and crawled and limped and flapped and hovered through the garden.

Found their places around the table, under the stars.

Rose bound Flynn to the ant chair, with curling vines and thorns. He couldn't completely stifle his pained cries. I could hear them from in here. Or maybe that was because the Beetle wanted me to hear them.

Funny how I'd once thought my mask and I had a genuine bond. The Beetle had since made it very clear that I was only a means to an end. That end would come now, and it wanted me crushed and hopeless all the way up to it.

Every time Flynn struggled, blood trickled from his torn sleeves. His shirt was already scratched to shreds.

Rose sent the Cockroach and the Mantis to the hedge maze, and they returned with the forgotten human faces, laying each out like they were setting the table for a feast. One per place, in front of the spirit who'd stolen the accompanying body.

Mom.

Vivi.

My grandparents.

Flynn's dad.

And all the rest.

Joseph Cragg, the first face from that lineup in the basement, was in front of the Moth.

Flynn and I still had our faces, so there was nothing to lay in front of him or the Beetle. But it didn't seem to matter that neither the Beetle nor the Ant had completed the process of taking over our bodies. It was enough that they held us captive.

If Flynn's dad was correct, then this Rite would destroy every human soul at this table, mine and Flynn's included, leaving our bodies breathing but hollow.

There was no further ceremony. A few white pillared candles littered the tabletop, having survived my and the Butterfly's tussle in hot wax, but Rose didn't bother lighting them.

Ellen's blue-rosed crystal ball, the original conduit, sat in the very center of the table.

Right there in front of us. And I couldn't reach it. Flynn couldn't reach it.

The spirits held hands—or, as close to hands as they had to offer—the way we'd done at our séances.

Mom was at one end. Vivi was at the other. Flynn winced as the Butterfly grabbed the hand of his broken arm. The Wasp grabbed his other hand. My body held hands with the Moth and with Rose.

In a low, soft voice—Mom's voice—Rose began to speak. In a language I didn't recognize. The wicks of the surviving candles hissed into blue-white flames. The crystal ball, with its rose at the center, glowed with a strange inner light, that brilliant, devouring blue.

From the bushes surrounding the patio, musty perfume burst into the air, dead drunken grapes wafting through, thick as a cloud. The rose vines strangling the pillars climbed higher, choked tighter. Bits of stone crumbled to the ground.

The insects from the yard came to join the spirits at the table. Humming flies and shiny cockroaches. Spring-green mantises. Screaming cicadas. Mosquitoes sucking at the dried-out husk that wore their mask. Dusty moths flitted gray wings over the faintest specter of them all, a body that rattled like an empty skeleton, its velour wings wearing so thin they faded into the chair behind them.

Butterflies swarmed over Vivi's neck and shoulders. They perched proudly atop the lace wings that unfolded from her back.

Something scrabbled at my leg. The Beetle let me feel it.

And, oh God. I was crawling with beetles. I couldn't move. Their tiny pinpricking feet hooked into me, six at a time, and writhed up my calves, over my knees. They climbed over and under my shirt, swarming toward my neck. Rustling and rooting through my hair.

The mask covered my face, but my ears were open, exposed.

I wanted to scream. But my body was heavier, stonier, than the chair it rested on.

Bloody vines wound out from Mom's arms and wrapped

around her body, weaving through her veil, her curls. Their buds burst into fat-fisted full bloom.

Ellen's crystal ball flared.

This was the spirits' moment.

The so-called Rite of the Stars.

And I couldn't stop them.

I was sitting here, watching everyone I loved teeter on the brink of that swallowing icy void—the same one I'd tried to hurl myself into before. I was aching to save them, and I was drowning beneath the weight of the Beetle.

It was telling me I shouldn't exist anymore. That I shouldn't even try.

The same feeling that had echoed in my brain for months. The Beetle had trapped and tricked me, and now it was stopping me from moving my body.

Weighing me down, locking me up—like the worst-ever catatonic low.

I was still in here. I wanted to move.

Body, please, I begged myself.

But nothing happened.

Nothing happened.

I was going to die. We were all going to die, because I couldn't help myself. I'd never figured out how to help myself. And that's why—

No. That wasn't true.

I flashed back to my recent terrible low, kneeling by the toilet with blue-rose tea lingering on my lips. I had helped myself then. I'd gotten myself to move.

I could do it again.

You have to move, I told myself now. *Your finger. Just one finger.*

I put all my effort into my left-hand pinky. One tiny part of myself. I hoped and strained and begged my body.

Move. Move. *You can do this, Libby.*

My pinky twitched. The tiniest, almost invisible twitch.

But a radiant sunburst of hope surged through me. This outside force seizing my body—I could fight it the same way I fought my lows.

These spirits thought they'd won. They thought I was gone, and that I could never claw my way back. They thought I was weak.

But they were using the exact bullshit psychological tactics I'd been training for my whole life. With each and every low and hypomania I'd survived, before I'd even known what to call them.

So, what if my mind—for all its ragged and jagged edges—didn't make me weaker?

I'm not made of glass.

The voice—*my* voice—came to me from somewhere deep inside. Like the first time the Beetle told me **You are not broken.** For a glorious moment, I'd thought that strong voice belonged to my own brain. Rooting *for* me, for once, instead of *against* me.

It hadn't really been my voice then.

But it was now.

I moved my thumb. Then another finger and another and another. Startling a beetle that had been climbing my ring finger.

Yes, I could do this.

And my newfound inner voice surged through me again, louder:

I'm not broken. I can break you.

In my mind, I smashed through the Beetle's glass wall.

There was another behind it.

I smashed that one, too. And another. Again and again and again.

Until there was no more glass. No more walls between me and my body. No more moving fingers one at a time.

I sucked in a breath, and it was with my own lungs. Tasting the actual air. Beetles were swarming all over my body. My chair was so charged, so hot, it burned the back of my thighs, searing the spot stripped tender by my fall into the candle wax.

Flynn must've heard some mental change in me. *Libby?* he whispered into my mind, a voice afraid to hope.

I'm here.

Behind the ant mask, Flynn's eyes relit.

And I spasmed into sudden motion. This time, it was me taking the Beetle by surprise, not the other way around.

I imagined the Beetle in a glass cage of its own.

I locked it up in my mind the same way it had locked me up.

It wrestled me for control, the muscles in my hands and arms fighting against me as I pulled free. Beetles tumbled from my thrashing body to the grass below.

Rose stopped chanting. Turned and saw me. What I was doing.

But Flynn shot to life in his chair. He yanked his hands free from the Wasp and the Butterfly. A splitting screech, like nails on a chalkboard, screamed into my head.

All the spirits around the table recoiled, and I realized: it was Flynn.

Hijacking the hive mind. Projecting that noise into all of our skulls.

A distraction.

For me.

I had to move *now.*

I ripped my hands free and jumped to my feet. Flung myself toward the center of the table. Toward the crystal ball, the conduit.

I raised a fist to smash it.

One of Rose's vines latched on to my arm, twisting it off course. My bare fist crashed down—not onto the shining crystal ball—onto the séance table itself.

The table cracked. And crumbled.

The crystal ball tumbled down with it—and everything stopped. Every single spirit was watching, glued to the fate of the conduit. But the ball didn't crack. It rolled. Out of sight. Under the debris.

All the spirits leaped up around us.

Rose redirected the vines to chase me, leaving Flynn free to tear himself out of his chair. He only had his left arm to work with, but he looped it around the Butterfly, yanking Vivi's body away from the table. The Mantis and the Centipede, with its wriggling, grasping legs, charged after them. The Wasp, too, with that throbbing red stinger.

My mask seared hot against my face, clutched in a panic to my hairline, trying to seize back control, seize back the strength I was stealing. It clawed inside my mind—a trapped animal, frightened and furious.

I didn't know how long I could hold it back.

I dove into the debris of the shattered table. Digging for the crystal ball. Tearing through Rose's coiling vines.

A massive body slammed into my side. Whooshing all the breath out of me, knocking me to my knees.

The Cockroach, oozing torso and all. Back for more.

I clutched my aching ribs, and the Cockroach hissed like it was a battle cry. Charged me again.

And I didn't dodge. Didn't even try.

I grabbed the Cockroach around the neck and wrestled it down. It gnashed its mandibles and its human teeth, dribbling spit and pus. It scrabbled at me with its wooden-spiked twisted human limbs. With its extra buglike legs.

It was one of those that I grabbed, by the joint growing from its armpit—and I tore it straight off.

With a hair-raising hiss, the Cockroach sank its human teeth into my arm. They were so old, so brittle, they cracked apart, leaving nothing but the slime of its pulpy gums. Its sagging jaw couldn't even close properly, and when I wrenched my arm away, it caught and ripped the rotting tendons.

The Cockroach's jaw flung to the ground, bone shattering.

I hurled the Cockroach away, flipping it onto its back, and chucked its leg after it. I didn't *intend* to clock it on the head with its own loose leg. But I wasn't sorry about that either.

The Cockroach spun in the grass, thrashing, leaking lumpy fluid—hissing for all it was worth.

I stomped off the vines wrapping around my ankle, and I was about to dive back into the debris pile when Flynn shouted inside my head, *Libby! Vivi's mask! Your mom's!*

Oh.

That's why he was wrestling the Butterfly. He had the mask of Vivi's face. The other spirits had been trying to stop him, but they didn't succeed. He shoved Vivi's mask back onto her face. Over the butterfly mask.

The Butterfly wasn't laughing now. It shrieked, clutching at Vivi's mask as Flynn pressed.

The mask of Mom's face had fallen into the rubble, too.

Rose saw me. Saw me scanning the rubble near the head of the table for Mom's fallen face. Saw me find it.

Rose was strong.

Here's hoping I was stronger.

I charged at Mom's body. In a blur of hard weight, I tackled her to the ground. It was like wrestling a marble statue. But with the beetle mask on, I could fight. Maybe I could even win.

I crushed Mom's face down over Rose's mask. Over the blue voids of Rose's eyes.

Mom's face stayed frozen, locked in its anguished scream, while I straddled her body, trying to pin it without destroying it.

And a vine wrapped around my neck.

Shit.

It tightened like a boa constrictor, thorns digging into my throat. Puncturing one spot after another, tearing at my veins, searching for one so big I'd bleed out.

Any second, Rose's thorns would find their target.

But I couldn't release Mom's face to grab the vine. I had to keep pressing down. Had to keep hoping that Mom knew how to find herself again.

"Mom, wake up," I gasped through my closing throat. "Wake up, wake—"

More vines coiled over the first, choking the air out of me. Blood streamed down my throat, trickled down my shirt and over my chest.

The world was smudging. The Beetle clamored at me from the inside, fighting for control. Burning me through its mask.

I was going to pass out. That swirling blue was returning to my vision. Those blue and gold walls. Not again. Not—

"Let go of Libby!"

That voice.

I knew that voice.

The vines around my neck did loosen. Enough that I could turn and see.

Vivi.

The butterfly mask was off.

It was her. Actually her.

She stood among the smashed remains of the table. In her hand, held aloft like a hostage, was Ellen's crystal ball.

The conduit. Flynn must've told her to grab it.

All around her, the spirits froze. Some had been midfight with Flynn. Others midstride toward Vivi herself. Others yet had been coming for me and Rose. Even the Cockroach was back on its feet.

For one awful moment, they held suspended, staring at the crystal ball in Vivi's hands.

And then they burst into raging panic. Lashing out in wild fury. They surged toward Vivi. In the thick of them, I lost sight of Flynn. An awful cry from him pierced the air—worse than when I'd broken his arm, worse than any cry I'd heard from him before.

It pierced straight through my heart. Because I couldn't see him. Couldn't see what they'd done to him. What they were about to do to Vivi.

The spirits were *desperate* not to be destroyed.

As soon as I could breathe, I shouted, "Vivi, smash it!"

Vivi didn't need to be told twice. She hurled it against the stone. Hard.

The crystal cracked.

And crunched.

Glass shattered. Sprayed out in tiny shards.

Just like that, the vines withered and dropped from my throat. The beetles squirming for purchase on my skin stood still. And then they dropped like the dead. Crashing into powder.

scared scared help

My mask clung weakly to my face.

I wasn't positive if the Beetle—if any of the spirits—*quite* deserved this. They had never wanted to be trapped in this house in the first place. They'd been fighting to free themselves.

But the Beetle had made it plenty clear: it was us versus them.

And they had lost.

The mask on my face unsealed with a pop. As it slid from my forehead, it cracked down the middle, like the normal glass it should've been, and shattered against the ground.

The Beetle—or, more accurately, whatever it had really been—was gone.

All around the table, pops and cracks. As the spirits lost their power.

Mom.

Oh God. I didn't know if her own face had rebonded in time.

Under me, her body gave a hacking, wet cough. Her hands were covering her face, and I couldn't see.

She pulled something free. Something mask-shaped.

This time, it was the withering rose mask that came off in her hands. Its blue blooms curled and blackened, the petals cracking to dust.

Underneath, Mom was gasping and wild-eyed. Bloody and burned all around the edges of her face. The skin by her ear ravaged and dangling.

"Libby?" Her voice came out ragged. Raw. But hers.

It was all she managed before we were tackled in a sudden hug.

Vivi. The lacy wings had wilted and dropped from her back. And she was coughing, too, sputtering out gobs of clear chrysalis slime, crumpled feathers.

I threw my arms around her shoulders. Smashed her shaking body to my chest.

Mom pulled herself up and sobbed into the tops of our heads. Her arms were wet and slick with the blood those roses had pulled out of her. She smeared it all over our sticky clothes.

Our frantic heartbeats pounded against each other.

Reunited.

All alive. All together.

And the house . . . It looked different. It was missing something. The color in the windows. They were gaping dark holes. The stained glass was gone.

Or . . . no. Not gone.

It had been crushed to powder—to glinting jewel-toned sand. It caught in the wind, drifting out from the house to mist down on the backyard.

Rich purples and reds and deep, dark blues coated the collapsing remains of the hedge maze. Frosted its shriveling vines with gemlike glitter.

It dusted my hair, brushed my bare arms.

I flinched, sure that it would cut like glass.

But it'd been blasted to smithereens, restored to its rawest material. The flecks were so tiny, soft like snowflakes.

It glittered in Vivi's dark curls. Mom reached out her palm and, mesmerized, watched it land in the cup of her hand.

I turned to look for Flynn. And found him, now free from the ant mask, by the broken stone table. Caught his green eyes, watching the three of us with a misty softness, the barest flit of his foxlike smile.

But something was wrong.

He staggered, clutching at the wasp chair to hold himself up.

"Flynn!" I ran to him.

Around us, as masks had dropped from bodies, they'd left behind faceless corpses. Shadows mercifully fell into the holes where their faces should have been, but the white of fractured bone shone through in the moonlight. The blood had long since dried and curdled, leaving a peeling mess of flesh and muscles.

I stepped, accidentally, on the skeletal arm of the Moth, of Joseph Cragg's body, and it puffed into ash.

I ran past them all and caught Flynn by the shoulder. "Hey, we did it. We won."

"Almost." He smiled. "Will you help me? My dad's mask . . ." He'd grabbed it from the wreckage with his good arm, was looking around the ruined bodies for what had been the Wasp. But his stare was taking on a strange glazed look. He looked right at the Wasp and then past it, like he couldn't see so well.

"Of course." I looped my arm over his shoulders.

And he stumbled full-on into me. His shirt was wet. Sopping.

There was no blue glass over my eyes this time. The blood wasn't purple. It was red. Very, very red.

There was a gash. There was a hole. Underneath his rib cage.

One of those monsters—that cry I'd heard—it had cut clean through him.

I gasped. "Your phone, Flynn. Give me your phone."

He nodded down at the pocket of his jeans, and I dug it out. The screen was cracked, the battery at 3 percent.

I tried to stay focused, calm. Even as his blood soaked into me. I blinked water out of my eyes. "We need an ambulance."

"Let me do that." Mom was behind me. Her and Vivi both. She took the phone. "It's okay, Flynn," she told him. "You're going to be okay, sweetie."

Was he?

"My dad," he said to me. With sharpening urgency.

Flynn shouldn't be moving. We should make him lie down, try to hold in the blood.

"Please." His fingers trembled where he gripped that mask of his dad's face.

This was what Flynn wanted. Maybe the last thing Flynn wanted.

Together, we stumbled to where the Wasp lay. Its paper wings were crumbling in the grass. Its stinger was smeared with blood. Blood that must've been Flynn's.

I knelt down with him, and Flynn put the mask over his dad's face.

It latched on, like Ellen's had latched to her body. Knitting together effortlessly.

Like Flynn's dad had told me in the tomb: *Souls know where they belong*.

The mangled corpse, brass and paper and old torn flesh began to melt away, into ash.

Now Flynn's dad could finally rest.

Against me, Flynn sighed. "There. We won." He closed his eyes. Sagged against me.

"Flynn. Hey. Stay awake, okay?" I laid him down as best I could. Looking as little as possible, I pressed my hands over the ruin under his rib cage.

Even his lips were white now. He was starting to look dead. Deader than when he'd channeled Ellen.

"Flynn!" I shouted, because I didn't know what else to do.

That did get his eyes back open. But they stared through me, unfocused. "Do you want me to stay with you?"

Of course, I didn't think about that twice. "Yes. Stay. Please stay."

He nodded. Like someone falling asleep, he mumbled, "I'll stay."

And then, with growing horror, I understood what he'd actually been asking.

"No," I said. "Flynn. Don't stay like Ellen. *Stay.* Really stay. Please."

This house had already seen too many ghosts. I had. Flynn had, too.

"Can't." His whisper was barely louder than a breath.

Maybe he couldn't. Maybe I was asking the impossible. But.

"Fight," I pleaded. "I know it hurts, but you have to fight. I don't know what's on the other side—where we'll go or what we'll become, if anything. But we have these lives now, and if we lose them, we can't get them back. Didn't you see what Ellen was willing to do, just to steal someone else's chance? Don't give up your own. Not if you can help it."

Sirens wailed from down the street, from past Flynn's house. They were close.

"One breath at a time," I told him. "Just one more. Then one more. One more after that."

He did fight. His chest inching up. Inching down.

The glass fell around us like snow as he went limper in my arms.

It flurried down on the bent and broken séance table, on the empty, ashy thrones.

It caught and stuck in the pooling white wax from all the burned-out candles I'd knocked down, forming glimmering, hardening puddles.

It lined Flynn's coppery lashes, their every tiny flutter, until they went still.

CHAPTER TWENTY-EIGHT

LIFE IS A FRAGILE THING.

This past spring, when doctors restarted my heart with electric shocks, I would've said it wasn't fragile enough. I'd wanted to die, and they wouldn't let me.

But when Flynn's heart stopped, I knew how truly vulnerable life was.

When the doctors saved him, like they'd saved me, I knew how precious it was, too.

Precious and tender and teetering.

He could have died then and there, no matter how hard he'd fought. How hard he'd tried. But one thing House of Masks had taught me: Sometimes the impossible did come to pass. Sometimes for worse, but sometimes, just sometimes, for better.

His recovery was painful.

All our recoveries were painful.

Our beaten bodies were a collective patchwork of blisters and burns and blood. Broken skeletons. Wounds that would scar.

My ribs were fractured.

The doctors said Flynn would take months to heal. He'd been stabbed through his large intestine and lost pints of blood.

While we'd waited for the ambulance, while I'd stayed by Flynn's side in the grass, Mom and Vivi had laid the monstrous corpses in our backyard to rest. Recovered their human faces from the rubble of the séance table and reunited them with their bodies.

Mom was the one who'd lifted her parents' faces back into place.

One by one, they'd all slumped and crumbled into dust, like Ellen had. And the wind had swept them away, along with the glassy snow.

When the paramedics arrived, we'd had to claim we'd been attacked. By intruders wearing masks and costumes. And then we'd had to endure police questioning—had to keep our stories straight enough, sane enough, to dead-end their investigation. To stonewall the over-interested media.

There were, after all, no culprits to catch. There was no story we wanted to tell.

After the ordeal, my family debated leaving.

A *new* fresh start.

But a fresh start wasn't what I wanted.

Not this time.

This house was the place where we'd all almost died. For each of us, throughout that nightmare, it would've been so much easier to let go. But we chose to fight.

We chose to stay.

We chose each other.

Every day, I wanted to remember that.

We spent the rest of summer rebuilding. New window by window, new flower by flower. Clear glass this time, and no more roses. We dug up the withered remains of the hedge maze. Repatched the broken walls. Scoured the attic. We took down the spiky white metal fence.

We started family sessions with Dr. Glaser. Stilted as they were. We'd had to feed her the same lines we fed the police. It was as close to the truth as we could expect Dr. Glaser to understand.

When September snuck up—that long-dreaded Monday—I wanted to be fearless. Ready, wholly and completely. But my ribs were still a little tender. Every breath was still a little raw.

After a summer that had served nothing but sunburns, the morning was cruel and unusual—chilly, and of all things, thunderstorming. Not lightly either. With big sloshing sheets of rain.

On the porch, Flynn stood waiting, slouched against the railing, swigging from a steaming thermos. His stamina wasn't back—he'd winded himself from walking the half block from his place. He hadn't been especially excited when his doctor said so long as his physical activity remained limited, he could start the school year as usual. His hood was up, but he was completely soaked.

I paused in the doorway, stunned at the water seeping into the shoulders of his red-and black-striped sweatshirt. "Why the hell won't you buy an umbrella already?"

Vivi poked her head out from behind me, buttoning her magenta raincoat. "Also, you can knock, you know. Instead of stealth-texting Libby whenever you show up," she reminded him. "Unless you actively enjoy hanging around our house like a creeper."

"Good morning to you both, too," Flynn said, his throaty voice raspy from sleep in a way that I not-so-secretly loved. It looked like he'd just rolled out of bed. Stubble lined his jaw, and his eyes were shadowed from restless nights. His hair was mussed in an effortlessly charming way, although that was business as usual.

Mom came up behind me and Vivi, slapping umbrellas into our hands. "Girls, first days are hard enough without catching pneumonia." And then she saw Flynn, dripping water all over the porch. "Oh no! Flynn, sweetie, can I lend you a rain jacket? A sweatshirt or anything?"

I stifled a laugh at the thought of Flynn sporting one of Mom's realty sweatshirts.

He had to bite his lip, too. "That's okay. Thanks, Sharon." To his credit, he did manage it with a mostly straight face.

Mom sighed. "Well. I'm off, then." It was a first day for her, too—back at work, meeting prospective buyers. She touched the curls in front of her ear, fluffing them for the thousandth time. Conscious, I'm sure, of the ragged scar underneath. She squeezed my and Vivi's shoulders, offering a flimsy smile. "Good luck today," she said.

I think she was trying to hide how nervous she was, letting all of us venture into the big wide outside world, pretending to be even halfway normal.

"Wait, Mom." Her lipstick was smudged. I scraped it from her chin. "Good luck to you, too."

"Thanks, sweetie." She couldn't help herself. She plopped a kiss on my forehead.

"Okay, well, now you totally ruined your lipstick again," I said. And my forehead, too.

Mom laughed. "I'll fix it in the car. Lock up, please, girls!" She pitched her umbrella and rushed to her car.

"You sure you don't want a ride?" I asked Vivi. It was admittedly Mom-ish of me, but I didn't love the idea of her waiting for the bus in a soaking downpour. And I had my license now, as well as a very clunky—but very safe!—used car, courtesy of Mom. After seeing how hard I'd fought to stay alive this summer, she finally trusted me enough to let me drive. She trusted me again with most things, even letting me keep my bedroom door closed—except when Flynn came over.

Of course, Mom wasn't fooling anyone that half the reason for my car was so that I could help ferry Vivi back and forth between school and ballet lessons. But I didn't mind. Not if it meant getting to see my little sister back in her satin shoes.

Vivi shook her head at my offer. "Nope, sticking with the bus. My first mission today is finding at least one person who doesn't suck. That seems doable, right?"

"Yeah." Flynn glanced at me, with one of his small smirks. A certain softness in his eyes. "One sounds about right." Then he glanced at Vivi. "Maybe two."

"You got this." I nudged her. Eighth grade. It was a big deal. And I was sorry she had to do it at a new school because of me, but if there was anyone who'd find somewhere to sit at the lunch table, it was Vivi. "Just, whatever you do, don't show anyone that book you're reading about spiders."

I *hated* that book.

I hated that Vivi, in general, still loved all things creepy and crawly. The sight of her book covers was enough to send me and Mom shuddering.

"Ooh! Did I tell you about the Brazilian wandering spider?" She tugged at my elbow, and then started pulling the book from her backpack. "You'll like this, I think. Most spiders are actually fraidy-cats, but these, when they're threatened, they refuse to run. And they've got this venom that—oh, crap!" Vivi cried suddenly. "Is that my bus? Gotta-go-byeeee!"

She was off, splashing through puddles in her rain slicker, waving her arms at the school bus on the corner.

Flynn blinked after her. "Were those words?"

Just me and him, then.

I locked up the house behind me and sidled up to Flynn. "Hey, you."

Tired as he was, he grinned. "Hey."

I moved to snuggle in, but he held up a hand to stop me.

"I must warn you," he said, "I am extremely soaked."

"Don't care."

"Great news."

I leaned against the rail beside him and cozied up—very carefully—under his good arm, against his good side, which was, as advertised, extremely soaked. The right arm was still in a cast, the one part of himself he'd managed to keep dry. I knew it wasn't me, not really, who'd broken it—but every time I looked at it, I thought of his splintered bone poking out into the open air. All his blood that looked so purple through the blue over my eyes. As always, I winced.

Flynn pretended not to notice. But he did. He always did. And it probably made him feel the pain of that moment all over again, too.

The aroma of hot bitter coffee wafted from his extremely large thermos.

"You have a bad night?" I asked.

He was struggling with recurring nightmares—we all were, but his were especially vivid. The one that got him worst was about channeling Ellen Clery. The worms he'd felt wriggling into her muscles as if they were under his own skin.

"Slept like shit. Feel like shit. What's new?" He took another deep swig of coffee and then offered it to me.

I shook my head. If anything, I needed a sedative.

After feeling low for the past two days, in anticipation of this morning, now my heart was pounding so hard Flynn could probably feel it against his own rib cage. My leg jiggled in time with every stabbing raindrop.

Despite my meds keeping me stable-ish, my brain was still my brain. My first day at a new school, especially after what had happened at my old school, was a foolproof recipe for an itching, anxious kind of hypomania.

He nudged me with his hip. "You seem a little twitchy."

"I am."

Flynn nodded. "Wish we had first period together. Or lunch."

"Me too." First period for me was Drama, to the delight of Dr. Glaser and Mom. But I was more nervous about meeting the theater kids than anything else. Here's hoping they were less awful than my last circle of friends.

Flynn and I had *seventh* period together. And that was it. I'd never been so excited for physics.

"You gonna be okay?" he asked.

"Yes," I blurted. "Definitely. Totally."

That should be true. I had a mostly clean slate here. No doubt people had heard about the masked-intruder debacle this summer, but I'd already practiced my avoidant answers to nosy questions. And Vivi had helped me set my socials back up, so I didn't look like a serial killer. Plus, I had a car. Most miraculously, I even had a boyfriend.

If last spring someone had told me I would spend the summer being accosted by rotting bug-shaped spirits and finding a boyfriend, it's the boyfriend part I would've found most far-fetched.

"Lib." He set the coffee on the railing and touched my hand, which had been on its way to my mouth, my teeth ready to tear at my nails.

I dropped it. Took his hand instead and squeezed it. "We'd better go, huh? We're gonna be late."

Flynn shrugged. "We can wait until you're ready." The smile he cut my way was the slightest bit worried. The slightest bit of a white-lie smile. "I don't really know, anyway, how it can still be school that scares you. After what we've seen."

I wasn't sorry that we'd stayed in the house. Not most of the time. Because every time I thought about how we were still there and the monsters weren't, I felt strong.

But I was sorry about how much Flynn hated going inside. How much he even hated looking at it. How much it clearly served for him as an ever-constant reminder that while we'd laid Ellen to rest and obliterated a house full of restless spirits, it was only one house's worth.

And now we lived in a world where we knew these things were real. Ghosts and worse than ghosts.

Spirits scared Flynn more than they scared me.

The living scared me more than they scared Flynn.

But he was right—I did need to learn to make my peace among them.

"Fine." I took a big swig of his coffee and then grabbed him by his soaking sweatshirt. Pressed the deepest, longest kiss onto his lips.

He blinked stunned and suddenly very dilated green eyes. Looking a lot more awake than anything the coffee had accomplished for him. "What was that for?"

"I'm ready." I patted him on the chest, hoisted my umbrella, and set off down the steps.

"Hey. Hey! You're gonna kiss me like that and walk away?" He threw up his hood and charged after me, into the rain. "Did I say *I* was ready? I take it back. I'm not. Get back here. Let's be later for school."

I grinned at him.

He was freshly soaked. He was about to make a mess of my car, and we were about to kiss and make a mess of each other. A mess of our attendance records.

And it would be worth it. Every messy little minute of it.

Because, yes, we lived in a world where ghosts were real, but I wasn't one of them—not yet.

ACKNOWLEDGMENTS

As a teen, I never got the chance to read a book with a main character who had cyclothymia (aka bipolar III). And of all the narratives I've drafted, this is the first time I've tackled one from the perspective of a mind like my own. A daunting task, in part because I know I can only speak for myself. I've done my best to reflect my experiences, but please know this book cannot and does not attempt to speak for everyone who shares that bipolar III lens, let alone folks with bipolar I and II, who may find that Libby's symptoms differ from their own. Regardless, I hope Libby's journey speaks to some readers, and can be a reminder that you are not even a little alone.

It means so much to me to get to tell this story, but in all honesty, it didn't come easily. If *What We Harvest* was my miracle book, the one that finally brought my dream of being an author to life, then *A Place for Vanishing* was the trial. I wrestled to discover what shape this narrative was meant to be. And I often felt like Libby, trapped in a House of Masks and fighting to find the way out. That said, I wouldn't change a thing. As Libby's battle was for her, this process was transformative for me. I learned and grew immeasurably, and I am beyond grateful to all those who helped me along the way—supporting this narrative as it matured into the book it is now.

On the front lines was the fantastic team at Delacorte Press. I owe a warm and infinite thank you to my editors, Krista Marino and Lydia Gregovic. *A Place for Vanishing* in its current form exists because of your keen insight and determination in ushering it from draft to draft until we uncovered the true heart of Libby's story. Thank you as well to Colleen Fellingham and Elizabeth Johnson for the thorough polish and care of your copyediting. To Trisha Previte for designing the perfect cover, to Zoe Van Dijk for gorgeously bringing it to life, and to Cathy Bobak for crafting the interior. To Madison Furr, my sparkling publicist, for helping me tell the world about it. To Tamar Schwartz and CJ Han for guiding it through production. And a huge thank you to Beverly Horowitz, Judith Haut, and Barbara Marcus for providing *A Place for Vanishing* with such an extraordinary home at Delacorte and Penguin Random House.

Of course, the first to believe in this book were my wonderful agent, Christa Heschke—my fellow horror-lover and staunch advocate—and the lovely Daniele Hunter. My deepest thanks to you both, to Kade Dishmon, and to the rest of the incredible team at McIntosh & Otis for all that you do.

I'm also very grateful to the writing community at large, especially the #22debuts, as well as the former Pitch Wars community, which includes my mentors and friends, Laura Lashley, Ian Barnes, Kylie Schachte, and Aty Behsam. A particular shout-out to those author friends who read and gave vital feedback on early versions of *A Place for Vanishing:* Amanda Quain, Laura Lashley, Ashley Winstead, Aty Behsam, Amanda Glaze, and Chandra Fisher.

Thank you, as always, to all the dear friends and family who have supported me throughout the years.

I would be lost without the powerful friendship of Emily Friend, Maia McWilliams, Katie Zelonka, and Sara Wilf. Maia and Emily were also tremendously helpful behind the scenes on *A Place for Vanishing*. Emily, your encouragement, visual brainstorming, and architectural know-how are a godsend, and Maia, your dedication, sharp literary eye, and attention to detail are truly invaluable.

And in writing, as in all things, my family is my anchor.

Love and hearty thank-yous to Dad, Pam, Shawn, and Mom for their support. Dad and Pam, thank you for reading and engaging even as I delve into fearsome horror-laden territory, for cheerleading every step of the way, and for being my very own grassroots publicity team. Shawn, the other half of my brain, thank you for always being game to leap in when my own mind is breaking—to chat through anything impossible until it is possible—for understanding me and my writing so deeply, and naturally, for being the best brother in the world. Mom, you may have read this book more than anyone. Thank you for your tireless edits and devotion, for catching small things and big things, and for jumping in time and time again with key feedback, no matter how tight the deadline. I would like to state for the record that while Mom's name is Rose Ann, she fortunately has less than nothing in common with the Rose of *A Place for Vanishing*—so no worries, world, it's not some weird Freudian thing.

Endless thank-yous to Grant, my treasured partner in *everything*. You are the best parts of every love interest I write, because you are the best love story I've ever known. And in a very new addition—one who is not yet with us as I write this, but will be soon—thank you to our own little Rose. I haven't met you yet, but even if I had, I know I'd struggle to sum up the enormity of what you mean to me. Your name, again I swear, has nothing to do with the Rose in this book.

Finally, my heartfelt thanks to you, reader, for not only taking this ride, but for sticking around to the end. Writing books is my dream, and you make it possible.

ABOUT THE AUTHOR

ANN FRAISTAT is an author, playwright, and narrative designer. Her coauthor credits include plays, such as *Romeo & Juliet: Choose Your Own Ending,* and alternate reality games sponsored by the National Science Foundation. When not engrossed in fictional worlds on her laptop, Ann has worked on stages across the Washington, DC, area as an actor and director. Other loves include all things spooky, baking, and drinking as much tea as possible. She is the author of *What We Harvest* and *A Place for Vanishing.*

annfraistat.com

@annfrai